Sív & THE BLOOD MOON

BY

GEOFFREY LEIGH

table of contents

part 1
solomon, the gatekeeper, and the prophecy

part II
age of the prophecy: present time

PART III
UNDER THE BLOOD MOON

There are a few Nordic and Gaelic names that need a little introduction to the American reader:

Siv .... *Seeve*
Seamus .... *Shay-mus*
Siobhan .... *Sha-vonn*
Ciarra .... *Keerah*
Aelhaeran .... *Al-ah-ran*

Cast of Characters

Old Wizard Council

Solomon
Simon
Seamus
Enzo
Gwendolyn
Camden
Leigh
Patrick

Followers

Elijah
Demetrius

Young Wizard Council

Elijah
Siobhan
Gavin
Margaret
Alexander
Hayley
Elizabeth
Demetrius

Dwarves

Siv
Ramsey
Teige
Elwin
Markus
Martha
Yuri
Aldwin
Raven Hair
Pudgy
Caitlyn
Tobias

Elves

Olaf
Ryanne
Osvald
Ciarra
William
Johann
Carl
Merckx
Naomi

Dark Forces

The Gatekeeper of Souls
Malkavic
Aelhaeran

Humans

Roarke
Drake

Places

Lindisfarne
Lavendelle
Mystic Forest
Haunted Forest
Nauren
Volcano
Bradán
Lake of the Serpent
Tower of the Wizards
Wastelands

Druids

Cael
Finn

Creatures

Fallon
Serpent of the Lake

X

For
Catherine

Part I
Solomon,
the Gatekeeper,
and
the Prophecy

Chapter 1
Rebekah

Siv pulled herself close to her father. His protective arm instinctively held her tight, but it was of no use. He could not protect his daughter from this evil. He knew someday Siv would have to face the Evil One—her mother Rebekah had told him as much. His mind raced back to Rebekah's words fifteen years before . . .

Rebekah cried out in agony, her breaths came in gasps. She looked up at Elwin and knew this was the end. She had to stay strong for him, for there was so much she had to tell him before she passed. She didn't know how much longer she would last.

Drenched with sweat, her matted red hair clung to her neck and the side of her face. She was in agony. Martha, Elwin's sister, looked up at Elwin and shook her head no. Rebekah was not going to live through the birth of the child. The injuries she sustained had crushed her pelvis and it had healed in a way that prevented childbirth.

Rebekah let out another loud cry as her abdomen became rock hard again as it contracted against the obstructed pelvis.

"It is no use," Martha said as she looked up at Elwin. "The baby won't be able to pass. There is no room!"

Elwin did not know what to do. He could not stand seeing Rebekah in pain.

"I cannot survive this," Rebekah began. "You must cut the child out of me and save her! I know it is a girl. I feel it inside of me!"

"I can't do it Rebekah! I can't," Elwin cried out, clearly racked with grief at the thought of losing his precious Rebekah.

"Look at me Elwin," Rebekah began, "look at me and do as I tell you!"

Elwin turned and faced her.

"I cannot have this child. I told you I would die when my time came. I told you I saw this coming. You have known this. My time has come, but this child must live! You must cut her from me, or she will surely die with me. I beg you, Elwin, I beg you, do not let this happen!"

Elwin looked at Rebekah and then at Martha. Martha nodded her head and went to retrieve the knife.

"Hand me my pouch," she said gently.

Elwin retrieved the pouch that she had set out earlier that morning, before her labor set in. He handed it to her and she removed the pendant from around her neck and placed it in the pouch. She held it tight.

"We will have a daughter. You shall name her Siv for me. I need you to do this for me, all right?" She clutched his arm.

"Yes, my dear, it will be as you wish." The thought of cutting the baby from Rebekah was overwhelming to Elwin.

Rebekah squeezed his hands and said, "Stay focused."

Elwin nodded.

"Do not talk to Siv about me. Do not tell her anything. Do not give her anything that is mine. Burn my clothes, burn my body after I pass. Do not leave any sign that she is my daughter! Promise me you will do this for me!"

Rebekah searched Elwin's face for his answer. She squeezed his hand with all her strength. "Promise me!"

He turned away from her as tears flowed down his cheeks. "I promise, Rebekah." Elwin turned to her and nodded.

"There is only one thing of mine that I wish you to give her." She looked up at Elwin to make sure he was focused on her instructions. *"You need to give this pendant to Siv when her time comes. You will know when it is her time. She will need this to protect her from the Evil One. Do you understand?"*

Elwin nodded yes. He wasn't sure if he really understood, but he did not want to add more stress to Rebekah.

She placed the bag with her pendant in his hand as another contraction set in. This was worse than any of the ones that had come before. She did everything she could not to yell out and further distract Elwin. She had to tell him one more thing.

Rebekah's breaths began to come in gasps once again. It looked as though she was fighting to stay conscious. Finally, she looked up just as another contraction hit and cried out: "You need to cut this child from me before I pass. I cannot hold out much longer."

Elwin nodded and Martha came over with towels and a knife. Neither of them had done anything like this before. Neither of them would know what to do if it was not for Rebekah. Both of them were in fear of what they were about to do.

The contraction abated. Rebekah grabbed Elwin's hands and looked at him. This time, more gently, she said "Raise Siv as your own! There is no one else to protect her!" She forced a weak smile, as a tear rolled from her eye.

Elwin understood Rebekah's tear. Rebekah had peered into the future and foretold Elwin of her fate. He did not understand the powers she possessed. She had tried to prepare Elwin for this day as she had seen it coming for many, many months. Nothing she said, though, prepared him for this day. As he caught the tear rolling down her cheek with his finger, he understood the deep sadness that Rebekah previously expressed that she would never hold her daughter, look into her eyes, watch her grow up, or share in any of the things she longed to experience with her.

Elwin's thoughts snapped back to the present. The memories

were too painful for him to continue. Elwin held Siv close with his left arm. His right hand reached down to his coat pocket and he felt the pouch that Rebekah had given him those fifteen years ago. It never left his pocket. He took it everywhere with him as it was his only connection left with Rebekah.

As he grasped the pouch, ready to take it out, Solomon, as if reading Elwin's mind turned and looked him in the eye and shook his head no. Elwin was shocked that the wizard seemed to know what he was thinking and even seemed to know about the pendant Rebekah had given him! He withdrew his hand from his pocket. He felt powerless to do anything to protect Siv from the evil that was descending upon her.

Solomon reflected on the times and the events surrounding the Prophecy that he scribed 750 years ago and all that had transpired since that time . . .

CHAPTER II
THE CHAMBER OF THE GATEKEEPER
(750 YEARS EARLIER)

THE volcano towered above all Lavendelle. Inside the volcano, empty chambers and a myriad of tunnels, once filled with magma and molten lava, were all that was left to bear witness to a once active and mighty volcano. These chambers and tunnels formed a labyrinth inside the volcano that was now the home of ghoulish beasts known as goblins and their demon lord, Malkavic.

Malicious beyond description, Malkavic oppressed all living, thinking creatures of Lavendelle by using an army of goblins as his tool of oppression, evil, and chaos. The goblins protected Malkavic from any who wished him harm. Though Malkavic was synonymous with the volcano and all the evil that flowed from it, the real power and evil was found several hundred feet below the mountain's surface, for there resided the nefarious and unspeakable Gatekeeper of Souls.

The Gatekeeper wasn't alive as one understood that to be, nor was he dead. He was just a presence that existed. His existence could not be described in words but rather was perceived by those who encountered him.

Within the volcano, a long trail, winding hundreds of feet ever downward along the walls of a pit, led to the Gatekeeper's chamber. Molten magma's eerie glow illuminated the walls with dancing colors of red, yellow, and orange. Gaseous fumes of sulfur, methane, and hydrochloric acid spewed forth, and an acrid odor ensured all but the hardiest would turn away. Hardly ever had this chamber been entered for the inhabitants of the volcano lived in great fear of the pit and the chamber below it.

At the far end of the chamber, a giant stone barricaded a passageway. This portal was used by only one entity—the Gatekeeper—as he entered and left Lavendelle. He only traversed this portal during the nights of the lunar eclipse in search of the lost souls of Lavendelle.

Solomon descended the dark trail winding along the sides of the pit by instinct rather than sight; down hundreds of feet below the volcano's surface. He was headed to the Chamber of the Gatekeeper. Solomon was a wizard—head of the order of all the wizards in Lavendelle. He cast a spell on all the inhabitants of the volcano so that his presence would not be detected, and despite all his sentries and patrols, Malkavic knew nothing of Solomon's visit that night.

Solomon was more than a wizard; he was a seer. Everything that Solomon had prophesied in his lifetime came to pass, with the exception of his visions that were in the far distant future, beyond his reach. Solomon didn't travel to the volcano to see Malkavic. No, he was there to meet with the Gatekeeper about a vision he had been given regarding Malkavic. The moon was fading from view and darkness began to settle across all the land. It was the night of the lunar eclipse.

As Solomon approached the depths of the chamber, a crashing sound shattered the quiet and filled the chamber with a deafening noise that echoed throughout the labyrinth of tunnels. A tremor shuddered throughout the chamber and shook the walls inside the mountain as the enormous stone rolled back, revealing a large portal into another world. Solomon estimated the circular stone to be at least three feet thick, twelve feet high, and twelve feet wide. In the blink of an eye, the presence of the Gatekeeper filled the entire expanse.

"So, Solomon, you have come to speak to me regarding your vision of Malkavic. Speak to me what you will," grumbled the Gatekeeper. His voice came from within a dense gaseous presence without specific form. His deep voice bellowed throughout the chamber.

Solomon was not intimidated. "I have seen the reign of Malkavic come to a swift end. I know this will not disappoint you as he currently occupies and controls most of your volcano."

A deep laugh resonated from within the formless cloud. "Malkavic controls nothing. He only thinks he controls this world. Both you and I know he has no vision for that which is unseen, and, therefore, he has no control. Tell me of your vision, Solomon."

"I see Malkavic's reign of terror ending at the next lunar eclipse," said Solomon. "I see him being entombed eternally in your chamber. But I have no vision of what happens once he gets beyond your gate. My vision ends there."

"Is that all you see, Solomon? I sense that there is more to your prophecy. What are you withholding from me?" the Gatekeeper growled.

"I need to know if you will entomb Malkavic if I have him delivered to you on the next lunar eclipse." Solomon continued on, ignoring the Gatekeeper's question.

"Solomon, you are not speaking to one without vision or understanding. I, too, see Malkavic coming to me very soon. But, if you manipulate the prophecy you have been given, to trick him and try to capture him, I will not entomb him. Your gift of vision is given to you to be shared by all—friend and foe alike. Your whole vision must be written by the next disappearance of the moon or I will not take Malkavic! What happens to the prophecy after that is beyond the reach of us both."

With that, the Gatekeeper's gaseous cloud exploded from the chamber like an arrow shot from a bow. His presence seared through the depth of Solomon's soul and out the other end of the chamber. Solomon felt the Gatekeeper's presence go through him like an arrow piercing its quarry. The Gatekeeper took something from Solomon that night, and he now felt that the Gatekeeper knew of the rest of the prophecy; indeed, he believed that the Gatekeeper now knew of his whole vision. For a brief moment, Solomon feared for Siv, a young and innocent dwarf not yet born whose life was now in danger because he was sure the Gatekeeper knew of her and her intimate role in the prophecy.

Solomon was not one to be underestimated. He took something from the Gatekeeper too when the Gatekeeper passed through him—something the Gatekeeper never intended to give away. Solomon acquired a key to much more power than even he wielded prior to this night.

His meeting was over. Solomon knew he had to scribe the prophecy, yet he did not want to reveal the whole prophecy because he did not want the demon lord Malkavic nor any of his agents to learn anything about a possible escape from the Gatekeeper once he was entombed. Also, he wanted to protect the unborn dwarf, Siv, with whom he already felt a close bond.

If Malkavic knew of his imminent capture, he would do everything to avoid it. And, if he knew of a possible escape once captured, he would make plans now to escape. This could never be allowed to happen.

Well, he had time to think. He had until the next lunar eclipse.

CHAPTER III
WIZARD FOLLOWERS

SOUTH and east of the great volcano was a large body of water known as the Lake of the Serpent. Reports of a giant creature trolling the lake were told with great excitement by those purporting to see the beast. On the western shore of the great lake, on a small finger-like projection of land jutting out into the water, stood a tall tower surrounded by lush, manicured grounds and walls that reached toward the heavens.

If the volcano could be thought of as the focus of evil in Lavendelle, then this structure was seen as the source of goodness and enlightenment for all. The tower, known as the the Tower of the Wizards, could be seen far and wide, and it was the seat of all power for the wizards. The many small libraries found throughout the structure held innumerable secrets and the treasured writings of various wizards who had lived through the millennia.

A great round hall, seemingly carved out of stone, just off the main entrance to the tower, had been built stone by stone by the dwarves, who were masters at their craft. When they had finished, no seam could be detected and the illusion of a solid stone wall had been perfectly created.

Arched doors at the entrance to the hall, adorned with heavy wrought iron hinges and clavos, towered twenty feet in height. Though the doors weighed several hundred pounds each, they were as light as a feather and easy to move on the series of well-oiled hinges suspending them.

Outside the doors was an antechamber where guests gathered and waited. It was the place where the wizards received their guests. Guests typically did not travel beyond the antechamber for this was the entrance to the wizards' home and private chambers.

The Wizard Council met inside the great hall and discussed all the issues that faced their world. Each wizard traveled to a different part of Lavendelle and would bring back news of all the happenings in that area. There were nine seats, one for each wizard. The wizards sat and deliberated around a great fire pit in the center of the hall. A large hood at the top of the room efficiently siphoned off the smoke created by the fire. Only wizards on the Council ever met inside the great hall. All others were received and conducted their business in the antechamber.

Elijah and Demetrius sat in the antechamber to the great hall of the tower and waited. Inside the hall, the Wizard Council was meeting. Elijah, follower of Solomon, knew of what his mentor was discussing with the other wizards. Solomon was head of the Wizard Council and had called this emergency meeting. Though the other wizards had followers, only Solomon brought Elijah along—and for good reason. Much was going to happen on this evening, and Solomon needed Elijah along to accomplish his mission.

Simon was the keeper of the tower. It was where he resided, and Demetrius was Simon's follower. Although Simon shared much with Demetrius, today Demetrius was in the dark about the meeting; he just knew something ominous was afoot. Demetrius did not like being kept in the dark. He had a curiosity that often got him into trouble. Demetrius' curiosity not only annoyed Simon but was now annoying Elijah. Elijah had information and Demetrius wanted that information. But it was not information for Elijah to share. Demetrius knew that too. Although Simon would inform him of everything he wanted him to know when the meeting was over, he continued to prod Elijah for information.

"What do you think is going on in there?" Demetrius queried his guest.

"I think they have many things to decide upon tonight," Elijah replied.

"Yes, I believe that is true. Simon told me that Solomon called for this special council. Surely, you have some idea what they are discussing?"

"Well, Demetrius, I have some idea of the concerns that Solomon has, but I am not his confidante. He tells me what I need to know, and that is enough for me."

"Elijah, soon you and I will be sitting at these council meetings. It is for us to know not only their ways but their words as well. I need to know what they know. It affects my very being. I want some say in decisions they make. Don't you feel the same way?"

"There is a time and a place for everything. The time will come when I will serve as part of the Council. It is not my time yet. My place is here for now. You will soon be on the Council too, I am sure. Simon will inform you of everything you need to know," Elijah reassured his counterpart. "Tell me more about this tower you keep for Simon and the Council. I have not seen all of its secrets," Elijah said to Demetrius, changing the focus and direction of the conversation.

"You are right, my friend," Demetrius said. "Our time will

come, and it will be soon. We need to be ready when it does. Come with me. Let me show you this place." With that, Demetrius rose and took Elijah around the tower to see its many mysteries.

Demetrius was sure that with time and showing his friend the secrets of the place, he would be able to uncover Elijah's secrets. He started the tour at the top of the tower. The uppermost chamber afforded an unobstructed view of the volcano. Interestingly enough, both the upper chamber of the tower and the summit of the volcano were above the level of the clouds on this day. Looking across at the volcano, the large lake that expanded between these two could not be seen below; only clouds could be seen. Elijah stared across at the volcano. Goose bumps spread across his body; he did not know why. He just sensed evil. And he was right: All of Malkavic's evil attention was focused on that tower at that very moment in time.

Demetrius took Elijah through all the rooms, the nooks, and the many libraries of the tower down to the main hall. There were many secret passages in the tower, and Demetrius revealed these to Elijah as well. Elijah was delighted with all he had seen and learned. The tower had always been somewhat of a mystery to him.

Demetrius ended the tour by showing Elijah the seldom used workers' quarters, entrances, and exits. There were no longer servants occupying this tower, but when it was being constructed, this was where the workers entered and exited the tower and where they stayed. Though the quarters had been abandoned long ago, Demetrius maintained them. They were standing outside of the workers' entrance when Demetrius let the door shut behind them. Elijah tried the door to let himself back inside.

"Demetrius, you let the door shut, and I cannot open it! Now we need to go all the way around to the front, and this will surely disturb the Council," Elijah exclaimed. He did not want to disturb the wizards. He wanted not to be seen nor heard this day for the matters being discussed were serious and demanded the wizards' utmost concentration.

"It is fine, my friend. Follow me," Demetrius said to Elijah. And he meant it. Elijah was his closest friend. They just did not always see eye to eye on everything. Elijah was a stickler for the rules and doing everything by the book, whereas Demetrius always lived his life on the edge of danger; it was in his nature.

Demetrius, though annoying, was Elijah's closest friend as well. Elijah just worried that Demetrius' wild streak would one day lead to his downfall. He had shared that with Demetrius on many occasions, but it never seemed to change his friend.

Elijah followed Demetrius to the lake side of the tower across an overgrown, rubble-filled path. A large boulder field was present almost straight down from the tower's edge to the Lake of the Serpent below. The boulder field was too steep and too treacherous to traverse. Even agile goblins would not be able to traverse this field. This was one of the reasons this site had been chosen for the tower. The north, south, and east sides of the tower were protected by the boulder field and lake, leaving only the front, or the west side unprotected. The south side of the tower was built of stone, and there were no entrances to the structure from this side.

Incredibly, Demetrius was leading Elijah down a barely per-ceptible path through the boulder field and to the lake. He moved swiftly on sure footing, and Elijah struggled to keep up. When Elijah thought it best to stop so as not to get too far from the tower, he looked back but could not find his way back. This forced him to move forward and try to match pace with Demetrius.

Halfway to the bottom, Demetrius stopped. The lake was clearly visible here. All creatures of Lavendelle had a natural fear of the lake and the serpent that lived there. Even Elijah feared the beast. He had seen the serpent himself on one occasion. It had revealed a long neck and large teeth as its head rose from the lake. Its body remained underwater with the exception of a massive hump that rose up well behind its neck. He had also seen the creature's powerful tail extend from the lake. The creature was massive. It reportedly feasted on other creatures in the lake as well as wandering ogres, goblins, and—rumor had it—even dragons that strayed too close.

Right now, Elijah felt vulnerably close. He was thankful Demetrius had stopped.

"Demetrius, how did you get down here so fast? And how are we going to get back?"

"Don't you see it, Elijah?" Demetrius asked.

"See what?"

"The path," he explained. Demetrius suspected that his friend did not have the vision.

"Look before you, Elijah." Demetrius pointed out to the lake.

"I am not going any farther, Demetrius. I have encountered the beast of this lake before, and I will not walk any closer," Elijah exclaimed.

"Do you see the three crafts at the edge of the water down the path? Those vessels belong to the wizards. They are ours! I have been out on the lake many times. The crafts are not visible to others of these lands, nor are we when we are on them. The serpent cannot even see us when we are on them!" Demetrius told Elijah excitedly.

"I do not see them, Demetrius," Elijah confessed.

"Elijah, you cannot see them with your eyes? Let me give you this spell. You will be given the vision to see. You will see the path we took and the remainder of the path to the lake," Demetrius explained.

Elijah looked out to the water. "I don't know, Demetrius. What spell are you talking about?" Elijah turned to his friend, but Demetrius was gone.

Elijah looked all around. There was no way for his friend to disappear in the middle of this boulder field. Elijah felt exposed and vulnerable to the serpent. There was nothing for him to do. He knew Demetrius was playing tricks on him. He decided to sit and meditate until Demetrius returned.

Demetrius sat obscured from Elijah's vision. He was always amazed at his friend's calm demeanor. There was no panic, no fright within Elijah. He decided not to prolong the mystery but would instead reveal himself and the secret.

As Elijah sat meditating, Demetrius appeared before his very eyes. If this startled Elijah, he did not show it. He just stared at Demetrius. "Now that is a spell," Elijah said to his friend. "I did not think you could use such powerful magic on me."

"Elijah, I did not use magic on you. I was in the secret passage to the tower. Don't you see it?" Demetrius pointed to the entrance to the tower, which was visible as plain as day to Demetrius.

"I do not see it, Demetrius," Elijah replied.

"Watch me," Demetrius stated, as he walked right into the entrance and vanished in front of Elijah's eyes.

Elijah walked over to where his friend had disappeared, but he did not see anywhere to go. Demetrius was amazed at the power of the spell that obscured the entrance from his friend, a wizard in his own right. He reached out with his hand and pulled Elijah through the entrance into the tunnel underneath the mountain. Elijah stumbled into the passage.

"What happened?" he exclaimed.

"There is a powerful spell guarding this entrance and the paths through the rocks. It is also the spell that keeps the vessel on the lake from being seen by other living creatures. You need to learn this spell, Elijah." Demetrius led Elijah back out into the boulder field.

"You are right, my friend. I need to learn this spell."

With that, Demetrius sat down on the ground with Elijah and said, "Close your eyes." Elijah did as he was told. Demetrius placed his fingers on Elijah's closed lids and said, "Repeat after me: *Oscail an súile an dall ionas gur anois is féidir liom a fheiceáil.*"

Elijah repeated the words and when he opened his eyes, he saw a whole new vision that had been obscured from him. There was a clear path, albeit small and treacherous, through the boulder field. The vessels were down on the lake, just as Demetrius had told him. And directly in front of him was a passage into the base of the mountain just beneath the tower. At the end of this passage was a room that held power beyond the comprehension of either Elijah or Demetrius.

CHAPTER IV
THE GOBLIN CHAMBER

WELL above the Gatekeeper's chamber, and just beneath the crater in the top of the volcano, there was a large chamber, which was now occupied by Malkavic and his goblins. Malkavic stood at the head of the chamber, addressing his legion of goblins. He was in a foul mood. His sword, an ornate work of art made by a seditious wizard of a time long past, never left his side and currently swung from his hip in its scabbard.

The wizard, Aelhaeran the Depraved, had created several enchanted blades during his time; this was one of them. A giant blood red ruby engulfed the sword's pommel. The grip of the sword was a hollow tube open along one side for its entire length. Inside the hollow tube was an ancient script written down the length of the grip. The meaning of the script escaped Malkavic.

Smaller rubies of lesser value had been polished and inset in the grip, allowing Malkavic's fingers to rest comfortably against them while the opening of the grip rested against the palm of his hand. The sword's value and beauty could barely be comprehended by Malkavic.

This enchanted sword was a goblin slayer. The presence of goblins lit an inner fire within the rubies, and the blade became a white beacon of light. The more goblins present, the brighter the intensity of the weapon. Another feature of the magical saber was that the energy that lit the rubies and blade also was transmitted through the grip of the weapon to its wielder. The brighter the intensity of the light, the more energy was transmitted and the more potent Malkavic became.

As Malkavic addressed his minions, he withdrew his sword. A powerful glow from within the giant ruby bathed the entire chamber in a red light and a blinding white light beamed out from the blade. He was filled with rage and wanted to use the sword on the creature nearest to him, but he managed to control himself. An electric fear flashed through the chamber. This enchanted blade thirsted for blood—goblin blood. Every goblin that looked at this blade understood this fact.

When left to their own devices, goblins would roam in packs and cause problems for the residents of Lavendelle. What made them dangerous, however, was their fear of power and their ability to be programmed to work together by a galvanizing force. Malkavic was such a force—they feared him *and* they feared his sword.

Now Malkavic was being threatened. Rumors reached his ears, whispered across the wind on voices more silent than spoken, of an impending threat. He did not know where the threat came from, but he did know who voiced it: Solomon the Seer. The rumor of a prophecy plagued him; a prophecy where he, the demon lord of the goblins, was to be overthrown and cast into the earth for all time!

According to his mysterious sources, the rumor told that the prophecy was still being scribed. Malkavic mistakenly thought that if he destroyed the prophecy, as well as the prophet, before it was scribed, the prophecy would also die. Malkavic failed to grasp the concept of prophecy.

CHAPTER V
THE SECRET CAVERN

"THAT is a powerful spell, Demetrius. Where did you acquire it? Did Simon give it to you?" Elijah asked. "My eyes have been opened! How could I have been so blind? How did this spell have such power over me? I am nearly a wizard in my own right, yet I had no idea that these vessels, this path, this hidden passage even existed. How could I not sense the spell or such magic? Simon is powerful indeed!"

"It is not from Simon, my friend," Demetrius replied.

"Does Simon even know that this passage or that this place exists?" Elijah asked.

"Simon has not spoken to me of this place. I do not know what he sees and what he does not see. He is powerful, and I believe he must know of this, but I am uncertain whether he knows!"

"How then did you learn?" Elijah inquired.

"Come, let me show you." With that, Demetrius led a mystified Elijah down the passage under the mountain and to the cellar of the tower.

Wizards were known for their discernment, judgment, enlightenment, and intelligence, not just their power. Whereas others valued material things, wizards valued knowledge above all else.

Demetrius was eager to show Elijah one such cache of knowledge he had found cast into the deepest, most hidden part of the tower.

Elijah's eyes adjusted quickly to the darkened surroundings. The small passage opened into a dank cavern. Roots of overhead vegetation penetrated the canopy above. Along the far wall, there was a path leading upward that led to stairs, the bottom of which were visible. These stairs led somewhere; Elijah imagined they found their way to the tower somewhere above. He had not seen where on his tour. This intrigued him.

A small underground creek flowed toward the lake; however, its appearance was not evident on the other side of the entrance to the cavern, even after he had learned the spell. It must have remained underground all the way to the lake.

On the far wall, the path that led down from the stairwell ended at a stone façade and two doors that swung outward to accommodate a wide opening. Two twisted columns of stone rose up on either side of the doors. Each door had six panels and heavy golden handles that had been ornately carved by a master craftsman. When viewed individually, each handle was of a peculiar design. However, when the doors were shut, as they were now, the golden handles interlaced, forming a massive, beautiful sword that pointed downward.

"What is a room like this doing down here?" Elijah asked as he struggled to take in the beauty of the room.

"I know. It makes no sense to me either. Here we are in this underground world, well beneath the tower, and rising up in front of us is one of the most unique finds in this whole place! Behind those doors is another library that will take your breath away. For me, it is my favorite of all the libraries I have come across. It is where I learned the spell I showed you."

As with the other libraries in the tower, the door was not locked. But something about this room was different as this library was far removed from the protection of the tower, and it was just a short distance to the outside and to the lake. As Elijah considered this, he concluded that there was no need to secure this place. No creature would ever stumble upon the passage for the boulder field alone was next to impassable. No one would ever approach the boulder field because they would have to cross the Lake of the Serpent. Finally, the passage was guarded by powerful magic, and that alone explained why it sat here seemingly unprotected. As he thought about it, it was as secure as any other place inside the tower.

Demetrius swung the impressive doors outward. They entered the room, and Demetrius quickly lit a series of lanterns that illuminated the library. Stone tile lined the floors and walls. An inlay pattern in what resembled the Serpent of the Lake—at least what Elijah remembered the serpent to look like—greeted the two as they entered. Fire and smoke were spewing from the beast's mouth in the tile work beneath his feet. Elijah hoped to never find out if this were true of the monster.

The room was a study of some wizard from long ago. This appeared to be where the wizard did much of his work. There was a large collection of writings throughout the library. Many enchanted objects lay scattered about. There was a bench that sat out in the middle of an alcove along one side of the room, and many objects sat on or around the bench.

A dagger and leather scabbard that were lying on the bench drew Elijah's attention. He picked up the scabbard and studied it. He slid out the dagger and held it in his hand. Emeralds decorated the grip, which slipped easily between Elijah's fingers as he held the dagger. A large green emerald was embedded in the pommel of the dagger. Elijah had never seen such a magnificent stone.

Elijah found the grip most intriguing. It was hollow and open its entire length. The open side of the grip met the palm of his hand when he held it while the hollow opening extended onto the quillon of the dagger. If this hollowing out of the dagger weakened the weapon, it certainly did not appear that way to Elijah. The metal was unlike anything he had come across and appeared to be rigid, strong, and light, with no give.

As he grasped the dagger, his eyes settled on subtle etchings in a foreign script, visible along the inside of the hollow portion of the grip.

Demetrius approached him. "Isn't that beautiful?"

"It is exquisite," replied Elijah.

"I have no idea what the inscription says," Demetrius said. "I have considered it many times. Half of the books down here are written in the same script. I believe it to be an ancient wizard script that I have yet to learn. Many of the books in this room have powerful magic that I can understand. I just haven't had the time to look things over as closely as I wish. And besides, it hasn't been too long ago that I discovered this place. Demetrius pulled a thick tome with a brown leather cover from a shelf and held it out to Elijah.

"Take a look at this book here. It is from this book that I learned the spell that allowed me to see the passage, the path through the boulder field, and the boats. There is so much knowledge here. I just want to soak it all in."

"Does Simon know of your discovery, Demetrius? What does he say? Knowledge not properly applied can be a dangerous thing."

"For all I know, Simon knows nothing about this cavern. I do all the work around here, and I do all the exploring. I came across this on my own. If you take the hidden passage that I showed you from the top room in the tower, there is a second hidden passage off of the path. I haven't shown you that one yet; I saved the best for last! I will show you. It leads directly down to this room. I have found no other entries to this cavern, other than the passage that I just showed you."

Elijah stared, fascinated by all that surrounded him. His curiosity piqued, he looked again at the inscription on the dagger in his hand, but he could not make out what it said.

"I have no idea what this inscription means. Let me copy it down, and I will ask Solomon to decipher it for me," Elijah said to his friend.

"I have a better idea, Elijah. Take the dagger. It belongs to the wizards anyway. Show it to Solomon, and tell him about this room and all you have seen today. He is the leader of the Wizard Council and he should rightfully know of this place. Technically, the dagger should belong to him. Give it to him, and maybe he will unlock the mystery of the inscription for us. But there is one condition: You must share with me what you learn from Solomon. If you bring him down here, please include me."

"That is a good idea, my friend. I will do just that." With that, Elijah tied the dagger to his belt. He was excited to possess it, even if it was just for a short while.

The two put out the lanterns and closed the library. Elijah took one last look at the beast in the tile and shuddered. He found his hand holding the dagger as he considered the beast and then chuckled to himself. What could a dagger do against such an overwhelming beast?

As they closed the doors, they headed out along the path

leading to the stairs and to the tower above. The steps wound up the inner wall of the tower as they spiraled upward. They came to the end of the path. It appeared to be a stone wall, a blind ending. Elijah stopped to catch his breath.

Demetrius caught up to him and smiled. "Watch this," he said. He walked forward, but instead of crashing into the wall, he walked right through it! Elijah was amazed. Elijah followed suit and walked toward the wall, but instead of passing through it, he hit the wall in full stride and crumpled backward. Demetrius appeared through the wall again and found Elijah crumpled on the ground, rubbing his head. He correctly surmised what had happened.

"I forgot to show you where to step, Elijah. Sorry."

Elijah's head was still spinning from hitting the wall. He had fallen down seven stairs. Demetrius came over and picked him up. "Watch this: When you walk to the wall, you have to step on this stone. When you do that, you pass through the wall. If you don't, you cannot pass." Demetrius disappeared beyond the wall again.

Reluctantly, Elijah followed. He carefully stepped on the stone and, to his surprise, he passed through the wall.

On the other side he found Demetrius. "Wow, that is tricky," Elijah said. Elijah looked at the wall he had just passed through. He could see no passage. He touched the wall, and it was solid stone.

"How do we get back?" Elijah asked.

"Look here," Demetrius pointed to a stone on the ground. All the steps were perfectly carved and smooth. At the bottom of this particular stair, there was a stone that was cut into the wall. It was barely perceptible to the eye, even while looking for it. Demetrius stepped into the wall on the stone, and passed through the wall.

Elijah quickly followed.

They were both in the blind ending passageway from the cavern below. "This is most extraordinary, Demetrius. How did you find it?"

"Let me show you." They both walked back to the main hall on the other side of the wall. "I was exploring the secret passageways. I have been through them all numerous times. While walking up the stairs, my eyes rested on that unusual-looking stone. I had seen it many times before but never made note of it. I stopped and looked at it. As I polished the stairs and the walls of this passage, I rested against the opposite wall right there," Demetrius pointed to the area opposite the wall, "before I went up to the upper chamber room, where this secret passageway leads. I kicked at the stone and fell through this wall. I was trapped on the other side for some time before I finally started looking for a similar way back through the wall, and eventually I found my way back. If you travel thirty-two steps down from the upper chamber room, you will find this stone and be able to get into the passageway out of the castle! Nothing in this tower is here without a reason. Seeming imperfections, when considered, lead to amazing discoveries. This room below is the best example I can show you to bear witness to what I am telling you, Elijah."

The two followers then traversed the thirty-two steps to the uppermost chamber room. They entered the room through the back of a fireplace. Even if a fire had been blazing, there was enough room for safe passage into the secret passageway. But one had to know how to access the secret passageway in a hurry, or he would burn in the fire. Demetrius had indeed showed Elijah all that he knew.

They entered the uppermost chamber and walked to the

window. The cloud layer over the lake had risen and now encircled the volcano's summit. Even though it could no longer be seen, Elijah could sense the evil surrounding the volcano. He peered down at the lake. The waters were turbulent. He saw no sign of the serpent as he scanned the enormous lake, but looking down across the boulder field, he saw something he had never seen before: three vessels. Indeed, his eyes had been opened. The wizards' boats sat there out in the open, just waiting to be used.

Demetrius stood behind Elijah, his gaze also focused on the lake. They watched as a dragon flew over the lake, swooped down into the water, and disappeared. Moments later, the dragon appeared and flew out of the water with a large creature in its claw-like feet. It flew off toward the volcano.

Amazingly, out of the middle of the lake, a giant beast erupted from the surface. Its mouth wide open, it sank its fangs into the neck of the much smaller dragon. Blood shot forth from the dragon and the creature dove head first with the dragon in its jaws, deep into the bottom of the lake, with only blood pooling at the surface to bear witness to the violent act that had just taken place.

Demetrius and Elijah stood stunned and speechless. Elijah shuddered, realizing how close he had been to the lake—and the serpent—just a little earlier in the day.

"Demetrius, you have shown me so much today. I want to thank you," Elijah said as he looked out the window, chills still running down his spine. "I feel compelled to tell you a few things that I know. I can only speak of what I know. Our time to join the Council may be coming soon," Elijah began. "There is trouble between the wizards and the demon Malkavic. Solomon has had a vision regarding that trouble and is sharing his vision with the Council. That is as much as I can tell you. I do not know all of the vision of Solomon. Be prepared when Simon talks to you about what was discussed."

Elijah felt guilty about withholding information about the prophecy. He knew that a significant role would be played by a young dwarf not yet born, but even Elijah did not know her role in all that was happening or even who she was. Solomon had mentioned a young female dwarf to Elijah, but he had not revealed much about her when he was speaking the prophecy to Elijah for transcription. Elijah was sure he would learn more about her as he finished the transcription. What could he tell Demetrius about her? Still, he felt conflicted about not mentioning her, especially since Demetrius had not held back anything on this day.

Demetrius knew there was more; he could feel the turmoil within Elijah. Still, he knew not to push his friend too hard. He knew what he needed to know: trouble was brewing for the wizards. He knew that the sudden meeting that Solomon called for would not bring good news. Trouble with Malkavic was about the worst kind of trouble he and the wizards needed. Elijah had given Demetrius what he needed to know. Now it was time to prepare for war—and to protect Simon and the tower. That was his duty.

Chapter VI
The Goblin Slayer

Goblins were everywhere. They hung from stone ledges. They even scaled halfway up the walls to hear their leader. Malkavic swung the blade in his hand to emphasize his points as he addressed the masses. Blinding light from his blade captivated the attention of every goblin, raising the creatures' level of fear with each swing.

"Solomon the Seer is trying to destroy us," Malkavic bellowed for all the goblins to hear. "His time has come, and we must put an end to him."

The name of Solomon spread terror throughout the goblins. No goblin had ever taken on a wizard, let alone Solomon, the head of the Wizard Council. A considerable buzz rose and echoed throughout the chamber.

"We cannot survive if Solomon lives. It is either him or us. He has brought this war to us!" Malkavic sliced the sword through the dank air. "Solomon will prophesize our destruction and cast a spell on us all very soon. We must get to Solomon before he casts that spell, or it will be the end of us!" Malkavic growled at the goblins.

The goblins knew if Solomon cast a spell on them, they were surely destined to die. The simple-minded goblins were easy to program: All Malkavic had to do was explain to them that either Solomon died or they died. Then they would be dispatched to kill Solomon.

So there was the strategy: An overwhelming number of goblins would be dispatched to destroy Solomon. The volcano would be left abandoned, but there was little worry for Malkavic's safety. He would be buried deep inside his volcano, confident he would not be touched. There would be no time for Solomon to react. Malkavic knew of Solomon's location at the tower of the wizards. He would be destroyed on this night, or they would all die trying.

Malkavic's plan depended on the element of surprise. No one suspected that they would be attacking tonight. To be sure, goblins attacking a wizard was a sure sign of doom and death for the goblins. That is what made the plan so brilliant! There would be no opportunity for Solomon to counterattack; there would be no time for organization.

Tonight was the night of the lunar eclipse. Solomon had worked out all the details of capturing Malkavic without manipulating the prophecy. He had manipulated Malkavic into attacking on this night, only Malkavic was unaware of Solomon's deception. The Gatekeeper would have to take Malkavic for Solomon had not crossed him. The only thing important to Solomon at this time was ending Malkavic's wicked domination of Lavendelle. Malkavic had to go, even if it meant that Solomon had to sacrifice himself.

Solomon was not certain that Malkavic could be contained, even with all the power of the wizards. That was because Solomon could not be there to add his strength to the attack. Solomon, by far, was the most powerful wizard. With what he had taken from the Gatekeeper the night he visited the chamber, Solomon's power had grown significantly. Solomon needed to be visible in the tower and implore the goblins to come for his plan to be successful. The wizards needed to strike Malkavic hard and fast while the goblins were out. Then they needed to get him to the Gatekeeper, who would have more than enough power to cast him into the earth for all time.

CHAPTER VII
INSIDE THE
WIZARD COUNCIL

INSIDE the great hall of the tower, the Wizard Council convened. There were places for nine to sit; however, only eight seats were occupied because only eight wizards currently belonged to the Council. There were plenty of others in Lavendelle who practiced magic, but only these eight were considered the most enlightened.

Indeed, there were many former followers of the wizards who practiced magic in these lands. There were sorcerers who were lesser than wizards and had incomplete skill sets or flaws. There were also the druids, who combined spirituality, healing, and magic. There were others who practiced the magic arts, but all of these magi paled in their ability when compared to the wizards. A wizard who sat on the Council was powerful indeed, and each was a force to be reckoned with. Combined, they were the most powerful force in all of Lavendelle.

Once one accepted an invitation to serve on the Wizard Council, it was a lifetime appointment, typically lasting eight hundred to nine hundred years. Occasionally, a wizard's life was unexpectedly taken, although this was unusual given that they were dangerous adversaries. Most wizards lived a solitary existence and traveled extensively throughout Lavendelle. If they came across one worthy to teach, a wizard would take on a follower and instruct that follower in the ways of magic and wizardry. Only the exceptional follower ever moved on and was asked to join the Wizard Council.

Two such followers were known to the Council, and those were the two followers who were currently present in the tower on this day: Demetrius, follower of Simon, and Elijah, follower of Solomon. Their fates would be determined by the eight.

Solomon was the greatest among the current era of wizards and he was the leader of the Wizard Council. He could peer into the future and see what was to be as though it had already taken place. There seemed no limit to his vision. There had been other seers in the past but none like Solomon. He was peerless in his world. He had his own library in the tower, and his status for all time among the wizards seemed set as one of their greatest. He called the special meeting on this day to discuss one of the most important visions he had ever been given: the destruction of the demon lord oppressing the enchanted world.

"Thank you all for interrupting your work to gather together for this urgent meeting," Solomon began.

All of the wizards gathered around the fire pit acknowledged his appreciation. He silently said the name of each wizard inside his head as he looked at each one: Simon, Seamus, Enzo, Gwendolyn, Camden, Leigh, Patrick. All had answered his call to meet at the tower. The one empty seat was next to Solomon.

"I have several things to discuss with you. One of them is urgent and in need of action this very evening. I have been given a vision that will affect the fate of all in Lavendelle," Solomon continued.

"Tell us more of this vision," Seamus, the elven wizard, urged of Solomon.

"In time, my dear Seamus. First, I have another matter I must address. I realize this is not the best time to discuss this issue, but this will be the only time I can speak about it with you. I want to discuss the empty seat at this table," Solomon told the Council.

"You summoned us, Solomon, and I am willing to discuss anything you deem important enough to put before us. But I am confused as to why this will be the only time you discuss this situation with us," replied Enzo, the youngest of the Council.

Simon, however, deciphered immediately from Solomon's words that this would be Solomon's last Council meeting. Great concern passed across his face as he realized the importance of the statement he had just heard from his friend.

"As I understand what you are saying, Solomon, you are talking about the two open seats on this Council. And, from what I gather, you would like to discuss young Elijah," Simon stated in a grave voice. Simon mentioned two open seats because he realized that Solomon no longer planned to be with them and, therefore, his seat would be vacant as well.

Those at the Council understood the meaning behind Simon's words. A heavy weight engulfed them all. Enzo sank in his chair. This indeed was a dark time, and he could see that this would be the most consequential meeting of his short time as a wizard. Indeed, Solomon was not one to waste their time.

"Yes, Simon, that is correct. As you have surmised, this will be my last meeting. It is my duty and obligation to inform you about Elijah's attributes prior to my departure so that proper consideration can be given to his appointment on this Council."

"And is your departure related to the vision that prompted you to call us together?" Seamus inquired.

The wizards leaned forward, holding their breath as they waited for the answer.

"Seamus, I have much to discuss with you. I will share my vision with the Council and then we need to act and act swiftly. Yes, my vision includes my departure from this physical form which is now present before you. But I have acquired power that will grow beyond your understanding. I will not leave these lands, and I will be vigilant in overseeing all your works, my dear friends. I will be able to help you in ways I never imagined possible even one year ago. But I do not have time to discuss all that has transpired this past year."

Seamus seemed satisfied with Solomon's explanation. He sighed and leaned back, steeling himself for whatever Solomon had to tell them.

"First, we need to discuss a new leader for the Council, and next we need to discuss both Elijah and Demetrius. They have both reached their maturity, but it is for the Council to determine their worthiness. Do not act in haste, my friends. It is my desire to help guide you in choosing a new leader. It is my belief that Simon possesses the experience and wisdom to guide the Council into the future. I realize that Simon is the senior member, and you may decide to go with someone with longer years to serve. That is for you to decide. But, after I share my vision with you, you will realize that with the upcoming turmoil in our lands, wisdom reigns supreme in serving the needs of those in Lavendelle. Without the Council's direction and help, mayhem, chaos, and destruction may spill out and overflow into our world," Solomon finished and sat back, waiting for his words to be absorbed by those around the table.

Over the next hour, Solomon discussed the attributes of Elijah, and Simon discussed Demetrius. There was no question in anyone's mind that both of these followers were capable and possessed adequate knowledge and skills to ascend to the Council. Elijah seemed a lock for one of the seats. In fact, some wizards expected that one day Elijah would become the Council's leader.

Demetrius, on the other hand, was an enigma. Underlying his personality, he was basically good. However, he was a wild spirit. That wild spirit could serve as a distraction both to the Council and to his duties. To deny him the opportunity to move on would also be difficult because he clearly had substantial knowledge and skills. The consensus was that it would be better to keep Demetrius close so that he could be controlled and closely watched. If he were to ascend to the Wizard Council, they would need to keep him in check. The wizards agreed that his considerable skills would benefit the Council.

Seamus brought up the problem an ancient Council had with a wizard who nearly destroyed the group: Aelhaeran the Depraved. Whereas Aelhaeran shared the same wild nature and curiosity as Demetrius, the wizards acknowledged that he did not have the good spirit that they perceived in Demetrius. But as Seamus pointed out to the Council, "Power corrupts," and Demetrius would need to be closely monitored if he were to be granted a seat on the Council.

The time had come for the wizards to listen to Solomon's vision. They had not yet come to a conclusion about either Elijah or Demetrius; each wizard pondered all that they had discussed. They first needed to listen to Solomon's vision and then consider how everything Solomon was telling them would fit together and how his vision would affect the Council. Only then would they be able to make good decisions going forward.

"I have seen a vision of the future of this land without the demon lord Malkavic," Solomon began. "I have seen the Council band together and overthrow Malkavic on this very evening."

The room was deathly quiet. Each wizard considered Solomon's words. The demon oppressed the land. He controlled the goblins that were his purveyors of evil and destruction. Malkavic was a potent force in his own right. To challenge him would be dangerous. No one stirred or spoke.

Solomon continued, "Tonight, the entire goblin nation will be dispatched and will attack this tower. The goblins will be after me, and after this." Solomon held up a large book that he had scribed.

"What is that you are showing us, Solomon?" Patrick inquired.

"This is the prophecy of the downfall of Malkavic. I have foreseen it. It will come to pass. It will be tonight, the night of the lunar eclipse," Solomon stated. "But even more than that, Patrick, this is a prophecy of the next millennium that involves the Council, Malkavic, the Gatekeeper, and a special dwarf not yet born named Siv. It is here for all of you to read and absorb, but for tonight, fulfillment of the prophecy begins with the capture and internment of Malkavic!"

Solomon then informed the Council of his meeting with the Gatekeeper and how the Gatekeeper agreed to entomb Malkavic. He reminded them that it was only during the lunar eclipse that the Gatekeeper appeared in Lavendelle. He explained that in his vision he saw the seven remaining wizards capture Malkavic and deliver him to the Gatekeeper. He told them that he felt Malkavic's power would be drained with the goblins gone and that together the wizards would overwhelm him.

After Solomon finished and the wizards asked their questions, they all agreed: Malkavic must go. The wizards understood their role and made plans for their attack. They would take to the boats and swiftly cross the lake to the volcano on the other side to attack Malkavic. The demon would never anticipate an attack from the lake side of the volcano. Furthermore, by crossing the lake, they would avoid the attacking goblins. Solomon had explained to them why the goblins would be attacking. He also explained that this was part of his vision.

The wizards implored Solomon to join them. There was no reason to stay alone, unprotected from the swarms of goblins, they argued. Solomon told them of the Gatekeeper's words: His vision could not be altered or manipulated. Otherwise, their plans would be doomed. The Gatekeeper would not entomb Malkavic, and the demon lord would become even more powerful and oppressive in the enchanted world.

Now the wizards understood that Solomon was sacrificing himself for the good of all in Lavendelle. What they did not understand, and what Solomon had not disclosed, was the secret of the incredible magic and power that he had taken from the Gatekeeper when the Gatekeeper blasted through him on the night of the last lunar eclipse. The Gatekeeper was trying to intimidate Solomon, but he had failed. Solomon's power and presence of mind had allowed him to take the Gatekeeper's secrets. Indeed, this was not the last time Solomon would face the Gatekeeper. Solomon could see a future, epic confrontation. But that was for another day. Today was about freedom for those of Lavendelle. Good and evil creatures alike.

The plans were set. The Council was ready to act. It was agreed that the wisdom of Simon was needed and that he would lead the Council but only if Solomon did not make it through the attack of the goblins. All were somber with the knowledge that Solomon would not be returning to the Council. Still, they were hopeful.

After agreeing that both Elijah and Demetrius should be invited to join the Council, the wizards concluded the meeting. One by one, each of the other seven members of the Council came up and bid farewell to Solomon. The wizards shared endearing, departing words. Each of them was given courage by Solomon's demeanor. Finally, Simon came up and exchanged words with Solomon. The two wizards embraced, and it was done. The time for action was now. The evening was setting in. The beginning of the lunar eclipse was merely five hours away. There was no time to dally.

"Malkavic has an appointment with the Gatekeeper tonight," said Solomon. "Let us not keep him waiting." With that, Solomon adjourned his final meeting of the Council. Simon was now in charge, and his first act was to be the most dangerous venture the wizards had ever embarked on—a venture directly into the heart of evil!

CHAPTER VIII
THE CAPTURE
OF MALKAVIC

THE wizards chose the long and narrow craft to take across the lake as it was the fastest of the three. Time was precious and they had little to waste. The goblins had left the volcano and were on their way to the tower, even as the wizards crossed the lake.

Simon sat at the head of the boat; the remaining wizards sat single file behind. Simon cast out a line and cast a spell. When he was finished, the line became taut, rapidly propelling the boat across the lake. The winds blew hard across the turbulent lake. Twilight settled in under the thick clouds. The dark craft sped across the lake through the ominous night.

The creature that propelled the craft across the open water did so unseen. All that was known was that it had to be something large, powerful, and fast. Within ninety minutes, the vessel arrived at the other side of the bank. The full moon rose in the eastern sky yet remained behind the clouds. The wizards needed to travel quickly and silently to get to the entrance of the volcano unde-tected. They surmised that they had less than three hours to get to the volcano entrance, find their way to Malkavic, subdue him, and then take him down to the Chamber of the Gatekeeper—a challenge even on the best of days.

After climbing for nearly thirty minutes, the wizards finally reached the entrance into the volcano. This was just as Solomon had said it would be. The silence was eerie as the volcano would normally be teeming with goblins.

The cloud cover was breaking up. The full moon had risen high in the sky and illuminated the ground below. It was time to enter the volcano and shield themselves from the light.

As they entered the volcano, Simon and Enzo looked toward the tower across the lake. Out of nowhere, a powerful blinding light shot out from the tower that drew the rest of the wizards' attention. Simon intoned, "It has begun." They all thought about Solomon and Elijah back in the tower and wished them well. Quickly, one by one, they filed into the volcano entrance.

The goblins had struck first, but it was the endgame that mattered. Malkavic never considered the endgame. The wizards began their counterstrike—a move that Malkavic never saw coming. It was true what the Gatekeeper had told Solomon about the demon: "He has no vision." That lack of vision left Malkavic vulnerable.

The wizards found the volcano abandoned. Even though he expected it, Enzo still found himself amazed to find everything just as Solomon foretold. They were reminded that though the mountain had not erupted anytime in the past several centuries, a fire still smoldered somewhere within. A wave of heat crashed into them, and the smell of the goblins overwhelmed them. The foul odor lingered in the tunnels despite the absence of the creatures.

They followed Solomon's instructions, taking the tunnels to the right to find Malkavic. Once they had captured him, they would return and take the pathways to the left to get to the Gatekeeper.

The wizard Patrick didn't need Solomon's guide once entering the tunnels. He had a strong sense for evil, and he was drawn toward the demon lord. He rapidly led the way down the tunnels, ever inward toward the center of the volcano.

The tunnel widened and spilled out into a large chamber. They noticed that a confluence of tunnels emptied into this chamber. Many of the tunnels were intertwined here. The wizards slowed their pace as they grew close. Though they had not come across any goblins, the noxious odor aroused their suspicion. Certainly, some of the goblins had stayed behind. They could handle the goblins; they just had to prepare for what they might encounter upon entering the chamber.

Simon raised his hand and whispered in a low voice, "Let us stop here and get a strategy together."

All of the wizards gathered around Simon. Their eyes darted around, looking for trouble, and yet so far they had not encountered any goblins or Malkavic.

"I believe that we can get clear around this chamber without ever entering it. I think these tunnels are all connected here," Simon said, voicing his thoughts. "Leigh, take Patrick and see if you can locate Malkavic," Simon directed two of the wizards.

"I think he is up ahead, Simon. The stench has intensified beyond even what I can stand!" Seamus exclaimed.

"You do have the keenest nose among us, Seamus."

"Simon, this has to be the chamber," Gwendolyn began. "All the tunnels converge here. The heat is overwhelming, I feel as though we are in the center of the volcano."

"I agree with Gwendolyn," Enzo said. "Seamus smells him too. I believe this is just where Solomon told us he would be. We must act swiftly. There is little time before the Gatekeeper arrives."

The last wizard, Camden, just listened. He sat as a vigilant guard against detection.

Patrick and Leigh returned on silent steps. "It is just as we thought, Simon," Leigh whispered. "I saw Malkavic! He is pacing in the chamber. He is clearly agitated. I did not see any goblins with him. Solomon is truly amazing!"

"How does it look to you, Patrick?" Simon queried.

"It looks to me as though we are approaching the front of the chamber. If these tunnels truly interconnect all the way around this chamber, then, conceivably, we could sneak up from behind him and attack."

"I think a three-pronged attack may be better," Leigh began. "This will serve to confuse him and will give us our best chance to take him."

"I agree with Leigh," Gwendolyn said.

"All right, then here is the plan," Simon began. "Enzo, you take Camden and Gwendolyn with you. Move silently to the right and take your positions on the right flank of this chamber behind Malkavic. Seamus, you take Leigh and Patrick with you and try to take your positions on the left flank. I will give you several minutes to get into position, then I will step out in front of this chamber and draw Malkavic to me. Once I have his full attention, then you all will need to attack him from each flank. Together, we will overwhelm him and take him down. We don't have much time. Are we all in agreement?" Simon asked.

"Simon, I have an idea that may help," Seamus started.

"Tell me," Simon urged.

"I like your plan, but it would be better if we had a signal to coordinate our effort. This signal could possibly distract Malkavic even more."

"What sort of signal are you talking about?" Simon asked.

"When you are ready to attack, cast a spell and eliminate this odor. We will all be aware that when this happens, you are going to confront Malkavic. He, I am sure, will be distracted by the sudden change in the air!"

"Brilliant! Let us move out!"

Simon sent the wizards to take up their positions. The plan started off well. The element of surprise worked to their advantage. Still, Malkavic was no pushover. His strength surprised all of them.

The odor left the hall. Malkavic rose to his full height of six feet seven inches tall and flexed his taut muscles. He looked around the room. Something had changed, but he couldn't quite put his finger on it yet. Then he sensed magic around him and looked up to see the wizard walking toward him. He mistakenly took this to be Solomon.

One lone wizard was not going to frighten him. A cagy smile crossed his face and he drew his sword as Simon approached. He did not receive any strength from his sword on this night; the blade did not glow. The ruby at the end of the handle remained dull. He had forgotten that all the goblins were gone, and the sword was merely a sword in their absence.

"Is that you, Solomon?" Malkavic bellowed.

Simon stopped thirty feet from the massive Malkavic. He was a powerful creature, and his sheer size—both height and muscular frame—dwarfed the seven smaller magi. Simon was not going to be drawn in any closer. Simon's power could be countered by Malkavic if he allowed the demon lord to get too close. "I am Simon, Head of the Wizard Council, Malkavic. I have come for you. For too long you have oppressed these lands and their inhabitants. Your rule ends now."

Malkavic let out a deep belly laugh. "You and what army, Simon? You are an imposter. Solomon is the head of your council," Malkavic snarled. With that, Malkavic raised his sword in one hand and then raised his other hand. A massive fireball appeared in his open hand, and he hurled it with great speed toward Simon. He then charged forward, swinging his sword.

Simon had been expecting this. He stopped far enough away from the demon to be able to deflect the initial charge. He realized the amazing speed and strength of the demon lord and knew that, alone, he could have been overwhelmed. Simon quickly pointed his wand forward. A bolt shot out of the wand and the fireball exploded in mid-air. Blinding light momentarily stopped Malkavic's charge.

Simon had drawn all of Malkavic's attention. Unexpectedly, Malkavic experienced excruciating pain in the back of his legs. He fell to his knees as pain that felt like fire rushed up from his feet through his legs. He emitted a deep, bloodcurdling scream. As he fell, he looked to his left and saw three wizards pointing their wands at him. Fire emanated from the wizards' wands as they incapacitated him. A deep, sharp pain wrapped around his spine and the strength from his arms melted away. He looked to his right and saw the counterattack.

He opened his mouth to speak and curse the wizards but Simon was too fast. Simon approached the demon and stuck his fingers into Malkavic's voice box. Then he uttered a quick spell and Malkavic's voice was gone.

Malkavic crouched, paralyzed, wobbling on his knees. He was about to fall on his face; all his strength was gone. His last conscious thoughts were that the prophecy was being fulfilled—and he was powerless to stop it.

Prior to losing consciousness, Malkavic looked Simon in the eyes. With the demon lord on his knees, they were face to face. Malkavic grimaced as Simon peered into his eyes. The wizard reached out with his right hand and relieved Malkavic of his sword. "Malkavic, you will not need this sword where you are going. In fact, you will never need this sword again."

The last thing Malkavic saw was Simon turning his back on him and walking away, carrying his treasured sword. Malkavic then fell forward on his face, unconscious.

"Time is of the essence, my brothers," Seamus began. "We have less than one hour to deliver Malkavic to the chamber."

The wizards quickly bound Malkavic with magic twine, and with the power of levitation, they escorted him, unconscious, to the Chamber of the Gatekeeper. They laid his body in the center of the chamber. His hands and feet were bound tightly. The seven wizards surrounded the chamber's perimeter, an area defined not by stone walls but by lava flowing around the floor. One massive stone stood at the end of the chamber, and from their discussion with Solomon, they knew that this was where the Gatekeeper would emerge.

As they waited for the Gatekeeper to arrive, Simon looked at the sword he had taken from Malkavic. He saw the script on the hollow of the grip and read it. It was in an ancient wizard script. The name of Aelhaeran was scribed into the blade. The words "Goblin Slayer" were scribed into the hollow of the handle. He studied the writing etched into the grip: "Cursed will be the possessor of this blade."

Simon realized the blade must be destroyed as soon as possible. He resolved not to keep it in his possession one minute longer than was absolutely necessary. Aelhaeran the Depraved was an infamous wizard. He possessed magic stronger than any of his time, and Simon chose not to be cursed by the spell of the long-since-passed Aelhaeran. Simon took the sword and used both hands to hurl it into the flowing rivers of lava that surrounded the chamber.

Simon did not realize that a spell protected the blade. Aelhaeran protected the sword from destruction even from beyond the grave. Molten lava would not melt the enchanted weapon. But Simon knew nothing about that.

Just then the ground rumbled. The moon had disappeared, and the large stone at the end of the chamber rolled back. The presence of the Gatekeeper filled the expanse. The wizards had never before faced this entity, and they each stood in stunned silence. "I see Solomon has delivered on his word," the Gatekeeper bellowed from his gaseous form.

None of the wizards spoke for there was nothing for them to say. They avoided the Gatekeeper as best as they could. The pathway out of the chamber was not blocked by any, just as Solomon had said.

"I have a meeting with Solomon tonight," the Gatekeeper announced. With that he disappeared. He left so quickly that the wizards did not see him go. When they looked out on the chamber, Malkavic was gone too. The Gatekeeper had taken him. Everything had happened just as Solomon had described. None of them knew what he meant when he said he had a meeting with Solomon tonight. But none of them felt that this was good news for Solomon.

CHAPTER IX
TOWER UNDER SIEGE

AFTER Elijah and Solomon saw the wizards off in the boat, they returned to the tower and locked the main door behind them. In order to avoid unnecessary risk to Demetrius, Solomon sent him on a mission to Bradán, home of the dwarves, to the west. But Solomon needed Elijah. They climbed the steep stone steps to the upper chamber at the top of the tower where Elijah thought he would be transcribing the rest of the prophecy, but little did he know that Solomon had already finished the work.

When they arrived in the upper room, Solomon sat Elijah down at an old hand-hewn table across from him. "Much will happen tonight, my dear Elijah. I have much to discuss with you. You have been a loyal and faithful follower, and your time to join the Wizard Council has arrived."

Elijah, shaken by the news, said, "I appreciate your confidence in me, Solomon, but I have so much yet to learn."

"Our whole existence is learning, Elijah. When you join the Council, your learning will really just begin. The Council has decided that you and Demetrius should take your seats at the next meeting. That will occur in the next few days. This will be much the same way Simon and I joined—at the same time. It will be good for the two of you to have each other as you grow in our ways."

Elijah meekly thanked Solomon for his confidence and support. Then he pulled out the dagger and passed it to Solomon. "Demetrius and I found this in a secret cavern of this tower today. We both felt you should have it and hoped that maybe you could decipher its inscription."

Solomon took the weapon from its scabbard and studied it with care. "I have heard of such metal, yet I have never held it in my hands," Solomon began as he looked at the blade. "I sense there is magic in this blade. Surely, you can sense it too, Elijah."

Elijah nodded affirmatively.

"This is certainly one of the enchanted blades of ancient lore. The inscription is an ancient language used by the wizards of centuries past. You will master this language as you grow. Many of our spells come from this ancient language. The creator of this blade is someone who served on the Council. I am sure you have heard of him. His name is inscribed here on the blade: Aelhaeran. Aelhaeran was a very powerful wizard, indeed. He was corrupted by his power, but in terms of genius, he was talented and gifted. Just look at the craftsmanship of this dagger." Solomon held the dagger gingerly, giving it his full attention before he continued. "Look here, on the inside of the grip, it says that this is a goblin slayer. That means it is an enchanted blade. It must derive energy from goblins. I have read about such a dagger in ancient writings. The script says that the possessor of the blade will be blessed."

Elijah peered closely at the blade, fascinated by its craftsmanship and history.

"Aelhaeran was dangerous, Elijah. I do not think he can be believed or trusted, even after his death. I would recommend depositing this blade back where you found it. It is your decision. As for me, I have no use for it." Solomon returned the blade to Elijah.

"I will do as you say, Solomon. I will return the blade tonight," Elijah promised.

"Do you know what happens tonight, Elijah?" Solomon queried his follower.

Elijah shook his head no as he was uncertain of the direction Solomon was going with his question.

"The prophecy that you started scribing for me will be fulfilled! Malkavic will be removed from these lands. As you are aware, the wizards are on their way to the volcano to overthrow Malkavic. Lavendelle will be free of his evil and his oppression."

As he spoke, the dagger that Elijah held in his hand began to glow. Elijah had not yet placed it back in its scabbard. Light emanated from the blade, and the green emerald began to shine from an inner fire. Both Elijah and Solomon stared. Solomon stared across the table at Elijah. "It has begun," he said.

Below, at the base of the tower, the goblins formed a chaotic group, many scaling the outside of the tower toward the light coming from the upper chamber window. They screeched in frustration at finding all other entries and exits secured. The only way in was through the upper chamber where Solomon and Elijah waited.

"I have never seen such an overwhelming force of goblins," Elijah said, mystified, as he gazed out the window. Waves of hundreds and hundreds overwhelmed the tower.

The blade glowed and Elijah gripped it harder. He felt the energy return from the blade. Even if this was the work of the evil Aelhaeran, Elijah needed the blade tonight.

"Elijah, come quickly! Back away from the window," Solomon said. "The goblins are upon us, and our time is limited."

Elijah retreated back with Solomon as the goblins teemed toward the upper chamber. As they entered the window, Solomon picked up his wand and cast a spell. Light shot out from the wand and spread throughout the tower. Every goblin in sight, every goblin in contact with the tower, fell to the ground, but the spell did not deter them. They had a mission and their strategy of over-whelming force was eventually going to overtake the two occupants of the tower. Even when facing massive annihilation by the great wizard, the goblins kept coming. They were programmed to be successful or face death at the hand of Solomon.

"We don't have much time, Elijah," Solomon began. "This is my last night with you."

"What do you mean, Solomon?" Elijah asked, shocked by Solomon's statement.

"Elijah, the goblins will not stop until they overtake me. You will be able to escape, but I cannot. I will leave this body; the goblins will never capture me. I have acquired power beyond your ability to understand or my ability to teach you. I will be among you and the Council, but I will not be in the form you see me in now."

Elijah stared mutely, overcome by the meaning of Solomon's words.

"The one thing we must do, Elijah, is keep this prophecy from the goblins. It never should have been written, but I put it into writing according to an agreement I made with the Gatekeeper of Souls. Now, you must escape with it, quickly."

As soon as Solomon finished talking, the goblins gained new strength. They burst into the room and attacked. Elijah slashed the dagger through the air, and before he knew it, seven goblins lay dead at his feet. The goblins had quickly separated Elijah from his mentor. They fell upon Solomon and as they attempted to ram a spear through his body, Solomon disappeared entirely. Elijah screamed in anger at the goblins. Fury drove him to drive the dagger through the goblin minions. But with every goblin slain, three replaced it.

The goblins, however, feared the enchanted blade, and they struggled to escape from Elijah. The more goblins that appeared, the stronger Elijah became. The emerald from the dagger cast a bright green light throughout room. Lightning flashed as Elijah slashed down forty goblins that raced at him from all sides. Elijah successfully countered every goblin attack and each aggressor lost its life. He rushed to where Solomon had dropped his wand and retrieved it. A goblin reached for the wand at the same time, and that mistake cost the creature its life.

Elijah was unable to keep the minions at bay. He took the prophecy and flung it into the fire opposite the chamber. Unfortunately, only a portion of it burned before there was a goblin there to retrieve it.

The goblins had the prophecy and were ferreting it out of the window when Elijah flung himself on the goblin with the prophecy. The goblin died quickly, but, while Elijah was distracted, another goblin tore at the prophecy. As Elijah stabbed out at the goblin, his blade sliced the prophecy down its spine. The goblin holding it fell to its death outside the tower, but it clung to half of the prophecy in its fall. There was no way for Elijah to retrieve that half of the prophecy. Elijah was left with the remnants of the burnt half of the book; most of this was the part scribed by Solomon himself. The goblins escaped with the first half of the prophecy, the part that Elijah had transcribed as Solomon had dictated it to him.

Elijah spun around to face more goblins in the chamber. It was his time to escape. Elijah dashed for the fireplace—the very escape route he had learned about from Demetrius earlier that day—and quickly leapt through the fire, out the passageway in the back of the fireplace, and down the steps. He took each step as he dashed down, counting them as he went. When he reached the thirty-second step, he found the stone he needed to step on and quickly burst through the stone wall.

He finally had time to stop, catch his breath, and allow his heart to stop beating so hard. He looked at the remainder of the prophecy. It continued to smolder; the final pages that Solomon had written were either severely damaged or destroyed. Elijah quickly put out what remained of the fire and salvaged what he could of the prophecy. He leaned his head against the cool wall and closed his eyes tight. He sensed defeat. The one thing Solomon had charged him with was to safeguard the prophecy. Solomon was gone. To where? Elijah had no idea. He was no longer of this world, Elijah was sure. He would never have left his wand. Well, it was Elijah's wand now, and it was a powerful weapon indeed.

He hurried out of the tower, raced down the secret passageway, and made his way as quickly as he could to the lake. Before leaving the secret chamber of the tower, he had stowed away the prophecy in a place where not even Simon would be able to find it.

He rushed down the secret path to the edge of the lake where the small boat rested on the calm water. If he hurried, he could head off the party of goblins that had the prophecy and get it back.

Elijah realized that he was invisible to the goblins out on the lake. He could make it to the volcano and take the prophecy back. He cast his own spell on the creatures of the lake and soon he was being propelled rapidly across. He had the green emerald dagger at his side, but he had the emerald stone covered so as not to warn the goblins of his coming.

Upon reaching the shoreline, he jumped from the boat, hauled it to the shore, and headed quickly to the entrance of the volcano. He watched, hidden, as the goblins entered their lair up ahead of him. Soon he would be on them and they would pay for their transgressions against the wizards!

He scaled the volcano to the entrance, where he encountered three goblins. They saw him and froze, but before they could react, a green light shot out from his hand and the three goblins fell dead. He leapt into the tunnels, the green light of his dagger eerily reflecting off the walls as he raced, hopefully, to retrieve the rest of the prophecy.

Elijah understood that the wizards had been there and were somewhere around; however, he had not encountered them. The thought of them failing to subdue Malkavic had not crossed his mind.

Rage filled him. He had no thought of personal safety, only the retrieval of what Solomon had entrusted to him. Only pure fury existed. His mind was focused. These goblins had attacked, and they would pay with their own blood.

In moments he entered the chamber of Malkavic. No goblin escaped his rage. He did not think about what needed to be done; he only reacted to the danger at hand. He and the blade were one, and no goblin had a chance against the combination of Elijah's rage and Aelhaeran's magic. It was as if the blade gave him a sense of where every nearby goblin was and exactly what movements it was making. There were no effective attacks against him for he knew where every danger existed and reacted the only way he could to save his own life. He anticipated each creature's actions and reacted with his own deadly force. He would find the prophecy he lost, or every goblin he encountered would be slain.

His battle raged for another twenty minutes, but when there were no more goblins left, Elijah sat in the chamber amongst the dead. The stench was overwhelming. The heat was overbearing. His grief was unimaginable. His heart had finally settled and his breathing had returned to normal. The light from the dagger still glowed, but he was calm. He was sure that the goblins no longer posed a threat. He had failed to retrieve the prophecy. He had killed every goblin in sight, but he could not find Solomon's works. He felt as though he had failed his master. It had been the most important request Solomon had ever made of him, and he had failed in this, the last request he would ever receive from his mentor.

The wizards quickly distanced themselves from the Gatekeeper. They were keen on escape from this burning inferno. Deep in the recesses of the tunnels, they became aware of a green light.

"What is that light, Simon?" Enzo asked as he gazed off into the distant tunnels. "It looks as if it is coming from Malkavic's chamber. Dare we go back?"

"I feel we must investigate and make sure our business is done. We must ensure we have not overlooked anything," Simon replied.

As the wizards approached the chamber, they passed hundreds of dead goblins.

"What has caused this destruction?" Seamus wondered out loud.

"I don't know, but I think we are about to find out," Simon replied.

The wizards had reached the chamber where they had subdued Malkavic. They knew they had a limited amount of time to escape before they were trapped by more returning goblins.

An eerie green light filtered from every crevice of the chamber; the light was bright, but no sign of life was present. Only dead and dying goblins lay before them.

Simon entered the chamber and stared at the sight before him. What appeared to be several hundred goblins lay strewn throughout the chamber. The source of the green light emanated from an emerald stone with an internal fire glowing at the end of a dagger. The possessor of that dagger was none other than Elijah!

PART II
äge of the prophecy
present time

Chapter X
Lindisfarne

AT the very northern crevice of human existence lay a tidal island called Lindisfarne. Lindisfarne was a holy land that brought travelers from all over the known world. It was one of the oldest known villages in human existence. Within its borders, people sought health, healing, and spiritual guidance.

East of Lindisfarne, out into the North Sea, there was a forest that could be accessed by a land bridge. Hidden somewhere deep inside the forest, like a needle hidden in a haystack, was a tiny gate that led to another world, a magical world: the enchanted lands of Lavendelle.

No one knew for sure what lay beyond Lindisfarne to the east, for no one who traveled through that gate ever came back. Rumors milled around among the local villagers as to why no one ever returned. Some said of the explorers that they never returned because they found riches beyond their wildest dreams and refused to leave paradise. But this was the less popular belief held by most. Stories of magic, of small creatures and giant beasts, of goblins and dragons abounded. Imaginations were ripe with incredible tales—tales that kept all but the most curious out. These rumors saved many a soul, for Lavendelle was no place for mankind.

Lindisfarne can be reached on foot from the mainland of the Northumbria region during times of low tide. During high tide, a boat is needed, for the rough seas are not forgiving to those caught unaware. The island, an outstanding area of natural beauty on the northeastern coast of England, is lush and green with little natural barrier from the harsh North Sea. At the far end of the island a whinstone hill offers some break from the elements.

Lindisfarne, a Holy Island, welcomed people with ailments from all known corners of the world. The land grew uncommon and hardy vegetation, including greens used as medicinal herbs that could be found nowhere else in the known world. Rumors of miraculous healings extended far and wide.

Because of the miracles witnessed in Lindisfarne, many clergy, monks, and friars were drawn to the region. Some chose lives of solitude and worship, whereas others sought to evangelize to the travelers of the region. The monks set up their own monasteries.

A small local community emerged in the center of the island where people from many walks of life and many different backgrounds gathered. Local hostels, pubs, a mercantile exchange, and other supporting businesses sprouted up to aid the travelers who found their way to this small and remote island.

During low tide, at the far end of the island, there was another path that extended down the whinstone hill and out into the North Sea for some distance. This path connected the flat and windswept Lindisfarne to a heavily timbered, uninhabited forest that stood tall and strong against the elements.

Though Lindisfarne was thought of as a holy place, the forest beyond was thought to be cursed. The locals referred to it as the Haunted Forest. Reports of sightings of unusual phenomena frequented the local taverns. Strange and often frightening noises from the uninhabited forest filled the nights. Though these sounds and sightings terrified most, nothing ever crossed the land bridge and invaded Lindisfarne from the forest. Over time, the locals wrapped themselves in a false sense of security.

Lindisfarne attracted another kind of traveler in addition to those seeking spiritual guidance and healing. It attracted explorers—those who had heard of the unnatural forest beyond Lindisfarne and the secret of the treasures it held. They sought vast riches, but there was one thing all of these explorers had in common: They were never seen or heard from again—none of them—except for one.

None of the locals ever traveled across to the forest, either by foot or by vessel. All the locals knew of travelers who had struck out on the journey into the Haunted Forest and had not returned. Every time this happened, the legend of the Haunted Forest grew.

The locale mercantile was run by a man named Roarke. He was thick-boned, heavily muscled, and gritty. His worn and callused hands reflected a lifetime of hard work. He looked as though he should be out in the land or on the sea or exploring. He was as rough and tough as any man who had ever passed through Lindisfarne. But there was one exception: Roarke had a shriveled up left leg that left him hobbled and dependent upon a cane.

It had not always been this way for Roarke. In his younger days, he had come to Lindisfarne to explore the Haunted Forest, drawn by the rumors of riches. He had made one trip to the forest and mapped out part of it. While there, he had heard the harrowing noises from deep within. Undeterred, he had searched but never found the source. It had been unnerving to be in the same forest with the noises rather than listening from the safety of Lindisfarne, but his curiosity overtook him and he had gone back for a second trip and then again a third time. Each time he had expanded his map and his knowledge of the forest.

On Roarke's third trip, a mysterious event had occurred and he had barely escaped with his life. He paid the price of traveling to the Haunted Forest with the loss of the use of most of his left leg. He dragged himself through the thick underbrush back to Lindisfarne. For three days he languished in the forest, unable to rise and walk. Each day, he struggled to get back to Lindisfarne. Finally, on the third day, he was found lying face down on the side of the hill on the south side of the island. Roarke had no recollection of the events that had occurred other than he was exploring one moment, and the next he found himself on the ground and an excruciating pain shot through his left thigh.

He was found by local monks who took him to their monastery and nursed him back to health. The monks healed Roarke's physical body, but it was up to him to heal his mind and his soul. The years passed slowly, and gradually the night sweats and nightmares that frequented his sleep abated, but every so often, the nightmares would return just to warn him to never again return. Roarke was acclaimed and honored in Lindisfarne as the only known explorer to travel to the forest and return, a living witness to its dangers.

Every year new explorers came looking to get their riches from the forest's hidden secrets. Roarke kept the shelves in his store well-stocked. He would also sell the explorers a copy of the map he had made for a healthy profit. He was often invited to accompany them to the local pub where he would sit and talk with them for hours. This was the only connection he had with his former life. He identified with these men, and he loved the camaraderie of like-minded folk. He understood them yet rejected their pleas to accompany them.

The tales of his injury did little to dissuade the travelers. It only emboldened them, as it would have him in his youth. Yet it was always the same: They would head out for the forest, never to be seen or heard from again. He always had hope, but disappointment washed over him when they didn't return.

For a long time, the legend of the Haunted Forest was repeated again and again for curious visitors. It was a land of wizards, ogres, goblins, and dragons. There were reports of dwarves and elves as well. No one knew the origin of these stories; they had been told for as long as any could remember. Roarke never recalled encountering any life during his travels, but he could hear it and sense it, especially at night. With the passing of each party of explorers and their failure to return, the myth of the Haunted Forest grew until it was difficult to separate the truth from the tale.

Even though Roarke could not confirm seeing life in the forest, it was quite alive. He had made contact with intelligent life; he just failed to remember the encounter.

The nightmares and sweats that came to Roarke at night were a consequence of his encounter with an elf named Olaf. Olaf was Prince of the Elves and the firstborn child of the High Priest of the Elves.

On Roarke's third trip to the forest, he had stumbled across a gate that led to an enchanted world—Lavendelle. Had he crossed beyond the gate at that moment, he would have run into a raiding party of ogres that surely would have torn him to shreds. Olaf chose to spare Roarke's life, and he shot an arrow of fire into Roarke's left thigh. The arrow dissipated upon impact and no trace of it could ever be found. That is why Olaf chose this arrow. Olaf knew that getting hit by an arrow of fire had devastating consequences, but at least Roarke's life was spared.

What Roarke, the locals of Lindisfarne, and the explorers who traveled to the forest were unaware of was that the forest was patrolled by elves. The elves killed creatures that attempted to escape the forest and enter the human world. The elves also guarded the gate that led into Lavendelle, for that passage led directly to the elves' home and their city, Nauren.

It was the elves' duty to keep the two worlds from encountering each other. Olaf spared Roarke's life that day, but had he been able to peer into the future, he might have let Roarke stumble through the gate into the wandering ogres instead.

Chapter XI
Lure of the Forest

In spite of the elves, man often found his way beyond the gate in the forest that led to Lavendelle. What all seemed to have in common was that they never found their way out. The world was too different and had too many dangers. They could not possibly stay safe in such a place. Lavendelle was lethal to humankind.

The wizards warned the elves and the dwarves among others of the dangers of interacting with human explorers. Though they may not have appeared hostile and confrontational, any contact with them could lead to pain and destruction. Helping these explorers, they warned, could lead to the arrival of more and more humans who would eventually look to take over their world and change everything.

The explorers were most commonly drawn to the volcano, deep within Lavendelle, well east of Nauren and the gate. The area east of the volcano was treacherous and filled with many dangers. By the time any of the exploring parties reached the volcano, if they reached it alive, the ogres and the dragons usually finished them off.

Roarke had encountered many men like Drake Scott before.

He was young, strong, full of life, and had a passion for the unknown. Roarke developed an immediate bond with the young man. He was a hard-looking man, dark, not as big as Roarke, but solid, agile, and strong. He wore his hair short, and he had a thick, full beard that he kept trimmed very short. He bore the scars of a hard upbringing. Drake found his way to Lindisfarne alone, much the same way Roarke had arrived.

He began helping Roarke with his work. At first he did a job here and there, but Roarke liked him and he found more and more work for Drake. Drake liked Roarke as well, but he was also drawn to Roarke because of the legend of Roarke and what the older man had done in the past. Drake longed to explore the Haunted Forest, and he longed to discuss his plans with Roarke.

Roarke, however, was not interested in filling the young man full of wild dreams and fantasies of the unknown. He knew what had happened to him, and he did not want that to happen to Drake. He was much older now and wiser. He had seen many a strong man and many an expedition party disappear into the forest never to be seen or heard from again. Every time Drake brought up the forest, Roarke would change the subject. He never talked about his explorations or the map of the forest.

One evening, after several months of working for Roarke, Drake convinced the older man to have dinner with him. The pub was a local favorite. They walked past the bar at the front of the room and beyond a dozen tables scattered about. On this night the patrons only filled half the pub. The room was dark and smoke lifted and lingered toward the low ceiling. Light from lanterns filtered through the smoke, appearing as clouds on a full-moon night. The two soon found themselves in the back of the pub in a dark booth.

"Let me buy you a pint," Drake began. "I owe you for all the work you've given me."

"Thank you, lad, but I am not much of a drinker anymore."

"Why is that?" Drake asked, curious to know more about his friend.

"It is not that I don't miss the ale—I do mind you—but it brings back nightmares of things not so pleasant."

"What do you mean?"

"Sometimes, after I drink, everything that happened back in the forest comes flooding back to me. It is more than I can take."

Drake ordered two pints. He needed to hear what happened. If he couldn't get Roarke drinking, he would drink them himself.

The ale came and their food soon followed.

"Tell me about the forest, Roarke. Every time I ask, you change the subject."

"That is because I know you want to go. It is no place for man, I tell you, Drake. It is no place for you. There are demons out there. I have struggled to shake those demons ever since I left that forest. It has taken me years." Sweat broke out on Roarke's forehead as the memories came flooding back. The temptation of the ale sitting in front of him was too great. He finally reached for it and took a long drink.

Drake kept the ale coming and soon he had Roarke talking.

"The forest is alive, Drake. I mean to tell you it is alive. It is eerie out there. You can get no rest. You have to sleep with one eye open. It is like nothing I have ever come across in all of my travels. I have sailed all over the North Sea, and I have scaled the great mountains across the channel, but I have never encountered anything the likes of what I saw in the forest out there." Roarke pointed in the direction of the forest.

"What do you mean?" Drake asked. He leaned in close to hear Roarke's whispered answers.

"I mean there is something out there I can't describe. When the sun goes down, you need to find a place to hole up. There is something on the prowl out there. The noises you hear coming from the forest at night here are infinitely more alive and bone-chilling when you are in the forest. The noises can paralyze you with fear. I can't explain it, but it is like your mind and your body freeze up; you can't move!" Roarke took another long drink of the strong ale—his fourth pint.

"How many times were you out there, Roarke? What was it, three times? If it was so bad, why did you keep going back?" Drake looked from side to side to be sure they were not overheard. He noticed what appeared to be two fishermen leaning ever so slightly toward them, trying to pick up on their conversation. He lowered his voice further.

"I went back for the same reason you keep asking me these questions: I had to know. I had to see with my own eyes. I didn't listen to anyone. I don't want that for you! I am old now, and I wish I had never heard of that forest. I wish I had never gone there the first time. And I tell you this as I no longer have any desire to go back. I have been cured. I lost the use of this leg because of that forest. It's not worth it." He finished his pint and banged the pewter stein on the table. "How many a good man must we lose that way, Drake? I have seen them all. They come to me; they want my map. They want my stories. But none of them wants my warnings and none of them listens to me. They all go and they never return."

Drake listened intently to Roarke's words. He heard the older man's warnings, but they could not overcome his curiosity about this mysterious land.

"Listen to me and don't do what I did! Don't be a fool!" Roarke hung his head. He was clearly drunk now, and he was going to pay the price for his foolishness, he knew it. He might as well make the most of it he thought to himself, so he ordered another ale and drank it down.

"Will you tell me about the map?" Drake asked.

"You are the same as all the rest, Drake. You are the same. You hear my stories, but you don't think anything will happen to you. I, too, used to be that way. Not anymore."

Roarke stood up and walked to the other side of the table. He steadied himself with his hand as the effects of the alcohol surged through him. He bent over and rolled up his pant leg. He never showed his leg to people, but he wanted to make an impression on the young man in front of him.

"Look at what happened to me out there! Look!" he said as he pointed to his shriveled up leg and the huge crater in his upper thigh where he had been pierced by Olaf's arrow.

Drake tried to look away from the grotesque image, but his morbid curiosity brought his gaze back to the mangled leg.

"This leg used to be as strong as the other one. Now it is useless! Useless! Don't go, Drake! Don't go! Nothing good ever comes from that forest!" Roarke stated emphatically.

Drake's stomach turned and he thought he was going to be sick. He couldn't imagine what force could have done this to Roarke's leg.

"And, Drake, I am the lucky one. This happened to me. I fear for the others who have not returned. I fear for their very lives!"

Drake could see the fear and the true worry in Roarke's eyes.

He knew the old man was doing everything he could to dissuade him, and yet he felt little remorse for tempting Roarke and getting him to drink just to pull his secrets from his friend. Roarke's horrendous injury and harrowing tale did nothing to diminish Drake's desire to explore this world. Indeed, it only further stirred curiosity in his heart and stoked the fire burning in his soul to explore.

Drake had thick skin. Roarke's disfigurement had little effect upon him. Growing up in an orphanage, he had seen a lot of bad things and he had experienced the worst side of man. He had learned to look out for himself above all else, because if he didn't, no one else would. He was not used to having someone care about him as Roarke clearly cared, so it was hard for Drake to know how to receive his friend's concern.

Drake was a loner. His whole life he had done everything on his own, so it was really no surprise that he learned to explore by himself. He grew up without any lasting friendships. Kids came and went at the orphanage. He never got close to anyone. And he was living his early adult life alone too. Roarke was the only person who had ever really shown interest in him. And he had gotten Roarke drunk to pry his closely guarded secrets away. Drake wasn't proud of himself for doing that, but it had allowed him to extract the information he wanted out of the old man. Now he was planning on leaving Roarke and heading out on his own again, heading out to explore and learn all he could. He hoped to find riches that would make him wealthier than all those who used to look down on him; all those who had treated him as a second class citizen because he was an orphan.

He rose early the next morning. He quietly walked down the stairs into the store and packed supplies to last several days. He already had a pack for his supplies. He filled two canteens with water. He chose dry food that would last for as long as he had it. He needed a blanket and some medicinal supplies and bandages should he get injured. Finally, he needed a weapon. He considered all the weapons Roarke had in his store. Drake was a skilled fighter. He had learned early on how to fight and look after himself. He was skilled with a blade, a sword, and an axe. These were the weapons of his youth, and these were the weapons he chose to arm himself with for his journey into the Haunted Forest.

He felt prepared to defend himself against any creature that might cross his path. He stole into Roarke's office, found the map of the forest, rolled it up, and tiptoed out of the room.

He quietly unrolled the map on a countertop and studied it. He was amazed at how detailed the map was. Drake left the store and forged ahead, over the hill on the far end of the island and across the land bridge connecting Lindisfarne to the forest, and deep into the heart of the forest itself.

An hour later, he stopped and opened the map again. He found his location and drew his finger across the map. He was heading to an area on the map that marked water. He determined to make camp halfway to the water hole the first night. By the second night, provided all went well, he would camp at the water hole. This would leave him close to where Roarke had been injured. He would explore that area thoroughly and add to the map prior to returning. He would be excited to tell Roarke of his adventure.

CHAPTER XII
THE MORDING AFTER

WHEN Roarke awoke, his head throbbed, his throat was dry, and his legs wobbled under him. The events of the night before wavered in a fog. He looked about his room, finally bringing his focus back to himself. He was fully clothed. At least his boots were off. He could not remember how he got there. The afternoon sun filled his room, bringing more pain to his eyes.

He sat on the edge of his bed. His head bent forward into his hands as he ran the events of the previous evening through his mind. He remembered going out to the pub the night before with Drake. He also remembered that he had a drink. That was his first mistake. It took him a little while to get his bearings straight. It was Sunday. His store was closed. It was the afternoon and normally he was an early riser. Then the conversation of his travels rang in his mind; that was the second mistake, the one he feared the most. He realized what he had done. He filled the boy full of talk of adventure and travel, and he was fearful that Drake would head out into the forest. His fears were realized when he walked down to the store and found a note on the counter.

Roarke:

I didn't want to wake you, especially after our long night last night. I helped myself to some of the supplies that I listed below. I am leaving payment here with this note. Please apply my wages to the rest.

After last night, I couldn't wait to get out and explore for myself!

See you soon.

D. Scott

Drake was good on his payment. In fact, he left too much. Roarke still owed him money. He felt like a fool. He got liquored up, lost control of his tongue, and fed Drake's desire for exploration. He knew Drake had it in him too; he could see a lot of himself in young Drake Scott. He did not blame the young man for setting him up with the alcohol. In fact, he thought he might have done the same thing himself.

He rushed to the back of the store, fearful of what he would find. He walked to his desk and saw immediately that the drawer had been opened. He knew what had happened. He pulled open the drawer to learn that his worst fear had materialized. The map of the Haunted Forest was gone. Drake had it.

Drake might have thought that it was the only copy, but he was wrong. Roarke yanked the drawer out of the desk, turned it over, and looked at the bottom of the drawer. There was a copy that he had burned into the bottom to ensure he would never lose his last copy.

He sat down and began the process of transferring the map contents to a leather scroll tablet. He hoped that Drake would return soon like his note suggested, but he feared the worst. He dropped the pen and sat staring at the empty leather scroll before him. What good would it do to transfer the map? The problem was that he was too old and too crippled to try the forest again. He had tempted fate too many times and had barely escaped with his life. There was no way he could physically hold up to the challenge of the Haunted Forest at his age and with his worn and damaged body. Roarke hung his head in total defeat. Drake was on his own; there was nothing more Roarke could do to protect him.

CHAPTER XIII
GATEWAY TO LAVENDELLE

DRAKE wandered through the forest, thick with trees that were wider than he was tall; trees that reached higher in the sky than he could see. His travels were treacherous and slow going as he struggled across the forest floor, which was scattered with rocks, tree roots, and broken branches. He saw very few signs of life other than a few birds, rabbits, and squirrels.

An eerie silence surrounded him, even as he stole through the dim light that barely trickled down from above. It was easy to get disoriented down at the bottom of the forest. The only security he had was the map he possessed, and he knew where he was on it. He was determined to press on, ignoring his friend's warnings from the night before.

As night set in, the forest became so dark that Drake could barely see his hand as he held it in front of his face. He had gathered enough wood to make a small fire that should last many hours and settled in for a long night. He made himself dinner and then worked the fire a bit, adding more fuel so that he could drift off to sleep.

There was no chance of seeing stars on this night, or the moon if it was out. The only things visible were the flickering shadows created by the firelight that reflected off the branches above and danced across the surrounding rocks and trees.

He had camped out alone many times before, but tonight seemed different. He didn't know if it was all the rumors that he had heard about this place, or if it was everything Roarke had told him or shown him with his leg, or if there was something more intimidating, more primeval to the forest itself. He had never been in such a place. He was sure it was the forest. Drake considered himself every bit as brave as Roarke, and Roarke had been here three times before, and he had been all alone as well.

As Drake drifted off to sleep, he considered why he was drawn to the unknown: his strong desire to explore and know more about the world than what he could learn from books. At least, that is what he told himself.

Sleep came fast for he was exhausted. But as soon as sleep enveloped him, he awoke to the sounds of the forest as it came alive. At first the noises seemed to be far away, but they seemed to be moving in from every direction toward him. Usually a fire kept the predators away, but for whatever reason, Drake felt as though his fire was drawing them in toward him. He heard a blood-curdling scream echo close by. A shrill cry made his heart leap from his chest. He had never been religious, but he found himself praying for morning to come and for the beasts to go away.

The noises had been intimidating on Lindisfarne where he felt safe, but experiencing them here in the forest was life altering. He experienced fear that shook him to his very foundation; fear like he had never experienced before. Adrenaline rushed through his body as he huddled close to the fire, waiting for the morning that seemed so long in coming. He was fully awake with the arrival of first light.

He didn't want to go through another night like the last one, and he didn't know if he had the courage to proceed. The one thing that drove him on was that he felt as though he couldn't go back and face Roarke as a failure. He determined that with the coming night he would sleep without a fire. Hopefully, this would make him less of a target to whatever had haunted the night. He hadn't seen it, but he did hear it and he could feel it.

He packed up his few belongings and his precious map and proceeded along to where the map said he could find the water. By late afternoon, he arrived at a watering hole. He found everything just as Roarke had described. He made a quick dinner and then just as quickly doused the fire and huddled next to a rock. He drifted off to sleep. The sounds seemed to have followed him through the forest, but they seemed more distant. From this point forward, he would never camp with a fire on this island again! He slept deeply while vivid nightmares crept through his mind, but at least he slept.

In the morning, he headed off in the direction where Roarke had been injured, his senses on full alert. He unfolded the map to find a skull and crossbones marked over the very location where he now stood. The whole forest felt dangerous to him, so whatever Roarke had encountered, Drake considered this to be worse than anything he had already experienced. This was the end of the map. He had gone as far as Roarke had journeyed.

He approached a large rock formation jutting up from the ground and found a cleft in the rocks. As he approached it, a strange sensation that he was not alone overcame him. Fear gripped him and he looked all about, but he could find no evidence that there was anyone or anything nearby. Perhaps something was lurking in the cleft of the rocks. He came to the cleft and something seemed odd about its appearance. Looking into the cleft, he expected to see a shallow hollow in the rocks or a small cave. He held out his dagger, prepared for confrontation should he encounter anything alive within the cave. What he found instead was that the cleft widened to just a bit wider than his shoulders and a steep path appeared downward in the forest where there should have been no hill at all. His curiosity overcame his fear and as he traversed the hill a whole new world opened before his eyes.

He knew he was entering a wondrous place and he knew he had found the secret to this island. Thoughts rushed through his mind, telling him he should turn around and run, never to return. However, he could not quench the desire to learn more and push forward. Roarke had never encountered this or he surely would have marked it on his map. Drake would push on and carry the tale of his findings back to Roarke.

The elf stood guard near the gate, watching the solitary human as he entered the enchanted world. Elves did not kill indiscriminately. He watched with incredulity as the lone man pushed forward, unaware of the dangers that lay in front of him. He let the man pass, thinking that the land, the ogres, the dragons, or the goblins would take care of him.

Drake stared at the expanse of Lavendelle that lay before him at the bottom of the steep grade. He looked back up at where he had come from, but he could not see the cleft he had just passed through or the entrance to the forest he had just left. He made a mental note of his surroundings, added them to Roarke's map, and proceeded forward.

The sentries were already aware of his presence and would watch him closely until he left their area. Once he left, the elves would no longer be concerned.

This was indeed a strange world. Drake had never seen any-thing like it. Off to his left, he saw a heavy forest with huge trees similar to the forest he had just passed through. He had no desire to go that way; he had had enough of forests for a lifetime with just the past two nights in the Haunted Forest. Off to his right, there were southern mountain ranges—ranges that he had not been able to see when he was in Lindisfarne. Straight ahead, three days in the distance by his best estimation, lay a giant volcano rising up above all the land.

It was the volcano that towered above all that piqued his curiosity. This was where he was determined to travel. He realized that to do this he must start living off the land because his supplies would not last. He felt a rush of excitement as he thought about all the stories he would have to share with Roarke when he returned to Lindisfarne.

CHAPTER XIV
THE SOUTHERN MOUNTAIN RANGE

THE day started out like any other for the dwarves who called the mountains their home. Their village, Bradán, sat nestled in between three large mountain passes in the southern mountain range of Lavendelle. The sun rose high in the late morning and the bitterness of the morning air slowly burned off.

The male dwarves labored in the mines around the mountain, above the many paths that led to the work sites. But on this day, one particular path held the interest of a group of young female dwarves. They carried baskets of food and drink to the mines to catch the attention of the young male dwarves who were just learning their trade. This tradition had repeated itself throughout the generations. It was the beginning of the courtship that would lead to lifelong relationships. The female dwarves were dressed in their best hiking clothes and they all wore their cloaks tied tight around their necks.

"Why is she here? Who asked her to come?" the raven-haired dwarf, clearly the leader of the group, asked the pudgy dwarf who was hiking next to her.

The raven-haired dwarf was annoyed with another dwarf who had flaming red hair and walked at the back of the group. "I didn't ask her to come. I believe it was Caitlyn," the pudgy dwarf replied in a whisper.

In the back of the group, Siv, the dwarf with the flaming red hair, was aware of the conversation at the head of the group. She always had a difficult time fitting in with the other female dwarves her age. There were a number of reasons for this. First, Siv was the only dwarf with red hair. Red hair had never been seen among the dwarves. Second, she always had a knack for knowing things that were about to happen that others of her age did not. She was more mature and more perceptive than her peers. Perhaps this was because her mother had died when she was an infant. It was only Siv and her father at home, and Siv didn't have any females in her life to relate to. This was perhaps the biggest obstacle in Siv's ability to integrate with her peers. Regardless of the reasons, the results were still the same: rejection, feelings of isolation, insecurity, and self-doubt.

"Tell Caitlyn to come up here," Raven-hair demanded of Pudgy.

Pudgy dutifully followed her orders. "Caitlyn, can you come up here for a moment?"

Caitlyn, a slender dwarf who was considered the most beautiful among the male dwarves she was preparing to visit, came up to see what the two in the front needed. "Yes, what is it?"

"Did you invite her?" Raven-hair pointed backwards with her thumb toward Siv.

"Yes. Why?"

"She is not welcome here with us! How could you do this? She is a freak. Just look at her hair!"

"I like Siv. She is my friend," Caitlyn began, but Raven-hair didn't let her finish.

"Get rid of her. She will spoil this whole day if you don't!" With that, the two dwarves in front walked ahead and left Caitlyn standing by herself; the rest of the group followed.

Siv approached Caitlyn and said, "Don't worry about me, Caitlyn. I didn't feel much like going anyway."

"Well, Siv, we can head back, or we can go on ahead together on our own."

"I really don't feel much like going today. I don't want to spoil your day. Tobias is expecting you, and you made that special pie for him. You need to go!"

"Siv, if you aren't going, then I'm not going."

Siv glanced ahead and saw that the group was not waiting for them. She took Caitlyn by the arm and said, "Caitlyn, you are my friend and I love you very much, but this is not your battle. This is your day to be with Tobias and I will be greatly offended if you stay back with me. Hurry up and you will catch up with them. I will be fine. I am going off to my Aunt Martha's and have a little talk."

Siv and Caitlyn embraced and Caitlyn hurried off to visit Tobias, something she had been looking forward to for weeks. She had made a special meal for them to enjoy and she was excited to see him.

Siv watched her go, then turned and headed back to the village. A thousand thoughts marched through her head. The biggest, however, was how much she missed her mother, a mother she had never known.

CHAPTER XV
OGRES

It had taken two days on foot for Drake to travel to the great volcano that lay enclosed by the clouds. He knew he could no longer be on the island for the land stretched too far. Somehow, he had passed through a portal in the cleft in the rocks that his mind had no ability to comprehend.

It was late in the afternoon, and Drake looked for a place to make camp. He stumbled on an old campsite. Stones were spread around a fire pit that had been abandoned long ago. He gathered wood to start a small fire. He was determined to put the fire out early and sleep in the dark as he had the night before.

After dinner and after his fire was doused, Drake looked for a place to sleep. He wanted some nook or cranny where he would be protected. He was scrounging around the campsite when he suddenly found a skull—a human skull! The skull remained encased in an old steel helmet. A few ribs, some of the backbone, and some of the pelvis lay scattered on the ground and were all that remained. The arms and legs were missing entirely. It was a gruesome sight. He didn't want to think about what had happened to the rest of the person. The sounds of the night made him think that he probably knew.

He rummaged around the site and found objects that he assumed were the belongings of this unfortunate person. He found a map of the land, a map written in an unfamiliar language, but the landmarks were unmistakable. He decided that he would study the map and decipher the language as best he could.

Near the remains, under a fallen tree, Drake found a sword in a sheath. The detail of the ornate handle amazed him. Polished rubies were embedded in the grip where the fingers rested when holding the weapon. The grip itself was hollow, open its entire length. On the inside of the hollow of the handle there was an inscription that he could not decipher. And, on the end, there was the largest ruby he had ever seen. The scabbard was made of leather, etched and carved with beautiful symbols and ornate designs. Drake was overwhelmed by his good fortune. He would be rich when he returned to Lindisfarne. The large ruby alone should fetch a small fortune, not to mention the sword itself!

He wondered only briefly about the body that lay before him and that such a treasure was never found. Certainly, one who possessed such a weapon was someone of importance, and one for whom a search would be conducted. And, if he was a thief, certainly the owner of this weapon would have wanted it back. If the person was from this world, the body was not in a particularly difficult place to find; indeed, the body was lying out here in the open. His attention floated back to his prize.

He withdrew the sword from its scabbard. The sword was as sharp as though it were new, not as if it had been sitting among ruins for an undetermined period of time. He tested the blade on some of the firewood he had collected. It sliced through the wood with minimal effort. Upon withdrawing the sword, Drake felt a raw sense of power at the thought of possessing such a weapon.

He felt a stirring in his soul to discover more secrets and treasures in this hidden world. He did not know where these feelings came from. He waved the sword above his head as if dancing through some ancient combat. The blade was made of a metal the likes of which he had never seen before. He placed it back in its scabbard and began searching the surroundings for more treasure. He tried on the helmet and it seemed to fit him well. He decided to keep it. The body also had a few coins on it. Drake did not recognize the currency, but he was sure he would find out more in due time. There was nothing else of value. He was thrilled with the map, the helmet, and the sword.

Despite the remains of the body he found, he decided to stay put. He found a covered area to lie down in and spend the night. He kept the new sword close to his side. It was far more of a weapon than the throwing axe or the dagger he had taken from Roarke's place. He drifted off to sleep with a sense of security, knowing he had a great weapon at his disposal.

As the night passed, so did his security. The screams and loud, vicious roars and grunts filled the night and terrified him. His hair stood on end and a thousand small goose bumps rose across his skin throughout the night. All he wanted to do was make himself invisible to whatever was the source of the sounds. He clutched the sword close to his body for a false sense of protection. But tonight, he was left alone.

The crisp morning air wrapped itself around him, chilling him to the bone. He felt the weight of his journey in his tired muscles. He had not experienced a good night's sleep since leaving Lindisfarne.

Drake made a healthy breakfast and quickly left camp, determined to get to the base of the volcano by nightfall. It was a clear morning and he could see the volcano in the distance. No clouds surrounded the peak. He watched, mesmerized, as steam rose from where the peak should have been. Drake had a determined purpose. He had a map that he hoped to decipher so he could avoid any pitfalls on the way to the volcano. He did not know the name of his benefactor, but the map and the sword were sure to serve him well. He liked the helmet too; it fit him perfectly. He studied the map, searching for the most direct route to the volcano, and it was apparent that he would have to veer to the north and approach from that direction. On the other side of the mountain was a huge lake, and before the lake a skull and crossbones had been drawn; this was a universal language easily understood. Roarke's map had the same warnings and he knew he would have to investigate, for it was at this point on Roarke's map where Drake had found the gate into this amazing new world.

He saw areas drawn on the map that looked like fire and tar pits. These stretched out west of the volcano and lay between the mountains to the south and the forest to the north. Curiously, the areas to the east of the volcano and to the south and west of the lake were not defined on his new map. He pondered the past few days. Now he had Roarke's map of the Haunted Forest and a new map of this amazing and hidden world. He also had treasure that would surely bring him a small fortune. He knew that now was the time to turn back; he would be excited to show Roarke everything he had found. But he no longer considered turning back. Lust had begun to stir in his heart ever since he had found his new treasure, the sword. He was headed for the volcano and, hopefully, more riches.

He packed up his belongings and traveled as much as he could under the cover of trees. He avoided open fields and skirted along the edges of meadows as he worked his way toward the north side of the volcano. Surprisingly, he did not encounter much in the way of living creatures, just difficult terrain. He did see a few birds and a few small animals, but that was all. He wondered about the noises he had heard in the night, and his sensibilities made him alert to the potential danger that always lurked before him.

Though he was adventuresome, he was not careless. Drake had always traveled alone. He had single-handedly fought off bears and cougars in his travels. He was a seasoned veteran in terms of exploring. He just had never traveled in Lavendelle before and, indeed, it was different than anything he had previously encountered.

As the afternoon wore on, a stiff breeze began to blow in the clouds over the volcano. He walked into the breeze, making his travel a little more difficult. As he walked up the small foothills leading to the volcano, loud noises erupted up ahead. He rushed to take cover and travel in the dark shade of the forest. He came to a large rock formation and crawled to the top of the rocks. He looked out ahead in the direction of the noises.

Two of the largest, ugliest, and foulest creatures he had ever seen were just below him, feasting on an unfortunate creature. These creatures were larger than any bear he had ever encountered. They had some hair on their bodies—one much more hair than the other—and they had muscles and were incredibly, powerfully built.

They each had two arms and two legs and apparently walked upright like he did. They ripped the limbs off what looked like a moose as though they were plucking petals off a flower. They were devouring the animal in short order, bones and all. The large animal looked as though it was merely a snack for these creatures.

These creatures had broad, round faces; their noses looked to be smashed into and spread across the center of their face. Their mouths were wide set, and they had powerful jaws and razor-sharp teeth. Their hands were enormous. Their worn fingers were gnarled and their nails appeared to be bitten to the quick. He could smell their odor; something the likes of a bear coming out of a long winter's hibernation in its den, only ten times worse. Their grunts were deep and resonated in their barrel chests. The mere sight of them paralyzed Drake.

As he watched these two devour their meal, Drake thought how small the unfortunate moose looked to be from his vantage point. He hoped this was true, for if it wasn't, these creatures were bigger than even he was calculating. He watched one of them stand up and walk around the moose to get to its head. They did indeed walk upright; he had surmised correctly. He watched the beast grab hold of the large antlers, wring the neck of the moose, and rip it from the carcass. Drake shuddered. He couldn't imagine the strength that required!

Though they had an awkward appearance because of their overwhelming size, Drake realized that much of this size was muscle—muscle that allowed them to move effortlessly with quickness and grace.

He correctly assumed that these must be the ogres that he had heard about in folktales about the enchanted world. They had always been portrayed as clumsy, but seeing them in their element, he was sure he would never underestimate them. These were two of the most dangerous creatures he had ever seen in his life—and he had seen a lot.

As they finished feasting, the ogres started fighting over the last of the moose. Their growling erupted from somewhere deep inside their massive chests. The effect froze Drake in place. His mouth became dry. He laid flat against the rock and waited for the beasts to finish. He was helpless in this first encounter with ogres. At least he would have the opportunity to prepare his mind for the next time they met—which hopefully would be never.

He was thankful for the breeze. If it were blowing the other way, the ogres might have picked up his scent. Now he had some idea of what the terror in the night was all about and he wondered what other horrors awaited him.

They gorged themselves for what seemed like an eternity to Drake, but in reality not much time had passed. Once the ogres were gone, Drake went to the moose carcass to see if there was anything he could salvage for himself. The ogres had left surprisingly little, but he was able to salvage enough scraps for a meal. Looking at the carcass, Drake could have easily crawled inside what was left of the rib cage of the beast. It was enormous. The realization of how big the moose was and how the ogres had shredded it in such a relatively short period of time reinforced for him how ferocious these beasts were. They were unlike anything he had encountered before. They would easily rip apart even the most ferocious bear he had ever faced.

Drake looked down at the ground and saw their footprints in the dirt. The prints looked almost human, except for the size. The prints were wider than his two feet put together and longer than his two feet end to end. Interestingly, the footprints were flat, and besides their enormous size, this differentiated them from human tracks.

Chapter XVI
By the River

Siv sat by the river, away from the path where the girls would return from the mines so she would not be seen. She, however, would be able to see everything that was going on. She did not want the other girls to see her.

Her crimson red hair with a hint of strawberry curled down over her shoulders, reaching more than halfway down her back. She loved her red hair, and she loved letting it flow free, waving in the light breeze. The boys seemed to like it as well!

She knew she was different from the other girls. She knew she looked different and she knew her red hair stood out. She didn't understand why she was the way she was, but she liked who she was. It hurt that the others didn't accept her. She had always tried to make friends, but other than Caitlyn, there was no one who accepted her.

Siv was waiting for Ramsey and Teige, two of the boys, to return from the mines. Ramsey and Teige were her cousins and they were a few years older than her. Siv, though not accepted by her peers, was loved by her cousins. It was the fact that her family—her cousins, their mother Martha, her uncle Markus, and her father Elwin—loved her that took away the sting of her peers' rejection.

Ramsey and Teige were the most popular of all the young dwarves. They were rugged, strong, good-looking, and very athletic. Siv loved hanging out with them. She often waited at this spot for them to return from the mines. She would go home with them and visit with Aunt Martha before heading to her home for the night. It was one of the things she looked forward to most days.

It had been several days since she had last visited Martha. She needed to go today. The rejection by the girls hit her hard. She was looking forward to visiting the mines, hanging out with the boys, and seeing Tobias and Caitlyn together.

She strolled along the riverbed, keeping an eye out for Ramsey and Teige as she walked. She picked a small bouquet of wildflowers for Martha. Martha loved flowers and always had fresh flowers around her home. Siv hoped to do the same thing when she had a home of her own.

Finally, she saw the boys as they walked and joked with a group of friends. She crossed the river by tiptoeing over the rocks in the riverbed and she joined the group.

"Hi, Teige," Siv said as she approached her cousin.

"Hi, Siv," Teige said as he slipped his arm around her shoulder and gave her a small embrace.

"Who are the flowers for?" Ramsey inquired.

"I was bringing them to your mother. I thought I would head home with you so we could talk. I haven't seen her in a week, and I really need to talk to her today."

"Well, come on," Teige said.

The group started to break up as they approached the village and each of the boys went his own way home.

"Siv," Ramsey started, "Mother wasn't feeling so well this

morning. She had a hard time even getting out of bed. I don't know if she is feeling better or not. She may not be up for a visit."

"Oh, I am sorry to hear that. How long has she been ill?"

"Just this morning, but she is probably better now. She is never sick," said Teige.

They were approaching their home when Siv backed away and said, "Maybe I will check in with her in the morning. I don't want to come over when she is not feeling well. Would you give her these flowers for me?" Siv handed the small, fragrant bouquet to Teige.

"Sure, but if you want to wait a minute, I will check on her and see how she is feeling," Teige said.

Siv really needed to talk to her aunt. Today had been a rough day. But the last thing Martha needed was to hear of Siv's problems when she was under the weather herself. Siv decided her problems could wait, at least until the morning. "No, I think I will head on home. Tell Martha I hope she feels better and that I will check in on her in the morning."

Siv gave both Teige and Ramsey a big hug, and then she headed off in the direction of her home. She had a hard time disguising her disappointment.

CHAPTER XVII
GOBLINS

DRAKE found himself drained from the encounter with the ogres and he knew it was going to be a long day. It had take him three days on foot to travel from the cleft in the rocks to the foot of the volcano. He saw small geysers shooting blasts of steam out the sides of the volcano. He knew these could severely injure him. He would have to proceed with caution.

Evening began to set in and he was hungry and needed rest. He decided to make camp and investigate the volcano the following day. Hopefully, his search would lead to more treasure. He needed to get back to Lindisfarne and share with Roarke all that he had discovered: his sword, his coins, his new map, his helmet. He was sure Roarke would be excited too.

He found a small, cave-like nook at the base of the volcano and made camp. He soon had a small fire crackling and began to prepare the moose scraps he had salvaged. After cooking the meat, he doused the fire. He was relatively certain the ogres would not be coming back this way because there was nothing left of the moose. Besides, he was tucked away and would be difficult to spot. With that he drifted off to sleep as darkness settled around him.

The scent of fresh kill brought out the ghoulish beasts. They devoured what was left of the once mighty creature down to the small sinew and the big bones. Not a scrap was left. The bones were left behind, for the goblins did not have the strength to crunch the bones with the few teeth they had in their mouths; otherwise, these would have been devoured as well. When they were done, they caught Drake's scent and tracked that scent directly back to his resting place.

A thick cloud cover blocked any light from stars or moon, and the night fell into a vast darkness. Lying in the hollow of a rock Drake had fallen into a deep sleep, but even as he slept, he became aware of a faint red glow. As the light became brighter, it roused him from his sleep and for just a moment he was disoriented. He quickly became fully alert and turned his attention to the ruby on the pommel of his sword. To his amazement, he saw a glow pulsating from it. He then felt the presence of others nearby. He could not hear them or see them. He did not know what was out there, but he knew something was there. As his hand reached down and slid his new sword from its scabbard, his senses immediately grew keener. The blade blazed in the dark and Drake felt a vibration return from the sword as he squeezed it tight. It was as if the sword itself were alive and alert. He had no idea what caused the ruby to glow, nor what made the sword respond in such a fashion.

Before he knew it, a swarm of goblins rushed toward him; at least fifteen strong surrounded him and closed upon him. Drake felt disaster approaching. These were surely the foulest creatures he had ever come across. The smell as they approached was overwhelming; how he did not smell them before they arrived, he was not sure. These creatures rushed at him from all sides. He was clearly outmanned and outnumbered, and Drake knew they were not interested in anything but killing him.

Drake faced the creatures as they approached from all sides. He was still confused and did not realize what he possessed in the sword. And yet, something drove him to pull the sword out and defend himself. He pulled it up in front of him to protect himself from the surrounding hordes and as he did, a certain energy charged through his body. Without thinking, he quickly attacked. In the blink of an eye, in one movement, he swung at the nearest creatures to his left and with one stroke of the sword three of the goblins' heads dropped to the ground. Drake stared at the surreal scene before him. The bodies remained standing in place as the heads rolled to the ground, their vacant and hollow eyes still wide open, staring out into space. It was as if the bodies were unaware that they were dead. A dark, viscous fluid shot out of the stumps of the necks, spewing in all directions, and the headless bodies tried to run away before falling one by one at Drake's feet.

A calmness came over Drake that he could not understand. Facing insurmountable odds as he was, he would have expected his heart to be racing, his breath difficult to catch, and his hands cold and trembling. But instead, he was calm, his senses keen and alert, and as he killed the first of the three assailants, he experienced a lust to kill more. Euphoria engulfed him; it was like nothing he had never experienced before. He was changing on the inside. He didn't realize it, but he was under the spell of the blade.

He was thirsty for blood and went on a killing spree. He slew eight of the twelve remaining goblins in mere moments. His weapon was like none he had ever possessed. It continued to glow and he, once the hunted, now became the hunter. He began searching for more goblins to kill. With the glow from the blade, he was able to see clearly in his camp. With senses he did not realize he had,

Drake quickly found the four remaining goblins huddled together in the dark recesses of the camp. Clearly, they realized the blade was something to fear, if not the man wielding it. He approached and cut down the first goblin. He could not help himself. The sword cut through the goblin's body like it wasn't even there. The goblin lay in two in front of the three remaining creatures.

He thirsted for blood but finally was able to control himself. He wanted treasure, and he was sure that the three creatures in front of him held the key to achieving his goal. He stepped back, still clutching the sword, and motioned for the three remaining goblins to follow him. Reluctantly, the three stepped out of the crevices. They were clearly in fear of this man and his sword.

They had been struck down by the famous goblin slayer, a blade that hadn't been seen by goblins for hundreds of years. The blade had been only a superstition among the goblins—until this wandering party stumbled upon Drake.

Chapter XVIII
Dwarves

DEATH comes like a thief in the night to some, but for others it is preceded by a long, slow march to the bitter end. Indeed, for some, the Grim Reaper can be seen slowly approaching, only to take away the life of a loved one once he arrives. Living beings who see him coming are powerless to stop him. They only get the ability to say good-bye and start their mourning early. Death is a somber time for the living, no matter how it occurs. On this day, in a small home among the dwarves, Death was taking his own sweet time to sweep away the life of a dwarf who should have many more years to live. Death was unpredictable, unfair.

The room was small and lit by only one tiny window. The three dwarves sat in silence as they listened to the adults in the adjoining room. Death was almost certain to come to this home. If something wasn't done soon, there was little hope.

The three were Ramsey, Teige, and Siv. Ramsey and Teige were twins. Twins were uncommon among dwarves. Siv was fifteen, two years younger than her cousins. Siv's father, Elwin, and the twins' father, Markus, were talking in the next room. Martha, Elwin's sister, the twins' mother, and Siv's aunt, was very ill. Markus did not know what else he could do for his wife of twenty years.

Smoke filled the room as the two elder dwarves puffed on their pipes and discussed the fate of their loved one. They sat next to a burning fire and drank ale together.

"We need the medicine from the Cassava root to treat her or she will surely die, Markus," Elwin explained to his brother-in-law.

"I know, Elwin, I know. I do not know where I can find this root. Elijah is the only one I know who can get it, and we haven't seen him for months," Markus replied, as his head sank deeper into his chest.

"If we don't see the wizard by the next feorwertyne niht, I believe she will be gone." Elwin's head also sank into his chest. The two dwarves sat silently in their despair.

It had been a long time since Elijah, leader of the Wizard Council, had made his rounds among the dwarves. Elijah, however, had many responsibilities and no one was ever sure when his next visit would be.

Siv stared at her cousins. They had all heard the older dwarves' conversation. Ramsey and Teige were moved to tears as their mother's health deteriorated. She was so ill; she hardly recognized her own offspring. She slept most of the time, fevering, and being tormented by her dreams. They grieved to see their mother this way; she had always been a source of strength for the boys when their father was working deep in the mines.

"I do not believe Aunt Martha will pass," Siv announced to her cousins. Siv was tall for a female dwarf of her age, but petite. She was delicate, yet even as petite as she was, she said this with authority and confidence.

"How can you say this, Siv?" Teige inquired. "You just heard what they said." Teige's voice sounded hopeful. He and his brother were aware that Siv had an ability to see things and sense things about the future that they did not understand. For that matter, Siv did not understand either, but she did have feelings about things yet to pass that she always seemed to accurately predict.

There were anomalies about Siv that made her different. She was small like a dwarf, but—unlike most dwarves—she had fiery red hair and emerald green eyes . She did not have the dramatic and strong facial features of most dwarves. She had a more delicate, almost elven, look about her. Because there was something different about her, she often stayed with her father instead of going out with other dwarves her own age. In fact, she frequently avoided her peers because they often ridiculed her.

She did not like being different; she was self-conscious about her unusual appearance and her gift of vision, and she did not feel as though she fit in with others. Most dwarves outside of her family did not understand her, so she was shunned. Enchantment, magic, and prophesy were not abilities dwarves possessed. Siv often cursed the gift that made her different. Most often, except among family members, Siv kept her visions to herself.

Siv was extremely agile and quick; in fact, she was the fastest among all the dwarves. To those who knew her, like her cousins, she was loved deeply. There was a purity about her. Siv's words had inspired Ramsey and Teige to feel confident that their mother would live despite hearing what the adults in the adjoining room were saying.

"I cannot sit by and do nothing to help my mother," Ramsey began. "I must find Elijah!"

"But how, Ramsey?" asked Teige. "How will you find him?"

"While Father and Uncle Elwin were speaking, I felt moved to go find Elijah. It is the only way. With Siv saying that mother is going to live, I know that I must strike out now and find him. It is the only way."

"Maybe Elijah is on his way here now. Where would you go? What would you do?" Teige asked.

"I must travel east through the Mystic Forest, to the Tower of the Wizards. It is the only way." Ramsey replied with such conviction that Teige did not question his brother. He wanted his mother to live too, but he did not feel compelled to travel with Ramsey.

Both brothers were among the strongest and most athletic of all the dwarves their age. They had the muscles and maturity of grown dwarves—and an unrealistic confidence in their own strength because neither of them had ever left Bradán and experienced anything else of Lavendelle.

"I know nothing of the tower, nor where to find it, Ramsey, nor even if it exists. It may be only folklore," Teige said to his brother.

Ramsey looked up and stared intently into Siv's eyes. "Tell me, Siv, what do you see? Am I wrong to go, or am I truly called? Is my trip essential to saving my mother, or am I destined for failure?"

There was a long pause. Initially Siv said nothing; she just stared back into Ramsey's eyes. When she heard Ramsey talk about finding Elijah, her heart became troubled. Fear welled up within her as she sensed impending doom for Ramsey.

Finally, she spoke. The room was very quiet. She spoke almost in a whisper.

"Ramsey, you will not make it to the Tower of the Wizards. I sense extreme danger in your trip. I have no idea if you will return to see us again or not, but my heart is troubled at the thought of you going," Siv stated bluntly. "I do not know if your trip would be in vain. I do not see your mother passing, but I cannot tell you if it is because of you."

"I do not have your vision, Siv, and I appreciate what you have to say. I will be careful and will guard myself. But deep in my heart, I know I must go. If my mother was to pass, and I sat by and did nothing, there would be no reason for me to live. I could not go on knowing I let her down. She has been everything to me. I must live and be successful for her," Ramsey stated emphatically.

"She has been everything to all of us," Siv said. Teige nodded in agreement.

Chapter XIX
Home of the Elves

NAUREN was located deep in the forest in the northern regions of Lavendelle. The trees of the forest provided shelter from the harsh winds that occasionally swept across the wastelands from the south. They were massive trees that reached several hundred feet into the sky. Immediately to the southwest of Nauren's forest was the tiny gate that led to the human world. Just as the elves watched over Nauren from the dangers of the surrounding world, they watched over this gate and dangers to Nauren from the human world.

Nauren was known as a grand city throughout all of Lavendelle. The elves who lived in Nauren were highly functional and highly organized. Their city reflected this degree of sophistication.

The elves were governed by a high priest, Osvald, who watched over all aspects of the city. The high priest's firstborn son, Olaf, was the next in line to be High Priest of the Elves and, as such, was in charge of the protection and security of the city as well as the army if it was ever needed. For the past seven hundred and fifty years, there had been no need for an army thanks to the actions of the wizards who had removed Malkavic from their world.

The citizens of Nauren were celebrating the new princess who had been born to Olaf and his wife Ryanne. The first day of the official celebration was over and the wizards had presented the elves with a large crystalline statue of the elves' goddess Naomi to mark Ciarra's birth. The crystal statue was made of one of the hardest stones in all of Lavendelle, and it had taken all the power of the Council to have it sculpted and delivered on time. The detail was meticulous, even down to the necklace Naomi wore and never took off.

Elijah looked down at the little princess, barely a week old, as he held her in his arms. His ancient eyes had seen a lot of new beginnings, and this young baby would someday lead all the elves. He was filled with wonder and amazement as he held this new life in his hands.

"She is beautiful, Olaf. You and Ryanne should be proud!" Elijah began. "And that goes for you too, Osvald." Elijah looked at the high priest, the baby's grandfather.

"She is a blessing for both of us," Olaf said as he wrapped his arm around Ryanne, and the two shared a look between them full of the joy of new parents.

"She is a blessing for *all* of us," Osvald corrected his son as he swept his hand out in front of him across his vast city. "For all of Nauren."

"Indeed, she is, Osvald," Elijah agreed.

Wizards were rare creatures. A wizard would serve on the Council for nearly a millennium until his or her time passed. Elijah recalled Olaf's birth and considered how Olaf had grown and matured. He remembered Osvald coming into this world as well. As he looked down at the tiny baby, he considered how much she favored her mother, Ryanne, more than Olaf. He knew that could all change as she grew.

An interesting feature that Ciarra shared with her mother, but a feature rarely seen in elves, was that Ciarra's ears were rounded on the top rather than coming to a sharp point. Elijah had seen this in the elves infrequently, and when it happened, it only happened in the female elves. Indeed, Elijah could not recall ever coming across a male elf with rounded ears. They were always pointed.

"She favors you, Ryanne, not just in the ears, but in the face as well," Elijah looked at her as he said this.

"Thank you, Elijah. Do you really think so?" Ryanne studied the old wizard.

Elijah returned her look and nodded his head. "I don't know if she will have your red hair or your green eyes. Only time will tell, but I see a lot of you in her."

"I would hope for my daughter to look like my wife and not me!" Olaf laughed.

"The crystal statue of our goddess Naomi is beautiful beyond words," Osvald said as he looked at Elijah. "I have the perfect place for it in the temple."

The high priest had a temple that lay nestled in the forest of the southeastern region of Nauren. This temple was considered the most holy ground to the elves. Osvald often sought out the solitude of the temple when he was weighing heavy decisions.

The temple had been built for the elves by the dwarves, who were the master trade workers. There wasn't anything they could not do; they excelled as carpenters, tinsmiths, and stone masons. This particular temple appeared to be carved out of one piece of pure white marble. The joints where the sheets of marble met were virtually seamless. It was a white shining beacon of purity and beauty unequaled anywhere.

"The temple is the perfect place for this amazing work, Osvald," Elijah said. "As you know, the dwarves carved this statue for you, and it will fit perfectly with the temple they built for all the elves as well!"

A darkness settled momentarily over Osvald's face, but he did not react to Elijah's reference to the dwarves. After the building of the temple—and many other structures in Nauren—something had happened to fracture the relationship between the elves and the dwarves. No one from either community could recall what had occurred between the two cultures, but never again was there a close relationship between them. Even Solomon, with all his wisdom, was never able to bridge the gap. The dwarves returned to their villages in the mountains well south of Nauren, where they had remained since.

"You are holding your meeting at the temple over the next several days?" Olaf began. "It will be nice to have all the wizards here during the festival to celebrate."

"Yes, Olaf, I am happy the other six wizards are here as well, and I can speak for all of us when I say how much we enjoyed this first day of the festival. We have much to discuss during our meetings, but I am sure we will be able to participate in many of the events you have planned over the next week. But, alas, I have many things on my mind and must depart for now." He gently passed Ciarra back to Ryanne.

Elijah took his leave from the royal family. He had big decisions weighing on his mind. Over the past four hundred to five hundred years, the temple had become the new home for the Wizard

Council. This had started during the reign of Seamus, the elven wizard, as leader of the Council. The elves were his ancestors, and he felt comfortable here. Where he did not feel comfortable was at the wizards' tower. Things there had grown increasingly acrimonious with Demetrius, who kept the tower. In fact, many of the wizards had expressed their frustrations in dealing with Demetrius. With the passing of Seamus, Enzo had taken over as head of the Council. Enzo continued in Seamus' footsteps by keeping the meetings at the temple rather than dealing with Demetrius. With the recent passing of Enzo, Elijah had been elected as the new leader of the wizards. This festival, the presentation of the statue of Naomi, and this planned meeting were his first acts as the new leader. He needed to set out a new direction for the Council right away.

The tower had been the seat of the wizards' power and knowledge for all time. It had housed a collection of all known knowledge within Lavendelle. Numerous volumes were scattered in eclectic libraries throughout its chambers. The wizards were now losing their identity with no grounding point. Deep-kept secrets were being lost as was valuable history in just half a millennium. Elijah and Demetrius were the only living connection to the previous Council and to the tower. When they were gone, the remaining wizards would be lost.

The wizards were meeting once again in the open air Temple of the Elves, which was located in the most remote part of the elves' lands. Old traditions long since lost on these wizards needed to be reborn and the new ways of the Council needed to be abandoned before they lost everything! Throughout the generations, timidity and avoidance had never been the wizards' legacy, and the leaderless times of the past several hundred years were about to change.

The temple sat on an island in the middle of a small pond in the southeast region of Nauren. The temple had four wings that met to create a large domed cathedral. The temple had a roof, floors, and columns but what seemed to be missing were the walls. Inside, four massive marble columns anchored the four wings and supported the cathedral ceiling. At the end of each wing a massive fireplace faced the cathedral and when all four fireplaces were burning, the entire temple stayed warm no matter the weather.

Inside, the white marble floors were so well polished that when visitors looked down they would be met by their reflection staring back. The same was found when looking at the ceiling above. Inside the structure a gentle breeze wafted through. The giant trees outside buffered the temple from most of the harsher elements.

On the second day of the festival, the Council was seated inside the temple. Guard posts sat recessed in the trees, unseen, all around to watch over the temple. Many high-level meetings were held here, and the elves patrolled all the grounds. In generations past, this had been crucial. But many generations had come and gone without trouble. This had been the longest stretch of peace ever recorded in Lavendelle. That peace had been achieved by the action of the wizards and the leadership of Solomon the Seer. The elven leadership did not see any reason this would ever change.

The price for the peace had been paid in full, but now trouble brewed in the land. Elijah could feel it. He was on edge, but he could not see from where it was coming or where it was leading. His time as leader of the Council was surely going to be difficult for all in Lavendelle. This made the wizards' efforts to reclaim their fortress, the tower, quite urgent.

There were seven wizards in Nauren to celebrate with the elves and to meet together as the Wizard Council. Eight wizards resided in Lavendelle, but Demetrius, the eighth wizard, had not met together with the other wizards for hundreds of years. Elijah wanted to bring Demetrius to the forefront of the meeting. He knew it was going to be a long and difficult meeting.

Elijah knew that things had to change. No one was able to effectively confront Demetrius, who had kept the tower since the time of the passing of Simon several hundred years earlier. The few times Demetrius had been approached, the encounters were confrontational and difficult. Many on the Council felt Demetrius was possessed by Aelhaeran the Depraved. During Aelhaeran's time, he had nearly destroyed the Wizard Council because of his wicked ways. It was known that Demetrius had discovered Aelhaeran's writings and had become obsessed with them. For most wizards, anything to do with Aelhaeran triggered alarm and they shunned it. Not so for Demetrius. He seemingly embraced all of Aelhaeran's ways.

They sat at the round marble table. Elijah sat next to an open chair on his right—a sign that Demetrius was still recognized as one of the eight. To his left sat the young and beautiful Siobhan, granddaughter of Seamus, the elven wizard of the previous Council and the past leader of the wizards. Then there was Gavin, Margaret, and Alexander. Then there was another open seat: Elijah's former seat prior to the passing of Enzo. This vacant seat also needed to be filled. Hayley, the former druid, was next, and, finally, Elizabeth, the newest member of the Council. It was hard for Elijah to believe, but other than himself, there was no knowledge of the tower among these wizards. In fact, few of them really knew Demetrius; rather they just knew the name and the mystique. Inwardly, many of the wizards were unnerved by him. The same feeling had existed among an earlier Council, the one that had dealt with Aelhaeran the Depraved. Demetrius was being called Demetrius the Demented because of his ways.

"Most of you sitting at this table have never stepped foot inside our tower, the Tower of the Wizards," began Elijah. "It is time that we reclaim this tower as our own. It will again be the symbol of our strength throughout Lavendelle. We risk fracturing the Council and the future for all wizards of Lavendelle. For the past five hundred years, I have watched as we have slowly drifted apart as a group. Our influence is diminishing, we have less focus among us, and we are not able to share our knowledge effectively," Elijah concluded.

A chill settled across the room. What Elijah was proposing was a formidable task.

"These are the lands of my ancestors, Elijah," Siobhan began. "I feel at home here in this temple. We have been meeting here for over four hundred years and this is all most seated here at this table have known. I favor keeping this as our permanent home." Siobhan's grandfather Seamus had moved the Council here, and Siobhan supported her grandfather's decision even long after his passing.

Siobhan's opinion was acknowledged with nods of approval from many sitting at the table. Elijah was aware of the sentiment but needed to stand his ground. He was not *asking* the wizards what needed to be done; he was *telling* them. The others lacked his long-term vision.

Hayley, the former druid, spoke. "This temple belongs to the High Priest of the Elves, and this is the land of the elves. It is not our land. We are guests here. The elves have been generous to us, but how can we come in and take this beautiful land and temple as our own? That is not our way. We are not elves, but now we are being identified as being of the elves."

"I think that we should approach the elves about this matter, Hayley," Margaret stated. "We have Siobhan; she could speak to Osvald and Olaf about it. It seems to be the better path. The alternative would be to approach Demetrius, and we have not been successful at approaching him in the past!"

"Who is going to deal with Demetrius?" Elizabeth, the newest wizard, blurted out. This is what all the wizards were worried about.

"Times change and we need to change. The tower is our past, but this temple, these lands, and the elves should be our future," Siobhan added.

"Margaret, Siobhan, we are not elves; we are wizards," Elijah admonished. "We will not be driven from what is rightfully ours any longer! The tower is our rock and our identity. Our identity and our place in Lavendelle has eroded over time. I remember the days of Solomon and of Simon and the place the Council held in this world. I was there when we confronted and destroyed Malkavic. We as a group could not accomplish something so monumental the way we are today. Look at us! We are all afraid to face the challenge of approaching one of our own to claim that which is rightfully ours! I hang my head in sorrow when I realize how far we have fallen. All of our knowledge and teaching is in the tower. The tower was built by our predecessors and it was built to be ours for all time. No one will possess it, and no one wizard will drive us from our home!"

Elijah paused to let the power of his words have their desired effect. The other wizards remained silent as he continued.

"I will go to Demetrius. He was once my friend. I will deliver our message to him and then determine how best to proceed. But, my friends, we must stand united. This may be the biggest challenge of the Council. It may be the biggest challenge since Simon led the Council in the capture and entombment of the demon Malkavic," Elijah concluded.

The wizards sat silently as the weight of Elijah's words rested upon them. Only Elijah had lived during the time of the oppression of Lavendelle by Malkavic. Inwardly, each of them shuddered at the mere mention of his name. It was clear to all that Elijah was unwavering in his conviction about his position on this matter. He would forge ahead on his own if needed.

Elijah looked at Siobhan, then at Margaret. They both looked down.

Gavin finally spoke: "I am with you Elijah. I too feel as though we need to reclaim that which is ours. I long for the teachings that are kept in the tower."

"I am with you and with Gavin," Hayley began, "and I will go to Demetrius with you if you need me."

"That won't be necessary, Hayley, but thank you," Elijah said. "Demetrius was once my closest friend. I need to go to him as a friend."

"I want to see all that is in the tower. You have my support," Elizabeth stated, emboldened by the others.

All eyes turned to Alexander. He had been quiet most of the meeting, absorbing all that was taking place. This was Alexander's way. When he spoke, he was always thoughtful and carried the weight of a well-thought-out response.

"I have listened to all that has been said. I am convinced by Elijah's words about the state of the Council. I agree that we as a group could not, at this present time, accomplish what our predecessors accomplished with the capture and destruction of Malkavic. I believe in Elijah and his words, and I believe that under his direction we can accomplish this task. More importantly, we should want to accomplish this task. We should long to re-establish our position of strength in all of Lavendelle. We have been blessed with seven hundred and fifty years of freedom because of the bold actions of Solomon and Simon and the wizards of that time. We have taken false confidence in these times of freedom and become soft. We have let our guard down rather than be vigilant. We can change this. I believe that together we can become great again, just as our predecessors Solomon and Simon and the wizards of their generation were great." Alexander paused, he looked at each wizard seated at the table, and finally his eyes rested on Elijah. He looked up at Elijah through his thick, bushy eyebrows, nodded in affirmation, and said, "Elijah, I am with you."

After Alexander's words, Siobhan and Margaret joined in and the Council was united and focused. All were in favor of Elijah, their leader, approaching Demetrius. No one knew what would come after that meeting, but they stood united behind Elijah's leadership. They all knew that the goal was to recapture the tower. The hope was that Elijah would be strong enough to handle Demetrius alone.

Chapter XX
Forgotten Treasure

DRAKE stood with the sword drawn and pointing at the three goblins. The fiery red ruby bathed the goblins in its light. They knew that escape was impossible. It was as though all their energy was being sucked out of them by the presence of Drake and the sword. Their legs nearly buckled under the weight of their bodies.

"I am looking for treasure," Drake growled to the goblins. They clearly understood his words, as he did their reply.

"What is this treasure you are looking for, master," replied the largest of the three that knelt in front of Drake.

"What do you have that is valuable? Where can I find treasure like this sword and this stone?"

The smallest of the three goblins pointed in the direction of the volcano. "That is our home; in there we have our greatest treasure. It is not like your sword, but it was taken from the great wizard long ago. It is all we have."

"Who is this 'great wizard' you speak of? Where is he now?" Drake queried.

"No one knows what became of him. He wandered the lands long ago. Then, on that great night, our lord sent all of our ancestors out to defeat him and steal this 'treasure' from him. The treasure was stolen, and we have it today, but no one knows what to do with it," explained the smallest goblin.

"Why did your lord want it if he did not know what to do with it?" Drake asked. His interest in the treasure grew as they spoke.

"When our warriors returned victorious with the treasure to present to him, he had disappeared, and he has never been seen since."

"Tell me more of what happened that night," Drake pressed.

"We know very little about that night, master," the goblin replied.

Drake instructed the goblins to build a fire. He oversaw their work. They looked as though the life had been drained from them. He did not sense any further danger from the night. The small fire was built in the shallow hollow of a rock. Drake had the three sit on the ground with their backs to the rock as he questioned them.

Again, the smallest of the three spoke: "It has been said that long ago our great Lord Malkavic, lord of all these lands, sent our warriors out to defeat the great wizard. War was brewing between the wizards and the goblins. We were once a great force, but since the disappearance of our lord, our power has crumbled. The great wizard was to strike down our clan and our lord, so our entire colony went out to defeat the wizard before he could defeat us. The wizard's name was Solomon. Solomon had great magic that would destroy us, so we had to steal his magic. But he was powerful, and he was protected in his great tower, so it was very dangerous. That night, the warriors attacked Solomon's tower, but he was not alone. There was another wizard there. His name was Elijah. Elijah lives today, and no goblin will go near him. Elijah is not like any other wizard before him or since. He is a warrior. It has been passed down through our many generations since the great night that

Elijah single-handedly struck down over a thousand goblins with his bare hands. He is a bloodthirsty warrior, and even though he is ancient now, he could kill again."

"Who is this Elijah and how could he still be alive? How do you know he could kill again?" Drake asked.

"Elijah is the head of all wizards in this land. He was young back then, but now he is very old. None of us knows how long wizards can live. None of us has ever heard of a wizard passing," the small goblin said. The two others nodded their heads in agreement.

"What is this magic you speak of?" asked Drake. "I do not believe in magic."

The goblins did not know what to say. They just sat there and stared at Drake. This made him angry, and he stood up and began to pace.

Sensing his agitation, and fearing for his own life, the third goblin spoke. "How is it that you understand us and can speak to us, master? We know you are using magic. No one can speak our language in all these lands."

Drake thought about what the third goblin said. It made sense to him. He did not know how he understood these creatures, or even spoke to them; he just did. Also, he did not understand why the ruby on his sword kept glowing. He never thought about why things were happening the way they were; he was just existing in the moment. He reminded himself that he needed to be more aware.

Clearly, something was happening that he did not fully under-stand. The goblins called it magic, but he knew there had to be an explanation for it; he just didn't know what it was. Moreover, he really did not know what a wizard was, but this Elijah must be extremely dangerous, regardless of his age, he thought to himself.

Drake finally sat down again, warming himself by the fire. The three goblins remained seated and quiet. They had no thought of escape, only self-preservation. That meant doing everything they were told and answering all of Drake's questions.

"So . . . you stole this magic treasure from the great wizard. Why did he not come back and get it?" Drake asked.

The smallest goblin spoke again; he was clearly the leader of the three remaining goblins. "No one knows what happened to Solomon. He has never been seen since. Rumor has it that he perished in the great battle, but no one saw him die. Only his absence is a witness to his demise. Even if he were to have survived, the treasure is buried deep in the volcano. There is a maze of tunnels in that mountain. One could get lost in there and spend his whole life trying to find his way out."

"And what happened to this Malkavic that you speak of?" Drake continued to press for answers. "Tell me more of him."

The name of Malkavic still brought shudders to those who heard it. Clearly, Drake was from elsewhere for there was no fear associated with the name. The mere utterance of Malkavic brought immediate emotions and remembrances of his tyranny to all in Lavendelle.

The goblins were frightened. They were seated across from a great warrior who had single-handedly cut down their entire band without even a moment's hesitation. He spoke their language, he had great magic about him, and yet he did not acknowledge the existence of magic. Now he did not even give a thought to the name of Malkavic. They had no idea who Drake was, nor where he came from. For that matter, Drake was already beginning to forget as the magic in the sword worked within him.

"Malkavic was the lord of all these lands. He lived deep in the volcano. We served him. In fact, that is where many of us live to this day. When the raiding parties were driven back from the tower of Solomon by Elijah, they returned to the volcano. They had accomplished their mission and stole the treasure away from Solomon. They went to present the treasure to our lord, but he was gone. Days, weeks, months, and eventually years went by. He was never to return. Now his name is only the name of legends past. So many generations have passed, and he has never been seen again."

"And you say that you have this treasure in the volcano now?" asked Drake.

The goblin nodded. "It still sits in Lord Malkavic's chamber. It is of no use to us. It has remained there, waiting for his return."

Drake knew he must see this treasure that they were talking about. He also knew that without the help of these three goblins, he would never see it—given the description of the volcano with all its passages.

"I want you to take me to this treasure now," Drake demanded. With that, the three goblins stood up, and the party set off for the volcano. Daybreak was still an hour away, but by nightfall, Drake figured to have his hands on this powerful—yet unknown—treasure.

Drake was not an introspective man, and he could not resist the temptation that lay before him. He lived in the moment. Unfortunately for him, Lindisfarne, though only a handful of days in his past, was already becoming a distant memory. Lust for treasure and for the unknown blossomed in Drake's soul, and the path to personal destruction was the path he chose when he struck out toward the volcano with the three remaining goblins.

Chapter XXI
The Old Dwarf

Yuri was an old dwarf. Much of the ways of the dwarves these days passed him by. The hustle and bustle of dwarf life was too much for the aged Yuri to keep up with, at least that is what the other dwarves would tell themselves. In Yuri's day, however, he had been the strongest and the leader of all the dwarves. He had been so strong that he had outlived his wife, his children, and all of his friends. Now he lived on the edge of the Bradán at the base of Mount Ollmhór in a small stone cottage that he had built with his own hands, forgotten by most except a few neighbors who would occasionally check in on him, essentially waiting for him to die.

The greatness of Yuri, however, was not forgotten by all dwarves, as Yuri soon discovered when on this night a young dwarf approached on the lightly trodden path to his cottage to pick his brain about the journeys of his youth.

The chilly mountain air misted her breath and she could be seen from a distance as she spoke her thoughts out loud, trying to work out what she was going to say. She was nervous, but there was no one around to hear her words. The sun had set beyond the mountains, giving a light purple hue to the cloudless evening sky.

Light from within the cottage illuminated the front porch as she approached. Smoke from the chimney rose into the evening sky, bringing with it a strong hickory smell. It was clear that the inhabitant of the cottage was home and still awake. She was uncertain if she was actually at Yuri's cottage because she had never been to his cottage before, nor had she ever met Yuri. She only knew of his reputation, and she hoped that the stories were true.

Siv arrived at the front door—tiny, fragile, and very alone. Finally, she reached up to the hammer-and-plate knocker on the door, picked up the small hammer, and rapped it three times on the plate. Then she waited. At first, she heard nothing. All remained still within the cottage.

Yuri heard the rapping at the door. It was late. Dinner was over. He was not expecting guests. In fact, he could not remember the last time he had heard the familiar rapping at the door. He sat silently, smoking his long stem emerald green pipe, wondering if his mind was playing tricks on him.

Yuri continued to examine the elfin ring in his hands. He held this ring often as he had always been curious about it. It had been years ago that he found it along the paths to the mines. He never understood how something belonging to an elf ended up in Bradán, for the elves and the dwarves avoided each other at all costs. Outside, Siv waited nervously for a response. She heard movement within the cottage and she hoped that her knock would soon be answered.

Yuri was sure he had heard the knocker. He was sure that his mind—as sharp as it ever had been—was not playing tricks on him. It was not his mind that was aging, only his strength that had been slowly eroded with time. Time, the ultimate force, wears life away, slowly, methodically, and without any way to stop it.

Yuri rose, picked up his cane, and proceeded slowly to his door to meet the uninvited guest or guests who were interrupting his evening. He opened the door and the light from the cottage spilled out onto the porch. He blinked his eyes and found himself looking down into the anxious face of a young female dwarf. His grey beard trickled down onto his chest, his body hunched over at the shoulders. It was hard to envision a great warrior once inhabiting this now seemingly fragile, old frame.

"Yes, what is it?" Yuri inquired.

"Yuri?" Siv uttered in a hoarse whisper.

"It is me," Yuri replied. "And who might you be?"

"I am Siv, daughter of Elwin."

"There is not much dwarf in you, daughter of Elwin," Yuri said bluntly. He had a keen eye, and at his age, there was little time to mince words.

Siv did not like having her obvious differences pointed out so directly.

"What business do you have with an old dwarf on this night?" Yuri asked. It was late, he was tired, and he was in no mood to let her into his home. "I know of Elwin. I have no business with him," Yuri finished. He stood his ground unyielding in the doorway. Even with his ancient frame, Yuri had a presence about him.

"Please help me, sir," Siv implored. "My aunt Martha is dying. You are the only one who can help."

Although little Siv looked distraught, Yuri saw a strength in her that he seldom saw in other dwarves. He backed up. "Please, come in," he said, in a much less confrontational voice, as he yielded the door and invited Siv into his cottage.

The sitting area was small and Yuri sat in a chair by the fireplace where he had been sitting prior to this disruption. Siv sat on a small bench opposite the chair.

"Your grandfather was Aldwin, is that correct?" Yuri inquired.

Siv nodded affirmatively.

"You might not know it, but Aldwin, your grandfather, was great friends with my boys. He was here often," Yuri softened as he began to feel a connection with Siv.

Siv began to relax as Yuri relaxed. She too began to feel a connection with Yuri as they found commonality in familiar dwarves.

"You have not told me what I can do for you," Yuri said, this time much more softly. "How can I help Martha?"

"My aunt needs Cassava root," Siv blurted out.

"I do not have this, my dear. I am sorry you have wasted your time. If I had any, it surely would be yours. Elijah, the wizard, is the only source of Cassava that I know. You need to see him."

Siv looked up at Yuri with her emerald green eyes and said, "I know you don't have any Cassava root."

Yuri shifted in his chair and waited for an explanation.

"I know that you do not have the Cassava root, and I know that there is no root to be found anywhere around. The only one who can help us is Elijah. But he is long overdue for a visit."

"I still don't see how I can help you. I do not know how to reach Elijah. No one knows the way of wizards; they come and go at their pleasure. For all we know, Elijah is aware of Martha's troubles and is on his way here now." Yuri tried to relieve her concern.

Siv was not persuaded. "But Elijah may not know about Martha, and he may not come before she passes. I must do everything in my power to try to save her," Siv insisted.

"And what is it that you propose? And how do I come into your plans?" Yuri sat back and relit his pipe.

"My cousin Ramsey, Martha's son, wants to go find Elijah and bring him back here to save Martha. We heard our fathers talking, and they said she only had a few weeks before it is too late," Siv explained as she looked into Yuri's eyes.

Yuri could tell there was a lot more to Siv than met the eye as he returned her stare.

"I do not know where the wizard is!" Yuri exclaimed. "Who told you that I would know?"

"You are a legend among the dwarves, Yuri. Everyone knows how you have explored all Lavendelle. I know you have even been to the volcano! Ramsey insists on going to the Tower of the Wizards," Siv began, "but I fear for him. I sense that he will not make it and that he will perish on this journey!" She hung her head. "I can't explain how I know this, Yuri; I just do. I get visions of things to come. I don't tell anyone about these visions as my friends make fun of me when I do. But I do see things, and they always come to pass. I can't let Ramsey make this journey. Ramsey asked me if he would make it. I told him that he would not reach the tower, but I was afraid to tell him that I saw him perish on this journey. I didn't have the strength to tell him. Besides, I do not think I could deter him from this journey regardless of what I said. He is coming to see you, Yuri. I just left my cousins, Ramsey and Teige, and they talked about coming to see you tomorrow night. I had to come tonight and see you first. I cannot let Ramsey make this journey! You have been there, haven't you, Yuri? I must travel there to find Elijah. I cannot let Ramsey make this journey." Siv began weeping as she finished.

Now Yuri knew the purpose of the visit tonight and the weight of Siv's story rested heavily upon him. He dropped his head and kept his thoughts to himself for the moment. She had no idea what she was asking of him. She had no idea of the dangers that lay outside of the mountains. Moreover, her innocence was all too obvious to Yuri. It was a noble cause, indeed. It was a cause that should be taken up by men, not an adolescent female dwarf. Indeed, if Yuri still had the strength in his ancient body, he would seek out the wizard himself, but not Siv. She was not ready to face the dangers of Lavendelle.

"You will not find the wizard at the tower," Yuri stated. He had nothing left to add. He did not want to add any more encouragement. "You should go now."

Yuri's words hit Siv hard and she sat in stunned silence. She had no response and so she said nothing. She stared intently at Yuri, waiting for more. He knew she needed his knowledge. But Siv affected Yuri like no other before. He knew by her stare that she sensed he held the answers for which she was searching. As if knowing her mind, he understood that she feared for her cousin Ramsey, who would go regardless of what she said to him. Yuri believed in her vision of Ramsey's demise, even though he did not understand how she could see into the future. Yuri knew he would not be able to dissuade Siv from striking out on her own. He also knew that Siv's only chance for success lay with him.

Yuri stared at his pipe, ignoring Siv's stare. He felt Siv's intense green eyes burning into the top of his head. He did not want to look up and see her staring at him, but he knew he had to. How could one so young, seemingly a child, have such a presence about her? How could he sense her presence without even looking at her? In all his many years, he had never encountered one such as Siv, ever.

Yuri lifted his head and looked into Siv's gaze. It was just as he had sensed: She was able to project her image into his mind and he knew he would do whatever she asked of him, even against his best instincts.

More was being accomplished by Siv and her nonverbal confrontation with Yuri than could be accomplished by all her words. She waited on Yuri for a reply.

Yuri had been alive for many years since the passing of his wife and children without having anything meaningful happen. He had often wondered why he was still alive, outliving all his loved ones and all his offspring. Today had started like any other day, but with that knock on his door, all the answers to the questions he had had for so many years were beginning to unfold. He still had purpose and could still add meaning to his world.

"You are the only living soul among us who has traveled Lavendelle," Siv began. "You are the only one I know I can turn to for help."

Siv paused, waiting, hoping for Yuri to feel the importance and urgency of her cause and rush to her aid.

"I will be gone this night," she continued, "with or without your help. It is not a calling for Ramsey for he will die. It is my calling. I must go! My aunt is on her deathbed. Only the medicine from the Cassava plant can save her. If we do not have that medicine by the next feorwertyne niht, she will pass. I would not ask you for your guidance if I had the luxury of time, but I do not." Siv's green eyes pleaded with Yuri. "My only hope is that I can make it to the Tower of the Wizards to find Elijah, or at least to call for him, or all is lost. Please, Yuri, I beg you not to turn me away. I need your help. You are the only hope I have of making this a successful venture," Siv finished.

Yuri tore his gaze away from Siv's eyes and looked upward to consider the weight of her words.

"Siv, I do not know how you can survive," Yuri said. "I was strong in my youth, and I had a strong desire to explore this world. But even with all my strength, I nearly lost my life in my travels. It is dangerous out there. Lavendelle is known as the enchanted lands for a reason; there is magic. That is the problem with dwarves: We cannot feel nor sense magic. Although, with you, it may be different given the visions you have regarding the future. But for most dwarves, it is as though we are walking blind and alone in a very dangerous world. You can trust no one when you leave these mountains. NO ONE!" Yuri was emphatic. "You will not find Elijah at the tower. I met Elijah on my journeys. At that time, he told me that he no longer visits the tower. Therefore, there is no purpose to your travels," Yuri stated unequivocally.

"It has been many years since you wandered Lavendelle, Yuri," Siv began. "How can you be sure the wizard has not returned to the tower in all this time?"

"You ask a good question. I cannot be sure of anything any-more . . . anything, that is, except the overwhelming danger you face in trying to reach the Tower of the Wizards. The last I heard, the tower was occupied by a demented wizard, one that I warn you to steer clear of!"

Yuri motioned for her to remain seated. He walked into the back room of the cottage where he remained for several minutes before returning. Against his better instincts, he laid an ancient pack on the table and slowly untied the straps.

Siv watched Yuri in silence. He puffed away at his pipe; the earthy scent of the cherry-flavored tobacco smoke filled the cottage. A candle flickered on the table where Yuri had placed the pack and the fire in the fireplace warmed the air. Darkness crept in from the corners of the cottage as the light in the windows began to fade away.

Siv focused on a map Yuri had unfolded in front of her. Bradán was easy to spot in the middle of the rugged mountains. Near the southeast corner of the map was the wizards' tower.

"There it is," Yuri started, pointing to the right side of the map. "It is rugged land, and dangers lurk throughout. You must avoid being seen, and if you are seen, you must strive to get out of sight. Trust no one until you find Elijah.

"Look here, you must scale this mountain, Mount Ollmhór," he continued. "This is a formidable task. You must leave hours before daybreak and reach the summit by the end of the morning. The trees stop growing toward the top and it is here you will be exposed. This presents an early and very real danger. If the day is clear, you must reach the summit by the end of the morning or lightning storms are likely to move in and you must take cover. If the day is not clear and weather sets in early, you must take cover before the tree line and let it pass. It is too dangerous to try to summit the mountain in bad weather and it will surely destroy your chances of getting to the tower if you attempt it."

Siv listened and stored this information in the back of her mind.

Yuri continued, "When you get to the summit, you do not have time to waste; you must scale down the other side of the mountain as quickly as possible. Look here to the north," Yuri moved his finger along the map. "This looks to be the quickest way down. If you take this route, you will surely be several days off of where you need to be when you reach the base. You must head south; this area along the north is not passable. You will have to go back up the peak and head south, so don't make that mistake."

Siv nodded and made a mental note of this instruction. The trip was becoming very real and she listened intently. She stared at the map and was able to recall every detail that Yuri was explaining. She also took in the vast lands drawn by Yuri's own hand. She noted that far to her north—and not in the direction of the pass—was Nauren, home of the elves. She had heard of Nauren, but she had no idea whether it was real or where it was located. Now she knew. She also saw the large lake and the volcano to the north and east of the tower. She was amazed at all Yuri had done and seen in his youth. Yuri was impressive, indeed, and she wished to know more of him. She would plan on visiting him often—provided she survived this journey.

"Once you head down, go south. From the top of Mount Ollmhór, it looks to be the harder way, but it gets easier as you go. You must head straight for the trees and get off the top of the mountain. Beginning around mid-day, dragons start flying over the mountaintops, looking for prey. Don't become prey. They are treacherous beasts and not something a dwarf is prepared to deal with. These boulder fields are dangerous as you head down the mountain. They cannot be avoided as you traverse the southern route. You must cross them with care. If you go straight down, you will surely cause a rock slide. A slide could trap you and crush you. You must zigzag down the mountain, always heading south and east. Once you reach tree cover and you are out of the boulder fields, you can head straight down from there." Siv listened in silence.

Yuri stopped speaking for a moment. He got up, walked to the mantle, and reached for his pouch of tobacco. He let the weight of his words sink in. His mind was sharp and his recollections clear. He longed for the strength to once more set out with Siv, but there was no strength left for him to call upon. He had lived long past his days.

Yuri had always been different than the other dwarves, much the same as Siv was different. He knew he had to help her or she would just waste her life in a vain attempt to help her aunt. He took a long draw from his pipe as he reflected on the situation and on Siv's powerful presence. Then he headed back to the table and the map.

"Look here," Yuri pointed to the map. "Once you reach the bottom, you are out of the mountains. You will be entering the Mystic Forest. This forest is an ethereal place. It is full of life and it is heavily overgrown with vegetation. This vegetation will be your friend if you are smart, Siv, provided you make it to the forest. Keep yourself among the vegetation so that you are not seen. There are all sorts of creatures you may encounter, and many of them are evil. Avoid every creature and pull back from any encounter. This is the only way you will be able to make it out of this forest. Trust no one. Live among the forest greenery and stay out of sight."

Siv nodded slowly as she began to understand the enormity of the task that lay ahead of her. Her attention turned back to Yuri as he began to speak again.

"Head due east when you come to the forest," Yuri continued. "After a few hours, you should come across a large stream. Follow it away from the mountain. It will guide you through the forest and to the vast plains that open up before the Tower of the Wizards and the great lake just to the east of the tower. It is the lake the stream seeks. You must hide along the banks of the river as you approach the tower. It is in these plains that you will be most exposed. If you have made it this far, you have done well, but the most dangerous part of your journey lies ahead.

Siv remained silent, but she felt her heart sink inside her chest.

How would she ever survive a journey filled with so many perils, she wondered?

"You may think it wise to travel at night along the river so as not to be seen," Yuri continued. "Do not do it, Siv," Yuri stated emphatically. "Your scent will give you away and you will most likely be taken by goblins, ogres, dragons, or one of the many predators roaming the plains at night. When you come to the great plains, follow the stream at daybreak and travel quickly to the tower. You should be able to make it in a half-day or a little more. I can help you no more beyond that. The rest is up to you. I do not know what you will encounter at the tower, but I am sure it won't be Elijah."

Siv sat back and let Yuri's words sink in. The task was formidable indeed, and there was no guarantee that the endgame of reaching the tower would provide the reward for which she hoped. Siv could not see the outcome of the journey in her mind, but she felt positive that Martha was going to live. Was it because of her journey? That she could not say. She also felt equally strongly that she could not let Ramsey make this journey or he would surely die.

"Look here at this pack, Siv." Yuri extended his hand. Her green eyes followed Yuri's outstretched arm. "Here is what I took on my travels: this pack, this map, a small blanket roll, a canteen, and this axe and dagger. They served me well, and they will serve you as well if you will take them."

Siv considered what was before her. She did not have anything she needed for such a journey, yet here before her lay all that she needed; ancient as the items were, they had served Yuri well.

"Thank you, Yuri. I will bring them all back to you intact when I return with Elijah and the Cassava root," she asserted. She didn't know how she was going to accomplish this task; she only knew that she had to go. With these supplies she would be able to leave this coming morning, before she had time to consider all that she had learned and well before Ramsey would start preparing for his journey.

Siv got up, took Yuri's pack, and placed all of the contents securely back inside. "Thank you, Yuri," she said. Siv looked into Yuri's eyes and he looked deep into hers. They both understood that this meeting tonight had been unavoidable now that they had met. They were kindred spirits. Siv approached Yuri and embraced him for a long time before she whispered, "I will come back to see you. There is so much I need to know. Thank you for helping me."

Yuri stood there and watched as Siv walked away into the night, wondering if he had just sent Siv off to her death or if she would be successful and save her aunt. If he hadn't helped her, he told himself, he was sure that Siv would journey in vain with no chance of success.

Heed my warnings, Siv, heed my warnings, Yuri said to himself as he watched her disappear into the night. A cool breeze chilled the old dwarf as he turned to his cottage and shut his door. It would be a long night, of that he was sure.

This night was Yuri's answer to why he still lived. This night was one of the most important nights of his life and certainly the most relevant for decades. Who would have thought this day so important? It started like any other day and went on like most. It was only as Yuri was settling in for the evening that a small rap on the door had changed his life. Little did he realize, but he had just played an important role in the progression of the 750 year old prophecy of Solomon. The realization of that prophecy was sensed by Elijah, but the wizard did not know what he was sensing other than a great and dark disturbance in the land.

CЂAPCER XXII
CЂE COWER

THE meeting of the Wizard Council was over, and Elijah
needed to act. Time was precious; each wizard only had a millennium to accomplish all of his works and then his time was complete. Solomon had been the last great wizard. Elijah would not
be considered among the great, he was sure, but at least it would
be said about Elijah that he took the tasks he had been given and
faced them head on and did not avoid the difficult problems of his
time. He wanted to be known for always doing the right thing and
always placing the good of the Council first.

Although Elijah had never considered himself great, those of
Lavendelle, and even the younger wizards on the Council, knew
Elijah as the Warrior Wizard. His actions on the night the tower
was overrun by goblins were of lore throughout all of Lavendelle.
His reputation had been sealed on that night, even before he
had become a wizard. He was held in high esteem throughout
Lavendelle. Even his friend Demetrius revered Elijah. However, the
very night that the enlightened of Lavendelle looked at as a stun-
ning victory over an overwhelming force of goblins was the night
Elijah looked back on as the greatest failure of his life.

He had failed to accomplish the one task that Solomon had

placed him in charge of: protect the prophecy. Little did Elijah realize—for it was in the destroyed portion of the prophecy—that the enemy was supposed to obtain the entire prophecy that night. Even Solomon had not recognized the great warrior within Elijah and his ability to savagely attack and beat back the goblins to protect the prophecy. Indeed, if the goblin who had grabbed the document had not fallen to its death with half of it, Elijah would have certainly been able to escape with the entire prophecy intact.

Elijah did not realize it, but on that fateful night even Solomon watched with awe at Elijah's savage and brutal response to the goblin attack. Elijah did not use spells but rather displayed savage fury in hand-to-hand combat. Only Elijah realized that the fury he unleashed was a result of the magic in the dagger. What Elijah did not realize was that it was his character and his makeup that allowed the magic to flow from the dagger and course through him. A lesser wizard would not have been able to accomplish what Elijah had accomplished.

Elijah took his time traveling to the tower. There was much to contemplate. Normally, he could have been there in one to two days; however, it took Elijah three days to travel from Nauren to the Tower of the Wizards. He was worried about how the approaching confrontation with Demetrius would play out. He was also concerned about neglecting those in Lavendelle who were dependent upon him. Elijah knew it was time for him to find a follower to help him fulfill all his duties. He resolved to face this task once he had addressed the issues with Demetrius.

Frustration mounted within Elijah as he approached the tower. How had the Council and, even more important, how had *he*, let it come to this? Elijah had not even come near the tower for decades. As he drew closer, he could see the neglect to the grounds and to the formerly magnificent tower. This was so unlike the Demetrius he had known in his youth.

The once wide path of stone to the majestic doors of the tower was now reclaimed by the living soil underneath his feet. No hint of the path existed. Trees had grown tall in the once treeless plain in front of the tower so that the previously unobstructed view of the land was gone. The manicured fortress was no longer; instead, the tower was falling into ruin. Security was certainly compromised. Granted, since the demise of Malkavic there had been an unprecedented peace, but something within Elijah told him that those days were quickly coming to an end.

By the time Elijah reached the entrance to the tower he was full of anger. If Demetrius had appeared at that moment, he would have received the full wrath of Elijah, a wrath that even Elijah did not know existed.

The beautiful entrance to the tower was now barricaded by dead logs. Nothing was formidable about the place. Elijah was not certain Demetrius was even alive or at the tower any longer. He knew of the side entrance, and he knew of the entrance from the boulder field, but Elijah was not going to reclaim the tower by entering it from the back. He was here to stay. He was here to reclaim the wizards' rightful home.

His anger now matched that of the night the goblins had overtaken the tower. Elijah looked out from the landing and raised his staff. He closed his eyes and channeled his emotion. He then smote all trees and vegetation as far as his eyes could see. The stone path suddenly reappeared as the vegetation overgrowing it was swept away in the blink of an eye.

From a distance, two druids, former followers of Demetrius, had been working their way toward the tower. They were slowly stealing from the wizards. They would enter by the servants' entrance and take from the once majestic tower. They had taken the keys to the servants' quarters with them when they were dismissed. Demetrius had never even noticed the keys were missing.

As they approached, they saw a blinding light shoot out from the front of the tower. All the trees and vegetation were instantly destroyed. They had never witnessed such overwhelming force before. When all the dust settled, they saw a lone wizard standing strong, his staff outstretched over all the destruction. A new day had arrived, and the days of robbing the tower blind were over. The two scurried off back toward their home, frightened that they would be discovered; frightened that Elijah would see their guilt. And so the fear of Elijah would spread once again as word of his wrath disseminated among those living in Lavendelle.

The destruction of the trees and vegetation did little to quell the fury within Elijah. All he had to do was turn and face the seemingly impassable entrance. He raised his staff once again and destruction spread in an instant from the top of his staff to the barricaded doors. The logs and remnants of the doors were obliterated into the tiniest of particles as the energy from the staff pulverized everything in its way.

Elijah entered the tower and slowly turned in a full circle, taking in the devastation before him. He saw nothing that resembled any form of the former residence of the once majestic tower. Dirt, dust, and an overgrowth of vegetation crept throughout the interior.

Instead of being calmed by the release of his fury, Elijah's anger grew. His arrival at the tower was generations too late, but now he clearly had a mission, and his strength seemingly grew as he released a fury like no living creature of his generation had ever seen or heard. He now knew the full power he possessed. But he was not done. He walked into the chamber of the wizards and approached the fire pit. The room was empty and cold. He knew a fire hadn't burned here for generations. He stepped down into the center of the fire pit, which represented the center of the tower. With both hands he took his staff and raised it above his head. He uttered a spell as he drove the spike of the staff directly into the center of the pit at his feet.

A cyclone appeared out of the ashes and engulfed Elijah. The cyclone continued to grow to enormous size, driven by the rage and fury within the wizard. Blue light emanated from the spike of his staff, illuminating Elijah and his surroundings in an awesome and fearful spectacle.

From his den in the cellar of the tower, Demetrius rose, aware that something very powerful was happening for the first time in many generations. He scaled the steps and burst into the ante-chamber, ready to confront the source of the disturbance. What he witnessed shocked him to his core, and for the first time in his life as a wizard, he sensed fear scuttling down his spine as he saw Elijah's full wrath displayed before him. The blue light emanating from Elijah's staff was casting an eerie glow around him. He stood at the center of the cyclone with his arms raised. Demetrius witnessed an intensity unseen in almost eight centuries, and he was now certain that all he had heard of Elijah was a watered down version of the true fury he had displayed on the night of the attack on the tower.

Everything not made of stone or bolted to the floors or walls of the tower was swept out of the front entrance: all floors, all walls, and all rooms, everything in the tower was scrubbed away; only the writings of the libraries were spared. The winds from the cyclone captured Demetrius and threw him to the corner of the antechamber. The shock of the power before him stirred something deep within Demetrius, something that brought him immediately out of the dark place he had been for many, many years and forced him back to reality.

Within moments it was over, and Elijah stepped out of the pit. He took his staff, pointed it at the fire pit, and a large fire sprang to life. He then pointed his staff at a cowering Demetrius and uttered the following: "Demetrius, you have disgraced our ancestors. You have disgraced the Council. You are relieved of your possession of this tower. I will be taking possession of this tower as of now. I will be in the upper chamber. I will meet with you in the morning after you gather yourself."

Demetrius had never been witness to such fury—or such overwhelming magic—in all his days as a wizard, even during his time as an apprentice with Simon. He knew his magic was no match for Elijah. He had been engulfed in the dark world of Aelhaeran for generations, and nothing he had done nor studied prepared him to face what he faced on this day: pure, raw, savage fury. As he reflected on what he had seen, he realized that nothing he had learned while studying the dark art of wizardry of Aelhaeran compared to what he had just witnessed from Elijah. Now, as if transformed back to the days of his early years as a wizard, Demetrius remembered his friend Elijah and his position on the Council and stood down.

Elijah ascended to the upper chamber. As he regained control of his anger, he found himself startled to realize that he did not know where such awesome power came from. Thankfully, he had the strength to control and channel that rage. He was aware of Solomon's words to him on the night that Solomon had disappeared: "I have acquired power beyond your ability to understand or my ability to teach you." Well, Elijah was learning; he was just beginning to experience the power of being leader of the Wizard Council. Elijah marveled at how he continued to learn about himself. Even after seven hundred and fifty years as a wizard, he continued to learn.

When Elijah had approached the tower on this day, he had been unsure of how he would approach Demetrius and address him. However, upon reaching the tower and observing its state, his actions became instinctive as he knew deep inside what had to be done. He had accomplished the hardest part of his task. Now he needed to be smart and make Demetrius an ally rather than a powerful foe. He recalled how Aelhaeran had turned against the Council in the ancient past. Demetrius had been his friend, and now he needed Elijah's help. Elijah was determined to help Demetrius if his friend would let him.

His work was not finished; there was still much he needed to accomplish. A terrible time for Lavendelle was coming, and the wizards were not prepared to face it. Elijah did not know if he had the time needed to help the Council face the coming danger. The problem for Elijah was that he could not see from where nor when the storm would approach; he could only read the signs of dark storm clouds gathering, storm clouds that had gathered quickly with the resurrection of Malkavic's sword and the presence of the human, Drake Scott.

Chapter XXIII
Inside the Volcano

THE day passed quickly as the party approached the entrance into the volcano. Thoughts of treasure were at the forefront of Drake's mind. He tried to evaluate the dangers. Clearly, Malkavic was dead and gone, and for that matter so was Solomon. But Elijah was another story. He was alive and feared by these ghastly creatures. And according to the small one, Elijah had killed legions to get this treasure back. Drake must find out more about that night and Elijah. He must proceed with caution.

"Tell me more of the night the treasure was taken and more of this Elijah," Drake said to the small goblin as they treaded ever closer to the volcano.

"Elijah is a warrior wizard. All of our warriors who reached the tower were wiped out; only a few escaped to tell about it, and those were the ones with the treasure. Even the warrior who escaped with this treasure was slain by Elijah as he fell to his death. This was witnessed by the raiding party below. After we captured the treasure, the warriors returned to the volcano to present it to our lord, but, as I told you, he was gone," the creature finished.

"Yes, but you said Elijah came to the volcano. Tell me about that," Drake implored.

"When the warriors returned, there was no sign of Malkavic. The treasure was taken to his chamber, but he was gone. Soon, a large search for him was made. It was still nighttime. Then, an ominous green glow was seen approaching. It was the same glow that was seen in the chamber of the wizards. The warriors were summoned to see what was coming and determine if it was Malkavic. It was not Malkavic; it was Elijah. The story is that he was mad, crazy with rage. No one had seen anything like it before. He came not with magic and a staff, no, he came with sword in hand. He cut down every warrior he saw. There was no escaping him. Ten would jump on him, and ten would lay dead at his feet moments later. He moved with such swiftness and power; he was unstoppable. The only way he was stopped was by us retreating into the volcano. Elijah made it to the chamber where the treasure was, but before he got there, the treasure was removed and taken away. I don't know where they hid it. Perhaps they took it through the maze of tunnels, or perhaps they took it to the Chamber of the Gatekeeper below. The fact is they kept it from him until he was gone."

"What is this chamber?" Drake inquired.

"It is a chamber deep in the volcano. It is the home of a powerful presence known as the Gatekeeper. No one goes down there! No one!"

"Why not? Who is this Gatekeeper?" Drake pressed the creature for answers, but he could get no more useful information about the Gatekeeper or the chamber. He decided to drop this line of questioning for the time being, but he was determined to investigate again when the time was right. "So what did this Elijah finally do when he couldn't find the treasure?" Drake continued.

"Elijah killed every remaining soul in the chamber; none could escape, and none could stop him."

"So what made him leave?" Drake asked.

"No one knows. He didn't find the treasure. He just finally left. No goblin stood a chance against him. He did not use spells, just pure raw power, rage, and a savage fury we have never seen before. We know of no warrior like him before or since," the goblin concluded.

Drake thought about this story and concluded that this treasure was something very valuable indeed. Maybe even still valuable enough to sell it to Elijah if Drake could not use it. As they continued their approach to the volcano, the light from the ruby on the sword began to increase its intensity. More goblins hovered in the distance as the three led Drake to the entrance of the volcano.

Darkness settled in as they approached the volcano. Heat flowed out of the entrance, making Drake uncomfortable. There was an eerie orange glow shining out the opening in the side of the mountain from molten lava that reflected out the passageways.

The red light of the sword brightly illuminated the passages for Drake as he entered the volcano. Once the red light had been a fixture in these tunnels; it had been present for Malkavic's entire reign.

Drake secured a cord around the smallest of the three goblins to be sure not to lose his way in the tunnels. He kept his sword drawn and his senses were keen. The light from his sword grew brighter as they descended into the volcano.

Multiple passages existed, and Drake's senses heighted for an ambush. However, with the sword, no goblin could prove any match for him, and he could not be overwhelmed by sheer numbers due to the narrow width of the tunnels.

The heat was brutal. Drake was sweating profusely and realized his dependency on water. He had two full flasks, but they would do little to help him fight the heat. He would not be able to tolerate this without a better source of water. Unfortunately, all the water he had seen around the volcano smelled of sulfur and was not drinkable.

"We are almost there, master," the small goblin warned Drake. The goblin knew he would be the first to die if Drake became alarmed.

"Where are we?" Drake asked.

"We are at the Chamber of Malkavic."

Drake entered a large chamber where he found himself facing a small army of goblins, all alerted to his presence, and all waiting for his arrival. The goblins did not challenge him. They stayed back. They had all heard about the Dark Lord and his red sword. They all wondered openly if this was the return of Malkavic.

The small goblin felt the blade of Drake's sword rest on his neck. Even in the heat, a chill went up the goblin's spine.

"Take me to the treasure," Drake said forcefully.

The goblins parted as the small goblin led Drake to the back of the chamber. All the goblins watched, not one challenging Drake. The other two goblins that were originally part of this party of three quickly dispersed in the crowd and the fear of Drake began to spread. The goblins had heard about his skills as a warrior and the story of how he had cut down the party of fifteen, which soon grew to a party of over one hundred by the time all the goblins in the chamber had finished retelling it.

Drake felt supremely confident. The presence of all the goblins caused him to gain new strength and energy from the sword. He eagerly anticipated seeing the great treasure that would soon be his.

The small goblin led Drake into the back of Malkavic's chamber. He pointed to a pile of half-burned writings on an unusual parchment that was sitting on a ledge. "This is our treasure, master," the small creature uttered.

Drake looked at the small pile of writings and rage filled him. He had traveled this far and risked his life entering the volcano and for what? A pile of half-burned scribbles that he could not read?

"This is your 'treasure'?" Drake screamed.

The goblin feared for its life. The creature knew its life hinged on its reply. The goblin knew Drake was dangerous, but when Drake had slaughtered the other goblins, he had been controlled and almost joyful as he did it. Now fury shot forth from his entire being.

"This is what we took from Solomon. This is what Elijah seeks. It is ancient. It is what Malkavic sent us for on that night!"

Drake held his emotion in check. He stared in disbelief, trying to comprehend how this one book, partially burned, had destroyed two of the most powerful creatures in the land and had led Elijah on a killing spree that had reportedly left hundreds of goblins dead.

Chapter XXIV
A Dwarf's Journey

Siv tossed and turned in her sleep. The nightmare captured and held her. Suddenly, she woke in a cold sweat. The adventure she was about to embark upon filled her with anxiety. She was sure this had triggered the nightmare.

She reflected on her dream. It was one that she had experienced again and again for as long as she could remember: *She was walking down into a void, a place where blackness surrounded her. Only a sliver of light filtered up from somewhere below. The strong metallic smell and the sticky sensation that drizzled across her body alerted her to the fact that she was covered with blood! She was all alone! She was all alone!* Every time she came to the realization that she was covered in blood and all alone, she woke in a panic. Tonight was no different. It had been a long time since she last had this nightmare. She decided there would be no more sleep tonight. It was time to get up and set out on her journey.

The crescent moon overhead illuminated the village and the mountain. It was a crisp night, and frozen dew sparkled, reflecting the moonlight. Long, dark shadows stretched out from the edges of the forest, warning inhabitants of the village to keep out. It was into these shadows that Siv intended to walk as she entered the unknown. Thanks to her meeting with Yuri just a few short hours before, she now had a plan.

She packed herself a small package of food, filled her canteens, and was ready to go. She felt weighed down, not just by the pack and all that she carried, but by the consequences of failure and by the fear of the journey on which she was about to embark. She wondered whether her nightmares were about to become real. She forced herself to put these thoughts aside and focused on the mission.

With that, Siv turned away from the only home she had ever known and set her course east, up the daunting mountain pass that now lay before her. Her plan was to reach the summit before the morning passed. She had no time to waste. The clear early morning sky gave her hope that bad weather would not delay her travels.

As she disappeared into the shadows, she wondered if she would ever see her home again. Moonlight filtered through the forest as Siv trotted ever upwards. She could hear sounds, and occasionally she caught glimpses of movement in the forest between the trees as she travelled. She tried to ignore these things and focus on her trip to the tower. She gripped hard on the throwing axe that Yuri had given her. It felt good in her hand and it gave her some feeling of security in this dark forest all by herself. She had never undertaken such an adventure, but there was no one else who could go. If Ramsey went . . . she shuddered at the thought as she already knew his fate. She put all thoughts out of her mind and instead focused on awareness of her surroundings and reaching her goal.

Even though the forest was thick around her, Siv was aware of the approaching dawn as the sky lightened. She moved quickly for a dwarf, but it would be difficult to reach the summit before lunchtime.

For the most part, the only sounds she heard were the crunching of leaves and twigs under her feet. When she paused to catch her breath, she could hear the breeze filtering between the trees. She could smell the strong scent of pine as she rested. She loved this smell, but she had no time to enjoy it; she had to press on. Her talk with Yuri had made her hypervigilant to dangers that seemingly lurked everywhere. She suppressed these thoughts because they were counterproductive to her mission.

By mid-morning, Siv broke free of the trees and saw that the summit lay in the distance before her. The sky was clear and free of impending storm clouds. The air was still brisk, but she found herself covered in a light sweat as she struggled to reach the summit.

She sat down to rest and took some food out of her pack. She needed food, and she needed to concentrate so she could prepare herself for the dangers that lay ahead. She knew she would be exposed on the climb from this point forward.

Siv did not see any predators as she looked around, plotting her route to the top. Once convinced that it looked as safe as it would get, she again set out for the summit. She tried to stay small and avoid being spotted, but it was in vain. There was no cover. She kept her hand tightly gripped on the small axe. It was a small thing, but she found comfort in this.

As Siv reached the summit, she was amazed by how much the day had changed within a few short hours. The peak was surrounded by clouds; the skies were clear on the top of the mountain, but looking down, she could not see the trees. All that was visible were the billowing clouds below. The view below was something she had never experienced before. Looking down on clouds! It was amazing; something she had never dreamed of before. As she stood and looked at the clouds below, she could feel the wind pick up and sweep across her hair. She loved the feel of the wind in her hair. The early afternoon sun felt warm on her face. She felt invigorated and had a renewed sense of energy as she moved forward on her journey.

Siv considered the clouds below. They didn't look that much different than when she would stare up at them when she was back home lying in a meadow. What lay beneath these clouds, however, remained a mystery as she had never been on this side of the mountain before. Finally, she pried her gaze away from the spectacular view she was enjoying and looked up. She saw dark storm clouds rapidly approaching from the west. She was startled as they seemed to have appeared from nowhere and without any warning. She should have known they were coming when she felt the breeze pick up. She told herself she needed to be more aware of her surroundings.

Siv knew from Yuri that the clouds represented danger and lightning. She would need to move as quickly down the mountain as she could because the storm clouds represented imminent danger. It looked much easier to head down and north rather than across the rocky terrain to the south. Siv was frightened as she could see the lightning in the approaching clouds. She was exposed. She decided to head north despite Yuri's warning. It seemed the quickest way out of the impending storm. The southern route seemed impossible at this point. Surely she would be caught out in this dangerous afternoon storm if she attempted the southern route.

As she headed north and east, Yuri's words kept coming back to her. She did not know what waited for her below. Yuri had said it would add days to her journey and the bottom was not passable. Siv did not really understand how that could be. Also, she remembered Yuri saying the path would get easier as she headed south. She hesitated and looked to the south again. Rain was pouring now, and the wind was blowing the raindrops sideways. The electrical storm was not far off. The thought of crossing the boulder field to the south was no longer tenable. She would have to make her own way despite Yuri's guidance. Her path and her fate had been chosen for her by this afternoon storm. She turned north and to the trees and ran as quickly as she could to get to shelter and away from the storm.

Chapter XXV
Treasure

DRAKE looked down at the writings in disbelief. The scribbles and scratches were written on a type of parchment he had never seen. From a distance, they looked burned and ruined, but as he got closer, he could see that the document remained intact and was only burnt on the edges. For being ancient, as he had been led to believe, the document seemed well-preserved. It must be the special parchment that kept it so. The writing was neat but not recognizable to Drake's eyes.

He scratched his head as he sat down to contemplate his next move. What could possibly be so valuable about these documents, Drake wondered. Elijah had risked his life attacking this volcano to get this document. Maybe the answer could be found in the words. Maybe it was the key to treasures unimaginable. He just didn't know. It was far from what he had expected.

The small creature waited for Drake. The cord was still around its waist, so it waited for Drake's command. The goblin just wanted to free itself and be free of the danger it still faced.

"Tell me more of this Chamber of the Gatekeeper," Drake said as he focused on the small creature.

"No one goes there, master. I myself have never been," the

goblin stated in a shaky voice.

"Well, we are going there now!" Drake said emphatically as he picked up the document and placed it in his satchel. With that, he exited the chamber, towing the small goblin behind him. He looked out at all the goblins and felt empowered.

"I am leaving you, but I will return. Fix me a place to stay," he began, "and have water for me when I return."

This caused a stir in the room. There was no doubt about it in the minds of the goblins: Malkavic had returned. They did not know what this meant for them, but they would do as they were told.

The goblin led Drake back in the direction of the opening. Drake questioned this, but the creature told him it was the way to the Chamber of the Gatekeeper. Shortly thereafter, they reached the opening to the steps to the chamber.

"It is down there, master" was all the goblin could utter. It was very close to the opening of the volcano. Drake knew where he was in this maze of tunnels, but it was clear he would require assistance for a long time if he were to really learn his way around.

With the tip of his blade, he prodded the goblin down the path into the chamber below. The goblin headed downward, but with each step, its legs became heavier. Its fear of the chamber was greater than its fear of death. Finally, Drake could prod his guide no farther. He felt certain there was no ambush waiting for him at the bottom of the path; the fear in this goblin led him to believe that all feared this chamber.

Drake refused to face the fact that he too felt anxiety in the center of his belly. He too felt the trembling in his legs. This was no place for a man. Not at this time.

Drake was feeling warmer and warmer as he scaled down

the stairs. He was almost out of water and drenched in sweat. He decided at that moment to cut the goblin loose. To his surprise, the goblin did not run away.

"It is too hot down here for me. I must return to the surface and get water," Drake said to the goblin.

The goblin nodded and with much more spring in its legs, ascended the path back to the top. It had taken them over ten minutes to go down the stairs. They would ascend them in only seven.

When they reached the top, Drake looked at the goblin, which appeared unaffected by the heat, and said, "I am leaving. I will be back soon. You will be my right hand when I get back. Prepare a place for me."

"Yes, master," the goblin replied.

With that, Drake turned and headed out of the volcano. He needed to get to the other side of the volcano to get to the lake and to water. The coolness of the night air was a relief.

CHAPTER XXVI
DRUIDS

THE storms blowing from the west urged Siv to change her course and head north. She focused on the quickest way to reach the trees. The electricity of the afternoon storms made the hair on the back of her neck rise and tingle. Siv descended rapidly. She needed to get off the mountain as quickly as possible.

When she got to the trees, she sat down at the base of an enormous pine that towered toward the sky. Her clothes, soaked from a combination of sweat and a blowing rain that came in with the weather, clung to her tiny frame. The thick forest gave her some protection from the gale that blew around her.

Siv drank and ate sparingly from her supplies as she tried to get her bearings. She knew she was off course, and she knew she needed to head south and east from this point forward. Hopefully, she would be able to avoid the trouble that Yuri had warned her about at the northern part of the mountain. While scurrying down the mountain, she had been able to see the plains stretch out in front of her, but she did not have time to search for landmarks; she had been focused on getting out of the storm.

As she continued down the mountain, her course turned more and more toward the east rather than south. Siv was unaware of her course change; it was just easier going downhill. By the time she reached the bottom of the mountain, night was upon her. She tried to get her bearings straight so she would know how to get back home.

She found a small cleft in some nearby boulders and settled in for the night. Taking advice from Yuri, she tried to make herself as invisible as possible to hide from the unseen dangers in the night. She clutched the axe in her hand as she drifted off to sleep. Her last conscious thoughts were of Martha and her resolve to push on at the break of day.

Despite her exhaustion, Siv rose before dawn and headed out on a southeasterly course. She knew she was much farther north of where she needed to be, but she didn't know how far off course she had wandered.

She spotted two odd-looking creatures near a small pond as she was walking. Siv did not think they spotted her and quickly took to the underlying brush. She did not feel threatened by these creatures. Though they were quite a bit taller than her, they appeared slightly built and nonthreatening. The most striking feature was their wide-set eyes. They had broad noses that drooped over their upper lips. Their heads tapered quickly to a small jaw and mouth. Siv had never encountered such creatures and didn't know what they were.

The two were in conversation, but she did not understand their words as they carried across the wind. When they looked in her direction, she felt for sure she had been spotted. She decided to come out from the brush and head directly toward them. If they tried anything, she was sure she could outrun these two.

"Cael, do you see what I see coming our way?" said one of the creatures to the other.

"I do indeed, Finn, and right out of the brush."

"It is a dwarf, Cael," said the taller of the two. On closer inspection, Finn had a scar from just below his left eye to the corner of his mouth. "What brings a dwarf to our forest?" Finn called out to Siv.

"How do you speak my language?" replied Siv confidently.

"We have seen many dwarves in our time, haven't we, Finn?"

"Indeed we have, Cael."

"I am called Cael, and this is Finn," Cael said. "And what do they call you?"

"I am Siv. I hail from Bradán on the other side of this mountain pass."

"What is a dwarf doing out here in our forest all alone?" Finn asked.

"I am searching for Cassava root. I must find the wizard Elijah and get the Cassava. I am headed to the Tower of the Wizards," Siv stated.

"Why do you need the wizard to get the Cassava?" Cael inquired. "We have plenty of it at our home. It grows abundantly in the woods where we live."

Siv's heart skipped a beat in her chest. It was hard for her to contain her excitement about the possibility of getting the Cassava so early in her journey. "Cassava is powerful medicine for dwarves," she stated. "My aunt will die unless I get it to her soon! If you have this, I would like to get it from you. Can you give me some, or tell me how I can get it myself?"

"We have plenty of this root near our home," Finn said. "We would be happy to share with you. You must come with us. Our home is a half-day's journey from here. We must head out right away so that you can get it and be on your way. It sounds as if you are in a hurry."

Siv marveled at her luck. In all her excitement of finding the Cassava root, Siv had let her guard down. She was happy now that she had taken the northern route. She felt by trusting her own instincts, rather than heeding the warnings of Yuri, that she had found what she had come for. If she had listened to Yuri, she may never have even found the Cassava, and there was no guarantee of finding Elijah at the tower anyway.

Chapter XXVII
Dark and Stormy Night

It was late in the evening, and the weather was not as favorable as it had been the previous night. The wind whipped through the canyons, bending the trees of the forests on the mountain to its will. Tall, strong trees arched over in unison, protesting this unseen force of nature. It was no night for these two dwarves to be out.

Ramsey and Teige forged ahead, arching forward into the wind. Ramsey carried a pack and two weapons: a throwing axe, with which he was proficient, and a dagger. Teige carried a small provision of food and water for Ramsey. The two were travelling later than they planned. They had waited for Siv, expecting her to join them on their journey to see Yuri. They had all discussed it the night before. They were to meet together and seek out Yuri's guidance for Ramsey's planned mission. They had no idea where she had gone off to.

The two were on a mission. They were the only creatures stirring outside on this stormy evening as they forged their way toward a tiny cottage built of stone that looked to be forgotten by time. As they approached the dwelling, Teige was relieved to see a light coming from within. Smoke trailed quickly away from the chimney as it was swept away by the storm.

He reached up to the hammer on the door, picked it up, and tapped it where it echoed each time the hammer struck the plate. The lone inhabitant of the cottage was sitting by the fire and smoking his pipe when the tap on the door interrupted the silence of the evening. If he was startled, he did not show it. He simply rose from his comfortable chair and walked to the door as if he had expected the intruders to appear on this dark and stormy night. He opened the door and stared at Teige and Ramsey, who looked back at the ancient dwarf.

"You must be Ramsey and Teige," Yuri began. "I have been expecting you."

Teige and Ramsey looked at each other, then back at Yuri. They were speechless. How in the world did Yuri know who they were and how could he be expecting them? No answers came to their minds.

Yuri invited them into his home and closed the door behind them. "Have a seat by the fire and get yourselves warm," Yuri began. "Let me take your packs and your cloaks so you can dry off." Yuri helped the two get out of their wet things and he set everything by the fire to help them dry. "It looks as though you two are off on a journey," Yuri said, noting the pack and the heavy provisions.

"We are," Ramsey started. "I presume you are Yuri?"

"Indeed, it is me, Yuri."

"How did you know who we are?" Teige asked.

"You two look just like your grandfather, Aldwin. You are both strong and handsome, just as he was." Yuri took a long pull on his emerald pipe and let the boys fidget. This was clearly not going as they had expected. "Tell me, is your father Markus?"

Both Teige and Ramsey nodded. They did not know where

Yuri was going with this. Moreover, they were not sure what was happening.

"How did you know who we are?" Ramsey repeated Teige's question. "And how did you know to expect us? The weather is horrible tonight. I wouldn't think you would expect anyone to be out on a night like this!"

"That is true." Yuri looked at Ramsey. "Now which of you boys is Ramsey and which one is Teige?"

Ramsey and Teige looked at each other. It looked as though it was going to be a long night.

"I am Teige, sir." Teige stood up and shook Yuri's hand.

Ramsey followed suit and introduced himself in a similar manner.

"I am pleased to make your acquaintance," Yuri said. He then picked up his pipe to fill his lungs once again with the cherry-flavored tobacco.

Teige and Ramsey sat back and waited. There was no use in rushing Yuri. This was his home and he clearly was in control of the conversation. Their plan for how they were going to handle this meeting had been completely usurped by Yuri.

They both took comfort from the heat pouring out from the fire. The smell of the tobacco reminded them of their home as their father often smoked a pipe in the evening. The darkness of the night was being held in check as the light of the fire kept it from overtaking the cottage. They sat back on the small couch and waited. They began to relax.

Yuri waited. He wanted these boys to relax so he could impart what had transpired just the night before. He waited until he felt they would be able to hear what he was going to share with them.

"I know why you are here," Yuri began. "Your mother Martha is very ill. She needs medicine from the Cassava root to save her."

"That is right, but how do you know all this?" Ramsey asked.

"Did someone come looking for the Cassava root?" Teige inquired. "Do you have any?"

"No, I do not have Cassava, and no, no one came looking for Cassava," Yuri said. "But—"

"Then how do you know these things?" Teige interrupted.

"I was telling you, my boy, but you must first be patient and listen." Yuri picked up his pipe and inhaled.

Teige and Ramsey waited. There was nothing else for them to do.

"I understand that you plan to go find the wizard Elijah and get the Cassava root. Is that correct?" Yuri asked.

"Not me—Ramsey," Teige said as he pointed to his brother.

"It is true. I intend to go at first light," Ramsey said. "I have brought all my gear. I was hoping you would be able to help me."

"You won't make it tomorrow, Ramsey. Your efforts are in vain," Yuri said.

Again, Yuri was interrupted before he could finish his thoughts. "You can't deter me, Yuri. I will surely leave by first light."

Yuri sat up in his chair. He set his pipe down and put his hands on his knees. He leaned forward and said, "You boys need to stop interrupting me before I finish what I have to say! I know you want to go. I know I cannot talk you out of going. You need to understand the land and what you need to do to accomplish your mission, or you will be doomed to failure."

Yuri leaned back in his chair and took a long draw on his pipe. He let the boys absorb what he had to say.

"There will be no travel in the morning unless this storm blows over," Yuri continued. "I have seen storms like this set in. They can last for days. This one came in late this afternoon, and I don't see any sign that it will let up by morning. You can head out in the morning if you want. There is nothing I can do to stop you. But the mountain pass is too dangerous to traverse in this weather. Lightning storms will surely keep you from your goal."

Ramsey listened. He knew that Yuri was speaking from experience, yet he grieved for his mother and felt powerless to help her. Everything seemed to be stacked against him and his desire to help his mother.

"Yuri, I understand that we may not be able to go until the weather passes, but will you help us?" Teige asked.

"I will tell you everything I know to help you be successful, Teige."

"I have another question for you," Ramsey began. "You still haven't told us how you knew we were coming, how you knew who we were, how you knew that our mother was sick, and how you knew our plans."

Yuri sat back and looked at the two boys. He was surprised that the answer had not occurred to them already.

"Last night I had a visitor," Yuri began.

Ramsey and Teige just looked at each other, wondering who this mysterious visitor had been.

"You know her. She is your cousin Siv." Yuri let this information sit and percolate with the two visitors.

Ramsey and Teige sat speechless. Now they knew why she wasn't with them. They just had no idea where she was now.

"Siv explained everything to me last night."

"Where is she now?" Teige asked, somewhat confused. He had not expected this turn of events at all.

"I believe she is on her way to get the Cassava root as we speak. She left before the break of day," Yuri explained.

"How could she do this?" asked Ramsey. "She is too young, too small to attempt something so dangerous." Ramsey shook his head in disbelief. "This was a mission for me to do, not Siv! How could she do something like this on her own?"

"You two discussed your plans yesterday afternoon after hearing your fathers discuss Martha's condition, isn't that right?" Yuri asked. He watched the brothers nod in unison. "You asked Siv if she thought you would be successful, correct?" Yuri looked at Ramsey as he asked this question.

Ramsey nodded his head affirmatively. "Yes. She said she did not see my mother dying. She did tell me that I would not make it to the tower, but that didn't mean my mission would be a failure. I just knew I needed to go after hearing that she thought my mother would live."

"Siv told me the same thing, Ramsey," said Yuri. "Indeed, she believes Martha will live. She told me exactly what she said to you. She also told me what she didn't say to you."

Ramsey and Teige sat on the edge of their chairs as they waited to hear what Siv had said to Yuri. "What did she say?" Teige asked, wide-eyed and eager with anticipation.

"Siv told me that she knew you would perish on your journey and that she did not think your journey was the answer to saving Martha's life."

"She didn't say that to me," a stunned Ramsey replied.

"She told me that she was sure you would not hear her warnings if she shared them with you. She told me she knew with every fiber of her being that you could not go on this mission. Therefore, she was going to go in your place. She said that either she went or you would go. I knew she wouldn't be deterred either," Yuri concluded.

"I can't believe she did this." Teige shook his head in disbelief.

"She has never even camped out before," Ramsey started. "How will she have a chance? She is too innocent, too young, too inexperienced. What did you tell her?"

"You should realize how much you two mean to her," Yuri began. "She loves you both deeply, and she is sacrificing her own safety to save you, Ramsey." Yuri looked at Ramsey and then at Teige as the realization of what Siv had done to protect him overwhelmed them both.

"We must find her, Yuri," Teige began. "You must tell us everything you told her. We must head out at first light."

"Teige, I know you want to go, but you must first wait out the storm. You will only hinder your chances, slim as they may be already, if you try to battle these elements. You must let this storm pass," Yuri gently admonished him.

"Will you help us if we do exactly what you tell us to do?" Ramsey looked at Yuri as he said this.

"Do you know what position you put me in? I am sure your fathers will blame me for filling your heads with adventure and the mysteries of Mount Ollmhór, the Mystic Forest, and even the Tower of the Wizards," Yuri shook his head incredulously. "First, Siv, and now you two?"

Ramsey and Teige sat silently. There was nothing else they could say.

Finally, he looked at the two boys and said, "I will do everything I can to prepare you for your journey, just as I did for Siv. It is going to be a long night with much to learn. You can rest here once we are done. From the sounds of this storm, you will not be going anywhere tomorrow. The mountain may be impassable."

They all looked to the roof as the cottage shuddered against the violent wind.

CHAPTER XXVIII
HYTTER

THE two druids and Siv approached the hytter. The weather of the day before had not let up. Rain came in bursts, the wind continued to gust, and the temperature had dropped. Siv was thankful to find shelter, if even for a short time.

It was a small hut constructed of heavy timber with two-inch chinking between the logs. A window was positioned on either side of the front door. A generous porch swept across the entire front. The roof was made of sod, and Siv saw grass growing on the roof. It was unlike anything she had ever seen.

"We are here, Siv. Let me show you the Cassava plants," Finn said. Then he looked toward Cael. "Can you prepare a meal for all of us? We cannot send our guest away on an empty stomach."

"Gladly. It will be no problem. I have a vegetable stew already cooking."

Siv felt at ease with these two. The thought of stew sounded irresistible after her long trek and it sure beat the rations on which she had been surviving. She was excited that she did not need to travel any farther. She would be on her way home tonight, after just one night away, with fresh Cassava.

Finn led Siv to the forest in the back of their home where

hundreds of small green plants grew in no particular pattern. They were small plants when compared to Finn; however, some of them grew half way up Siv's thigh.

Finn knelt down and dug up one of the plants. To Siv's surprise, there was a large plant growing under the surface of the ground. "Here it is, Siv. Fresh root or Cassava."

Siv was so excited; she took it eagerly from Finn. The plant slipped out of her wet hands and she had to pick it up off the ground. It was heavier than she had expected. "Thank you so much, Finn. I cannot believe my luck. Two days into my journey and I have what I need. I would have never known that for which I was looking!"

"I don't know how you intend to use this root, Siv, or how much you need, but often Cassava needs to be dried out for several days to get medicinal use out of it. I don't know if there is time for your aunt to wait."

Siv's heart sank. "Perhaps I should head off to the tower and search for Elijah. He has always had what we needed. I cannot afford to be wrong on this, Finn."

"I have dried root in our hytter. Perhaps you can take this fresh Cassava and some of my dry root with you. Then you will have done all that you can do. As you can see, there is no shortage of Cassava around here," Finn stretched his hand out and panned his fingers across the expansive forest.

"Thank you so much for doing this for me, Finn. I will gladly take you up on your offer."

"Come, let us eat stew and then get you on your way. You still have some daylight left this evening. Or you can stay with us and wait for this storm to pass."

"I think I need to get on my way after dinner, but thanks for the offer," Siv replied.

Siv followed Finn back to the hytter. He opened the front door, and she entered freely, relaxed in her feeling of great fortune at running into these two.

"Sit, Siv," said Cael as he pointed to the table. The strong aroma from the vegetable stew was about as good as anything she had ever smelled. The warmth of the small hytter was comforting as well.

Finn walked into the area where Cael was cooking. He reached up on a shelf and grabbed something off the top. Pulling the object down, two large objects on a ring fell from the shelf to the floor.

"What are those?" Siv inquired as she pointed to the fallen objects.

"Oh, these are interesting," Finn began. "Let me tell you the story." He set the huge objects down on the table. They were as long as Siv's thigh.

"Let me first give you this," Cael said, handing Finn a leather pouch that was tied at the top.

"Open this up, Siv," Finn said, passing the pouch to her. "This is dried Cassava root."

"It is important to dry the root, Siv," Cael interjected. "This unlocks the medicine."

Siv listened intently. She peered into the satchel; it was full of dry root. She couldn't imagine more was needed than she already had. If she needed more, she was sure her new friends would be able to help her. The great part was that she was days ahead of schedule. Wouldn't Ramsey, Teige, and Yuri be surprised!

"How is that stew coming, Cael?" asked Finn.

"It is coming, Finn. You cannot rush a masterpiece. It will be ready in just a short time. By the time you get done telling your story about those keys, the stew will be ready."

Siv looked down at the keys, her curiosity piqued.

"These keys belong to the Tower of the Wizards," Finn said, as he let the weight of his words sink in on Siv.

She raised her eyebrows in surprise, sat quietly, and waited for an explanation.

"A long time back, we were followers of the wizard Demetrius, who lives in the tower. These are the keys to the servants' quarters at the back of the tower. We used to come and go through this entrance. We were followers for years; however, Demetrius became more and more erratic. We were afraid for our own lives at times. We never knew what we would encounter when we came to the tower. He was involved in all sorts of dark wizardry, deep in the dungeon of the tower!"

"There is a dungeon in the tower?" Siv exclaimed. The thought of a dungeon sent shivers down her spine. She only thought of benevolence when it came to wizards and that translated to the tower. Siv had set her belongings against the wall near the fire. She was nowhere near her axe anymore, and she felt at ease inside this home.

"Indeed, I know it is hard to understand, but there are dark things going on at the tower. You may be fortunate you did not make it there and encounter Demetrius!" Finn said.

Finn knew that Elijah had returned to the tower, for he had seen him arrive and witnessed his wrath after coming to the tower just the day before, but Finn did not mention this to Siv.

"So you two would have been wizards too, if it had not been for this Demetrius?" Siv asked.

Both Cael and Finn nodded in agreement.

"So why do you still possess the keys? Didn't Demetrius want them back?"

"That is just it, Siv. We never went back," Cael said.

Siv just looked at him, not completely following the conversation.

"We were down in the dungeon of the tower one evening with Demetrius," Finn explained, "when he was studying from a book of spells. He was repeating spells from the book when he looked as though he had become possessed by a spirit. He began to float, and the room started to glow with an eerie green light from which we could not determine the source."

Siv moved to the edge of her seat, entranced by Finn's words. Surely, this was a powerful wizard, she thought to herself.

"He seemed to forget about our presence and was completely absorbed in his spell," continued Finn. "We were so frightened; we backed out of the room, but just as we got out, a loud boom shot out from the room, and a green light bolted from the door. It was blinding. He seemed crazed! Indeed, his behavior became more and more crazed in our last days with him. We had become fearful to approach him. When that happened, we ran from the tower never to return. In fact, we don't know whatever became of Demetrius, if he even survived that night!" Cael nodded in agreement. "So you see, Siv, we never returned, and so we still have these keys. Maybe someday when we encounter Elijah again, we can pass these on to him. I had quite forgotten about them until I knocked them down getting the dried Cassava."

Cael walked over and placed two bowls of stew in front of Siv and Finn. "Dig in, Siv. You have a long journey ahead of you."

She devoured her meal. It was divine. "I am so thankful for all that you have done to help me. If I can ever repay the favor, I will," Siv said as she sopped up the remaining stew with a slice of bread.

"I am sure you will repay the favor," Finn said as he watched the dwarf consume the hearty meal.

Siv wasn't sure, but she thought she detected a different tone about Finn as he said this. She also noticed that Finn hadn't touched his stew. She looked at Finn and then at Cael. They stared back at her expectantly. Siv's head suddenly felt funny. Her eyes drooped; she could hardly keep them open. A sense of danger overcame her and she tried to look around for her axe. She could feel the strength leave her body as she slumped onto the table. Although her eyes were closed and her body limp, Siv's mind remained awake; however, she was unable to comprehend what had happened to her. As if through a fog, she could hear Finn and Cael speaking, but she no longer understood their words. Then everything drifted away to complete darkness.

CHAPTER XXIX
ELIJAH AND DEMETRIUS

ELIJAH looked out at the volcano from the window of the upper chamber. He sensed evil in the land, and even though the manifestation of such evil had yet to materialize, the source was always the same. Everything evil flowed like lava from the volcano and entrapped all the inhabitants of Lavendelle in its fiery grip.

Just as evil had emanated from the volcano, goodness and light used to emanate from the tower, but the presence of both had diminished since the night Malkavic had been subdued. The two structures had been a stark contrast of good versus evil, and now Elijah feared the volcano was once again becoming the focus of evil and destruction.

This was something Elijah sensed, and he knew the wizards needed to reestablish the tower as a source of goodness and power in these lands. No longer was Elijah going to subject the wizards to the status of interlopers on the elven land. No longer was the tower going to be ignored. Elijah's purpose was to restore power, respect, and order to the Wizard Council.

This seemed timely as he looked out at the volcano. Dark clouds were forming around the volcano and he wondered if these clouds were an omen of things to come. No longer was he the pupil in this tower with the wizard he followed, Solomon. No, now Elijah had all the weight and responsibility on his shoulders, just as Solomon had so many years ago.

He reflected on the ebb and flow of life. Everything happened in its own time. Solomon had restored order to the enchanted world by disposing of Malkavic, but trouble had returned. It was his time to face these challenges. Elijah's current predicament was nothing new; it was nothing that others who had walked in his place hadn't faced. What was different was how his predecessors had faced their problems. For Elijah, he always found that the direct approach worked best.

Elijah felt the solitude of the room disturbed. Without looking up, he said, "It has been a long time, Demetrius. Too long."

"Yes, Elijah, too long," Demetrius replied.

Elijah turned and faced his former friend. He was not sure who Demetrius was anymore. He was not sure if he was friend or foe. Elijah lifted his staff and pointed it into the fireplace. No fuel was present, yet a flame ignited and warmed the room.

"Please, sit," Elijah said as he pointed his hand at the chair opposite where he sat down. Elijah's request clearly demonstrated to Demetrius that Elijah was now in charge, and he was taking possession of the tower.

Demetrius had lived in the wizards' tower as its caretaker for over seven hundred and fifty years. Elijah had been present for less than twenty-four hours. He had given Demetrius one day to gather his belongings, and he was now offering Demetrius a seat as if he, Elijah, owned the place. Demetrius took his seat and waited.

After witnessing Elijah's power and intensity, Demetrius had no intention of challenging him. His old friend was not the young follower and new wizard who had joined the Council at the same time he had joined. No, Elijah had grown in stature and power and there was a gravity and purpose to him that Demetrius had never seen before. Nothing was the same.

Demetrius did not know where he stood with Elijah or the Wizard Council. One thing was for sure: Once one was a wizard, one was a wizard for life. Indeed, the Council never relieved Aelhaeran, the wizard whom Demetrius had studied extensively over the last several centuries, of his position on the Council.

Aelhaeran, Demetrius thought to himself, was a devil. Demetrius could not pull himself away and separate from his grip. At the same time, Aelhaeran had been unable to pull Demetrius all the way over to his dark world.

"I have cleansed this place, Demetrius. I am sorry that this tower has fallen into such a state of disrepair," Elijah looked at Demetrius as he spoke. "We have abandoned you and left you alone too long."

Demetrius looked at Elijah, not knowing where the conversation was headed. It was as if Elijah was extending an olive branch and Demetrius sorely needed that branch. He needed help. He had been unable to pull himself from the clutches of evil that continued to pull at his very soul.

"We all need each other, Demetrius. We all learn from each other and grow together. The Council is not and has not been whole without you. We need you. But your fellow wizards fear you."

Those words did not come as a surprise to Demetrius. He had been quite difficult to deal with over the centuries and, indeed, had become unapproachable for a long time. He had not wanted to give up the secrets of the tower to anyone. Now, it had all been taken from him and instead of being angry, he felt a sense of relief.

He did not know what he was going to do, but he knew what was no longer available to him and he felt liberated. He felt as if he were being offered an escape from the evil influence of Aelhaeran.

"I have much to do to repair the damage I have caused, my friend," Demetrius looked Elijah in the eye as he said this. "I am prepared to assume my position with the Council and repair relationships."

"There are so many on the Council who do not know you, Demetrius, so you will be able to start with a fresh slate with them. They do, however, know of your reputation, so that you will have to repair on your own."

"I feel relieved that I am leaving, Elijah. You warned me—what seems like an eternity ago—to avoid the writings of Aelhaeran," Demetrius acknowledged.

Elijah nodded his head in remembrance, but deep inside he felt a visceral reaction to the mere mention of the name Aelhaeran.

"I did not heed your advice, and I have paid dearly for my mistake. I feel as though Aelhaeran is still living here in this place. I feel as though he has a hold on me and is driving me to the dark world. I have done everything I can to resist, but I have been unable to escape. Now you come here and relieve me of my position with the tower. It is like you are offering me a chance to escape Aelhaeran's reach."

Elijah could see the relief in Demetrius and knew he was telling the truth. Elijah knew that though he had a wild and untamed spirit in his youth, Demetrius was basically good. He knew that Solomon had felt the same way too; otherwise, Demetrius would never have ascended to become a wizard.

Maybe it was Aelhaeran who was causing the turmoil in his own being; maybe Aelhaeran was the source of the disquiet. There was no doubt, however, that something was on the horizon.

"I have cleansed this place, Demetrius. Now I need to get it back into shape. I will go down and take care of Aelhaeran's study, and I will go to the libraries and begin to restore them too. You must go to the dwarves and tell them I need droves of mason, steel, and wood workers at the tower as soon as possible. We are going to rebuild this tower and restore it to all its previous glory and then some!"

Demetrius stood tall, invigorated by the thought of rejoining his wizard companions and helping to do something good for a change.

"I am long overdue for a visit to the dwarves," continued Elijah. "They need to see a wizard, and they will need your help. It is an easy task but an important one. You should know what to do when you get there. Send my apologies to the dwarves for my long overdue visit. I will be there again soon. But bring the dwarves here to work as soon as you can."

Demetrius nodded to show his understanding and assent.

"And, Demetrius," Elijah said as he looked at his old friend sternly, "I saw those druid followers approaching the tower yesterday. They ran when they saw me. I don't trust them, and I don't want to see them around here again."

"They are no longer my followers, Elijah. As far as I know, they have not been here for many, many years! I do not know what they are doing approaching the tower!"

"Their intentions are not and never have been honorable; there is nothing about those two that is good. I will deal with them in my own way if ever I come across them again."

"I, too, will deal with them Elijah, since I brought them here. I need your help to keep me on the right path, but first I need to escape Aelhaeran. He haunts me from beyond the grave, all day and all night. Oh, how I wish I had listened to you and Simon all those years ago. I just felt invincible. Now look at what has become of my life!"

"That is precisely why you need the Council, Demetrius! It is not good for a wizard to remain alone and isolated for centuries. When you isolate yourself, you are consumed by your own desires; you can be led astray, against sound judgment. The Wizard Council works as one in these lands. You are disconnected from us, so you wither away, and we are weakened by your loss. Together, as part of the Council, we can share your burden of Aelhaeran and defeat him. He was but one wizard; he cannot stand against us all!"

Demetrius never again returned to the study of Aelhaeran. He helped Elijah for two more days prior to leaving the tower. He felt as though all the weight of Lavendelle had been lifted from his shoulders as he walked away from the tower with his meager belongings. It had been a long, long time since Demetrius had left the tower. He felt his former self returning and darkness leaving him. He would have to take it one day at a time.

No one in Lavendelle should underestimate the power of a single wizard, regardless of his or her condition. A wizard of any level is a formidable foe, and Demetrius was no exception. In fact, Demetrius knew the dark arts of wizardry and was perhaps one of the most formidable wizards to ever walk the lands of Lavendelle. That being said, Demetrius knew in his heart he was no match for Elijah. Elijah would be revered as one of the truly great wizards, just as his mentor Solomon was revered. Elijah was now helping restore what life was left for Demetrius and for that, he would give Elijah his undying loyalty.

CHAPTER XXX
RESCUE MISSION

YURI had not slept. Siv had greatly affected him over the past several days. Ever since she first stepped into his cottage, he had been unable to stop thinking about her. There was magic about her, he could sense it; magic that she did not know she possessed. He believed in Siv, and he believed what she said about Ramsey. He knew in his heart he had done the right thing to let her go in place of Ramsey. Now Ramsey was here along with Teige. He knew he needed to help these two rescue Siv for she was bound to get into trouble out there all alone. Lavendelle was dangerous for anyone, let alone an adolescent female dwarf.

The winds and storm lasted all through the next day and night. Ramsey and Teige were stuck. They returned home during the day but made their way back to Yuri's that night. This time, both Teige and Ramsey were armed and packed for the journey.

Thankfully, the winds had died down in the night. It was a few hours before the sun would rise. The two young dwarves had slept restlessly. Yuri leaned over Ramsey, placing his hand on his shoulder. "It is time, Ramsey."

Ramsey opened his eyes and sat up. Teige, sensing his movement, awoke from a light sleep as well. Yuri had made breakfast for them. They spoke little as the gravity of the day that lay before them rested heavy on all. They needed to get off soon, well before sunrise, if they were to have any chance of getting over and down the mountain in one day.

As they bid Yuri good-bye, Ramsey stared into the old dwarf's eyes. "Thank you, Yuri, for giving us a chance. We will return with Siv and the Cassava root!"

Yuri reflected on Siv. Those green eyes! It was as if she knew him for all time. He would do anything to help Siv; she had a pure heart. He hoped she was safe, but he was worried. She had been gone for forty-eight hours with no word. He watched the two as they headed out after her. He remained at the door until they faded into the distance and out of his ancient eyes' ability to see. He watched for some time after that too. Finally, slowly, he turned and shut the door to his cottage and retreated to its warmth and comfort. It would take a miracle for them to all make it back, he thought.

Ramsey and Teige headed for the forest at the base of the mountain. The moon was not out in these early morning hours before the sun rose as it had been for Siv's journey. Instead, clouds blocked the moonlight and darkness was everywhere. At least the storm from the previous night appeared to have moved out of the canyon. Ramsey and Teige stayed close; the forest—and every sound coming from it—was frightening.

In the dark, it was hard to talk. Ramsey and Teige kept to the business of climbing. They feared their voices would travel and alert some unseen creature of their presence. The darkness played tricks on their minds. They found the comfort and strength in each other to push on.

The dawn broke and they found that they were making good time. They were halfway through the forest and scaling the mountain at first light.

"We should reach the summit before morning is over!" Ramsey said excitedly. "I am happy for the sunlight; it sure was eerie climbing in the dark!"

"I agree. It looks like the storm is over, and we have a clear sky. We need to get over the top and off the mountain before afternoon storms set in."

"I am concerned for Siv. We must press on!"

With that the two dwarves climbed at a rapid pace, reaching the summit before the morning was over. On the way down, the skies were clear and visibility was as good as it ever got.

"Ramsey, look here. The south looks treacherous. See that boulder field over there? We have to cross that if we are going to follow Yuri's directions."

"I think we have to, Teige. Remember, he said it was impassable at the bottom if we take the northern route. I agree with you, though, the north looks so much easier. However, if we go to the north, we will probably miss Siv's trail. Yuri stressed going south. I can't think she deviated from the course as time was critical. She didn't have the luxury of time to make a mistake."

"I agree with you, Ramsey, so across the boulders it is!"

They set out across the boulder field, which challenged the diminutive dwarves. They had to scale some of the larger boulders that others may have been able to step over. They found that many of the boulders were loose and went tumbling down the mountain as they worked their way across and down the field.

"We need to make time across these boulders, Ramsey. We are sitting ducks if the dragons come. I don't see any other living creatures up here for them to prey on."

The two quickly scurried across the boulders. Soon they found their path becoming more vertical. Teige noticed it first. He stopped completely in his tracks.

"Hey, Ramsey, look at me!" he shouted excitedly.

Ramsey, not too far behind, looked in Teige's direction. Teige was standing still, yet the rocks were all sliding down the mountain, carrying him with them.

"I think you better be careful, Teige. Remember what Yuri said about zigzagging these rocks and staying clear of rock slides," Ramsey shouted to his brother.

Teige decided to get out of the rock slide and that is when panic set in. His feet were trapped at the ankles by heavy rocks.

"Ramsey, come quickly! I think I am in trouble!" he shouted.

Ramsey looked and saw the problem. More and more rocks were piling up around Teige and trapping him in the rock slide. It looked dangerous. Boulders were starting to come crashing down the mountain as they were freed by the slow-moving slide. One of the boulders crashed dangerously close to Teige.

Teige was able to free one of his legs, but the other was stuck. A large boulder was coming his way. Just then, he felt himself being jerked out of the rock field by the shoulders. It was Ramsey! And just in time. He could have been finished by the last boulder. It had barely missed.

The two went tumbling down the side of the mountain before they finally stopped on a flat area. Both were the worse for wear. Thankfully, they were out of the rock slide.

"I almost didn't make it, Ramsey," Teige said breathlessly as he looked at his brother.

Ramsey lay on his back, sucking in as much air as he could to fill his lungs.

"Thank you," Teige said. "Are you all right?"

"Yes, I am fine. Mostly bruised I think. Give me a moment." Ramsey lay still a few more moments before he said, "I can see how that rock slide can catch up with you fairly quickly. I looked and you were on top of the rocks one moment, and the next you were trapped and the boulders started raining down on you. We have to follow everything Yuri told us. He certainly has a reliable vision of what is to come. Let's get off this mountain." The two were close to the tree line. They hurried to get off the mountain and out of sight of the dragons, though they hadn't seen any as of yet. They found a place in the woods to sit down and eat. Thankfully, they had made good time and had gotten over the mountain. Unfortunately, they had not seen any sign that Siv had passed through the area. They sat quietly and finished their meal.

"I can see how it got easier once we were over the boulders," Teige started. "I guess it is good we had Yuri's knowledge of the area. I would have never tried that boulder field if he hadn't insisted that it was the only way to go."

"I am so glad we are out of it. I kept looking up to make sure nothing was going to swoop down out of the sky and eat us! There was nowhere to hide!"

"I agree. When you grabbed me, I thought it might be a dragon!" Teige laughed. "Near as I can tell, we should reach the bottom of this mountain by early evening. If we really move, we could possibly make the stream by nightfall."

Ramsey nodded in agreement. "I agree with you. We need to get to Siv and the Cassava root as soon as possible. I believe time is of the essence."

"I am amazed Siv would do this alone. I can't believe she did it," Teige said as he shook his head. "I do not know what happened to her, but perhaps it is better she went alone given her vision of something terrible happening to you. I hope we will all return home safely."

Ramsey thought about this. "You may be right, Teige, you may be right. It is scary to think about Siv being out here all alone. Knowing what I know now, I don't know if I would have volunteered for this journey alone. I won't feel safe until we are all home together, sitting around a warm fire."

"I think we need to keep moving and never stay in one area too long. When we get to the bottom of the mountain, we need to stick to the overgrowth and hide in the brush. Avoid all signs of life and we should be all right. That is what Yuri recommended."

Chapter XXXI
Sacrifices

Long fingers of light reached through the trees and implored her eyes to acknowledge their presence. Siv had no energy to open them. She did not know where she was, and she did not know what had happened to her. Her mind had not fully awakened from the effects of whatever drug was circulating through her body.

Her arms and legs felt like lead weights. The light kept flickering on her closed eyelids. She became aware of movement and the sound of voices. She did not understand the voices or what was being said.

She tried to call out but became aware that there was something covering her mouth. In fact, whatever was covering her mouth was held tight to it. She tried moving her head back and forth, but to no avail; whatever was there had been secured tightly.

She could feel her mind and body awakening. She could feel strength flow out to her arms and legs. She tried opening her eyes, but the light from above was too intense. She began to focus her mind and her eyes. The voices she heard were those of the two creatures she had encountered in the forest. The movement she perceived was her body being pulled in a cart. She tried to move her arms and her legs, but they were strapped tightly down to the cart. She was pinned down with her arms and legs stretched out to all four corners of the cart, and she could not move.

The light shining through her eyelids was coming from the sun. Beams of light streamed down between the tall trees like arrows straight into her eyes. She was able to turn her head ever so slightly and avoid the direct light. This helped her focus as the light stirred her mind and brought her back to full consciousness.

The events that had led to her current predicament all came crashing down on her as she fully regained consciousness. Her heart raced; she panicked. Sweat broke out across her brow. Siv knew she was in mortal danger. She could hear the two creatures' voices, but she could not see them. She assumed they were pulling the cart somewhere.

The young dwarf had to think quickly to save her life. Even worse, she now remembered Martha lying on her deathbed. She had the Cassava root in her hand. Why hadn't she taken it and run? Overwhelming grief washed over her as she realized that she had failed in her quest and her failure would not only cost her her own life but probably that of her beloved aunt as well.

It felt like it was mid-morning. The ache that gripped her body told her that she had been tied down all night. Her body was stiff. Her wrists and ankles were sore. Her hands and feet had a prickling sensation, and her arms and legs screamed with pain. She did not know what these two had in store for her, but given her current condition, she was sure it was not good.

Finally, the trees were parting. They had come to a clearing and the cart had stopped. She could smell the fresh morning air after the rain from the night before and she could smell the scent of honeysuckle thick in the air. She loved honeysuckle. She should be out enjoying the beauty of the land instead of being tied down as a prisoner. Tears began to stream from her eyes; she could not hold them back. She could see the two creatures approach. She tried to speak, but all the sounds were muffled because of the gag in her mouth. She tried to implore either one with her eyes and plead for her release. The two did not even acknowledge her. It was clear that they were on a mission.

The cart had two wheels connected by an axle. It had two handles so that it could be pulled by one or two. Cael lifted the handles and the cart came to rest on its tail. Siv slid to the ground, still strapped to a pallet.

Finn lifted the pallet by the bottom while Cael swung around and lifted the head of the pallet. Siv could sense she was now being carried out into the clearing. She tried to wiggle with forceful movements of her body, but it was no use. She was pinned tightly. How could she have been so naive?

As they laid her down in the middle of the clearing, she saw an enormous bird circling overhead. Clearly, this was not a good sign. These two had done this before. Then, from somewhere nearby, she heard a loud grunting sound and knew something large was moving just beyond the edges of the clearing, just at the edge of her sight. Her heart jumped as she watched a huge bear lumber into the clearing. Siv realized there was no hope of escape—or survival.

Cael and Finn efficiently staked her to the ground at a site where the stakes were seemingly permanent—and just the right size for dwarves! Obviously, they had experience with this sort of thing. She fought them as they relocated each extremity to the permanent stake, but her efforts were useless. They were too efficient. Even though these creatures were slight, her strength failed her. She had clearly been taken in by them and underestimated them.

Finally, they removed the hard pallet from under her and carried it back to the cart.

She realized she was about to be sacrificed; to whom and for what she had no idea. Obviously, it wasn't important to her captors for her to know. They no longer even acknowledged her as a living being, but rather treated her as an object with no value.

She struggled until she was able to move the gag out of her mouth. She shouted out to the two, even calling them by name, but there was no response. They were done with her. She watched in panic as the two creatures started some sort of ritual that she did not understand. They painted her body with what looked like blood. They spread feathers around her in a circle with the end of the quills pointing inward, toward her. They began chanting, and it was as if they were talking to the great bird and the bear. Siv wasn't sure which creature she was going to be a meal for, but she was sure that she only had moments left to live.

In the distance she could see a red light approaching. The light frightened her as well. Her heart pounded in her chest. What could that light be? Each successive thing she encountered was worse than the last. The unknown was surely going to frighten her to death before the bear or the bird got her.

Chapter XXXII
Encounters

AFTER three days walking and exploring and really covering little ground, Drake still had not decided on what to do with the document he had taken from the volcano. He was gaining confidence daily, and capturing this writing from all those creatures left him supremely confident. The way he controlled the goblins and his possession of their "treasure" left him with a false confidence in his own abilities. It was the magic of Aelhaeran that was doing the work, but Drake did not understand this.

Drake was aware that for the first time in three days goblins were present. The ruby on the sword began to faintly glow. He was sure they were not following him; rather, he sensed a band of goblins ahead as he moved farther into the heavy forest of trees. The place he was walking was known as the Mystic Forest, though this meant nothing to Drake. As he pressed forward, the light on his sword grew brighter.

The Mystic Forest was full of those who delved in magic. Wizards were often encountered here. Many sorcerers and former wizard followers lived in this forest. The forest sat just east of the mountains and mines of the dwarves.

Most of the dwarves lived deep in the mountains and hardly

ever ventured out. Deep inside crevices and caverns within the mountains is where the dwarves worked, mining the mountains. They created a vast network of tunnels underneath the hills. When the dwarves did venture out from the mountains, they usually avoided the Mystic Forest. Most dwarves, like humans, had no sense of magical beings, and this put them in peril here.

The two druids, former followers of the wizard Demetrius, lived here as well. These odd-looking creatures worshiped nature and had a connection with the animals of the forest. They seemed to be able to communicate with them and have them do their bidding through spells. They seemed perfectly content to have no connection with others. They lived in nature, worshipped nature, and communicated with the animals.

Most creatures knew of these druids—and the strange happenings around them—and steered clear of them. Occasionally, dwarves wandered across the druids' home, usually to their demise. Such was the case today. But today, Drake unexpectedly entered the druids' lair, much to the surprise of all parties.

Drake could sense something happening up ahead. The forest had become silent, and the ruby on the sword hilt brightened. Drake rested his hand on the sword's handle, and he felt a calmness come over him as well as a sense of aggression. He could not see them, but there were goblins all around, and he knew it. They were not aware of him; they were watching the druids and their prey.

The two druids had captured a dwarf. They had her pinned to the ground with a stake at each arm and leg.

Drake entered the circular clearing where he saw the two druids standing over the dwarf. He did not have a direct view of the dwarf; he could only see a small creature staked to the ground.

This unfortunate creature was covered with some sort of ritual paint and blood. She was hardly recognizable in her current state. Drake watched a raven swoop down and land on the dwarf's head. As it went to peck at her eye, she quickly jerked her head and then she had the head of the raven in her mouth. She bit off the bird's head before the druids could react. The body of the raven flew off to the side as the dwarf flicked her head to the other side and spit out the bird's head. Blood sprayed out from the neck of the decapitated bird as the body flopped around for the next several seconds.

Overcome with rage, one of the druids cursed the dwarf and raised his staff to bludgeon her. Drake reacted without thinking. In a matter of seconds, he had crossed the clearing. With the handle of his sword in hand, he slammed his fist into the back of the druid's skull. The druid fell to the ground, bleeding and dazed. No one had seen this coming. Indeed, no one had known Drake was even there. The other druid held his staff out in front of him and tried to back away. Drake swung his sword, splitting the staff in half.

The druid stumbled backward and mumbled something incomprehensible to Drake as he fell to the ground. As soon as the druid had uttered his words, the large bear, which had been watching events unfold from the edge of the clearing, suddenly rose on its back legs and marched straight toward Drake. At the same time, a large bird of prey swept from the sky toward him.

What happened next occurred in the blink of the eye. The goblins were watching. They feared the sword. Even more so, they feared the human, Drake, whom they were watching with keen interest.

Drake had never been as skilled as he was at this moment in time. His mind was clear, but his instincts took over. His senses were much more alert with the sword in his hand. The bear confronted him, but he could sense the large bird diving from the sky toward him.

The angry bear was up on its hind legs and at eight feet tall, it towered over Drake. Only the helpless dwarf came between him and the bear. The bear swiped at Siv, missing its target, but its claw severed the tie that was holding her right wrist to the ground. The bear was a mass of fury with its loud roar and saliva flying everywhere. Its booming roar thundered from deep in its chest.

With his left hand, Drake grabbed his throwing axe and hurled it, point first, in one swift motion, at the bear. At the same time, he turned his body three hundred and sixty degrees and cut into the air with his sword. The bird was in a deep dive and in full attack mode, aiming straight for Drake. Drake's blade cleaved the winged predator in half, separating its claws from its wings. The bird fell at the foot of the bear. The bear fell dead on its face; its body thumping to the ground, just missing Siv. Blood erupted from between its eyes where the point of the axe was buried. The bear's body convulsed in protest as its last attempt to hold on to life failed. The axe had been thrown with such force that it penetrated the thick skull of the bear to the deepest point of its brain. With two hands on the handle of his sword, Drake straddled the bear's neck and plunged his blade through the base of the bear's neck, severing its spinal cord. In one swift movement, he withdrew the sword and had the bloody tip at the throat of the druid who had cast the spell on the animals. Drake knew what the druid had attempted. He did not understand the words the druid had uttered, but he was well aware of the consequences.

During all the commotion, the dwarf, with one hand free, had worked herself free of the remaining ties that bound her and ran off in the direction of the mountains and her home. As she turned to look back, she stood in sheer amazement at the dead birds, the dead bear, the dazed druid, and the other druid who was about to lose his life. She ran for freedom, never turning back again to see what happened next.

The goblins could have hunted the dwarf down, but they were in raw fear of the blade and did not move, fearing that they might be its next victims. Slowly, they retreated from the carnage, moving in the direction of the volcano.

The druid tried to utter something to Drake, but only incomprehensible sounds came out. The druid had soiled himself and was giving off a foul odor. He had used his best spell to attack Drake on two fronts, but the magic Drake possessed had overcome the druid's spell. He had just witnessed Drake's fury.

Then Drake heard from behind: "Do not kill my brother. We will give you whatever you want."

Drake pressed his sword into the neck of the druid lying on the ground and turned his head to the druid who was speaking. "Why should I spare his life? He was going to kill me and that small creature on the ground. For that matter, why should I spare your life either?"

Drake felt aggression and lust in his desire to kill these two creatures. Aelhaeran, maker of the blade, continued to sow his evil spirit inside Drake's soul.

He did not realize it, but the druid who had been hit in the skull was using all the magic he could muster at this time to speak to Drake in a language the man could understand. He recognized Drake as a human; very few had ever been seen in Lavendelle. This human, however, possessed great magic, and the druid respected it.

"You are human, are you not?" The druid kept Drake talking,

trying to calm him.

"I am, and what is it to you? What are you?"

"We are druids, the servant priests of this, the Mystic Forest. My name is Cael. My brother there is Finn."

Drake recognized that he was in complete control of the situation. The druid at the end of his sword was dead with even the slightest movement. Both the druids recognized this. The blood trickling down his neck from where the tip of Drake's blade rested attested to this fact. The other druid was spent as well. It was all he could do to try to talk Drake down from ending both of their lives.

"I have never heard of priests killing like you were about to kill that small creature you had pinned to the ground."

Cael looked in the direction of the dwarf and saw that she was gone. That in and of itself was painful enough, but now he had to focus on salvaging his own life as well as that of his brother.

Chapter XXXIII
Escape

Siv finally looked back at Cael and Finn. She was unsure if they would survive the encounter with the man. At this point it did not look good for the druids. She hoped the man would finish them off.

After she got far enough away to feel safe, Siv stopped and turned around to survey her current surroundings. She was unsure of her location, but the tracks of the heavy cart that had transported her were easy to follow in the rain-soaked ground. Soon, she was fairly sure of the direction of the hytter. She needed to get there, get the Cassava root, get her supplies, and escape before the druids returned—*if* they returned. They were tricky, and if the man let his guard down at all, they would turn the tables on him.

After running for quite a long way, well past the morning, Siv finally could see the sodden roof in the distance. She approached with caution. Adrenaline pumped through her body and kept her on high alert. It masked the exhaustion she would otherwise surely have felt after the trauma of being drugged, staked to the ground, and nearly eaten by a bear.

Just because she hadn't met anyone else here before she had been drugged, it didn't mean that there weren't other creatures to fear. How foolish she had been not to heed Yuri's words: "Trust no one." She had learned this lesson the hard way, and she was lucky to be among the living at this point.

Siv reflected on what had happened and realized that if she had headed across the boulder field to the south on the mountain, she probably would have never come across the evil druids. Experience is the best teacher, she thought; however, from this point forward, she would be paying a lot more attention to Yuri's words.

The home looked empty. There was no smoke rising from the chimney. Siv was reasonably sure that no one else was around. She approached the door, put her ear next to it, and listened. Only the sounds of the forest could be heard. Silence was all that came from the home.

She lifted her hand to the handle of the door, quietly opened it, and entered. Her pack was still leaning against the fireplace, undisturbed. The fresh Cassava root sat on the table. Next to it was the satchel with the dry Cassava root and the keys to the Tower of the Wizards. It looked as though nothing had changed since she had been drugged. The two must have taken her right after she had passed out.

As quickly as she could, she stuffed everything into Yuri's pack, including the Cassava root and the long keys to the tower. These keys protruded out the end of Yuri's pack, but no matter. She would give these keys back to Elijah herself, if she ever saw him again. Certainly, these two had no intention of returning them. Siv worked quickly despite her aching body. She needed to stay strong and focused.

After gathering her things, she needed a distraction in case the druids appeared (although the likelihood of that happening seemed remote to her given their predicament with the man they had encountered). Still, a distraction seemed appropriate. She went to the fireplace and started a fire. She stoked it until it was good and hot. She continued to look out the windows to make sure no one approached. Once the fire was ablaze, Siv took the red hot flaming logs and tossed them all around the hytter, making sure they would do maximum damage if left alone for even a short amount of time. This certainly would keep the druids occupied for a while. They would have a lot more to be concerned about than her if they ever returned. For all Siv knew, they were already dead.

Siv then left the hytter and, without looking back, headed toward the mountain as swiftly as she could. This time she would head south to the river and avoid returning the same way she had come. She would backtrack the way Yuri had told her to go in the first place. This too would be insurance in case the druids tried to track her. She was careful to leave as little trail as possible. They would expect her to head back north where they had found her. They would never expect her to head south as though she knew her way around. In fact, if they had escaped the man, they might bypass coming to their home and instead head to where they first met her in the hope of preventing her escape.

By early evening Siv had found the stream. She would follow this stream until she got closer to the mountain. This time she was far to the south of where she had come off the mountain. There was good light in the evening sky and Siv did not want to waste it. She was afraid of what lay behind her. If she had not been through all that she had, she felt surely she could make it to the tree line on the mountain well before dark.

Siv reflected on her situation. Hopefully, she could correct her ways, follow Yuri's advice, and this time stay safe. The danger she had experienced had engulfed her and left her with no way out before she had ever realized she was in jeopardy. A new appreciation for Yuri came over her as Siv considered her fate.

She pushed on as far as her body would allow before exhaustion set in. By late evening, she could go no farther. The trauma to her body, on top of her exhaustion, forced her to stop. She sat beneath the underbrush next to the stream Yuri had told her about. She washed the dried blood and paint from her body and face and then headed for the mountain as the shadows of the evening sky settled across the peak. She searched her bag and found what was left of her food and contemplated the trek to the mountain and then home. She lifted her eyes toward the mountain—only to receive the shock of her life.

CHAPTER XXXIV
ALLIANCES

"WHAT can we do for you? Anything you want. All you have to do is ask. Please spare us. We are your servants." Cael was doing everything in his power to communicate with Drake and to save him and his brother from this human who possessed such great magic.

Drake lusted to kill. He had never been like this before, but he loathed these weak creatures. He wanted to take the blade on Finn's neck and connect it with the scar on his face so that Finn would have one long scar. He restrained himself and listened to what they said while he struggled to control his drive to strike down these creatures.

"There is something I want," he said.

"What is it, master?" Cael asked. Finn remained still, lying on the ground with the blade pressing into his neck. The sharp blade had already drawn blood.

"I have the goblin treasure," Drake uttered.

"Goblin treasure? I have never heard of it," said Cael. "Tell me about it."

Drake thought for a moment and realized that these two might be able to help him. He saw the fear that engulfed them. Slowly, he removed the blade from Finn's neck. He took the tip and wiped off the blood using Finn's clothes. Then he placed it in its scabbard, withdrew the manuscript from his satchel, and showed it to Cael. "Tell me what this says," he demanded and thrust it into Cael's chest.

Finn remained on the ground, trying to get his faculties about him as Cael studied the ancient manuscript. "This is very old," Cael began. "It is written in the script of the wizards. Where did you come by this?"

Drake was relieved that what the goblins had told him was being verified by this creature. Obviously, the creature was doing what he said he would, hopeful that Drake would not kill them both with one slashing arc of the sword.

"We can translate this for you, master," Cael continued, "but it would be better if we take it to our home to work on it. It is quite an extensive document."

Drake thought about this proposal. "That seems reasonable, but if you try to cross me, I will not hesitate to strike down both of you!"

Cael and Finn both shuddered. They were relieved that they could help this man, but they knew they were in no position to attempt anything here. Perhaps they could make him some stew when they reached their home, they thought to themselves, but they would have to be careful. This man was no simple dwarf, no indeed. This man possessed greater magic than they did, yet they did not understand how this was possible. Men, like dwarves, were thought to be oblivious to the enchanted.

Cael reached down and helped his brother to his feet. Finn needed to change his soiled clothes; he smelled awful. Next, he placed the ancient wizard script into the cart they had used to haul the dwarf to this holy place of sacrifice. With that, he and Finn pulled the cart away toward their home. They were frightened. They did not know how the day would unfold with this stranger in tow. Certainly, nothing had gone as planned.

As they approached their home, they smelled an unfamiliar scent wafting through the air. At first they could not place it. Both Cael and Finn had a keen sense of smell. Drake did not sense the odor.

"That smell is getting stronger, Finn," Cael said as he looked at his brother.

"Indeed," Finn answered.

A few moments later, both recognized the smell of smoke in the air. At the same moment, both the druids and Drake saw smoke rising in the distance. A sinking feeling began to settle in the pit of the druids' stomachs for they knew of only one place where the smoke could be coming from: their home. Their pace quickened.

Cael looked at Drake and said, "We must move quickly. It looks as though our home is burning. Many of the things we need to transcribe this text for you are inside our home!" he lied.

"Then let's move," Drake said and the three rushed toward the cottage.

When they arrived at their hytter, flames roared from every side. Flames, smoke, and soot rose high into the air, snapping at the branches of nearby trees. There was no way to salvage anything. Cael and Finn looked at each other. They had no idea what had caused this disaster. Their spirits sank. There was nothing left. There was nothing to help them free themselves from Drake.

"What happened here, Cael? Look at our home!" Finn wailed.

Cael thought about it. "There was no fire when we left, Finn. It has been out since last evening."

"It had to be the dwarf! That is the only possibility. If we move quickly, we can catch her. She will be sorry she ever crossed our path!" Finn seethed.

In their devastation and anger, Cael and Finn had forgotten that they were Drake's prisoners. They heard the sword scrape the scabbard as Drake withdrew it.

"If you value your lives, you will not move!"

Reality quickly came crashing home as Finn and Cael turned toward their captor. The wound on Finn's neck began aching as he turned and a thin line of blood began to trickle down his neck.

Chapter XXXV
Reading of
the Prophecy

THEY sat at a small table some distance from the hytter as it burned. Only the hytter burned; the surrounding forest escaped the flames. When the heavy sodden roof collapsed, it put out much of the fire. The remaining flames seemed to be dying out slowly, but the heat from the fire was still intense. Cael and Finn, while devastated at the loss of their home, were at the same time amazed by the document at which they were looking. It had been written by Solomon himself—an ancient wizard who was a legend throughout Lavendelle. Indeed, Cael and Finn had read much of Solomon's writings when they followed Demetrius. However, they had never seen this prophecy. Apparently, this was the last prophecy of Solomon before he disappeared. No one ever gave an account of what happened to Solomon. All that was known was that the night the wizards had overthrown Malkavic was the last night Solomon had ever been seen.

"This is an amazing find!" Cael looked up at Drake. "You said the goblins had it? Incredible! How did you get it from them?"

"I demanded they take me to their greatest treasure," Drake

explained, "and they took me to the depths of their volcano and showed me this."

"This prophecy is centuries old. How did they keep it all this time? And how did they let you walk out with it?" Finn stared at Drake as the question hung in the air.

"I cut them down until they cooperated," Drake scowled. "What is this document? What does it say?" he demanded.

The two could see bloodlust in his eyes and felt fear. They believed what he said. "It looks to be a prophecy dating back to the dark times," Cael began. "Times when these lands were ruled by a malevolent force, Malkavic, who lived in the land of the volcano and had the goblins do his bidding."

"Tell me more of this Malkavic," Drake said inquisitively.

"As Cael said, he was an evil force in this world. He controlled all the lands by controlling all the goblins," Finn explained. "The goblins alone or in small bands are not too dangerous. They are more mischievous. What Malkavic was able to do was to organize the goblins. Instead of small bands and unfocused missions, he was able to build armies of goblins and focus their aggression on whatever he wanted. There wasn't anything that could stop them. All the inhabitants of these lands, Lavendelle, lived in fear."

"How did he organize these goblins?" Drake asked. "If there were so many of them, why did they not turn on Malkavic and kill him?"

"How did you walk into the heart of the volcano and take their manuscript which they have had for centuries?" Cael asked. "Obviously, this is important to them."

"Malkavic was a warrior," Finn explained. "He was reported to be of great stature and strength, and he was ruthless. He supposedly killed multitudes of goblins during his time. They lived in fear of crossing him because if they did not please him, they died." Finn let his words hang in the air.

Drake thought about their response. Obviously, these were intelligent creatures. He would be careful not to underestimate them.

"What happened to him?" Drake inquired. "If he was such a great warrior, how did the wizards overcome him?"

Cael and Finn looked at each other, then at Drake. "You don't know much about wizards, do you?" they asked.

"I have never met one," Drake replied. "Are they great warriors?"

"Not great warriors, but they possess great magic," Cael stated.

"What is this magic you speak of?" Drake asked.

Cael and Finn were astonished. This man possessed more magic than they did, yet here he was asking them to explain magic. Did he think they were fools? What game was he playing with them? Even more important, was he going to let them live? Independently, they both decided to appease him.

"Wizards possess great powers. These powers are called magic. Magic is an unseen force that allows them to accomplish their will and does their bidding," Cael explained. "It is as if they have a thought or an idea and they are able to focus their mind to be able to achieve their will. The way they accomplish this is what we call magic."

Drake listened intently, absorbing everything Cael said. He needed to know as much as possible about this strange world if he was to have any chance of finding the treasure he so desperately wanted.

"Typically, wizards are a force for good," Cael continued.

"They tend to work independently of each other and do their work on a small scale. Never before had they banded together and changed the course of Lavendelle on such a grand scale as they did the night Malkavic was overthrown. Alone, a wizard is a powerful force. Together, wizards are the strongest force in all of Lavendelle. Control, however, does not appear to be their desire. They seem to want to work in lives on an individual basis or in small communities. The direction and course of one's life is up to that individual. This was just the opposite of Malkavic's desire. He sought to bend all creatures' wills for his benefit," Cael finished.

"Tell me what this says," Drake said as he placed the tip of his sword on the prophecy.

Cael and Finn leaned closer to look at the manuscript. "This was written seven hundred and fifty years ago," Finn began. "It is from the seer, Solomon. This is the prophecy regarding the demon lord, Malkavic, and the end of his days."

Finn and Cael did their best to decipher the manuscript for Drake. Some of the manuscript was unreadable. There was a detailed account of every transgression Malkavic had committed and all that he had done to oppress those living in Lavendelle. The manuscript also included a long section that explained exactly how he had accomplished his evil deeds. In his writings, Solomon portrayed a picture of pure evil. Every instance of Malkavic's misdeeds was listed, including a full account of the evil perpetrated on each individual.

After hours of reading, Drake and the two druids had a palpable understanding of the environment in which the inhabitants of Lavendelle had lived: No community or individual had been unaffected by the terror that was Malkavic.

Cael, Finn, and Drake did not understand Solomon's diligent

documentation of all the transgressions or why he took his valuable time to document them. Perhaps it was to chronologically list the evils and to provide insight into the thinking of the Wizard Council, which led them to the unprecedented actions taken against Malkavic.

The thought began to unfold in Drake's mind that Malkavic had to have accumulated riches beyond his wildest dreams during his reign of terror. Perhaps the goblins did not appreciate these things. He was sure of the terror of the goblins he had encountered, and he convinced himself that they would not cross him in any way. If he could just lay hands on these treasures that his spirit lusted after, he would be more powerful than anyone in this land: Malkavic, the wizards, even those who ruled beyond. He looked down at his sword and knew it was a testament to the riches that could be found here.

It was late afternoon and there was still more to be read. Drake lusted for more. He was in no mood to stop. Clearly, Finn and Cael were exhausted from the day; they were fragile and not as sturdy as Drake. Moreover, they were distraught over the destruction of their home and the loss of all that they possessed.

"We will stop for the night," Drake said as he warily eyed them, "but come the morning, we will finish this reading. At that time, I will release you from my service."

"Thank you, master," Cael mumbled. Finn and Cael gathered food that grew wild and drew water from their well, which fortunately had been spared.

They ate, drank, and then collapsed from exhaustion. They were certain they would make it through the night; the human needed them to finish the translation of the manuscript. Why he was so focused on this ancient document, they had no idea; however, they would dutifully serve him and hope for the release he had promised. As they huddled together on the ground, their last images of Drake before they drifted off to sleep were of him pacing with his sword drawn. The fire had died to just a few embers and lit Drake from behind. The ruby at the end of the sword glowed in the light of the small fire that remained.

Finn and Cael did not understand why the red stone seemingly glowed from within. All they understood was that this human possessed great magic. That he did not acknowledge this to them meant he was a dangerous foe who was not to be underestimated.

The stone glowing in the hilt of the sword meant that goblins were near, although Drake himself could not sense their presence. The goblins had a mortal fear of the man and the sword and they remained in the shadows. Drake felt energy, but he could not identify the source of it. He could not sense magic, and he could not sense that it was the sword in his hand that made him feel so alive and vibrant.

Drake had so much to contemplate after hearing the story of Malkavic and his transgressions. He was developing a very good understanding of Lavendelle and its inhabitants. If he had to, Drake would search every corner of this land and find Malkavic's treasure. If need be, he would organize the goblins, just as Malkavic had done, and search these lands until he got what he desired!

The chronology of Malkavic's transgressions clearly spelled out how the demon had worked. Drake could follow Malkavic's blueprint for leading the goblins if he had to. He had learned much from this ancient manuscript, but he had much more to learn. He was more determined than ever to find Malkavic's treasure. He would have to watch out for the wizards and give them wide berth, especially the one he had heard about from the goblins: Elijah.

CHAPTER XXXVI
Long Journey Home

Siv wasn't sure if she was awake or if she was dreaming. She had to be delirious because what she was seeing was unbelievable. Still, there could be no denying what her eyes were telling her brain. She watched as the two worked their way toward the southern bend in the stream. If she was not mistaken—but she had to be—it looked as though Teige and Ramsey were on a direct path toward her.

"I knew we could make it to the stream by nightfall, Teige," Ramsey said excitedly to his brother.

"You were right again," Teige replied. "I think we should find a place to settle for the night. I do not think we want to be right on the water as this is a place many of the night creatures may seek out."

"We have come a long way in a day, a lot longer than I thought possible! Still, there are a few more hours of daylight left. Perhaps we should press on."

"Yes, I realize how far we have come, but we had a clear direction. Now we need to think hard about the next step. I think it is time we stop."

Teige did not get a response from Ramsey; in fact, Ramsey

wasn't even paying attention to Teige any longer. He was walking away from him and toward the stream. Teige didn't know what he had said for Ramsey to tune him out, but as he followed Ramsey's gaze, he received his answer. He saw Siv, battered and torn, but moving directly toward them! The sight of Siv rattled Teige and Ramsey. Seeing Siv, they knew Yuri was right: Siv needed them, and they were glad they were there for her. Ramsey ran to her.

"I am so glad we found you! Come with us and let us help you!" he said as he embraced his cousin.

Teige was quick on Ramsey's heels, and he embraced her as well. Without speaking, he put his shoulder under Siv's arm and helped her away from the stream. He also took Yuri's pack from her shoulder and carried it in his free hand.

"I am so glad to see you two," Siv began. "I could hardly believe my eyes! How did you know I needed you?" The tension was significantly relieved by finding her family, but she knew they were not out of danger even though there were now three of them.

Teige looked at Ramsey and then Siv followed his look. "Yuri knew, Siv. He knew you needed us. He told us what you did for Ramsey and for our mother. I am glad we listened to him. He guided us to you!"

"I am glad too. I am glad too," was all an exhausted Siv could utter.

"Did you find Elijah? Did you get to the tower? Did you get the Cassava root?" Teige asked.

"I did not find Elijah, nor did I make it to the tower, but yes, I have the Cassava root!" Siv had a big grin on her face as she told Teige and Ramsey the great news.

Finding the Cassava root lifted everyone's spirits and new energy shot through the group. Even Siv felt reenergized as the other two dwarves contemplated the enormity of her accomplishments.

"We are not out of danger," Siv stated. "We need to get some distance from here."

Judging from her condition, both Ramsey and Teige knew she must be right.

"Let's get moving," Teige stated. "Siv, will you be able to move on?"

"We have the Cassava root," she began. "We need to get it back to Martha as soon as possible. Time is our enemy! I think I am being hunted by two druids. They are evil and they tried to kill me. I escaped and I don't know if they are even alive, but if they are, and if they are free, they will come after me. We need to get out of here and quick!"

Upon hearing this, Teige reached into his satchel and pulled out his axe. It felt good in his hands. If the druids attacked tonight, they would not be counting on reinforcements, and they wouldn't be counting on facing him!

Siv witnessed the darkness wash over Teige and his determination as he pulled out his axe. "It is good I have you and Ramsey to protect me, Teige, but I believe distance from the druids will be our better ally than facing this danger head on. If we can make it up the mountain, we will be able to see a great distance and prepare for the druids if they approach."

"I agree with Siv," Ramsey said.

"Seeing you two has renewed my strength. We need to stop talking and start moving. I don't want to face those two again. They are crafty and attack without being seen. They are evil." Siv started toward the mountain.

Teige absorbed what she had said and shifted his focus. The task at hand was to put distance between them and the unseen danger that was coming from behind. With that, the three headed out into the evening, back in the direction of the mountain and their home.

The three had gained renewed energy from Siv's success. They also knew they had to get home as quickly as possible because Martha was living on borrowed time. She needed the medicine from the Cassava root.

They had great fortune on this evening. The sky was lit by a bright moon; though only a half-moon, it gave them good light for their journey. They continued into the night until they reached timberline and the edge of the boulder field.

"I almost lost my life here, Siv," Teige began as he pointed upward toward the boulders. "I got caught in those boulders and nearly got crushed. Thankfully, Ramsey saved me."

"Yes, I did, and I think it is a good place to stop for the night," Ramsey concluded.

Siv looked up at the boulder field and considered what she had learned from Teige. As she was looking, she noticed something lying amongst the boulders. It was massive and it was moving. Teige followed Siv's gaze and froze in his tracks. There was a dragon stretched out on the boulders. It was not a very big dragon, as dragons go, but it was a dragon nonetheless.

"Ramsey, look!" Teige exclaimed as he pointed at the dragon.

Ramsey looked up to see what Siv and Teige were looking at. They stood silently and watched. They were trapped with no way to go up the mountain if the druids came. They could not go back as there was too much danger in that. They could stay put, but they would face the same problem in the morning. They could easily be seen and eaten by the creature above as they tried to pass. There was no good solution. There was nothing to do but retreat and take a new path. The druids would certainly gain the upper hand if they retreated.

The dragon expelled several loud snorts. It moved its head back and forth but remained in the same place. It let out a loud cry. Finally, it stretched out and lay on its side as though it was exhausted and dying.

"I think it is hurt," Siv said as she looked at her cousins.

"It is awfully strange, Siv. It isn't moving from that spot!" Ramsey said.

They stood silently for another few minutes and watched. It whimpered several more times.

"I think it is trapped in the rocks, just like I was trapped," Teige said as he wiped his hand across his brow.

"We have to do something," Ramsey started. "If we are pursued by the druids, we will be trapped. There is no way around that thing either. What are we going to do?"

"I think we need to help it. I can feel the dragon. I feel as though it has given up," Siv said.

"Siv, are you crazy? That thing could kill us all in seconds and think nothing of it!" Teige responded, incredulous at his cousin's proposal.

Siv just shook her head. Ramsey and Teige knew they were in trouble as there was no changing Siv's mind once she set herself to it. They knew she followed her own path.

"I can feel the dragon inside me; I know it won't hurt us. It is dying and needs our help. We can do this! The dragon senses me too. It will be all right."

Teige's jaw dropped as he watched Siv walk toward the dragon. Ramsey stood still and shook his head in disbelief. There was nothing to do but follow her. They hoped it did not get them all killed. There appeared to be no other way.

The dragon lifted its head as Siv approached. It snorted and Siv stopped in her tracks. She was nervous, but she could feel that the spirit of the beast was resigned to its fate. The dragon set its head back on the ground and Siv slowly approached once again. Teige and Ramsey stayed back and watched their cousin.

Siv had a connection with the dragon that she could feel in her soul. It was something she could not explain, but she knew she had to be there for the beast. She could feel the dragon imploring her for help. The dragon opened its eyes and Siv met its stare. The two locked eyes for a long time without moving. Siv's green eyes penetrated into the dragon, and somehow the dragon knew she was there to help. She reached out and stroked the dragon's muzzle. It was grizzled and rough. Next, she took her water flask and let a few drops sprinkle on to the great beast's nose. The dragon quickly lapped up the drops.

The dragon looked young to Siv. She had little experience with these beasts, but the ones she had seen before were much larger and showed much more wear and tear on their hides than this one had. That being said, this creature appeared as though it could be alarmingly dangerous.

Siv slowly poured out a few more drops of water. The dragon eagerly lapped up each drop. Siv had had a full flask, and it was quickly gone in a few moments. It was not much to resuscitate the dragon, but it was enough to establish trust.

"Ramsey, Teige, come down here and look at what's happened to this dragon for me." Siv said this as though she expected both to do exactly what she requested. Surprisingly, they both sprung to their feet before they even considered the risk they were taking.

They were mesmerized by what Siv was doing. The dragon lifted its head and watched as the two approached its trapped leg.

"Its legs are trapped by several boulders. The situation looks serious."

"Is there anything you can do?"

"We can push a few of them off, but there is a large one that I don't think either of us can move."

"Do what you can." Siv then turned her attention back to the dragon. She kept close eye contact with it, and the creature seemed to understand that she meant it no harm. She maintained eye contact with it while Teige and Ramsey worked to free its legs. Her green eyes penetrated deep and the dragon was calmed by her presence despite the pain it was experiencing.

The two dwarves had been able to move a significant amount of weight from the dragon's legs, but there was still one large boulder that pinned the beast to the ground. Had it been a more mature dragon, it probably would have had the strength to break free, thought Teige, but alas, the injured beast was probably stuck here for good.

"Ramsey, we have done all that we can do. Siv, come over here and look. I don't think we will be able to do anything else."

Siv approached the dragon's hindquarters and assessed the situation.

"Isn't there anything else you can do? I feel there is more that we can do to help!"

Teige considered the problem. They could probably all make a break for it now and leave the dragon behind and be safe. He could tell that Siv wasn't going to have any of that. She was determined to free this beast. He just hoped they wouldn't become a meal for the dragon once they set it free.

"Ramsey, see if you can find something in the forest to use as a lever," Siv said as she pointed to the trees.

Siv returned to the dragon and again did her best to comfort it. She could feel the dragon relax and calm down as she approached.

Teige followed his brother into the forest. They soon returned with a long, sturdy tree trunk. They positioned it as best they could under the boulder and placed as large a rock as they could lift under the log near the large boulder. They were used to this kind of work in the mines. They hoped it worked.

Ramsey swung the log over by Siv and by the head of the dragon. He was certain the three of them were not strong enough to move the boulder that was trapping the dragon, but perhaps Siv could get the dragon to participate in its own release.

He explained to Siv, and soon he and Teige were pulling with all their might on the log. The boulder did not budge. Siv joined them, and the three together were still not successful.

Siv walked over to the dragon and stared into its eyes. She had a connection with the beast and did her best to get the dragon to pay attention to her. The dragon lifted its head and stared up at the three dwarves. With its head up, the creature towered over them.

Somehow Siv was able to communicate with the dragon. Ramsey and Teige had seen their cousin do a lot of amazing things, but this was perhaps one of the most amazing things they had ever seen. With Siv at the dragon's head, never taking her eyes from it, the dragon lifted its front leg and rested it on the long lever arm, and then rested its chin on the lever arm. Siv stood up and all three together did all they could to push the lever arm down. Siv concentrated on the dragon and it began to push as well. All of a sudden a great force was applied to the log as the dragon began pushing down!

The boulder started to move. Then the log snapped under the enormous stress. The log snapping sent Siv, Ramsey, and Teige crashing to the ground and rolling down and away from the dragon. Their spirits were crushed; they had been so close. But as soon as they looked up, they realized that the dragon had pulled itself free of the boulder. It was moving quickly around, clearly favoring the bad leg. Then, without any further hesitation, the dragon took to the air.

Siv could feel the life flow back into the dragon, which only moments before had seemed resigned to its fate. The next thing she felt was Teige's hand on her shoulder pulling her into the forest. She did not resist. They all scampered off quickly so as not to become the next meal for the newly freed dragon.

"Wow! That was amazing, Siv! Truly incredible!" said Teige, shaking his head.

"I agree," Ramsey said. "How did you talk to that thing?"

"I don't know. I just did. At least now we have a free path to the top of the mountain. Let's make camp here and rest for the evening," Siv said. "That took a lot out of me and I am exhausted."

"You are a kind soul, Siv. I can't believe you made us help that beast. We could have been its next meal!" Teige said as he handed his full flask of water to his cousin.

"I know, Teige, but I could feel the dragon suffering as we watched it struggle. I felt a connection with it. The dragon could feel me too, I am sure."

"I don't understand how that is possible. I just hope we never have to face it again, and if we do, I hope it remembers us favorably!" Teige shook his head as he said this.

CHAPTER XXXVII
A PLAN IS FORMED

THE early morning light crept into the sky; a heavy mist lay across the ground. This was like most mornings in the Mystic Forest. Only one thing had changed: the hytter of logs and the sodden roof were no more. Only smoke trailed high up from Cael and Finn's home.

Cael spotted him first. Drake sat with his back against a tree, his sword still in hand, the blade's tip resting in the sod outstretched beyond his feet. The nightmare that had unfolded the previous day continued. Cael wondered if this would be the last day he and Finn would walk this land. Would this human strike them down, or would he release them as promised?

There was no protection for them. Bringing the man back to their home offered some hope of protection and escape, but when they found their home destroyed by that evil dwarf, all hope had been lost. Cael resolved to pay back Siv if he ever got the chance.

Drake started a fire as Cael and Finn awoke to the day. Drake's energy had not lapsed, and Cael and Finn wondered if he had even slept. They were still exhausted and overcome by all the events of the prior day. They felt completely overwhelmed by this man and totally under his power.

Cael and Finn were but slight creatures, and though they possessed magic, this powerfully built man possessed more magic than they had witnessed in any creature other than a wizard. And yet, he denied possessing this magic! They could not understand it.

They sat around the fire and Drake pulled out the writings. He handed them back to Cael. "Finish reading this to me," Drake demanded.

"Yes, my lord," Cael said as he bowed down. Cael brought the writings over next to Finn, sat down, and began to read.

" 'Because of these great transgressions and the destruction of lives, property, and prosperity, committed by Malkavic, the Wizard Council had elected to take action against him. With the next disappearance of the moon, Malkavic will be delivered to the Chamber of the Gatekeeper by the wizards of this Council where he will be entombed for all time.' "

"Who is this Gatekeeper?" Drake demanded. "I have heard of him once before. I believe I was on my way to his chamber in the volcano, but I could not continue down because of the heat!" Drake cursed himself. Had he gone to the chamber, he might already have the treasure! Anyway, he had his first real clue. The Gatekeeper probably had Malkavic's treasure. Now he had a place to start his search!

"Yes, the Chamber of the Gatekeeper is somewhere in the depths of that volcano, or at least that is the rumor," Cael started. "So you know where it is? You have been that way?"

"Yes, I know where to find it. I started on the path to the chamber, but it is a long way down into the very depths of that volcano, and the heat is overwhelming. I didn't have any water and I could not keep going forward, so I turned around and left it for another day." Drake hovered over the druids, slowly waving his sword back and forth. "Who is this Gatekeeper?" Drake asked.

Finn and Cael shuddered, disturbed by the question. Finn's eyes widened, the scar across his face reddened, and for the first time he spoke with force. "Not who but *what* is the Gatekeeper is the real question. No one knows the answer. The Gatekeeper has not been seen by anyone who has lived to tell about it. All the creatures of Lavendelle know to take cover when the moon disappears in the night sky to avoid coming across this thing. Beings disappear, never to be seen again. Stay away, I caution you. Stay away!"

Cael sat with wide eyes and nodded in agreement. These writings were dangerous and dealt with unspeakable things—things that had driven these druids away from the wizards, the tower, and the volcano and deep into the Mystic Forest where they could live free from all of them.

The druids' words utterly entranced Drake. He sensed their fear as they uttered the name of the Gatekeeper. He was beginning to understand the fear the goblin had shown on the path down to the Gatekeeper's chamber. His thoughts overwhelmed him; he became driven by what he might find at the Chamber of the Gatekeeper. The treasure had to be there. He would have to be more prepared the next time he went to the volcano. He would also have to prepare for an encounter with the Gatekeeper.

Drake shook his thoughts aside. "What else is written?" he asked, eager to hear more. As he realized that the druids were coming to the end of the prophecy, his excitement grew, for he now had direction. That direction seemed to point him back to the volcano.

" 'Malkavic will be entombed for all time.' " Finn began where Cael had left off. " 'For all time or until the day when the firstborn to the Prince of the Elves is brought to the Chamber of the Gatekeeper in exchange for the release of Malkavic! This will be the sign that Malkavic is about to return: The moon shall turn to darkness and then reappear as blood in the sky. On that day, the Gatekeeper shall open his chamber and take in the royal offspring, and Malkavic will be returned to Lavendelle.' That is all that is written, master," Finn said to Drake.

"It looks as though more was written after this, but where is the rest of it?" Cael inquired.

"That is all there is. That is what I took from the goblins. There was no more." Drake's voice trailed off, his mind wandering elsewhere.

Both Finn and Cael stared at Drake, waiting for instruction. They received nothing. Drake remained deep in thought. He held his sword in his hand and stood up. He began pacing as he had the previous evening. He was clearly trying to absorb all that he had learned.

As they sat there, they thought about trying to escape. Clearly, this would be next to impossible as this man was too swift and too powerful for them. Even with their best magic, Drake had struck down the eagle and the bear in mere moments. Cael imagined the point of Drake's axe being buried in his skull if he attempted to flee. Drake's magic trumped their magic. To try to escape would mean certain death for them. So they sat quietly, hoping above hope that this was not their final day to breathe the air, smell the land, and feel the soil under their feet. He had yet to release them as he had promised. The prophecy had been read, and they were still there. However, it wasn't looking good for them at the moment.

Drake's thoughts focused on these two creatures who did not appear to be all that timid; however, the mere mention of the Gatekeeper and his chamber seemed to frighten them. It seemed to terrify them more than being held by him even though he could snuff their lives out faster than what they had planned for the little dwarf the day before. That little creature, he laughed to himself, had gotten her revenge on these two.

Perhaps he should proceed with caution. It seemed as though there was another way to approach the Gatekeeper and get to Malkavic. Surely, if he were to free Malkavic from hundreds of years of captivity, he would be handsomely rewarded. Treasure was all that really motivated Drake. He did not need dominion over those ghastly creatures, the goblins. He could hardly stand the heat or the stench emanating from their lair. Malkavic could have all that. All he wanted was the treasure and to return to Lindisfarne triumphant!

And who was this Prince of the Elves? How would he find this being? How long could he sit around, waiting for a baby to come along? And how could he possibly retrieve a baby from this prince? Still, that being said, it may be the only way he could approach this Gatekeeper.

The longer the druids waited for Drake, the more their thoughts tortured them. They had to think of something. Surely, this human was planning their demise. They had no doubt that this was what he was lost in thought about. They had to do something.

"Master?" The word called Drake back to the moment and away from his deep thoughts.

Drake looked at Cael. "Yes?"

Cael was nervous about what he was about to propose. He did not know how it would be received. His thoughts would tie together his own fate as well as that of his brother and Drake.

"The baby elf was born last month," Cael said timidly. He stole a glance at Finn. He was not sure what Finn was thinking, except that the scar on his face was turning dark and blood began to ooze again from the wound Drake had inflicted. Cael knew that Finn also felt nervous about what he was leading them into. Finn sat quietly.

"Last month?" Drake inquired. His mind raced as he waited to hear Cael confirm that he had heard correctly.

"Yes, my lord," Cael nodded as he looked at Drake. "And, as I recall, the next disappearance of the moon should occur eight nights from tonight!"

Electricity shot through the air. Drake's mind began racing so fast that everything else seemed slow. Drake believed that his time had come. He had the prophecy, he understood the prophecy, the baby had been born, and the Gatekeeper was scheduled to come again in eight nights. It was Drake's time and he was in control. All he had to do was reach out and take what he wanted. The prophecy had clearly been written for him; everything was aligning for his success!

"Let us turn that moon to blood!" Drake uttered powerfully as he stood and turned his gaze toward the heavens.

And so it began: the prophecy had been discovered by Drake, it had been deciphered by Cael and Finn, and it was all as the Gatekeeper had planned when he insisted that Solomon write out his vision. Solomon might have won the victory all those years ago, but the war was coming to a head and the final battle had been set in motion by Drake and the two druids.

In a distant place, the Gatekeeper sat patiently; time was not relevant to him. This was his time and these pawns were about to do his bidding. With the next disappearance of the moon, everything this world knew would change.

Chapter XXXVIII
Medicine for a
Sick Dwarf

After a long night of hiking and the dramatic rescue of the dragon, the dwarves arrived back at Yuri's cottage by early afternoon the next day. As they approached Yuri's home, they all felt a sense of excitement. They had the Cassava root and were excited to finally be home again. Yuri, who had been an excellent source of wisdom and guidance for them, would certainly know how to use the Cassava and whether the fresh or the dry Cassava plant was needed. Moreover, he would be able to identify if this was indeed Cassava root.

Siv had no doubt that she had the root. There was no reason for the druids to lie to her about this. But even more important was that Siv felt strongly that Martha would live. Martha needed the Cassava root, and there was no other around, so this had to be it!

Yuri stared in disbelief as the three approached. He sat outside his cottage on a comfortable chair, pulling drags on his long stem wooden pipe. He enjoyed the warmth that filled his chest; he enjoyed watching the smoke as he exhaled. Over the decades, he had become quite talented at exhaling a variety of shapes. However, his favorite was exhaling rings. This always fascinated his guests.

Today, however, he forgot all about rings and smoking. His attention focused on the approaching group of dwarves. He had feared he would never see these three again, let alone two days later. He reflected on Siv's appearance. She didn't even resemble a dwarf by his estimation. Small, yes, but slightly built and agile, she also had flaming red hair and eyes a penetrating green. None of these features was dwarf-like. She was a very strange creature; strange but special and Yuri felt a connection to her that he could not explain.

Upon reflecting on Siv and her seeming power over him, it was not really that surprising that he was seeing these three again. Something about her transcended the present; she seemingly knew how everything worked and fit together. There was no explaining her presence other than as a gift. Certainly, most dwarves were unable to perceive—let alone understand—all there was to Siv. Ramsey and Teige had obviously put their faith and trust in her.

When the three saw Yuri sitting and waiting for them, their pace quickened. Siv burst forward with what little energy she had left and ran to Yuri with her arms wide open.

"Yuri, we found the root! We owe everything to you!" Siv embraced him so tightly that he could feel her love flow out to him. He returned her embrace. He had not felt so connected to anyone for a long, long time. He was happy these three had come into his life.

"I did not know if I would ever see the three of you again," Yuri said as Ramsey and Teige approached. They all sat on the ground and Yuri sat back down. "I sent you into a dangerous world, and I didn't know how I was going to live with myself if you were harmed in any way. I just wish I could have gone with you, but time has eroded my strength and all that is left is this withered old body before you."

"But time did not steal your mind, Yuri. The gift of your knowledge and experience saved us, saved me, and, most importantly, may save Aunt Martha!" Siv said excitedly.

"Then you found the root?" Yuri looked at them.

Siv took the satchel and pulled out the fresh Cassava plant and root, and then she opened up the pouch with the dried Cassava root. "Here, Yuri, this is what I found. Tell me that it is what we need and that this adventure wasn't all for naught!"

Yuri took the fresh root and the dried root and looked at them.

"This dried root is of no use to your mother; it is only food. But this root from the fresh Cassava plant will be life-saving! You have done well, Siv."

"Why is the fresh root what we need and the dried root not helpful?" Siv looked at Yuri.

"The skin of the root has the medicine. Once the root has dried, the medicine seeps out of it. Moreover, the correct preparation and the correct dose of the medicine is important: too much and the medicine becomes a poison; too little and there is little more benefit than if you prepare this dry root here."

Siv placed her hands on her hips and said, "Those druids told me that the dry root was the key and that the fresh root would not be helpful. They lied to me!" Siv felt further betrayal from these two, if that was even possible. As she reflected on Yuri's words, she realized that the story of the dry root was another way they had lured her back into their home.

"What did you say?" Yuri's turned his full attention to Siv. "What about the druids?" A dark shadow had come over Yuri's face at the mention of the druids.

"I came across two druids who said they could help me find the root. Little did I know, they were only trying to trick me so that they could kill me!" Siv said.

"You took the northern route, didn't you?" Yuri began. "I told you to stay south and trust no one!"

Siv's head dropped as though she had disappointed her mentor. "I am sorry, Yuri. I fully realize all my mistakes and how I should have listened to you. I almost died because I didn't listen to you. I got caught in a terrible storm at the top and I just had to get out of it. The only way down was to the north. I couldn't have crossed that boulder field in the lightning storm. It was terrifying. When I found shelter, I tried to correct my path and head south, but it was too little, too late." She stared at the ground, shaking her head at her own mistakes.

"How is it we found you then?" Teige inquired. "Ramsey and I headed south across the boulders and that is where we found you."

"I know, Teige, I know. I headed south during my escape and I was careful to cover my trail. They were chasing me, I am sure, but I had a head start. I figured they would head back north, thinking that was where I was headed."

Yuri was amazed at all he was hearing and he needed to hear more about this adventure. He was well-versed on these druids as he had encountered them in his youth. One of them still bore the scar Yuri had left on his face! He had no idea how long druids lived, but he was sure these two had been around for generations.

"We must save these stories for later." Siv refocused the attention of the dwarves. "First, we must make the medicine and get it to Martha. How long will it take you, Yuri?"

Yuri felt those piercing green eyes penetrate him again and his mind refocused on the task at hand. "It will take the balance of the day, but it should be ready by nightfall. We must get started. I will teach you all how to prepare this medicine so that you will always have this knowledge with you."

With that, Yuri stood and walked into his cottage. The three young dwarves got up and followed. Martha had precious little time left, but at least now there was hope.

CHAPTER XXXIX
A BOLD AND
AUDACIOUS PLAN

DRAKE devised a single, bold plan. He had no time to plan for contingencies. He and the druids had traveled two days to get back to where everything had started. He now had six nights left until the disappearance of the moon. Six nights or there would be no further opportunity for Drake.

He could not fail. He had been looked down upon his whole life; he had been an orphan with no one who loved him. He had lived on the streets, out in the cold, without a place to call home. He was always left with the scraps of other men's successes. Well, no more! This was his time. He either achieved, or he spent the rest of his time in poverty and misery. He couldn't allow that to happen.

The heat of the volcano bore down on them. The stench was beyond putrid. The creatures scattered around the cavernous chamber, some of them clinging to the walls to witness their new leader. It was not too dissimilar to a night seven hundred and fifty years earlier in this same chamber; only he and none of the others present could recognize that irony.

He stood at the head of the chamber as he spoke. In his hand the hilt of the sword throbbed with an eerie red glow; the blade was almost blinding in its intensity. It had not taken the goblins long to learn to fear this man. He had slain scores of them without thinking twice about it. The goblins were powerless against him. They were all convinced that this was Malkavic who had returned. Indeed, the first thing he wanted was the treasure Malkavic had sent them after.

Two odd-looking creatures stood behind the man as he spoke. They were dressed in long, hooded robes from their head to their feet. Gold tassels hung from the point of each hood. One wore a green robe, the other brown. One of them, the larger one in brown, had a scar from his left eye to the corner of his mouth. The two had wide-set eyes that took everything in and they constantly surveyed the goblins as the man spoke. Although normally his words would not be understood by any living creature in the room, the cursed sword of Aelhaeran allowed the man to communicate with the goblins. The druids watched this display of powerful magic—a magic so powerful that they could not begin to understand it despite all their time with Demetrius.

Drake stood on a table high above the goblins. "You will attack in three groups. The first group will attack from the south with the setting of the sun. Your goal is to take control of the Temple of the Elves." He had determined that this was the easiest way to get the infant princess from the elves. "You will attack until successful or until you are driven back. If you are driven back, you will retreat to the wastelands and circle back and reinforce the second wave of attackers. Should you need to do that, the second group will attack from the southwest. This attack should come well into the night. Hopefully, you can press on deep into Nauren. If successful, you should take control of the temple."

The goblins listened as Drake carefully explained each part of his audacious plan in detail. He had thought about all possible contingencies and wanted to make sure these foul creatures understood exactly what he wanted them to do.

"If the elves mount a resistance," Drake continued, "they should be weakened by the first two waves of attack. The first two attacks may or may not be enough to take the temple. If the elves counterattack, resist them as long as you can and then fall back. All remaining attackers need to gather due west of Nauren for the final assault just as the morning breaks! It is here we may break their will and capture Nauren. Drive all the way to the temple and capture it."

Cael and Finn held Drake's maps for him and Drake used the point of the sword to identify points of importance as he spoke.

"As you battle, we will attack from behind and cut the legs out of their reinforcements. If we are successful, we will take over all of Nauren, but that is only the beginning. Even if we are not successful at taking Nauren, we will draw the elven resistance out of the city. If the third wave of attacks is successfully resisted, you will all flee to the Mystic Forest where we will regroup if necessary, Drake pointed on the map to the area of the druid's hytter, and attack the elves who pursue us."

Cael and Finn watched intently to see how the goblins would react to Drake's plan. The foul creatures gave Drake—and his blazing sword—their full attention. They watched as Drake brought down the map, pointed the sword toward the group, and waved it across them all.

"This is the beginning of the goblins' return to power. We will regain control of these lands once and for all. We will either succeed or we will never return to power again. This is our only hope!" As he spoke, Drake jumped from the table and slammed his fist down on a stone to emphasize his point.

The goblins hung on Drake's every word. They shuddered in mortal fear of the blade. The blazing light pierced their minds and there was no thought of dissent among the ranks. Whether it was Drake, the sword, the curse of Aelhaeran, or a combination of all three that galvanized them, the goblins were ready to leave that very night. They would march all night and the next two days to get into position to attack. This human gave them no time to waste. Time was critical he kept saying. Time was critical. Two nights from now they would attack!

What was not critical was the ability of the simple-minded goblins to think. These were vessels to be programmed. After hearing Solomon's words, Drake had a full understanding of how to program these creatures. The what, the why, and the how were unimportant. The when and where was all they needed to know and that is what he gave them. Those answers were simple: The when was now, and the where was the elven home of Nauren. The promise of taking over and restoring the power of the goblins was meaningless to these simple creatures.

With the charge he gave the goblins, the chamber emptied quickly. Cael and Finn looked on in awe at the power they witnessed. Was this man a wizard from another land? Was he indeed the demon Malkavic returned? They could not match his power or his magic. Had they realized this sooner, they never would have sent the bear and the eagle raining down an attack on him. These mindless creatures did not stand a chance against one so powerful. Cael and Finn wondered how they had missed picking up on this power.

Cael and Finn were powerful, but few in the lands ever came close to possessing the magic of Aelhaeran the Depraved—the powerful, diabolical wizard of the generation before Solomon. Drake possessed the cursed sword of Aelhaeran, which bestowed upon him many powers—all powers that Aelhaeran had allowed the possessor of the blade to acquire. Aelhaeran's spells transcended his time and his passing. There was no one in the enchanted world who could possibly know of the existence of this blade or the power it bestowed upon its possessor—and few who even remembered the creator himself, Aelhaeran.

Drake turned his attention to the two druids who had a focused stare. Now they completely acquiesced to him. He was their leader by total fear and intimidation. Any thought of escape or of trying to trick Drake fled from them.

"We are down to six nights. It will be two nights from now when the goblins attack. There will be three nights left by the time we have the baby. We have not a moment to spare. Are you sure you will be able to locate the child?" Drake directed his question to Finn.

He still had a lust to kill Finn. He was not sure where that came from, but he had come close before as witnessed by the wound on Finn's neck, which still continued to intermittently ooze a greenish discharge mixed with a dark red fluid.

Finn looked back at Drake. "We will be able to find the baby. What we need to be sure of is whether we will be able to remove the baby from her mother. A big part of being able to extract that child depends on the goblins' ability to draw the Elven Guard off and away."

Drake nodded as he considered the truth of Finn's words. Indeed, much of his plan was riding on the ability of these creatures to distract the elves and keep their attention focused on the temple outside of Nauren, rather than Nauren itself.

"Once we have the child," Finn continued, "hopefully the goblins will be able to draw the elves into the Mystic Forest. Once the elves are in the forest, Cael and I should be able to keep them occupied, giving you just enough time to get the baby to the Gatekeeper. Indeed, once in the forest, they will be out of position and out of time to react even if they are able to figure everything out!"

"I believe we are destined for success! It is written right there in the prophecy of Solomon," Drake said with a feeling of extreme confidence. "They will never know what we want. If anything, they will think we are after something in the temple. Who would want a baby? No one knows about this prophecy; it has been buried in the volcano for a millennium. Moreover, when the baby disappears, they will follow the trail to the Mystic Forest, where you will detain them until the moon disappears. By then, we will have accomplished our mission!"

Drake's supreme confidence inspired Cael and Finn. They too were completely committed to the plan. The plan had been quickly conceived, and there was no time to think it through properly. It was a bold and audacious plan with a slim window for everything to work. As it was now, all the stars seemed to be aligned for success.

PART III

UNDER THE
BLOOD MOON

Chapter XL
Reflections

Elijah sat alone in the tower. The last time—and in fact the only time that he had been alone in this tower—was the night the goblins had attacked. It had been the night when Solomon informed him that he was going to be invited to join the Wizard Council. As exciting as that news should have been to Elijah, he was overwhelmed with the gravity of the situation and he was aware of the evil and oppression that was omnipresent.

He gazed out the window toward the volcano. Clouds scattered across the evening sky. The light of the setting sun reflected off the volcano; pink and gold scattered with purple highlights spread across the azure blue sky. The night was calm and there was no breeze, but Elijah could feel evil in the land just as he had all those years ago.

As he looked out at the volcano, his mind reflected back on the details of the night the goblins had attacked, 750 years ago. He recalled the disappearance of Solomon.

"Elijah, the goblins will not stop until they overtake me. You will be able to escape, but I cannot. I will leave this body; the goblins will never capture me. I have acquired power beyond your ability to understand or my ability to teach you. I will be among you and the Council, but I will not be in the form you see

me in now.

"*The one thing we must do, Elijah, is keep this prophecy from the goblins. It should have never been written, but I put it into writing according to an agreement I made with the Gatekeeper of Souls. Now, you must escape with it, quickly.*"

Elijah recalled how the goblins had gained new strength, burst into the room, and attacked. He had slashed his dagger through the air and quickly killed seven goblins. He remembered their attack on Solomon and how his mentor had disappeared entirely. Elijah could still recall the fury that had driven him to attack all the goblins within his sight.

Elijah thought about that moment. Solomon had told Elijah they needed to keep the prophecy from the goblins, and then he was gone. Elijah was able to keep a portion of the prophecy from the goblins, but they got a significant part of it. This was something that had always bothered him. Each time he thought about this night, he remembered this great failure. In all the years since, he had never been successful in retrieving the missing portion of the prophecy.

Again, he reflected on that fateful night where all had been lost. He had flung the prophecy into the fire, but only a portion of it burned before a goblin retrieved it. Elijah had attacked the goblin, but another of the foul creatures tore at it. When Elijah had stabbed out at the goblin, his blade sliced the prophecy down the middle. The goblin with the prophecy had fallen to its death outside the tower, but it had clung to half of the prophecy in its fall. Elijah had no way to retrieve that half of the prophecy.

The latter half of the prophecy is what Elijah had saved. The first half of the prophecy is what the goblins had stolen. This was the part that Elijah had scribed. Where this part of the prophecy was now nagged at Elijah, and he was concerned that this was the source of trouble he was detecting in the land. To this day, he still recalled the details of the prophecy. He recalled detailing all of Malkavic's transgressions. He remembered writing about the capture and entombment of the demon lord. What worried him most was one of the last things he had written: the possible return of Malkavic. *Malkavic will be entombed for all time. For all time or until the day when the firstborn to the Prince of the Elves is brought to the Chamber of the Gatekeeper in exchange for the release of Malkavic!*

Elijah had just returned from Nauren and the festival celebrating the birth of Ciarra to Olaf, the Prince of the Elves! These were dangerous times and he needed to know more. He needed to know everything Solomon had prophesied.

Elijah had never read the remainder of the prophecy—the part of the prophecy scribed by Solomon. That part of the prophecy lay before him now on the hand-hewn table, ready for his review. As he looked at the writings before him, most of the prophecy remained intact. Only the last part of the prophecy had been destroyed in the fire. The only other object on the table before him was the emerald dagger that he had used to fight off the goblins hordes so many years ago. With his aged and withered hand, he lifted the book to his lap and began reading.

Chapter XLI
Reconnaissance

THE two druids and Drake had reached their observation point near Nauren. They were far enough away not to be seen by the elven sentries, but they were close enough to be spotted by nomadic elves. There were four nights left until the lunar eclipse.

The three sat tucked away under a rock formation in a shallow depression where they were able to sit and not be spotted. They had a clear vision of Nauren in the distance and a clear vision of the evening sky.

The rock formation sat a short distance up on a hill and was out of the way of the foot traffic to Nauren. They had to be quiet, and they could not light a fire. There could be no indication of their presence or their entire plan would be jeopardized. Their location was ideal. A slight breeze blew from the east and their shelter prevented their scent from giving them away.

Drake was completely oblivious to these things; however, he could see that Cael and Finn were cunning. He had been smart to make them allies instead of adversaries. The fact of the matter was that these two were terrified of Drake. They were with him on this venture not only to save their lives but because they shared a common goal: to disrupt the peace in Lavendelle. They were afraid of Elijah, the new leader of the wizards, and they needed to turn Elijah's focus toward other problems. When Enzo had led the Council, there had been little intrusion on their lives. Now, however, Elijah was a problem. They had always feared him and they knew of his dislike for them.

They knew now that if they were successful in their pact with Drake, the wizards would have a new set of problems to keep them occupied. They were amazed at all they had learned from the prophecy of Solomon. How this prophecy had been kept quiet for almost eight hundred years was unfathomable to them. To know that this prophecy had been sitting in the volcano under the noses of the goblins all this time was equally amazing.

"What do you see?" Drake looked at Finn.

Finn looked to be in deep concentration as he sat cross-legged with his hands folded in his lap, his head turned upward, and his eyes closed. The scar that Drake had put on his neck was swollen, red, and draining.

"He cannot speak," Cael answered in place of Finn. "He is connected with the great eagle you see in the distance." Cael pointed high in the sky directly over Nauren.

"What can he see?" Drake asked.

"That great eagle is a hunter and has incredible vision. That predator vision can help it spot rodents, rabbits, fish, and other prey from great heights, even higher than it is flying now. From where we are sitting, that eagle could look into the very heart of Nauren and see everything!"

Drake stared, wide-eyed, as the eagle circled overhead. He was fascinated with all the possibilities of this newfound armament.

"What the eagle sees," continued Cael, "it is trained to see from very early on, even as it learns to fly. The bird sees movements, shapes, and patterns of movements that help it identify the prey it is seeking. The bird's vision can penetrate deep into the lakes and spot fish that are not visible to us when we are standing on the shore. Eagles are truly remarkable creatures."

Drake nodded in agreement. What an amazing creature—and how fortunate he had someone who understood its power and could use it for his own benefit.

"When Finn or I channel the eagle," explained Cael, "we can see in our minds what the eagle is seeing. The difference is in what we choose to focus our vision. I am limited to what the bird is seeing and my vision is therefore limited. Finn, however, has a deeper connection with our flying friend. He seems to be able to connect with the eagle and control its flight and its vision. Finn has quite a gift," Cael finished.

Drake could not comprehend how these two were able to speak and communicate with animals. Had he not seen it with his own eyes when they tried to get the giant bird and the great bear to sweep down upon him and kill him, he would never have believed it. He looked at Finn's neck and took pleasure in the wound he had left to remind Finn who was in charge and that he was alive today only because Drake had spared him.

Drake looked off into the distance and watched. The great eagle soared back and forth over Nauren. It was quite unusual to watch the eagle fly as Drake had never seen such a methodical flight pattern from a wild creature. It must be as Cael had said: Finn was controlling this eagle. Drake would patiently await the results of tonight's "flyover" as Finn had referred to it. The information the bird gathered would be vital to the success of their mission.

Drake leaned his back against the large boulder and watched

the bird in the distance. He closed his eyes and considered his plans for the coming day. He needed all the information he could gather. He needed to know where the sentries were located on the way into Nauren. To make sure that the druids were not leading him into a trap, he would be taking Finn with him. He hadn't shared this piece of information with Finn yet; he would spring it on the druid after Finn told him all that he had learned from the bird. If Finn betrayed him, his life would end as soon as Drake discovered the betrayal.

CHAPTER XLII
ATTACK OF
THE WIZARD

DRAKE was not the only one watching the unusual flight pattern of the bird: Siobhan, daughter of Seamus, looked up into the sky and considered the eagle. Its flight was methodical; it was not the normal flight of a predator. She had been watching it move as if with a purpose—as if it were searching Nauren. What that purpose could be, at this point, remained a mystery.

A dark and overwhelming feeling of evil overcame Siobhan. She did not know where it was coming from. This should be a happy time, a time of celebration. She and the other wizards had just presented a beautiful stone statue to honor her kind. The heir to the throne, Ciarra, had been born to Olaf and Ryanne. All Nauren was in celebration and she had stayed to continue celebrating with the elves, all of whom shared a common ancestry with her.

She now knew that what Elijah had said was true. She had believed him when he spoke of the evil he felt in the land, but it was different now. Now the evil was tangible. The evil of which Elijah had spoken was now more than words. She believed evil was being projected from the sky down upon her and upon Nauren. She knew that the secret of that evil lay in the bird she was watching.

But wizards were not to be underestimated, nor should creatures attempt to use magic against a wizard. It never ended well. She knew what she had to do. Siobhan moved across the pond to the temple that sat empty. She walked into the great chamber and lit the fires from all ends of the room.

Next, Siobhan spread out her robes in the center of the temple and sat. She placed her staff in front of her and closed her eyes. She could feel her friend nestled in the high hills above Nauren. He was resting but alert. Her mind connected with the great winged predator and the bird was ready to act on her command.

A large, multicolored but predominantly grey and white condor with a sharp, hooked black beak and menacing claws became aware of its master's summons for their minds were now connected. The bird looked out upon Nauren and looked toward the temple, the place from which it was being summoned. The mighty bird stretched out its massive wings, wings that extended eight feet on either side of its body, and took flight. When the condor was flying, it reigned over the skies. There was no equal to this great bird. It lived to serve its master, the wizard Siobhan.

With lightning speed, the condor streaked through the sky, racing toward the temple. If the eagle flying in patterns over Nauren noticed the bird, it did not pay attention to the condor. This was unusual as most predators from the heavens became prey when the great condor of the wizard circled above.

Siobhan noticed this as well. She stayed seated in the temple, awaiting her escort. From high above, she felt the great disturbance in the air as the massive wings of her condor slowed its descent in preparation to land. Siobhan took her staff and raised herself up.

She walked out to find her companion.

"Fallon, it is so good to see you!" Siobhan reached out her hand and stroked the condor's giant head. The bird was clearly excited to see its master.

Siobhan pulled out a fish from her satchel and offered it. Fallon gulped it down with one swallow.

As Siobhan drew close to the bird, she closed her eyes and pulled its head next to hers. She rested her head against Fallon as the bird stood still. In a few moments, Fallon turned its beak to the sky and locked on to the bird flying in the curious pattern over Nauren.

Siobhan stepped clear and with one last look between the two, Fallon raised its giant wings and took to the skies. This time, the eagle did not miss Fallon. The large condor raced toward the smaller eagle.

High in the hills to the east of Nauren, the druid shrieked and fell on his back, flat on the ground. Sweat poured from his face and his eyes burst wide open. He could feel his heart pounding in his chest as he lay on the cool ground. Both Drake and Cael spun around and stared at Finn; they sensed imminent danger as his scream announced their presence.

Fallon had done well; the eagle broke off its pattern and dove in a panic into the forest canopy below. Fallon began closing in, but as the eagle dove into the safety of the forest, Fallon had to break pursuit of the smaller bird and pull up. Fallon lumbered back to its perch in the hills above, waiting once again to be summoned by its master.

Siobhan was pleased with her results. Like all of elf ancestry, she had incredible hearing. She heard the disturbance in the hills to the east and she knew Nauren had been under surveillance. By what or by whom, she did not know, but to be sure, malevolent forces were watching Nauren. This information needed to be relayed to Elijah. He would want to know what had happened and he would know what to do. Sharing information was the key to the wizards' ability to work together for the good of the lands. Elijah had expressed his concerns; Siobhan needed to reinforce his concerns. All the other wizards had already left Nauren. She was the only one left, so it was up to her to inform Elijah. She would leave in the morning after conveying her goodwill to Olaf and Osvald, the high priest.

Chapter XLIII
Assault on Nauren

"WHAT was that?" Drake spun around as Finn's scream shattered the calm of the evening.

"No matter," Cael began, trying to deflect Drake's wrath. "We must leave here at once or we may be discovered and this plan will be thwarted before we begin."

"What?" cried Drake. "No one is going anywhere until I have answers! If someone comes here to attack me, I swear you two will be the first to die by my sword."

"Cael is right," Finn insisted. "We must move away now. The wizard's bird attacked and nearly killed our spy. I was looking down at Nauren and I was approaching the Temple of the Elves when out of nowhere that bird approached like an arrow. I felt my heart jump; I never saw it coming until it was almost too late. I was startled and I lost contact. That probably saved the bird as it reacted instinctively to save its own life."

"Master," Cael started, "we pledge our allegiance to you. You do not understand our ways, but we are not trying to trick you. If there is a wizard in Nauren, Finn is right; we are all in danger. Our magic cannot compete with theirs; they will destroy us! I fear our location may have already been discovered, and we must move quickly, or we will be found out. We have four nights left to accomplish our mission or all is for naught—for all time."

Drake listened intently. His frustration grew as he felt his trust of these two dissipating, and yet the problem was that he had to trust them. He could not accomplish the mission without them. There was no time left. He was convinced he was living out the ancient prophecy and would successfully fulfill it. But Finn's scream had reverberated throughout their hiding place, and it was clear they had to move to have any chance at success. "Let's get out of here and fast!"

Their only recourse was to retreat to the rugged hills north of Nauren, but this was away from where they ultimately needed to be to launch their counterattack in just a few short hours. On top of that, they now would most likely have to deal with elves patrolling these woods, which could also hamper their success.

The plan had been brilliant in conception. Now, in reality, they were rushing through contingency plans left and right. Clearly, this rapidly conceived plan was flawed, but perhaps not that flawed, and perhaps they could still be successful. It all depended upon the attacks from the south and west, and the ability of the goblins to draw support away.

With the cover of night, Cael, Finn, and Drake were able to make their way due north, away from Nauren and away from the sentry outpost they had occupied. It was too bad; the outpost had been an ideal location to scout the land. They were careful not to leave a trail that could be followed. They stayed among the rocks, away from the soft ground. Unfortunately, they had little time to cover their presence at the outpost and they had to be careful in their retreat.

They slowed down as they approached the hollow of a gully.

Thankfully, it was dry. It provided good cover as they were obscured and disappeared into the darkness of the night.

A stiff breeze blew in a westerly direction, stirring up dirt and sand across the plain. Dust was thick in the air. Visibility had been limited across the barren wastelands all day. There had been days like this before, but the visibility had never been quite this poor.

The new sentry had taken his position at the southernmost post guarding Nauren after chatting with the elf he was relieving. The elf who was leaving warned him of the problems with visibility. Neither elf was too alarmed given that other than a wandering party of ogres or the occasional dragon, there was little chance of anything unusual happening at this southern observation post overlooking the wastelands.

Twilight was upon the land. The sentry was not surprised about the unusual appearance of the horizon. Dust was rising in the sky and the dust cloud was getting larger and closer, yet the breeze had settled for the most part and the breeze was westward, not north. However, as he continued to watch the horizon, it became clear that something highly unusual was occurring.

He felt uneasy but continued gazing south, waiting to see what might happen. He had sharp ears, but all he could detect was a dull rumble. He had never encountered anything like this before. His heart began to race, and sweat broke out across his brow. It was a sinister night. He had never experienced anything like this before.

Despite his unrest, still he did nothing. He did not want to become a laughingstock because he had panicked on the watch. He would live with that shame for the rest of his life. Suddenly, he saw the creatures coming at him. He had little time to react and realized he was in trouble. His inexperience and youth would cost him greatly. He looked at the little bow and arrow, but against so many, they would be useless.

He was not sure he had been seen by these goblins, but he knew he had only two choices: sit quietly, let them pass, and then sound the alarm, or sound the alarm now. Yes, that was the only thing to do and with that he put his lips to the twelve-foot wooden horn that rested nearby on the ground below. The elf sucked in a deep breath and blew as hard as he could into the horn. He could feel the air oscillate inside the conical wooden pipe as it rushed to exit and sound the alarm. He heard the horn blast, but as soon as he heard it, it was muffled. He looked down and saw the goblins plugging the horn and racing up toward him. Before he could react, three were on him, dragging him out of the tree. His last thoughts were of falling into the swarm of goblins. He landed hard on his outstretched neck when it snapped. He would not make it to the end of his shift and see the morning. His failure to be vigilant and act had cost him his life. Hopefully, his warning had been heard!

Olaf's sharp ears did hear the brief blast of the horn, but then it was gone. He did not know what to think. At that same moment, he saw Siobhan approaching and he knew something was wrong. Siobhan had heard the horn too.

"What is it, Siobhan? I heard the alarm from the south, but just as quickly it was gone. I am concerned."

"I fear evil is upon us, Olaf," Siobhan began. "Just this evening I discovered that we were being spied upon from the east. That is what I have come to tell you."

"How did you discover this?"

"A great bird was flying over Nauren. It flew back and forth as though it was searching for someone or something. As I watched the bird, I realized that it was flying as though it was under the control of some unseen force. I sent Fallon after the bird and discovered that it was being controlled from that knoll east of Nauren."

"That knoll used to be a sentry outpost. We no longer keep a sentry there. We must be quick then. The alarm came from the south, and that is the direction we must head. But I will also send a patrol to search the outpost to the east."

With that, Olaf sounded the alarm, and Nauren sprang to life. The sentry may have been slow to react, but the wisdom of Siobhan and the life experience of Olaf were much more formidable. They knew of the dangers that could exist and their quick reaction was the only thing that could save them from being overrun.

Though the unfortunate sentry had been slow to react, his alarm did waken Nauren and the goblins were soon to be met by an elven army that they had hoped to catch off guard.

As they rested, it was apparent that Nauren had come to life. Though they were no longer in a position to see what was happening, they could hear the horns blowing and they knew that the first phase of their attack had begun.

Drake was amazed at the power he now possessed. He was directing an army of hundreds and they were following his commands exactly as outlined. As he reflected on what was occurring, he once again felt supremely confident. He would see this plan through to the end, even if he had to march into Nauren himself, right through the front gate.

He despised the two druids with whom he shared the gully,

but he needed them, and they feared him, just as the goblins feared him. Drake enjoyed wielding power. It would be hard, if not impossible, to return empty-handed from his adventures. He needed the treasure he was sure to collect to establish himself when he returned home.

As the night wore on, the three could only imagine what was occurring below and to the west. Thanks to that wizard, they had lost their viewing post. Then it happened. As the three sat there, they all saw it together. With the night sky providing background illumination, three stealthy figures approached the sentry viewing post. They all sat quietly, without making a sound. Drake knew that the two had been right. He was still wary.

The elves took their time at the sentry outpost. Drake could tell they could not find any indication of the direction the three had taken. They watched as two of the elves headed back to the direction of Nauren to report what they had seen.

One sentry remained behind. This would be a problem they would have to address.

CHAPTER XLIV
DEFENSE OF NAUREN

WITH the alarms trumpeting throughout Nauren, elves scrambled in groups of forty, fifty, and sixty, gathering at their assigned posts surrounding Nauren. The reason for the alarm had not yet been determined, and each squadron of elves waited anxiously for its commander.

Attacking the elves was a dangerous if not foolhardy proposition. The elves of Nauren functioned as close to a military as there was in all of Lavendelle. They had always been able to withstand attacks from Malkavic a millennium ago, but Malkavic had been able to contain them at least to Nauren.

The elves learned how to survive during Malkavic's reign of terror. Those survival skills had been passed down and preserved for generations. Despite this, the sentries were sometimes lax in their obligations given that they had not faced any serious threats since Malkavic's reign.

Though the sentries may have been soft, Olaf's response to the alarms proved the senior leadership of elves still had an edge to it. Siobhan and Olaf addressed the twelve senior commanders of the elves.

"We are being attacked from an unknown force," Olaf began.

"Siobhan discovered Nauren was being spied upon at the old sentry outpost on the knoll to the east this evening." Siobhan nodded in acknowledgment. Olaf continued, "Shortly after Siobhan disrupted the observers, a muted alarm echoed from the south. There is little time to act. We must send our troops to the southern border of Nauren to repel whatever is coming our way. If nothing is found, we need to regroup close to the city.

"Johann, Carl, and William, I need you to keep your troops here in the city. The rest of you will take your troops as quickly as possible to the south.

"William, I need you to dispatch a party of sentries to investigate the disturbance at the knoll."

The leaders quickly dispersed. There was precious little time to respond to an attack, and the commanders realized this. The attackers, whoever they were, had the advantage of surprise, but Nauren was well-run and well-protected. They would repel the attack and chase down those responsible. It was foolhardy to attack Nauren; there were no forces in Lavendelle strong enough to defeat the elves.

Each leader disseminated the information about the attack to his squadron. The alarm signals were no longer going off in Nauren; they were no longer needed. All lanterns were lit, and the city was buzzing with activity. The elves were well-schooled and worked together as a cohesive unit. As each squadron of infantry received its orders, the troops headed south to investigate and repel any possible attack.

As each squadron arrived at its post, the troops fell into disbelief. They were overwhelmed by goblins. They had never seen such a band of goblins working together before. Even with their entire army, the elves were easily outnumbered three to one.

The focus of the goblin attack seemed to be the sacred temple. There was no time to think; this was full-scale war. Kill or be killed. The elves, organized, offered a stiff resistance to the attacks. The goblins reacted with a strong drive to break down the elves' defenses. An intense battle was shaping up along the southern border of the temple. The commanders of the elves were amazed at the savageness of their attackers and how far they had been able to penetrate into the land of Nauren.

As wave after wave of attacks were deflected, the goblins were soon in full-blown retreat. The elves pursued initially, but broke off their pursuit to re-gather, rearm, and try to figure out what had just happened to their city.

Many elves had been injured and maimed, and several had lost their lives that night. But it was apparent that the goblins had suffered a much higher number of losses. Nothing made sense. As quickly as the attack had begun, it ended. The elves had to collect themselves and debrief. The leaders went back to meet with Olaf at what had once been Nauren's town center; now it served as their command post.

For his part, Olaf was trying to make sense of all that was happening. He was head of the defense for his city. One day he would be High Priest of the Elves. He was a new father. And just a week ago Nauren had been on an unprecedented high with the birth of Ciarra, with the five-day-long celebration, and the beautiful statue presented by the wizards. Now, everything had changed. Nauren was experiencing an attack from an unknown force—something dark and sinister that had not been present in the land since the time of Malkavic.

Olaf and Siobhan sat together. It was always comforting to have a wizard by your side in times of trouble, Olaf thought.

Two of the three sentries William had sent east had reported back of their findings. They concluded that several observers had recently departed from the sentry outpost to the east, but there was no sign of them now. One sentry was left behind at the outpost per William's order.

"Olaf, it was like nothing I had ever seen before," began the senior member of the field commanders. "Hundreds of goblins swarmed the southern border. They killed our sentry and many others in the attack! As soon as we were able to take hold of a position south of the temple, the goblins broke off and retreated. They were gone as quickly as they had come. But when they were fighting, they fought with ferocity."

"It doesn't make sense, Siobhan," said Olaf as he looked at the wizard and then at his men. "Goblins don't behave this way. I have never witnessed goblins organizing, attacking, and acting in a coordinated effort. What is to be gained by their attack? What is the purpose?"

It was the middle of the night. The warriors were haggard and worn, the leadership confused. With his question, Olaf did not receive the answer he wanted or expected. Instead, alarm horns once again sounded, this time to the southwest of Nauren. Thankfully, Olaf thought, the elves had always remained vigilant about their security. But now, everything had changed; nothing would ever be quite the same. He needed to report back himself to his father, but there was no time. Alarms were again sounding and that could only mean that the goblins were on the attack again.

"William," Olaf began, "you must take your command and reinforce the southern border. At first light, we must send out a tracking party and find out where these goblins went and what they are after. The rest of you return quickly to the border and resist the attack being launched.

"Johann, it is up to you and your troops to protect Nauren. There is no one else left. Our city is under siege!

"Carl, you need to take your defenders and reinforce the temple guard! These are desperate times, but I know we can withstand this attack. Once we get through this, we will hunt down those responsible and make sure this will never happen again!"

Inspired by Olaf's words and strength the elves were quickly dispatched. Times were indeed desperate. There was no time to get caught up in the why. There would be plenty of time for that in the future. For now there was only time to react and repel their attackers.

CHAPTER XLV
WAR

DRAKE, Cael, and Finn hid, trapped in the gulley. They could not move for fear of giving away their position. The sentry was still sitting in their previous observation post. Curse that wizard, Drake thought. He kept his sword hilt covered as it was like a beacon of light with all the goblin activity around. He could not afford to be discovered by this sentry. Up on the knoll the sentry sat, alert, vigilant, and very much alone. The elf strained with all his senses to detect any intruder. Even with his keen hearing, it was no use. He felt isolated, alone, and useless. He had been the youngest of the three sentries sent out to inspect this knoll, and because he was the most junior, the other two had given him the dubious task of remaining behind. He felt as though his skill as a warrior was being wasted.

The young elf heard the horns ring out again. He thought about answering the call, but he was afraid of the repercussions if he left his post. It was not good for Nauren and the elves that the alarm horns were sounding again. Their whole world had been shattered. By what force, this elf did not know, but he longed to join the fight. The young elf did not realize how important his outpost had just become to Nauren. He was protecting the city's flank and was critical to its defense. Unfortunately, he was too young and too ill-prepared to understand his role. Fortunately, however, he stayed at his post.

After the elves dispersed, Siobhan looked at Olaf and reflected on the situation: "It may not be goblins attacking from the southwest, Olaf, just because they were the first to attack."

"I was thinking the same thing myself. Something has to be driving this, Siobhan; goblins just don't work together in coordination like this."

"I believe the outpost to the east is the key. Clearly, there was evidence of someone or something watching over Nauren, and just as clearly there was evidence of the great bird being used to spy on us," Siobhan said.

"Thank you for your quick work in discovering that outpost, Siobhan. That was important information you provided."

"Elijah warned us just before he left that he felt an evil disturbance creeping over Lavendelle. He said he did not know from where the evil came or how it would be manifest. I think we are about to find out!"

"Elijah is wise, and he needs to know what is happening to us! We need him, Siobhan; we need all the wizards now. Evil has descended upon Nauren this night!"

"I agree, Olaf. Elijah predicted this. I must fly to him at first light and seek his direction for all of us!"

"That is good, Siobhan. Everything we can do to overcome this evil we need to do right away! At first light, I wish you speed in your travel!"

The goblins returned to attack again. Their numbers had

increased since the first attack. How could this be, the old elf thought. This made no sense. What was driving these mindless creatures to attack?

The goblins were attacking the lines of defense he had set up. They attacked fiercely but were met with fierce resistance. This time, the goblins did not retreat so quickly. Wave after wave of goblins attacked the elves' lines of defense. As they broke through, many elves were killed, but not as many elves died as goblins.

The goblins had incredible night vision, much better than even the elves. This is what made the strategy of attacking at night so brilliant. It was more difficult for the elves to respond. Difficult as it was, the attack was stopped before it reached the temple. Then, as quick as the attack had come, the goblins retreated again to the south and to the wastelands.

As morning approached, the elves hoped there would be calm so they could make sense of all the chaos of the night. Each squadron of elves reformed with its leader. Each group had lost members, but the elves were still strong and unified. Each group felt anger at the attack and the loss of its comrades. It was all so senseless. What was the purpose?

Squadrons of elves were left along the southern and southwestern borders to protect Nauren until all could be discussed among the leaders and new direction provided.

A hint of light peered over the eastern horizon, but darkness was resisting the light. It was a futile effort.

Drake, Finn, and Cael had made the most of their time by going over the plans for this morning again and again. This was the first time they had to plan for whatever possible contingency they faced. Finn had meticulously recalled all that he had learned from the scouting expedition with the eagle before the vicious attack by the wizard. He had learned so much, but this was his first chance to share with the others what he knew.

Finn drew a hastily sketched map in the red clay soil at the bottom of the ravine. He leaned forward and explained to Drake and Cael, "Nauren is arranged around a town center that appears to be the lifeblood of the community and very busy. Through the bird, I observed, as we already knew, that to the southeast is the Temple of the Elves, their sacred meeting place. I also determined something we did not know. Apparently, this temple is currently home to a wizard as this was the launching point of the attack!"

Drake pointed to the map and asked, "What is this area, here?"

"To the west and to the northwest of Nauren, most of the elves' homes sit nestled in the trees. They are expertly camouflaged and hard to see. The palace is over here," Finn pointed, "to the northeast of the town center, and this area over here is the location of the scouting outpost that we had originally used before we had to relocate." Finn moved his finger along the map. "The palace of the high priest sits behind this wall. It has large grounds within its walls and behind the palace are what appear to be several personal residences. From what I channeled from the bird, one of those, the one farthest to the north, and perched highest overlooking the palace, is the prince's home. I say this because of what I witnessed: The home has a terrace on the second level, and that terrace appears to lead directly to the quarters where the baby lives. Indeed, I saw a baby lying in a bassinet on the terrace with what appeared to be its mother!" Finn announced triumphantly.

Drake and Cael arched their eyebrows at this revelation. The three whispered among themselves and came up with a plan of attack. With the third wave of attacks coming in the next one to two hours, Drake would sneak up on the sentry and silence him. There was no other way around it as the elves clearly suspected malfeasance coming from this outpost. The sentry had to be dealt with as there could be no additional disturbance from the east or their plans would fail utterly.

Once the sentry was silenced, Drake and Finn would approach the palace where the new baby lay and would find some way to retrieve the child. Cael would stay back and prepare to receive the child. He would also scout out a more secure and more remote location where they could hide from any possible pursuing parties.

The great danger, Finn and Cael warned Drake, was the wizard. The wizard could be the end to all of them. They would have to abort their plan if the wizard were present. Drake heard what they were saying, but he was not going to let a wizard interfere with his plans. The time was now; success lay just within his grasp. Everything was aligned and, for the most part, their plans had succeeded. Drake would know more once he took care of the sentry and reclaimed their lookout. With the dawn of the new day, there were now only three nights left until the Gatekeeper came calling.

Chapter XLVI
good fortune

Olaf sat with the leaders of the squadrons. He listened to their reports. What did the goblins want with the temple? What was their purpose? Who was behind these attacks? He agreed with his commanders: The goblins were simply mindless drones being organized by some force bent on the destruction of the elves.

As the commanders finished their briefing, the horns due west of Nauren were sounding a new alarm. Nauren was again under siege. Would it end anytime soon? Olaf declared that the leaders could not give up Nauren. They needed to repel the attacks and stay back and defend Nauren. What he feared was the pursuit of the goblins. If the commanders led an all-out attack on the goblins, Nauren could be left vulnerable.

Now, with the light of day, the elves could gather enough information to understand what was going on. Siobhan would bring back Elijah, and Nauren would be fortified.

The sentry heard the horns to the west. He was too inexperienced to understand his role in protecting Nauren. All he could think about was that he was doing nothing while his friends were battling some dark force bent on attacking his home. The alarms were coming from the west, which meant the enemy was approaching his home. He felt compelled to join the fight. He felt as though he was wasting precious resources sitting alone at the remote eastern outpost while all the action was occurring to the west of the city.

Drake watched the elf abandon his post. He could not believe their good fortune! Drake took this as a sign that he would succeed. He summoned Cael and Finn back to their post as soon as he had seen the elf flee his position. They had watched the post all night and Drake was sure that no one else had been left behind.

Cael and Finn could not believe their good fortune either. As they sat back to make their final preparations, Finn saw it first. He quickly got the attention of the other two. They all watched in amazement. Drake was not sure what he was witnessing other than the large bird of the wizard leaving Nauren for the wastelands with a passenger on its back. Cael and Finn explained that the passenger was the wizard fleeing. Drake saw this as another sign to move forward.

Johann stretched his troops in a thin line along the southern border. They were the only guard left to protect Nauren's flank. Carl had his troops in position around the temple, which appeared to be the object of the goblin attack. Either group could fall back and defend the city. William had sentries along the northern and eastern outposts. At least he thought he had the eastern outpost covered. The rest of his troops he took to the front lines of attack on the western border of Nauren.

Though the goblins attacked in great numbers, the light of the morning sky significantly aided the elves. They were invigorated in their defense as they could now see the goblins from a distance.

No longer were the goblins on them before they could repel their attacks. Even still, the sheer number of goblins made them a formidable force.

CHAPTER XLVII
DAWN THE NEXT DAY

DRAKE and Finn left the outpost on the east of Nauren and worked their way carefully to the northeast. They had in their minds the place where the infant Ciarra could be found. Cael, as instructed, retreated north to the gulley. From there, he would look for better cover where he could keep and care for the infant before they moved her to the volcano.

"We must move farther north, master, or we will be coming to the front gates of the palace. Surely we will be discovered! Let us head under the cover of these trees as we head farther north!" Finn finished.

Drake followed. It was apparent that they were on the edge of the town of Nauren. The whole town looked abandoned. They saw homes and roads, but there were no signs of elves anywhere. The grand diversion that they had planned appeared to be working flawlessly.

Soon, Finn and Drake were under the cover of the forest on the edge of town. They moved silently among the trees as they headed to the back side of the palace grounds.

Olaf considered the way he had his troops amassed to protect

Nauren. The original site of attack had been due south of the temple. The goblins had penetrated deep into the city before being repelled. Johann had his troops thinly stretched along this border in case any of the original attackers returned, or if any were found alive to continue their attack. Johann's troops extended to the southwest border as they responded to the second wave of attacks.

Carl and his troops were positioned as a final guard to protect the temple. The attacks had seemed to be aimed at the temple for some reason. This temple was sacred to the elves and had to be protected at all costs. They were the final line of protection.

William had half of his troops serving as sentries surrounding Nauren. The other half was positioned along the western front. Word had gotten back that the elves had been outnumbered three to one and four to one in the first two attacks. Olaf could not understand how such an army had amassed and the elves had been caught so unaware. Life would never be the same in Nauren, regardless of the outcome of the day's battles. The elves would have to be more vigilant to prevent such a tragedy from occurring again.

Olaf could not figure out the motive behind the attacks. There had been no warning of trouble brewing, at least according to his sources. He was more disturbed after getting Siobhan's report of Elijah's concern. Though Elijah had only recently been named the head of the wizards, he was well-respected among the inhabitants Lavendelle as a serious wizard, a warrior in his own right, even though wizards were not thought of as warriors. Elijah had suspected trouble. Upon hearing this from Siobhan, Olaf knew that Nauren was in jeopardy. It was his swift decision to mobilize his troops that had saved Nauren the previous night.

Olaf moved his own private guard from his estate to the western front where there were no more elves left to protect the city; there was no second line of defense. The attacks of the night had left all of Nauren stretched thin. They needed to repel the attacks or risk being overrun. There was no other backup protection if the western defense broke.

There was no protection to the north and east other than the sentries and the terrain. It would be difficult to mount much of an army to attack Nauren from the north or the east as this was rugged land and it would be next to impossible to amass a large army without it being quickly detected. That explained the attacks from the wastelands. There was nothing out there. Large armies could form and attacks could be quickly launched, which was exactly the tact that had been taken.

CHAPTER XLVIII
ABDUCTION

THE defenders had a new ally: light. With light came the ability for the archers to deploy their arrows. This was particularly effective in thinning out the masses of goblins that attacked. But the goblins struck hard and battled fiercely. They hid behind the trees and rock formations and launched small attacks from the flanks. The main force of goblins charged the front right down the middle. Their only advantage was in their sheer numbers.

On the other side of Nauren, Drake and Finn scaled the fence surrounding the palace grounds and moved undetected to the back of Olaf's home. The home sat behind that of the high priest, right in the middle of beautiful gardens.

Drake and Finn ducked behind a hedge that ran along the eastern wall of Olaf's home. Above their heads on the second level was a large terrace that extended off a room that led to the interior of the home.

"This is where I saw the baby yesterday; we have to be in the right place. I recognize these grounds!" Finn said excitedly.

Drake shared his excitement. When they had drawn up their malevolent plan, this place had seemed so distant. The fact was that they were carrying out their plan and they were indeed here at the precipice of their final point of no return. With their next action, there would be no turning back. Their hearts raced in anticipation.

"I don't know what lies inside those doors besides the baby," Finn whispered to Drake. "We could be facing an army when we go through those doors; there is no telling. With all the excitement caused by the goblins, I would be surprised if the baby and the family are not heavily guarded."

Drake listened. "Is there any way you can get another look inside?" he whispered.

Finn thought about it. It would be ideal if he could summon his drone spy back for another look. It would depend on the affect the wizard's bird had caused the night before. But Finn knew the wizard and her attack bird were gone; he had seen them fly away that morning.

"Let me try to call on our bird friend and see what we can see."

Finn sank back into deep concentration. There were no sounds outside the grounds. Normally, elves would be scattered around the grounds, maintaining the gardens. Today was a different day. Today, every spare elf had been dispatched west to protect Nauren.

The diversion had been grand, and the results equally spectacular. It had worked better than even Drake, Cael, and Finn had planned. But this was only the opening salvo in the war that they had started. The three had given no thought to the response that would come from the elves. They had not thought beyond springing Malkavic from the Gatekeeper. Drake had hoped to be rewarded with treasure for his part; treasure that he could take home and use to live in the lifestyle of a king.

He sat silently. He watched as a menacing bird approached from the northwest. It was huge and had a six-foot wingspan.

Seeing this predator up close gave him a whole new appreciation for the size of the wizard's bird, which was the largest bird Drake had ever seen. This one was, however, a formidable predator. He watched as the great talons sank deep into the branch on which it chose to land. It sat perched on a tree with a perfect view of the terrace above.

Finn sat silently as the bird peered into the room. Drake waited patiently. They needed to act soon, but time was currently on their side.

Finn finally opened his eyes. "The baby sits in a basket just inside the doors on the terrace above. The baby's mother has apparently just finished feeding the baby and the baby appears to have drifted off to sleep."

"That is great news, Finn! It is amazing all that you can do with that bird!" Drake removed a rope with a hook from his pack and threw it onto the terrace. The sound of the hook landing on the terrace boomed out in Drake's and Finn's ears, but in reality it hadn't been that loud. Their senses were on heightened alert.

Finn sat back again, apparently channeling the bird. Drake knew he had to take it from here. At least Finn would be watching and might be able to help if something unexpected happened. Drake pulled on the rope slowly to make as little sound as possible. Finally, the hook took hold of something. Drake tested the rope. It felt as though his weight would be supported. He scaled the outer wall of the home and quickly reached the terrace. He crouched down in a corner and studied his surroundings.

He pulled up the rope and placed it in the corner recess where he sat. He did not want any elf to see it hanging from the terrace and get curious. Even though there were no elves out now, he could not be sure an elf might not wander by.

Drake hid behind a trellis that was overgrown with vines as he contemplated his next move. He slowly moved to the window and peered inside the home. A fire blazed in the hearth opposite the window and a chair sat with its back to the window. Next to the chair sat a large bassinet with a handle arching widely over the middle so the baby could be moved without disturbing her. She was sleeping comfortably, apparently with a full belly. She appeared so tiny to him.

He swung the door outward onto the terrace. A gentle breeze followed him into the room where he was welcomed by the warmth of the fireplace. A wonderful smell of baking bread tickled his nose and made his stomach churn in response. He approached the bassinet and lifted the handle. He was afraid to handle the baby inside the home for fear of waking her and causing her to cry out.

Finn watched as everything unfolded before him through the channeled bird. Everything was going according to plan. All of a sudden he saw Drake move quickly, rushing out of the home with the bassinet. What was he doing? That was not part of the plan. Obviously, something had happened inside and Drake had had to act fast. He saw Drake remove the infant from the bassinet, place her into the sling around his neck, and quickly take cover behind the vine-laden trellis on the side of the terrace. What was it? Had the baby cried out?

Finn's heart raced as if he were up there himself. Drake was clearly in trouble. Finn could see into the room. He saw the door swing open. Someone was coming. With that, Finn had the bird take flight and head toward the porch. Within seconds the bird had the bassinet in its massive talons and had taken flight to the northwest.

The baby's mother saw the door swung open. She raced onto the terrace and cried out as she watched the predator fly off with the bassinet and, presumably, her baby.

Drake sat paralyzed by the noise. He heard the grief in the mother's voice as she cried out for Ciarra. He saw her on the opposite side of the terrace staring out at the bird as it flew away. He listened to her sobs, but they were not strong enough to crack his hardened heart.

The predatory drone turned south toward the wastelands. The mother watched until the bird was out of sight. Then, as quickly as she had raced onto the terrace, she turned and raced back into the house and toward the front to see where the bird was headed. She never noticed Drake tucked carefully away behind the vines.

As soon as the mother had fled from the terrace, Drake moved into action. He placed the hook back over the wall and then quickly lowered himself to the ground as fast as his arms would allow. He would have to drop the last several feet, but he was strong and his adrenaline was quickly racing through him, making the drop almost unnoticeable. He flipped the rope up to release the hook so he could pull it down and then quickly stowed it inside his pack.

He and Finn heard the disturbance at the front of the property. There was only one way to go. Finn looked Drake in the eye and pointed to the back of the property. They sped out of the palace gardens, undetected by anyone as there was no one left to spot them. It was unbelievable to both of them, but the baby slept through the whole event.

CHAPTER XLIX
ESCAPE

WHAT happened?" Cael asked excitedly as he saw Drake and Finn take cover in the gulley. He could see that they had been successful as Drake was carrying Princess Ciarra in the cloth slung around his neck. As the baby began to stir, Drake removed the sling and passed her to Cael.

"That was brilliant!" Drake said as he struggled to catch his breath. "They will chase south after the bird, the same direction the goblins will be headed! What made you do that?"

"I could see the mother coming, and I knew I had to act fast. If you killed the mother, the elves would have hunted us down for all eternity. With the help of the wizards, they would find out everything, and they would find us!"

"How can you be so sure?" Drake inquired. "We will unleash a firestorm when we free Malkavic! They will have more trouble on their hands than worrying about us."

"Do not forget," Finn began as he looked at Cael, "it was the wizards who subdued Malkavic in the first place."

Drake simply did not have the same appreciation for the power of the wizards as Finn and Cael. He was a foreigner in these lands and he was oblivious to magic. The two could sense Drake's confidence when it came to the wizards. They thought it was because he possessed powerful magic of his own—magic that they had witnessed not only in their initial confrontation but on this very day. The way he commanded the goblins proved to them his undeniable power. The day had gone brilliantly!

Drake did possess power—that of the evil sorcerer Aelhaeran. Drake was unable to perceive it, but evil was overcoming him. He was overconfident of his abilities and severely underestimated the wizards of this land.

"What is the difference if I killed her or not? We have the baby. Won't that make them hunt us down now?"

Finn shook his head no. "If you killed the mother, our presence would have been immediately known and we would have been found out! Militant parties of elves would have been dispatched to hunt us now, even as we speak. Elves are not stupid." Finn let his words sink in before continuing. "What is so brilliant is that they will all assume the great eagle took the princess in the basket as it flew south. They will follow that bird as far as the trail will take them. All we need now is a little time to escape and we will be gone for good. We will never be discovered! That bird has given us a window of opportunity to escape unseen!"

"As I said," Drake began, "it was brilliant!"

Cael just listened and took care of the tiny princess. "Well, if that is the case," Cael began, "then I suggest we put distance between where we are now and the elves. I searched while you two were gone and though I haven't found a place to stay—there was no time—I did find an escape route north."

"North will take us away from the volcano." Drake shook his head. "We need to be heading east. We have to deliver the baby in three nights, before the moon disappears, or all of this was for naught!"

"No. First we need to get as far away as possible from Nauren. I don't know what their response will be, but there is nothing to the north, and I believe it is the best way to go. If we head east, the terrain is treacherous, and though it is not much better north, there is a way. We don't have time to debate the matter. You can tell me all about what happened on the way," Cael said emphatically.

With that, the three were off.

Chapter L
Reaction

OLAF walked along the last line of defense for Nauren. His elite guard was there to destroy any invader who was able to break through the lines along the western edge of the city. Word had gotten to Olaf that the fighting on the western border had been the most intense since the raids had begun the preceding night. Despite what seemed to be a wholesale slaughter of the goblins, the enemy's latest attack was fueled by its greatest force yet. This truly was Nauren's last line of defense.

Olaf had never witnessed such ferocity amongst the goblins. They were simple creatures that had always been nothing more than a nuisance. He was just beginning to get a taste of what life had been like before the wizards had dispatched Malkavic. During those times, the elves had been much more wary.

He reflected on what was happening. His militia had grown soft and discipline was lacking. But how could they stay sharp and focused when there hadn't been a threat for three generations of elves? It had been almost a millennium since there had been any true threat to Nauren. Neither he—nor any living elf—would forget the events of this day.

He reflected on all that had gone on in the last month: all the great things for the elves and for Nauren. The goblins had robbed them of that joy in one short night. But what had driven them to attack? The answer to that may indeed lay to the east where Siobhan had discovered the spy. Siobhan was gone. He knew it would be at least two days before she was back, or before Elijah could get back to Nauren. He needed their counsel.

Why could this not have occurred while the wizards were all still in Nauren? Olaf considered this, and the answer was immediately apparent. Clearly, the goblins were driven by a foe that was not yet manifest to him. That foe had waited until the celebrations had ended and the wizards dispersed. A chill swept over Olaf as he realized that Nauren must have been under observation for some time by a malevolent force. How could they have missed this?

Olaf summoned William, his chief of intelligence and the one responsible for all the sentry outposts. Olaf headed south to meet William; he could not wait to discuss his thoughts.

"William, I fear Nauren has been under observation for some period of time. The timing of these attacks could not have been better for our enemy. They caught us at our most vulnerable time! Indeed, had the attacks occurred five days ago, the wizards would still have been among us!"

William thought about what he was hearing and his heart was troubled. Clearly, he had missed this and now the city was under attack. He had to agree with Olaf: This was the most vulnerable time for Nauren, and his failure had left the elves even more vulnerable.

Olaf continued, "I need you to gather intelligence for me, starting east at the sentry post. See what you can find out about who has been spying on us." William nodded his agreement as Olaf continued. "The goblins come from the volcano. I think we need to search all the way back to the volcano to find answers. Since the goblins attacked from the wastelands, send another party south and trace their trail back to the volcano. See if you can track anything other than the goblins. We will find our answers this way."

"I will do it at once, Olaf. I am sorry to have failed you."

"You have not failed me, William. You have not caused this savage attack. Siobhan told me Elijah sensed evil creeping over Lavendelle. He did not know from where it came, but evil was upon us. Evil had to drive these goblins; they are incapable of organizing such an attack on their own! We need to find the source of this evil and deal with it so that it never harms another elf!"

"We will find this evil and destroy it before it destroys us."

The two elves looked up and saw one of the high priest's servants rapidly approaching.

"I bid you come right away, Olaf. Your father summons you with the utmost urgency. He said to drop everything you are doing and come immediately!"

Never before had the high priest issued such an order to his son. Something dire must be happening at the palace.

Olaf turned to William and said, "I must go now. You have your orders!"

"It will be as you wish, Olaf. I will send Dylan to the palace to assist you."

With that, William turned back toward the front and headed off. Olaf turned and retreated to the palace of the high priest as quickly as his legs would carry him.

Chapter 11
Revelations

Upon arriving at the palace, the servants directed Olaf to his own residence. His heart started to race in his chest. Something had happened to his home, his family.

He flung open the door and saw his wife, Ryanne, weeping in his father's arms. There was no sign of Ciarra. Where was the baby? Ryanne never left her side except to lay the child to rest. Olaf bounded up the stairs to Ciarra's nursery and found the door open. He stepped in, but the baby was not there. The bassinet was missing and the porch door was open.

Olaf raced back down the stairs. "What happened, my love? Where is Ciarra?"

Ryanne looked at Olaf and reached her hand out for him. "I am sorry, Olaf, I am sorry," she whispered before she sank back into her father-in-law's arms and began weeping again.

Olaf was beside himself with grief. He dropped to his knees and looked at his father. "Where is my child? What happened here?"

"We don't know, Olaf," Osvald began. "While you were out protecting Nauren, Ciarra was taken from her room. Ryanne had just finished feeding her and had laid her down to sleep. She came

311

back to check on her just a few minutes later, but the door to the terrace was wide open, and a massive bird, a great eagle, had the bassinet in its talons and was flying south with the baby. I just came here myself. I sent for you as soon as I heard about the disturbance at your home. I had no idea what I would find."

Olaf approached his wife and placed his hands on her shoulders. She lifted her head and looked into his eyes. "Will we ever see her again?"

Olaf ignored the question for the answer was overwhelmingly negative. He needed information, and there seemed to be no time to search for answers. The time for action was now. He had been played for a fool, and so had Nauren. Clearly, the bird was under the control of evil creatures. He needed Elijah, for Elijah would know what sort of creature was capable of controlling the birds of the air. By now, Elijah would surely know the source of this evil.

"I need to know what you saw, Ryanne, everything. I need to know where the bird took Ciarra. This was not an accident. This is what all these attacks have been about this past night. This was all a well-engineered ploy that took the lives of many elves, all to sneak in the back door and steal our baby, the Princess of Nauren!"

A chill set in with Olaf's words. His father knew them to be true, for he could feel it in his soul. It was a dark time for the elves. Ciarra's life hung in the balance.

Olaf learned little else from Ryanne other than that the eagle flew due south over the wastelands as far as her eyes could see. For an elf, that was a long way indeed.

"I must leave you, Ryanne," Olaf said as he embraced her. "I will find Ciarra!"

Olaf directed his servants to gather supplies for his journey.

He was filled with rage, but he had his rage under control. Dylan waited outside for him, not knowing what had occurred inside, but he saw the change in Olaf's face, indeed, in his entire presence. He had never seen Olaf like this before. There was now a hardness to his features and darkness had swept over him.

"Dylan," Olaf looked at the young elf as he spoke, "I need you to go to the temple and tell Carl to remove his guard from the temple. He should leave the normal sentries, but he needs to come to the palace as swiftly as he can, and he needs to bring his troops with him. When you have given Carl my orders, you will go to the western front and ask my commanders about what is happening. It is my belief that the attack will be broken off shortly. Tell William to send half of our defenders to chase down the goblins. Do not let them regroup! The remaining elves must fall back and take positions around Nauren in case I am wrong."

Dylan quickly departed to deliver Olaf's orders.

Olaf reran the events of the previous night in his mind, and he realized how simple the plan had been. With only a few moving parts it had been very effective. Now it was his turn to reply. Any creature involved in this evil would pay with its life!

Chapter LII
Siobhan's
New Position

Elijah finished reading what was left of the prophecy that he had salvaged on the night of Solomon's disappearance. He did not have it all, but he knew enough. He knew what he had scribed for Solomon. He reflected on the prophecy as a whole and now knew what Solomon had feared because he felt the same fear creep up inside him. There was evil in the land, and with the birth of Ciarra, the timing seemed right for the unfolding of the prophecy. He needed to be strong and decisive.

Elijah closed the ancient manuscript and placed the old familiar dagger with the green emerald pommel on top of it. He made his way down to the front of the tower. There was so much to be done to restore it to its former brilliance. It was sad that he and the rest of the wizards, including Demetrius, had let it fall into such a state. If he had not acted, it would not have been long before the tower had been reclaimed by the wastelands to the north and east.

The sun melted downward toward the horizon; the heat of the day was receding. Elijah stood looking at the tower and considered all that had to be done. His attention diverted north, away from the tower as he sensed something behind him.

He looked into the northern sky and was not surprised to see her approach. Siobhan coming on wings could only mean one thing: trouble had come sooner than he expected. Elijah knew his fears were becoming manifest; he was sorry he had been so slow to act. He should have been better at anticipating what was to come, and he should have left more support for Nauren.

The wings of the huge bird stirred up a shower of dust as it came to rest on the ground. Elijah felt the sting of sand against his cheek. The bird knelt down and carefully let Siobhan off its back. She stroked the bird's head and quickly set it free from her service, at least for now.

"I must say, Siobhan, I am not surprised to see you," Elijah said to her as they watched Fallon take to the sky. A great current of air rushed over them as the bird soared away. "Come in and tell me the trouble that brings you here on Fallon's wings."

Siobhan looked around nervously. Elijah could sense her unease, and he said, "We are alone here, Siobhan. I have sent Demetrius to Bradán."

Elijah was glad he had acted as soon as he had. Trouble was upon them, but he had reclaimed the tower, and he had come to an understanding with Demetrius. Now he had to come to an understanding with the other six to help Demetrius and to make the Council whole again; whole and able to add a ninth.

As they entered the tower, Siobhan was filled with awe at its presence and immensity. Elijah escorted her to the upper chamber, showing her the tower as they moved through it. When they came to the upper tower room, Elijah turned and faced Siobhan as he said, "Trouble is upon us. I can sense it!"

It was no great mystery that trouble was upon them, Siobhan

thought to herself, for she was here, a place where she had never set foot, and she had come on the wings of her great condor. "You are right, Elijah. You told us that you sensed evil. I am here to inform you that Nauren is under siege! There have been multiple attacks throughout the night. Goblins attacked from the wastelands in waves! We were all caught off guard! Olaf sent me to appeal for your help in saving Nauren! He implores you to come quickly."

"Siobhan, you are a wizard and our representative to the elves. Olaf has a wizard, yet he calls for me. Your place is in Nauren with Olaf. Your departure, I fear, has caused a great calamity to fall upon the elves." Elijah hung his head. He grieved for Olaf and his wife; he grieved for Nauren. But, mostly, he feared for the life of Ciarra. He did not need to be told what had happened in Nauren for he had written the words of prophecy from Solomon all those years ago, and he knew in his heart they were living out the prophecy even as they spoke.

Siobhan was stung by his words. She had no response. What could Elijah know that she did not? She had come to him with words of the attack, yet Elijah seemed to know more than she or Olaf about what was happening.

"Elijah, I don't understand," she whispered, imploring him to explain. His words had only added to the sense of hopelessness she already felt inside.

"Why did the goblins attack, Siobhan? Do you know? Does Olaf know?"

"That's just it, Elijah. There is no feasible explanation. We fear that malevolent forces are behind the attack, yet all that we witnessed were goblins. Just before the attack, though, I did discover spies in the east. There was a great eagle flying in a pattern over the city as though it were being controlled. I sent Fallon to retrieve the eagle if possible, or to at least break up the pattern. As soon as Fallon engaged the eagle, it broke pattern and a large cry rang out from the eastern outpost. I am sure this was the spy or spies! Unfortunately, Olaf sent out a sentry patrol and they found nothing other than that the outpost had been visited recently."

Elijah listened. "It is strange for goblins to work together in a coordinated effort."

"That is right, and that is what Olaf and I discussed. But there was no further evidence of another's presence."

"Well, Siobhan, there was evidence of malfeasance to the east as you told me."

"Yes, but we don't know who or what was watching over us."

"True, but you can be sure that no goblin would be able to communicate and direct an eagle as you described. It had to be a being or beings that are enchanted. That certainly should make you more nervous and more alert!"

Siobhan looked to the ground and absorbed Elijah's words. He was right, of course. She had reacted and abandoned Nauren to recruit Elijah for their aid. The fact that Nauren was facing enchanted creatures and she had left them unprotected made her feel shame. It had been an unwise decision.

"What were the methods of the attacks? You said they attacked from the wastelands?"

Siobhan shook her head. "Yes, they seemed to be headed to the temple. They attacked from the wastelands in the south initially. When they were repelled, they regrouped and attacked from the southwest, again driving to the temple where they were again turned away. As I flew out this morning, Nauren was again under attack from the west!"

For a moment Elijah considered what he was hearing. Finally, he spoke: "Siobhan, perhaps the purpose of the attacks was not to overrun the temple, but to draw the protection away from Nauren so that the real attack could come from the east."

"But what was left to attack with, Elijah? The terrain to the east is difficult. I don't see how an army could mount much of an attack from the east, and certainly it would leave them with no possibility of retreat if they were overcome!"

"Yes, Siobhan, what you say is true. No army could mount much of an attack on Nauren from the north or the east. But I was not referring to an army. I fear that Olaf's family was the true target of the attack. The attack required Nauren's defenses to be drawn away from the palace so evil could fill the void left behind."

Siobhan frowned, deep in thought. "Why would they attack Olaf's family?"

The time had come to share his fear with Siobhan. She was obviously in turmoil over her decision to leave Nauren unprotected against what was clearly a malevolent, enchanted force. He looked at Siobhan as she stared at him, waiting for him to speak.

"Siobhan," he said, letting the weight of his words fall on her slowly so that she understood the gravity of what was happening, "the object of the attack was to capture Ciarra and steal her away as a sacrifice for the Gatekeeper of Souls. As you realize, the Gatekeeper is scheduled to make his appearance among us again in three nights."

Siobhan's heart sank at what she was hearing and the overwhelming burden she felt at the critical error she had made. She had abandoned the elves when they needed her most. She would always carry this with her.

"How can you know this, Elijah?"

"Siobhan, you are witnessing the fulfillment of a prophecy

scribed long before your time. I know because I scribed half of that prophecy when I was a follower of Solomon. I just finished reading what was left of the prophecy, the part that was scribed by none other than Solomon himself. It is what sits before you here on this table." Elijah pointed at the charred manuscript.

"What can we do?" she asked in a weakened voice. "What can I do?"

"I need to take Fallon at first light to Bradán. Will that be possible?"

"Yes, of course. Fallon is strong. He can fly us both! But why Bradán?"

"There is no time to explain; there is too much to discuss. The dwarves are Ciarra's only hope! I need you here, Siobhan. This is your new home. We shall never abandon this tower again, and this tower will always have a wizard's presence!"

"What do you mean, Elijah?"

"This tower needs a caretaker, Siobhan, and I have chosen you for that position."

Siobhan was stunned. She had not seen this coming at all. She liked her home with the elves; they shared a common ancestry.

"What happened to Demetrius?" Siobhan inquired.

"He is no longer here. He is on a mission for me as we speak. I have relieved him of his obligation to this tower."

Siobhan reflected on all that Elijah had shown and told her. She could feel the spirit of those who had come before her in this place. Despite the barrenness and all that was missing, thanks to Elijah, the tower was still the seat of power for the wizards. Siobhan could immediately feel it and had some understanding of Elijah's insistence on reclaiming it. How had Elijah taken care of Demetrius in such a short period of time? Her imagination wandered.

"I love this tower, Elijah, but why me? I am content in my position with the elves."

"Siobhan, it is time for a change for you, and in fact for all of us. In my mind, there is no better place for you than here. In my time as a follower, to serve as caretaker of this tower was a position of prestige reserved for the most senior among the wizards. Indeed, Simon was caretaker here when Malkavic was captured, when he assumed his position as head of the Wizard Council." He let these words sink in for a moment.

"But as I said, this tower will always be occupied by a wizard. I must go, and that leaves you to watch over this place for all of us. Ciarra's life and the fate of all Lavendelle hang in the balance!" Elijah felt Siobhan's suffering. He reached out to her and placed his hand on her shoulder. "Siobhan, I fear there is little any of us can do. I believe that forces beyond our control are in play and our actions were prophesied over seven hundred years ago. We are witnessing an unfolding of the prophecy. Solomon saw it all. He was a great seer, a great prophet. Now, with what is occurring, his final and perhaps greatest prophecy is being fulfilled. Come with me. There is much to show you before I leave."

Elijah walked to the burning fireplace and then disappeared behind the fire. Siobhan did not know where he had gone. She stood and stared into the flames. Elijah, realizing that she had not followed him, returned to her and showed her the way down the secret path behind the fireplace.

Soon, Elijah imparted his knowledge of the secret passages in the tower. He took her outside behind the tower to the Lake of the Serpent. It was clear to him that Siobhan, a wizard for many years herself, was oblivious to the spell that had shielded his eyes in his youth. He imparted his wisdom to her and her eyes were opened. She could see the boats on the lake, the paths among the protective boulders, and the entrance to the back of the tower. She had been oblivious to all of these things just moments before.

After reflecting on all she had seen and learned, Siobhan said, "It is quite impressive, Elijah. I am happy you were able to reclaim it."

"Siobhan, I will be sending Fallon back to you with three dwarves; not tomorrow, but the next day. They will need to reach the volcano before that evening falls. They will need to reach the Chamber of the Gatekeeper before the Gatekeeper comes, or I fear we will never see Princess Ciarra again! The dwarves are her only hope. There is nothing you can do. The prophecy makes it clear that a wizard is not present. Unfortunately, the prophecy is burnt and I do not know what the outcome will be." Elijah looked across the Lake of the Serpent and stared out at the volcano in the distance.

Siobhan followed his gazed, but she remained silent, deep in thought. She worried about the words Elijah had spoken. She worried about Nauren and all the elves. She worried about little Ciarra. "When the dwarves arrive," Elijah continued, "you need to give them the emerald dagger that is resting on the prophecy in the upper chamber where we sat. You need to bring them to this boat and then send them on their way across the lake as quickly as possible. This is all you can do to try to save the princess. Then, all we can do is wait to see what happens. It is out of our hands. It is now up to the dwarves."

"Why the dwarves? Which dwarves? Do you know whom you are sending?"

"I do not know myself, Siobhan. All I know is that I need to go and meet with the dwarves. I can only hope that the answers will become clear when I get there. I do have an unexpected ally though," he said as he looked up at Siobhan. "I sent Demetrius to the dwarves to seek their expertise in restoring our tower. Hopefully, I can meet up with him when I get there."

"Can he be trusted?" she whispered.

Elijah sighed. There was so much to be done to repair relationships among the members of this fractured group of wizards. They could not have division amongst them; they were only eight. If this discord and distrust continued, they would be less effective and their influence would further diminish. Now, more than ever, the Council needed to come together.

"Siobhan, we need him. We all need each other. Demetrius needs us. Demetrius is my friend. We started as wizards together. He has a good soul, and we need to help him. The spell I just taught you is one Demetrius taught me when we were both followers. He opened my eyes to all of this just as I opened yours. I will not abandon him. None of us will! We need each other now more than ever. I fear that this is only the beginning of a new evil in Lavendelle. We need to be whole, or we will crumble and become irrelevant. That will not happen as long as I am Head of the Wizard Council!"

CHAPTER LIII
MARTHA

FIVE dwarves were gathered around Martha's bed. All were family with the exception of one ancient dwarf at the head of the bed. All eyes were on Yuri.

"I have given her the Cassava root. It will take time for the root to do its work. She is very ill; her heartbeat is irregular and very weak," Yuri said with great sadness in his voice.

"I hope she is not too far gone," Markus said, looking at no one in particular as he held her hand. Indeed, it was not a good sign. Martha had received her second dose of Cassava root that morning, yet she looked as though there was not much life left in her. She remained asleep. She only had enough strength to briefly wake and sip the medicine down before she fell back asleep. She was as far gone as any of them had seen another dwarf, and that included Yuri.

Elwin looked at his sister and then at Siv, Ramsey, and Teige. "It is a good thing what you have done. Martha would not have had a chance without your efforts."

"I would have never given you permission to go—had I known," Elwin added as he looked at his daughter.

"That is why we didn't tell you," Siv said as she looked back at her father.

"I can't believe you went, Siv. You are but a child," Markus said.

Markus and Elwin had learned of the three younger dwarves' adventures the night before. They had lost track of their children as Martha lay on her deathbed and had given them little thought. They had supposed that the impending death was too much for the younger three to cope with, and so they had kept their distance. Besides, the three were old enough to look after themselves.

When they had arrived with Yuri, Markus and Elwin were so overwhelmed with joy by the fact that they brought with them the Cassava root that the adventures of the younger three were lost in their joy. Their joy and hope were shared by Siv, Ramsey, Teige, and Yuri as well, and Yuri had gone straight to work.

But Markus and Elwin were beginning to be overtaken by the shock of hearing about their adventures as their hope for Martha began to dwindle.

"I just know she is going to pull through," Ramsey began. "I know it because everything Siv told me has come to pass, just as it always has, and Siv said she is going to live!"

Elwin and Markus were too close to Siv to understand her gift. Besides, she was a mere child. They gave little thought to what she had to say. They thought Ramsey was simply voicing the words of a son overcome with grief.

"Tell them what you see, Siv, tell them," Ramsey implored.

Yuri was amazed at what he was hearing and seeing. Ramsey especially, and Teige as well, recognized Siv's gift of foresight. Yuri knew it too. Yet her uncle and her own father were oblivious to this gifted soul. She was youthful, yes, but Yuri knew she was far more than a child.

Siv felt uncomfortable with all the attention. Telling Ramsey and Teige what she saw and thought was one thing, but telling her father and her uncle was another. They had always dismissed the things she said, not because they were malicious in any way, but because they never really truly believed in her words; they just thought her words were those of a child.

That being said, Siv decided to say what she felt in her heart. This was her way, and she only said things that she truly felt.

"I feel that Martha will live. Nothing I have seen since arriving here last night makes me feel any differently. We have done everything we can to help her, and I believe in my heart she will live."

Elwin put his arm around his daughter and gave her a hug. Markus looked at Siv and gave her a smile. It was clear to him that Siv loved Martha.

Yuri looked at the two men in amazement. Siv's words were received as those of a starry-eyed child full of wild dreams. The weight of her words seemed to be missed by these two.

Yuri looked at Ramsey and then at Teige; it was clear that these two had full belief in their young cousin. They too believed Martha would live. They believed because they had seen Siv and had faith in her words.

Yuri looked at Martha. He had never seen anyone recover from such an advanced stage of illness. By all accounts, it appeared to him as though they had arrived too late. But then he looked at Siv; she was staring at her aunt. Even though he couldn't see her eyes, he could see them in his mind. He believed with his whole heart in what Siv had said. He didn't know how she would do it, but he believed Martha would pull through.

Light streamed through the windows as the morning sun sent blinding beams into the room. The air, however, felt heavy and full of sickness. Yuri rose to open the window and let air flow into the room. Then he walked over to the door to open it and let fresh air flow through the entire cottage. Upon opening the door and looking out, his heart leaped. His faith in Siv grew even more. He was sure of what he was seeing, yet it appeared different in ways he had not seen before.

"Come quick! Look!" Yuri pointed. The other dwarves ran to the door to see what all the excitement was about. They too were confused, but their spirits were bolstered as well.

"It looks like Elijah," Teige said, "but I don't think it is Elijah."

"I don't think that is Elijah," Yuri said, "but it looks like a very old wizard indeed!"

Siv bolted from the door and ran across the field toward the old wizard. The wizard was quite a distance away, but she made good time as she sped across the field.

Demetrius stopped and took in all that he was seeing. The last time he had been here was in his youth, and though he was seeing the area for the first time in over seven hundred years, his keen memory had not been dulled; things had not changed much since his last visit. Of course, all of the dwarves of that time had long since passed, but Bradán and their descendants lived on.

He looked out and saw a youthful dwarf approaching at a fast clip. Elijah was right; he was needed. There was life outside of the tower. With every step he had taken since he left the tower he felt reinvigorated. He was discovering himself all over again now that he was freed from the bondage he felt at the tower—the bondage of the evil Aelhaeran. The thought of Aelhaeran sent a chill through his body. Yes, he was starting to recover.

Demetrius let Siv approach him and he said, "Slow down there, dear. What is all the hurry about? You look as though you haven't seen a wizard around here in a long, long time."

"It is true then," Siv gasped between breaths. "You are a wizard! Who are you and where is Elijah? Elijah is the only wizard I have ever met. And yes, it has been a long time since we have seen him. Is he all right?"

"He is fine. He sent me to you as he is unable to come. Elijah is very busy, but he will return as soon as he can. He told me that you all are long overdue for a visit. My name is Demetrius. What do I call you?"

Siv's heart skipped a beat upon hearing the name Demetrius. She recalled what the druids had said about him. But as she reflected on this, nothing those druids said was to be believed.

I am Siv, but you must come with me quickly," she said as she reached out and pulled at Demetrius' hand. Siv was no taller than the old wizard's chest. He towered over her. He let Siv lead him back toward the cottage.

"Where are we going, young Siv?"

"My aunt is sick. I think she is dying. We need you. I know you can save her."

Demetrius could hear the desperation in her voice. He knew the matter was urgent. He needed to help this poor child save her aunt.

When they arrived at the cottage, he was led to Martha. Martha was dying and it appeared that if Demetrius did not act soon, there would be nothing anyone could do. Demetrius gazed down at the ailing woman. Her eyes were closed, and her face was ashen in color. Dried saliva crusted around her lips and her skin had lost all turgor. It was clear that she was extremely dehydrated. She looked to be clinging to the last threads of life.

He reached down and placed his hand on her chest. His hand was large and it covered her whole chest. Her breaths were coming in bunches, and then they would stop. They were all shallow. She was barely moving any air through her lungs.

He could feel her heart beat as his hand rested on her chest. There appeared to be little force inside her chest. The heartbeat felt weak, thready, and irregular. Her heart was also beating very quickly.

He looked up at Siv. "Bring me water. She must drink, or surely she will perish."

Demetrius roused Martha and made her drink the water; a few sips at first and then a little along. "She is extremely dehydrated. She must take in more or the Cassava root will do very little to help her. I want you to make her drink a sip or two of water every few minutes. When she gets strong enough, we will give her this." Demetrius reached into his bag and pulled out a packet of powder.

"What is that?" Markus inquired.

"It is from a plant that has a lovely lavender flower with the shape of a finger of a glove. We call it the Folks-glove plant. But I caution you: The plant is a poison and it must be handled cautiously to get medicinal value from it."

"Will she get better?" Markus looked to Demetrius for hope.

"Yes, I believe she can get better, but we have much work to do to get her there," Demetrius said. He felt great compassion for all the dwarves in the room.

Yuri watched with amazement. It was just as Siv had said: Martha would survive. And Siv said this not knowing that there was a wizard around the corner. Even though Siv had declared it, it had fallen on deaf ears with Markus and Elwin. But when Demetrius said it, the elder dwarves were filled with hope and with joy.

Yuri looked at Siv and considered her. He was glad he had the opportunity to know her. He now knew why he had lived so long. He was needed and his life had meaning once again.

Chapter LIV
Healing

DEMETRIUS led a round-the-clock vigil through the night. Martha was given sips of water every quarter hour and by midnight she appeared to be getting better hydrated, her skin had more fullness, and the deep cracks on her tongue slowly faded. However, she still had a weakened and erratic heartbeat that raced in her chest. Siv was awake with Demetrius.

"I feel she is getting better, Siv. The time has come to give her the medicine I brought. Can you bring my bag to me?"

Siv got up and retrieved his bag. "How will this help her?"

"This is powerful medicine, Siv. We start out slowly and keep administering it until we get the desired effect."

"How do you determine how much to give?"

Demetrius eyed Siv. She was intelligent and it was a good question. Perhaps the knowledge he imparted would help Siv save someone else someday.

"That is a good question, Siv. Let me see your hand." Siv came close to Demetrius and placed her tiny hand in his. Demetrius placed her hand over her own chest and said, "Close your eyes, Siv, and feel your chest. Concentrate and you should be able to feel your heartbeat."

Siv did as she was told. "I am not sure if I feel my heart or not."

"It takes time, Siv. Let me see your fingers." Demetrius took her fingers and moved them to her wrist, just below her thumb. Feel here, Siv. You should be able to feel the effects of your heart beating, but I caution you, do not press hard. Use only a light touch."

Siv kept her eyes closed. "I do feel this, Demetrius." There was amazement in her voice.

"Now, Siv, do you feel how even and regular your heart is beating?" Siv nodded. "I want you to feel this same spot on Martha's wrist."

Siv reached over and rested her fingertips lightly against Martha's wrist. She waited for some time. Her eyes widened. "Wow! It is so soft, I can hardly feel it. And it is not regular like mine. It is fast, then slow, and then it is fast again."

"Exactly, Siv. Now, with practice, you should be able to place your hand over any creature's heart and feel it beat through its chest. Remember, I have been at this for over seven hundred years! It takes time."

Siv smiled and laughed softly as Demetrius continued to share his knowledge with her.

"Now, we start with just a pinch of this medicine, mix it in her water, and give her a drink. Then we wait. The next time we come to give her more water, we feel for her heartbeat again. With time, the heart should slow and the strength of the heartbeat you feel should be stronger. It is at that time you will know you have given enough."

"When she gets better, will she need the medicine anymore?"

"That is another good question, Siv, and the answer is sometimes yes and sometimes no. We will know with time as we see how she responds. I expect her to regain her strength starting anytime. I believe she has been through the worst part of this illness. If we can get her heart beating stronger, the medicine from the Cassava plant should be able to reach its target and cure her. She may require more Cassava, or she may not."

"I am so glad you came, Demetrius." Siv reached out and squeezed his hand and held him close. He could feel the love flow out from her and knew she was sincere.

"I am glad too, Siv. This has been as important for me as it is for all of you. I don't think Martha would have made it much longer without more help than what you all were able to provide. Now you know some important principles: Keep your patient well-hydrated, make sure her heart is strong, and soon you will see how to witness the effect of your intervention and how to adjust it. That is your next lesson."

Siv stayed with Demetrius and helped him tend to Martha through the night. They had given two doses of the Folks-glove powder with no response. After the third dose, Siv could feel that Martha's heart was much slower, much more regular, and felt much stronger. She looked down at her aunt, and Martha opened her eyes. Martha reached up and stroked Siv's cheek.

Demetrius watched as Siv smiled at her aunt. He sensed the relief on Siv's face. He felt joy in helping these dwarves. Internally, he wondered how he had wasted so many years trapped by Aelhaeran. He wondered also if he would be able to fully escape Aelhaeran's evil influence. He would have to rely on help from his friend, Elijah.

As morning arrived, Martha had clearly taken a turn for the better. A combination of the Cassava root and the Folks-glove powder from Demetrius, as well as tender loving care from him and Siv, and it looked like she might make it.

Demetrius rested his eyes as he had been up all night. He had taken to the hills outside of the dwarf village and found a spot along the hillside that seemed just right. It had been a long night, and he had done a good deed. He had forgotten how good it was to give of himself to others and share in their joy. Elijah had provided Demetrius just what he needed and at just the right time when he would be receptive to hearing Elijah's message. He drifted off with these thoughts in his head.

It was afternoon when Yuri looked out the cottage window. Martha was starting to regain her strength. His time here was nearly done. He felt useful again, needed and accepted. He had missed this for a long time. It is hard growing old and outliving all your friends and loved ones, he thought to himself. Well, he had new friends now, and as long as he had strength, he would do his best to preserve these relationships. He was going to start now.

He watched Siv from the window. She was sitting on a small chair that she had turned to the southwestern sky. Her focus was out on the horizon.

Yuri approached Siv and pulled up another weather-beaten chair next to her. He lifted his gaze to the hot afternoon sky as well. It was bright out.

"What are you looking at Siv?" Yuri inquired as all he could see was a clear blue mid-afternoon sky.

"I am not sure, Yuri," Siv replied. "It is more that I sense something out there rather than see."

"What do you mean? What is it that you sense?"

"I tell you because you chose to believe me, Yuri. My father doesn't always understand me or believe me, so I often keep these thoughts to myself. It is really hard to explain, and I am not sure I understand it myself. But my heart keeps drawing my attention to the horizon out there," she said as she pointed in the direction of her gaze. "I get feelings all the time, feelings about things I am not even thinking about. It is as if I can sense things that are going to happen and even anticipate things that will happen . . . things that I don't really know anything about." She continued to look wistfully at the horizon.

Yuri looked at her and thought about what she had said. He did not reply immediately but let her words settle. Being honest with himself, Yuri did not fully understand what she was saying or feeling, yet he knew what she said was true to the best she could explain herself.

"Siv, to be honest with you, I don't have any experience with anything like that. I am not the one who can help you. I will say this: I believe you with my whole heart for I have only known you a few short days and all the things you have told me or said to me or your cousins about what is to be have happened."

Siv turned her gaze toward Yuri. She got out of her chair and walked over to him and hugged him. "Thank you, Yuri, thank you. That means so much to me, especially coming from you."

Siv returned to her chair. Yuri had been sincere, and he realized how difficult it had been for this young dwarf to grow up being so different from everyone else. He could see she longed for acceptance. Well, he was determined to be her friend.

They sat back in their chairs and Yuri said, "Siv, I really think you should talk to Elijah about all of this. He would be able to help you understand. I will go with you if you like. Or better yet, you could talk to Demetrius as he is already here! Who knows when we will see Elijah again?"

"Yuri, I know."

He looked at her curiously. "You know what?"

"I know when we will see Elijah again."

"Tell me, Siv."

Siv turned from Yuri and looked to the horizon again as she said, "He is coming now."

CHAPTER LV
TWO WIZARDS

YURI and Siv sat for some time watching the sky to the southwest. Soon, they were joined by Ramsey and Teige. Markus and Elwin stayed in the cottage with Martha. Everyone's spirits were lifted by her amazing improvement over such a short period of time. It was due to a combination of the Cassava root and Demetrius' care.

"What are you looking at?" Teige asked Yuri and Siv.

Before Yuri could reply, Siv lifted her hand and pointed to the southwest sky. "Look! Over the mountain, up in the sky."

Everyone's gaze followed her finger out to the horizon. Yuri had not seen it, and he had been sitting, watching, for some period of time.

"I see it," said Ramsey. Not too long after that Teige saw it too. Yuri was the last to see the small dark dot in the late afternoon sky.

"What is it?" Teige inquired.

"I don't know, but it seems to be headed this way," Siv replied.

"I know what it is, or I should say who it is," Yuri said. All three looked at him. "It is Elijah!" he said it with great conviction.

"Elijah? But why? We have Demetrius here with us," Teige

said. It didn't make any sense.

It made sense to Siv; it meant Yuri believed in her. No adult had ever taken her visions seriously before.

All three watched as the dark dot on the horizon grew larger and larger until it started to take form.

"It looks like a dragon!" Ramsey pointed as the beast grew larger.

"No, I think it is a great bird!" Teige replied.

"I think Yuri was right, Teige. Do you see what is on the back of that bird? I think it is Elijah!" Ramsey said with amazement.

Yuri sat silently. He exchanged glances with Siv and he saw her smile. She was amazing and had a truly precious gift.

Elijah and the bird seemed to be heading toward the center of the village. All four dwarves followed. They watched as the massive bird landed and loose debris scattered under the great draft created by the condor's wings. The dwarves approached Elijah and were happy to see him. Siv, Ramsey, and Teige welcomed the wizard.

"It is so good to have you here with us again," a voice in the small crowd of gathering dwarves shouted out.

"It is good to be back," Elijah responded.

Elijah saw Yuri and looked at him. "Yuri, you old dwarf, it has been too long. It is good to see you out in the village."

"I don't ever recall two wizards being here in Bradán at the same time, and I am talking about a *long* time," Yuri started. "I fear something dire must have brought the two of you here."

Yuri's words quieted the dwarves who had gathered to witness Elijah's grand yet unexpected arrival. What he said was true. There had never been two wizards here at the same time before that any could recall. They had seen other wizards, but they mostly remembered Elijah. No one had ever met Demetrius before his arrival here the day prior.

"It is as you say, Yuri. So I take it Demetrius has arrived?"

All of the dwarves nodded.

"I need to speak with him; it is urgent. And then I need to speak with all of the dwarves as soon as possible. Does anyone know where Demetrius is right now?"

"I know, Elijah," Siv said.

Elijah looked at her; he could not help himself for he had always been drawn to Siv. He opened up his arms and knelt down. He embraced her and spoke to her as if she were still but a child. "Siv, it is so good to see you. Please hurry and request Demetrius come to me as soon as you can find him."

"I will, Elijah!" Siv ran off.

"Now the rest of you, go to everyone in the village and bring everyone to me. We shall meet here as soon as all of you can get together and as soon as I speak with Demetrius."

"Demetrius, wake up!"

The old wizard slowly opened his eyes and found himself staring back at Siv. She stared at him, and he could feel her bright green eyes imploring him back into consciousness.

"What is it, my dear?"

"You must come quickly!" Siv reached for his hand and tugged at it until the old wizard sat up. He had been lying on a pallet, stretched out on the soft soil under the cover of trees to shield him from the light of the sun. It had worked well and the spot had been a good one. If Siv had not roused him, he could have slept until the night. Reflecting on those thoughts, he could see evening was not that far off.

"How is Martha?"

"It's not Martha," Siv started. "She is getting better thanks to you. She has woken up several times today and has been talking some. You have worked miracles with her! But you must come quickly. Elijah is here and he sent me for you!"

"What? How can that be? Elijah sent me here so that he could stay back at the tower. There was much work to be done. He would never leave the tower alone; I know him."

"You must come quickly!" Siv said again as she tugged at his arm.

Demetrius did not understand what Elijah was doing here. Elijah would have had to leave just one day after him to get here so quickly. Nothing made sense, but Demetrius quickly followed the young dwarf back to the village.

When Demetrius saw the great condor resting in the middle of the village he knew that it had to be Elijah, and he also understood how Elijah had made such great time. It was as Siv had said. Elijah was there, in the middle of the village, talking amongst the gathering dwarves.

"It is good to see you, Demetrius," Elijah said as he saw his friend approach.

"And you, Elijah, but I must say it is quite a surprise to see you again so soon!"

"Demetrius," Elijah began, "we must talk."

Demetrius felt Aelhaeran stir inside of him, and he knew something sinister had brought Elijah here unexpectedly.

CHAPTER LVI
THE THREE

THE sun had set behind the mountain, but the light struggled to keep its presence felt. Darkness was slowly beating back the light as it crept across the sky from the east. The still night air felt heavy to match the mood of the gathering. Elijah had gathered all the dwarves in Bradán's town center to speak to them. They were all filled with anxiety about the unknown.

A large fire burned in a pit. Dwarves sat on benches, chairs, and rocks at their local gathering spot as well as on the ground surrounding Elijah and Demetrius. Almost the entire population of the dwarf village was present.

Elijah began to speak. "I hoped never to have had to meet with you all like this."

The dwarves each individually felt that something bad was going to happen. They were a simple village and lived simple lives. They did not want the outside world to spill over into their peaceful existence. It looked like their world was inevitably facing danger.

"Nearly a millennium ago, I was a follower of the great wizard Solomon. As some of you may recall, Solomon was a great seer, a prophet. He could see the future. There has never been one like him before, and I must say, there has never been someone like him since his passing."

Yuri stirred and then looked at Siv. At Elijah's words, Siv had looked at Yuri at the same time. Yuri wasn't so sure that Elijah's words were correct. He believed in Siv. The dwarves remained silent and just listened.

"When I was a follower of Solomon," continued Elijah, "I scribed a prophecy for him about Malkavic."

Malkavic's name shot terror into the dwarves. They remembered the times of danger and oppression that the wizards had freed them from generations before. The memories had been passed from generation to generation.

"The prophecy was about the defeat of Malkavic and his removal from Lavendelle. Solomon never wanted this, his greatest prophecy, ever to be known. Unknown to most, Solomon approached the Gatekeeper of Souls." Another gasp rumbled through the dwarves. It was as if their greatest fears were coming true.

Yuri knew in his heart it had to be a dramatic event that had brought both the wizards to them, let alone Elijah on the wings of the great condor. Elijah had always come quietly; never before had he made such a grand appearance. It was a sign of dangerous times, of that Yuri was sure.

"Solomon planned to have the Gatekeeper entomb Malkavic when the wizards brought him there. The Gatekeeper agreed, provided Solomon put his prophecy in writing. I know this, for I am the one who wrote Solomon's words."

Elijah spoke slowly so that the dwarves could absorb what they were hearing. He needed them, and he needed them to understand their role in all that was occurring.

"Unbeknownst to me at the time, Solomon had finished

writing the prophecy himself. I just read Solomon's final writings. Unfortunately, the prophecy did not remain intact. On the night Malkavic was entombed, goblins attacked the Tower of the Wizards."

Another loud gasp rumbled through the gathering.

"I know it is inconceivable, but it was Malkavic who ordered them to attack. Hundreds and hundreds attacked. I know because I was in the tower with Solomon when it occurred. Solomon and I were able to kill scores of goblins in our defense, but we were overwhelmed as we were only two."

It was the first time Elijah had acknowledged slaying goblins. Elijah was legend among the inhabitants of Lavendelle and his reputation as the Warrior Wizard was acknowledged with his words that night. Demetrius had witnessed the aftermath of the wholesale slaughter of the goblins, but even Demetrius had not heard from Elijah of his part in the attack. He had heard from Simon about Elijah being found alone in Malkavic's chamber with hundreds of dead goblins. Demetrius could only imagine what had happened. Hearing Elijah speak of that night sent shivers down his spine.

"During this attack, the goblins overwhelmed Solomon. I witnessed Solomon disappear before my own eyes. I do not know what became of him. He told me he possessed magic I could not understand. To this day, I still do not understand what Solomon knew. He was the most powerful wizard I have ever known."

Demetrius felt a stirring. It was Aelhaeran letting Demetrius know that he was a powerful force as well. Even this far away from the tower, Aelhaeran was able to reach out and grasp him. Demetrius fought to suppress these feelings. What had he done, letting Aelhaeran into his mind? He needed to be free of the curse within. Just as he was having these thoughts, Elijah looked at him as though he were reading his mind. He felt shame. Elijah was perceptive and powerful indeed.

"When Solomon disappeared, the goblins stole the prophecy. I was momentarily able to retrieve it from them and I tried to destroy it by casting it in the fire. Unfortunately, the prophecy was retrieved by a goblin. However, the foul creature paid with its life for that mistake!"

Anger welled up within Elijah as he recalled the night. The feelings of that evening raced through his mind and body; his passion surged through the dwarves and Demetrius. As he relived the night, those around him witnessed the events unfold before them. The story was critical to what Elijah would request of the dwarves that very night; it was crucial that they understand his request for the great sacrifice that would be asked of them.

"I was able to retrieve part of that prophecy from the goblin before it fell to its death. It was the part scribed by Solomon; the part that burned in the fire before it was retrieved. The goblins got away with the part of the prophecy I scribed. I followed the goblins and tried to retrieve the remainder of the prophecy, but as much as I tried, I never saw it again!"

"What did you do with Solomon's prophecy all these years?" Demetrius inquired of Elijah.

"You would not believe me if I told you, Demetrius."

Demetrius looked at him, inquiring, waiting for a response.

"I hid it in the tower. Indeed, I wondered all these years if you would stumble upon it. After you headed here, I went searching for it. It took some time, but I was able to recover it. I hid it well."

"You never cease to amaze me, Elijah. I thought I had discovered all the secrets of the tower years and years ago." Demetrius shook his head in disbelief.

"Demetrius, I believe that the tower holds boundless mysteries and knowledge. One could live a millennium and never discover all that is locked inside its walls."

"It must be true, Elijah, if you could keep this from me for over seven hundred years."

"Seven hundred and fifty years to be exact, Demetrius."

The dwarves sat back in amazement as they watched the two wizards converse.

"What does all this have to do with us?" Yuri inquired. "This is ancient history; how does this affect us today?"

The dwarves all nodded as the same questions consumed their thoughts as well.

Siv did not nod her head; she sunk in to her father's body as fear welled up within her. She felt as if Elijah had come specifically to speak to her and his words terrified her. She felt her father's arm around her shoulder and she found comfort in him.

"This has to do with Malkavic," Elijah said, pausing to let the demon lord's name shock the dwarves and refocus their attention on the dangers at hand. "The prophecy was not only about the wizards removing Malkavic and freeing Lavendelle from his evil," Elijah began, "but it was also about the return of Malkavic to Lavendelle and the threat of his evil once again taking over and suppressing all of Lavendelle!"

The dwarves shuddered and were collectively afraid. They were terrified of the prospect of Malkavic's return to Lavendelle. A millennium ago, despite their rift with the elves, the elves had helped protect the dwarves. Now there was no relationship between them and no hope for the dwarves.

"The reason that the Gatekeeper made Solomon write down the prophecy is for the very reason we are here tonight. The Gatekeeper wanted Solomon to put in writing a guide for some future generation that would explain how to unlock his gates and set Malkavic free. I know because I wrote the guide. This is what the goblins took that night! This is the reason Solomon never wanted to put the words in writing. This is the reason Solomon never wanted to make known this, perhaps his greatest vision. Solomon could not control his visions; he could only report them. This was a particularly dark vision, and Solomon preferred to keep it to himself. But he needed the assistance of the Gatekeeper, and they came to an understanding."

The dwarves listened with rapt attention. The name of the Gatekeeper made them shudder. What part had they to play in these events, they wondered as Elijah continued.

"I feel that Solomon hoped to keep the latter half of his prophecy to himself and so he scribed it in his own hands. Even I was shielded from his vision. I am not unaware anymore. For some time, I have felt an evil creeping over Lavendelle. I have not known from where it came nor where it existed. But recent events have helped me understand the source of this evil! You need to understand what has recently happened: Nauren was attacked by hundreds of goblins just the night before last."

A collective gasp rose through the crowd as they listened. They leaned forward and gave him their full attention.

"Goblins can be motivated to work together if there is a strong enough force to unite them. Indeed, this is how Malkavic was able to control Lavendelle during his reign of terror. They would do anything that Malkavic desired them to do, and they would do it without question. I fear an unknown evil force has taken control of the goblins. I fear the source of this evil emanates again from the volcano!"

"Why would the goblins attack the elves, Elijah?" Yuri asked. "That makes no sense." He was clearly the wisest and most discerning among the dwarves. His body was ancient, yet his mind was still as sharp as it had been in his youth.

"As you may know, a princess was born to Olaf and Ryanne, and indeed to all the elves. Princess Ciarra. She was born a few weeks ago. The prophecy of Solomon predicts that the firstborn of the Prince of the Elves shall be taken and brought to the Gatekeeper of Souls. In exchange for this pure child, Malkavic will be freed. We are two nights away from the next disappearance of the moon; hence, we are two nights away from the return of the Gatekeeper to these lands for one night!"

"Everything is in place for Malkavic to return! All the inhabitants of Lavendelle are in grave danger," Demetrius added.

"Yes, it is as Demetrius has said. The baby princess has been born, the Gatekeeper is coming, and the goblins have attacked. Clearly, the capture of Princess Ciarra is the only logical reason the goblins attacked the elves. It has been foretold that this would happen. We all know that the goblins are not strong enough or smart enough to organize and attack on their own. As I have said, I have felt evil welling up in Lavendelle. I am now convinced an evil force has discovered the prophecy and has discovered the key to unlocking Malkavic from his crypt."

"That still doesn't explain what it has to do with us other than the fact that we are now in danger, but that danger will extend to all creatures in Lavendelle if Malkavic returns," Elwin said as Siv pulled herself closer and closer to her father, burying herself under his outstretched arm.

"Do we know if the goblins took the princess?" Yuri inquired.

"I know in my heart it is so, Yuri, but I have not received confirmation," Elijah replied. "Unfortunately, there is no time for confirmation. As of tonight, we have two nights to act, or Princess Ciarra will never be seen again. Moreover, Malkavic will be released and return to Lavendelle and to his evil ways," Elijah finished.

"What do you expect us to do?" Elwin inquired. "You said we only have two nights to act. What do you mean by 'we'?"

"That is the reason I am here tonight, Elwin. That is why I flew here on the wings of the great condor. There is no time to waste. Indeed, there is no time to plan. There is only time to act and to follow the prophecy!"

Siv was riveted by Elijah's tale. She felt a stirring deep inside her as if all the greatest fears of her short life were becoming manifest with every word that Elijah uttered.

"As I said, I just finished reading the rest of the prophecy, scribed by Solomon's hand. I have an understanding about the only chance there is to save the princess and ensure Malkavic's entombment is permanent. The prophecy talks of the abduction of the firstborn of the Prince of the Elves. It talks about the baby being delivered to the Gatekeeper. The prophecy also talks about three of the least among the creatures of these lands, three dwarves, who journey into the heart of the volcano and into the chamber of the Gatekeeper himself to save the princess. My vision beyond these words is impaired as the remainder of the prophecy was destroyed by the fire that night a millennium ago. I am not a seer and I have no vision for the outcome. If I did not have Solomon's words to guide me, I would not be here. Indeed, I would be with the elves, guiding them. I would tell them what I knew and lead them in an all-out assault on the volcano myself."

Siv felt her heart ready to burst inside her chest as she thought of the tiny baby being stolen from her family and taken to such a foul and evil place. She grieved for Ciarra.

"But Solomon does not mention a wizard rescuing Princess Ciarra," continued Elijah. "He does not mention elves attacking the volcano and retrieving the child. Any attempt outside of the prophecy to rescue this child is doomed to certain failure. Solomon was a great seer, and now with the fulfillment of this prophecy, everything he foretold has come to pass. It is useless to try to go against his vision. That is why I have come to you this night. As soon as I heard of the goblin attack on the elves, I knew what was happening. We are living out Solomon's vision; his last and greatest prophecy is unfolding! I had to act on my part the only way I know to have any chance at saving the princess and keeping Malkavic entombed for all time."

At these words, Siv and Yuri exchanged an anxious look. They both understood the danger implicit in the task Elijah was describing.

"I need three volunteers among you to come with me and help us save the princess. Unfortunately, after reading Solomon's prophecy, I do not have any insight into who is supposed to come. All I can request is that if you feel compelled to answer the calling, tell me. I do not have time to analyze and plan; we only have time to act, but we must act swiftly or all will be for naught."

"Elijah, I feel compelled to help. My mind is sharp, but my body lacks the strength. How can I help?" Yuri inquired.

"Yuri, my great friend, we could all use your wisdom in guiding those who feel the urge to respond to this calling."

The request was overwhelming. Elijah was asking for three of them to attack the volcano on their own, work their way down to the Chamber of the Gatekeeper of Souls, confront the evil that had abducted Princess Ciarra, and retrieve her for the elves. The plan was pure insanity and certainly a death sentence for those who attempted such a mission.

Siv sat riveted to her father's side. She felt compelled to respond, but her experience in the forest this past week overwhelmed her with fear. She had experienced only a fraction of the danger that she was now being asked to expose herself to, and that was almost more than she could bear. She convinced herself that she lacked the fortitude to attempt such a journey, which was most surely to end in demise for the three unfortunate dwarves who volunteered to go, if there were any.

Finally, Teige stood up and said, "Elijah, I just returned from the other side of the mountain. I learned a lot in my travels. I feel compelled to respond to your calling."

Elijah acknowledged Teige with a nod of his head.

"Elijah, I too traveled to the Mystic Forest last week. I also feel compelled to respond to your calling," said Ramsey as he stood up.

Elijah reflected on Teige and Ramsey. They were brothers and would be loyal to each other. Looking at them, he could tell that they were stoutly built dwarves. Elijah felt good with these two, but he needed a third. As he waited, it was apparent that no other dwarves were willing to volunteer themselves.

Elijah didn't want just any dwarf; he wanted the dwarves that Solomon foresaw in his prophecy. This was the only chance for success and, indeed, Princess Ciarra's only hope. These were desperate times.

Siv felt compelled to answer Elijah's calling and her father could sense that she was stirring beside him. He pulled her closer to his side, trying to shield and protect her.

It became apparent that there were no more volunteers. But as the dwarves sat there, a small but very bright light began to show in the night sky. It captured the attention of all at the meeting that evening, including Elijah and Demetrius. All attention turned to the light as it whimsically flitted down from the sky, moving closer and closer to the gathering. In a short period of time, the light had come to settle right in front of Siv. There was no denying that she was being singled out by the light.

Elijah and Demetrius approached Siv to investigate. Siv peered directly into the bright light. She was startled to see a face looking back at her.

As startled as Siv was to see the face looking back at her, Elijah and Demetrius were shaken to the core of all their knowledge as wizards. Elijah stared at the face looking back at him for some time. It was a face he hadn't seen in almost eight hundred years. Finally, he uttered, "Solomon."

Elwin held Siv close with his left arm. His left hand reached down to his coat pocket and he felt the pouch that Rebekah had given him those fifteen years ago. It never left his pocket. He took it everywhere with him as it was his only connection left with Rebekah.

As he grasped the pouch, ready to take it out, Solomon, as if reading Elwin's mind turned and looked at him in the eye and shook his head no. Elwin was shocked that the wizard seemed to know what he was thinking and even seemed to know about the pendant Rebekah had given him! He withdrew his hand from his pocket. He felt powerless to do anything to protect Siv from the evil that was descending upon her.

CHAPTER LVII
WILD GOOSE CHASE

To the north of the Mystic Forest, at the southernmost part of the wastelands, they found it. Olaf stood looking down over it. None of the elves spoke. Ciarra's abandoned and broken bassinet lay strewn over rocky ground, as though it had been dropped from some height. This was a particularly difficult time for Olaf as this was the last link he had to his daughter.

Olaf bent over and picked up her blanket and held it to his face. He could still smell his daughter's scent. Tears welled up within him, but he held it all inside. He felt anger, but he kept that inside as well. He needed to be decisive and make good decisions. He needed to find Ciarra. He feared what they would find next.

Grief-stricken, Olaf huddled with William and Johann. "We need to make the right moves. I fear for my daughter's life. I fear the next thing we will find is her body strewn among the rocks. How can I return to Ryanne with that news?" He turned to Johann and said, "Johann, you have chased the goblins to this point. It is the same direction as the eagle flew, and now we find evidence of Ciarra being brought this way. What is happening? We were deliberately attacked, but by whom? Did you find any clues along the way?"

"None, my lord. The only thing that is apparent is that hordes of goblins surrounded Nauren and attacked. They broke off the final attack and we chased them here, where it appears they headed deep into the forest. There is no sign of any other force being involved."

Olaf considered what Johann had said and then turned to William. "What do you have to tell me, William?"

"Although only goblins were present during the assault on Nauren, it appears that other creatures were involved in the assault on you and your family, Olaf. The eagle taking the bassinet and dropping it here clearly points to a more cerebral attack than what the goblins could muster. I believe it is all connected and that the goblins were a tool used for a higher purpose. That purpose appears to be the abduction of the princess. Why they would want the princess is beyond my ability to understand at this point in time."

"What did your sentries find to the north and east of Nauren?" Olaf asked as he considered William's words.

"They reported in this morning. Nothing was seen to the north or east to the volcano. All appeared quiet. They did confirm that there had been a recent visit to the eastern outpost, but there was little in the way of clues as to who, what, or when that site was visited other than it appeared to be recent. The sentries scoured the area and covered as much ground as they could. As you know, our numbers are limited due to the events of the night before last, but there is no indication of anyone or anything to the north or to the east. Given the magnitude of the attack, it is hard to conceive that any significant force could have come from or escaped in that direction."

"Thank you, William," Olaf began, "but let us not discount

what Siobhan told us: We were being watched from the east. And let us remember what Elijah told Siobhan: Evil is brewing in Lavendelle. I have to consider why there was such a significant attack on Nauren to the south and to the west. The only logical conclusion I can come up with is that the evil force we were coming up against was small and needed to draw our strength away from their objective: Princess Ciarra. But why would they want the princess? I do not have an answer for that.

"William, you must return to Nauren and keep your sentries on the lookout. You must keep your elves searching to the north and to the east but concentrate on the east where the sentry outpost is located.

"Johann, you and I will continue our push forward. I have no clue as to Ciarra's location other than to follow the flight of the eagle. This bassinet confirms that we are either on the right track or we are being led into a trap. Either way, we must move forward. I promised Ryanne that I would return with Ciarra. I plan to keep that promise." Olaf turned to William and handed him the bassinet and blanket. "William, when you return to Nauren, take this bassinet and blanket with you. I want to show the elves of Nauren that we are on the trail of Ciarra—and we don't plan to return without her!"

CHAPTER LVIII
NORTHERN ROUTE

EVENING was settling in and no elves had been seen in over two hours. Prior to this, the elves had been scurrying around, carefully searching the area. It was no use; Cael had scouted out the perfect retreat that would keep them invisible.

The clock continued to tick down. They had just two nights left. Cael knew if they did not have Princess Ciarra in the Chamber of the Gatekeeper by the time he came the following night, all this risk would be for naught. They would never get Malkavic; the elves would hunt them down once they figured everything out, and he was sure they would figure it all out. And this human with the sword would probably finish them off first!

"We must be moving soon," Cael began. "It is over a day and night's travel to the volcano, and then you only have a little time left to get this baby down to the Chamber of the Gatekeeper. I will help you with the baby to that point, but after we reach the volcano, you will be on your own."

This had been the agreement among the three. Cael and Finn were not interested in any treasure that Drake was seeking. They were interested in escaping from Drake and for Malkavic to return and hold the attention of the wizards. Then they could go on living undisturbed, offering their sacrifices, practicing their art, and living in their remote corner of the world, seldom visited by others.

Clearly, now that Elijah was head of the Wizard Council, things were going to change. It was apparent from what they had witnessed at the tower when Elijah had returned, that the tower was going to once again be established as a seat of power for the wizards. That was too close to their operation in the Mystic Forest, and certainly they would be under heavy scrutiny. With all that they had pilfered out of the tower under Demetrius' watch, they didn't need any wizards looking around. A lot of what they had taken appeared to be lost in the fire, but they hadn't had time to sift through the rubble.

"I think it is imperative that we put time and distance between us and Nauren. Certainly, the elves will figure everything out once they have time to consider all that has happened. Once they do, they will return to this area with many more elves and study it very carefully. This looks to be the only time when we can get away unseen. The elves they sent this way have cleared the area. It is time for us to depart," Finn said, emphasizing what Cael had been saying.

"I have not seen any disturbance for over an hour. I agree that the time to move is now," Drake said, convinced by what he had heard. "We will have to travel all night if we are to arrive at the volcano on time."

"Let us cover our tracks as best we can so if the elves stumble upon this site it won't look like anything more than a bunch of animals has been here. It is especially important that we hide any signs of the baby," Cael added.

"You just take care of that one and keep her quiet! We cannot afford any cry or noise or those elves will be on us and we will have to fight our way out." Drake shot a warning glance at Cael. "Finn and I will cover our tracks As soon as we do this, we need to head out," Drake said. He was clearly in charge of the group.

"I believe all the elves who came through here headed south. If we stay to the north, we should be all right. It is a longer distance to the volcano, but there should be less traffic. The terrain, though rough, should be our friend as it will be easy to hide our retreat, and it is doubtful the elves will come this way unless they find a clue that leads them to us. If that happens, we will be on higher ground and know about their approach well in advance. We will have enough time to mount some kind of defense!" Cael had clearly given this a lot of thought.

Finn and Drake hid any evidence of their stay, and then the three took the northern route to the volcano. The terrain was treacherous, but as they climbed, they could see that they had not been followed. This was the same route Drake had taken on his first journey. Everything had come full circle. Drake was no longer the same person he had been prior to entering this world and prior to possessing the cursed sword of Aelhaeran. No, indeed, he had become possessed by the evil of the sword.

Drake thought to himself about the plan; it had worked to near perfection. Their only hope had been to remain undetected; otherwise, the whole plan was doomed. The fact that they had not been seen nor heard gave Drake great confidence that everything was about to succeed. He could already count the treasure. He couldn't wait to see Roarke's face. He would return a king and show everyone who had thought him nothing more than an orphan peasant that he had become someone—someone quite different than the man he had been just a few days earlier. He gripped the sword that was now a permanent fixture at his side—the sword that was a curse to anyone who bore it. So said its maker: Aelhaeran!

Chapter LIX
Final Instructions

Siv, Teige, Ramsey, Elijah, Demetrius, Yuri, Elwin, and Markus were all gathered at Martha and Markus' home. It had been decided that the three dwarves would head out that very night. The three young dwarves were there to get their final instructions and say perhaps their last good-byes.

"I don't want you to go, Siv," Elwin said as he looked at his daughter. "You're all I have in this world. We can hide from Malkavic; he won't be able to reach us here."

"I must go, Father. I believe I am the only hope for the princess. I know that you say we can escape Malkavic, but we don't know that! I can't live in a world of oppression, the likes of which we have never seen, knowing all the time that I had an opportunity to prevent it. I refuse to live that way!"

"You are so brave." Elwin embraced his daughter.

"I am not brave; I am afraid. I am very afraid! I am afraid for my family, for my friends, but I am even more afraid for the princess. Her life will surely end tomorrow night without my help, and I can't have her blood on my hands!"

It was as if Elwin and Markus were seeing Siv for the first time. They saw her as Yuri had seen her since he first met her. She was no longer a child but a blossoming young adult with a mature way of thinking about the world. When had this transformation happened, they wondered.

It wasn't just Markus and Elwin but Elijah too. How had he missed seeing these qualities in Siv during all his travels? He had seen her, spoken to her; he knew her family, yet he had missed everything. Elijah didn't feel like much of a wizard on this evening, let alone the leader of the wizards.

"You have until tomorrow evening to get to the Chamber of the Gatekeeper! When the moon disappears completely, the Gatekeeper comes and moves across the land. It is when he first appears that the exchange for Princess Ciarra will be made! Solomon, when he first approached the Gatekeeper, met him just as he was appearing from his lair. He told me of his journey to the chamber in the abyss. I will tell you how to get there. I have drawn a map of the tunnels as I remember them from when I visited the volcano. As you see here, if you continue to go to the right and follow the tunnels deep into the volcano, you will come to a massive chamber. This is the chamber Malkavic occupied, and this is where I went to retrieve the prophecy. This is not the way to go! You will be trapped by goblins, I fear, if you travel this way."

Siv listened intently. She did not want to miss a single word for fear she might overlook some piece of information that would be vital to the success of her mission.

"You must head left and downward," continued Elijah. "You will reach a large hole in the earth; it will open up before you. That is the way to the abyss. There is a stony path that winds and winds down the walls of the pit. There is only one path like this in the entire volcano. If you find yourself going down into the abyss as I have described, you have found where you need to go! If you look up, all light will disappear above and only the glow of molten lava, flowing at the base of the pit, will guide your path. Once you get to the bottom of the path, follow the narrow path to where it widens and opens into the grand chamber. This will be the Chamber of the Gatekeeper."

Ramsey and Teige exchanged anxious looks. Were they really going to do this? Enter the Chamber of the Gatekeeper? It seemed so unreal. Siv gently nudged them both and brought them back to reality as Elijah continued to explain exactly what they must do.

"Once you arrive at the chamber, you will be on your own. The Gatekeeper will appear once a giant stone is rolled away to reveal the gate. You will most likely find whoever took Princess Ciarra down there too at some point; either they will arrive before you, or they will come after you. They will have the princess with them. They won't be expecting you! Remember that the Gatekeeper is without form and only comes once the stone is rolled back! I do not know what you will be able to do. I do know that the prophecy discussed the three of you and your journey to save the princess. Solomon's appearance tonight has validated the prophecy. I have not seen him since he disappeared in the upper chamber all those years ago. He did tell me that he would always be with us. I thought I felt him guiding me in the past; now I know those feelings were true."

Elijah then turned to Siv and looked directly into her eyes as he spoke. "If Solomon has chosen you, Siv, and you two as well, Teige and Ramsey, then who is anyone to stand in your way? You need to get to the chamber. That is the most important task on hand. Once you are there, the rest is up to you. It would be my suggestion to find a way to retrieve the princess and flee as fast as your feet can carry you! It is important for the three of you to get to the tower by morning. The only way that is possible is to fly on the back of Fallon. Fallon will deliver you there by first light. The keeper of the tower is Siobhan," Elijah said.

He looked at Demetrius to let the words settle with him. He had not gone over this with Demetrius prior to this, but these were desperate times and Demetrius would have to understand. They could discuss it all later. Demetrius looked at Elijah and nodded his head slightly. The relief in Demetrius was substantial, but Elijah would not have been able to detect it. It was next to impossible to know what a wizard was thinking, even for other wizards.

Elijah continued, "Siobhan will know I sent you when you arrive on the back of Fallon for he belongs to her. She knows I came here for you. She is a wizard and she will guide you. You must give her a message from me. She is to see to it that the three of you get on the boat to cross the Lake of the Serpent and get to the other side before the afternoon is over, or you will not have time to reach the Chamber of the Gatekeeper. Once on the other side, you will be at the base of the volcano. The goblins will not welcome you, trust me. Do not waste time on the ones you come across; cut them down for they will surely do the same to you if given the chance. It is my belief that you will be met with minimal resistance. Most of the goblins are most likely still away from the tower and fleeing a pursuing force of elves. I don't think they will have time to worry about the three of you!"

The idea of the Lake of the Serpent put fear into Teige and Ramsey. If Siv felt anything but resolution to see this through, no one in the room could see it.

"Siv, Teige, and Ramsey already have weapons. They have their heavy throwing axes and daggers. You cannot go unarmed, even if you don't know how to wield a weapon. I want you to have

Siobhan escort you to the upper chamber. From that chamber you will be able to look out across the lake and see the volcano. All of you will gain perspective of what lies ahead as you look out at the volcano.

"In the upper room, Siv, there is the prophecy sitting out on the table by the fireplace. I left my dagger on top of the prophecy. It has a green emerald on its pommel. I want you to retrieve this dagger and keep it at your side. The dagger is enchanted and will glow when you get to the volcano. The green emerald can cast almost a blinding light at times, for its fire comes from within. You may find that the light from this dagger will help you find your way as you pass down the abyss."

Demetrius recalled the dagger from the remotest part of his memory. He considered what Elijah was telling Siv. He wondered if this dagger could be a key to everything that was to happen.

As Fallon rested, Demetrius and Elijah secured three sheets around the great bird's chest. These sheets were all that the small dwarves would have to hold on to during the long flight to the tower. They said their good-byes and were loaded up on Fallon's back. They were so small in comparison to the great bird. They could hardly be noticed.

Elijah seemed to be communicating with Fallon as he stroked the giant condor's head. The two of them seemed to come to an understanding as Elijah stepped back.

"Safe travels," Elijah said as he took one last look at the three dwarves. With that, Elijah looked at Fallon and raised his arm and pointed in the direction of the tower. The giant bird took flight with great speed.

Fallon and the three dwarves were quickly out of sight, lost in the night sky. Elijah, Demetrius, Yuri, Elwin, and Markus all stood silently as the three flew away, each lost in his own thoughts.

Elijah thought about his position. He was Head of the Wizard Council, he knew all that was about to happen, and yet here he was in Bradán, and he had no influence left in the outcome of the confrontation that was to take place in one day's time.

As he reflected on this, he remained amazed at how accurate Solomon's vision had been. How could Solomon have known of the limited role the wizards would play on this most important night—perhaps the most important night in Lavendelle since the wizards took Malkavic?

chapter lx
uncertainty

Siv was up front, wrapped in the sheet that held her tight
against the great bird. The crisp night air felt comforting against
her face. She tried looking down, but when she did, she experienced a wave of nausea at the dizzying height. She closed her eyes
and tried to forget all the pressure that burdened the three young
dwarves. Soon, the rhythm of Fallon's wings stroking through the
night sky and the sound of the wind whipping over her drew her
into sleep. She was followed shortly thereafter by Ramsey and
Teige.

The light of the sun peeking across the horizon greeted her
as she opened her eyes. At first, she couldn't remember where she
was or what she was doing. She tried to move, only to find herself
tethered down. Gradually, the events of the evening wandered
back into her consciousness and she realized this was not all just a
bad dream.

This was the most important day of her life. Would it come
to define her life for the rest of time, or would this be the last day
she walked Lavendelle? For all her gift of vision and of foresight,
it failed her today, the day she needed it most. In fact, she could
not see anything beyond today, and that frightened her. She knew

without a doubt that she had to see this through. She knew it when Elijah spoke; she knew that Elijah had come for her before he even began speaking. She had tried to hide in her father's arms, but it was no use. This was her time, her responsibility, and she needed to answer the call. Seeing Solomon sealed her fate. There was no looking back.

Siv looked behind her and saw that her cousins were still sleeping. She peered down to the ground below; they were amazingly high in the sky. She looked east but could not see the tower. She could, however, see the volcano, and she convinced herself she was seeing the massive lake, but she wasn't completely sure. How much longer, she wondered.

As the sun gained altitude in the morning sky, the coolness and crispness of the night air began to recede. Ramsey and then Teige soon joined Siv in her reflection on the upcoming events of the day. The tower came into view and Siv knew it would not be long before they arrived. Siv was amazed at the steadiness and strength of this great condor. She would never forget this time in her life.

"That looks like the tower ahead," Teige called anxiously over the wind as he covered his eyes from the bright morning light.

"I agree," Ramsey joined in. "It won't be long now."

Fallon dipped into a rapidly descending glide with his wings stretched out. The three young dwarves stared over their tether-sheets to see the tower rising before them. They watched as someone came out to observe their descent.

"That must be Siobhan," Siv said.

"Indeed," Teige replied.

Fallon came to a gentle landing and Siobhan approached. "How was your flight? I have been expecting you."

"That was the most amazing thing I have ever experienced in

my life," Ramsey said as he bounded down off the great bird.

"I totally agree!" Teige said excitedly. The brothers jumped so quickly to the ground with their packs and weapons that Siobhan didn't have time to instruct Fallon to let them down gently.

Siv stayed put. She was perched at the highest point of the condor and hadn't decided how she was going to negotiate getting down.

Siobhan put her hand on Fallon's neck, and the great condor lowered itself down, allowing Siv an easy exit. Once down, Siobhan removed the sheets and released the bird for a much-needed rest.

"I am Siobhan, the caretaker of this tower. Elijah told me to expect you three this morning."

"I am Teige, and this is my brother Ramsey," the young dwarf said excitedly. Ramsey waved to Siobhan at the mention of his name.

Siobhan turned to Siv and said, "And whom might you be?"

"I am Siv, and these two are my cousins."

Siobhan looked at Siv; she was not what Siobhan was expecting. Siv was young, tall and slender, petite, and did not look like the type to be attacking anything. The other two dwarves were perhaps more than she hoped for; they were clearly energetic, athletically built, and had a very sturdy appearance about them. She hoped Elijah knew what he was doing.

"Come in and let me get you all something to eat. I have prepared something for you as you have a long journey ahead of you today!"

Siobhan turned and walked into the tower, which was still missing its front door thanks to Elijah.

After the dwarves had straightened the kinks out of their bodies and filled their bellies, Siv said to Siobhan, "Elijah mentioned to us that you would help us cross the Lake of the Serpent and get to the volcano."

"Yes, Siv, that is correct. You have a little bit of time before you need to be on your way, but not much. You all need to prepare yourselves," Siobhan replied.

"Have you ever been there?" Teige inquired. "I mean to the volcano?"

"No, Teige, I have not. I am sorry I won't be able to offer you much in the way of insight when it comes to what you will find over there. Elijah has been there, and all of the wizards went once many years ago, but there hasn't been a need to return until now. It is not a desirable place, as you can imagine."

"Elijah wanted us to look out at the volcano from the upper chamber room. I believe that is what he called it," Ramsey told Siobhan.

"Yes, I think that is a marvelous suggestion. Let me show you up there now!"

"Siobhan," Siv began, "Elijah also mentioned to us that he left the prophecy on a table by the fireplace."

"That is correct; it still sits where he left it."

"He also mentioned to me that there is a dagger with an emerald at its pommel and that it sits on top of the prophecy. He told me that he wanted me to take that dagger with me when we leave for the volcano."

Siobhan thought about what Siv said. If Elijah wanted Siv to have the dagger, then she would see to it that Siv had it. "We will look for it now, Siv. Let us go. I believe Elijah said something about that to me as well."

Siobhan escorted the dwarves to the upper chamber. The more she considered the three visitors, the more she felt concerned for them. Granted the two male dwarves were stout and looked to be good choices for the journey, but even still, she did not see how they had much of a chance of success assaulting the volcano and going up against the Gatekeeper.

The more she thought about Siv, the more her concern grew for the child. She was small and delicate and had a mild manner, almost timid. Siv had to be the least among the dwarves. In fact, Siv hardly resembled a dwarf.

She didn't blame Siv for being there. It was not Siv's idea. It was up to Elijah to choose who was to forge ahead. Siobhan respected the prophecies of Solomon; he was a legend. She had read the prophecy that Elijah had left behind. Solomon was clear that it would be three dwarves who stepped forward to save the princess. But Siobhan wasn't convinced that the princess had even been taken. Now, Elijah was acting on only partial information; there was no confirmation that Princess Ciarra had been taken, and he had chosen these three to approach the volcano and the Gatekeeper. Siobhan was amazed.

It was unlike Elijah to act so swiftly and without all the facts needed to make good, informed decisions. In her opinion, his second irrational act was to choose Siv to assault the volcano. Now, Siobhan felt that she, herself, was a party to Elijah's eccentric acts because she was facilitating the actions Elijah had set into motion. She still doubted that they were living out Solomon's prophecy.

Elijah was too close to Solomon and his prophecy, she thought to herself. The fact that Elijah had written half of the prophecy for Solomon only proved that he had waited nearly a millennium for the prophecy to unfold. Now, Elijah had convinced himself that he was right. Moreover, the more she thought about what Elijah had told her about her actions being a mistake by abandoning Nauren the more she questioned his criticism as well.

She had never before doubted Elijah. He was held in esteem by all those on the Council, by her grandfather before her, and, indeed, by herself all these years. Yet, what if Elijah was wrong? She had come to him for help at the bidding of Olaf. Olaf was a strong, considerate leader. She had concurred with Olaf. She had come as swiftly as she could to bring Elijah and his wisdom back to help Nauren, and how had Elijah responded?

Looking at the situation from an outside perspective, Siobhan felt that Elijah's actions could perhaps be viewed as irrational in Nauren's time of need, not hers. Instead of going immediately to Nauren, Elijah flew to Bradán and chose these three to return and assault the volcano. What did any of that have to do with helping the elves?

All of the actions Elijah had taken were because he was convinced that he was living in the times of the prophecy foretold by Solomon. She had read what Solomon wrote and remained unconvinced.

She did not know what the outcome would be for the three dwarves Solomon wrote about in his prophecy. She was fairly certain that the outcome for the three dwarves in front of her would not be good. What she did feel was that Elijah had acted swiftly and decisively without a full grasp of what was happening to Nauren. He had made a huge assumption that Princess Ciarra had been taken when there was not even the remotest suggestion that the princess had been the target of the attacks on Nauren. In fact, the focus of the attacks appeared to have something to do with the temple, not the princess.

Instead of returning to Nauren as requested by Olaf, Elijah had fled to the dwarves. There he had selected Siv to lead the charge against the Gatekeeper. Nothing made sense. Either Elijah was making a big mistake, a mistake that may jeopardize his position on the Council, or he was making a brilliant move, the only move he could make to save the princess. Siobhan did not know which was true. It was neither her time nor her place to challenge Elijah. She must do her part to support Elijah's leadership and help see his plan through. Otherwise, she would be the one who would carry the burden of the criticism of the Council. Moreover, she had always believed in Elijah. It was the pressure of the times and of the unknown that made her question everything.

They arrived at the upper chamber. "Siv, there is the dagger; come let us look at it."

Siobhan took Siv over to the table. Meanwhile, Teige and Ramsey went to the window to look at their objective for the day. They had to scoot a chair over to the window to stand on it and see out.

"That is a big lake, Teige," Ramsey said.

"It will take the better part of the day to get across it, let alone down into the volcano," Teige replied.

"I will be able to help you get across." Siobhan had overheard their conversation.

"I hope so," Teige started. "I don't know how we will be able to do it without your help."

Siobhan turned her attention to Siv. "Look here, Siv. Let us tie this dagger in its scabbard to your waist. See how it hangs there? Now you will have quick access to it the moment you need it."

Siobhan had quickly and masterfully suspended the dagger from a makeshift belt at Siv's waist. It was comfortable at her side.

It was positioned just inside her cloak. It did little in Siobhan's mind to make Siv look any more intimidating. In fact, it only made her appear even more out of place.

"Siv, come over here and look at where we are going," Teige said as he waved her over.

Siv hopped up on the chair and looked out the window. It was a long way! She looked down at the base of the tower and pointed. "Look! There are the boats, just like Elijah told us."

Teige looked and Ramsey pushed his way to the window to see as well. "I don't see them," they both said. "Where are they?"

Siv looked again and pointed, "Right there, plain as day! I can't believe you two can't see them."

Siobhan was intrigued. How could this little one see the boats? It wasn't until Elijah had opened her eyes that she had seen them herself. But there was no time to waste; it was time to send these three on their way or their journey would be for naught.

"Siv is right, there are boats down there. Let me get you all down there so that you can be on your way. Time is of the essence."

With Siobhan's words, all three of them felt the gravity of the situation. They stared at the volcano, and the impact of what they were about to attempt hit them all hard. They were not quick to move; they felt the weight of it all come crashing down on them. Siobhan looked at the three, and she understood that they all realized the enormity of the mission they faced. She felt great compassion for them, but she was surprised because before she could speak herself, Siv stood up and addressed her cousins.

"Come on, guys, we didn't come this far to quit before we even began. That poor baby is out there with evil forces. She is being taken to the very heart of that volcano as we speak. If she is going to be there, I will make sure she won't be there alone. We are her only hope. Either we save her or we go down trying!" Siv had hoisted the dagger above her head to emphasize her final words.

Siobhan was shocked. There was clearly more to this dwarf than met the eye. She had hoped that her initial criticism of Elijah's selection was wrong. She decided to wait and see what transpired.

Siobhan took them the secret way out to the lake, and after helping Ramsey and Teige see the boats, she helped them onto the smallest of the three vessels. She gave them some food and filled their flasks. Then Siobhan raised her hands over the waters. She told Ramsey to cast out the lines in front of the boat. He did so as Siobhan uttered a spell. The lines became taut and the boat began to move with great swiftness toward the volcano.

Siobhan watched them as they sped away. Teige and Ramsey looked back at her; Siv, however, stood at the bow of the boat with her eyes focused forward. There is so much more to this dwarf than was apparent on meeting her, Siobhan thought to herself. So much more indeed.

CHAPTER LXI
TRAIL GOES COLD

IT was mid-day the next day when they came upon it. There were still small pockets of material smoldering into the ground. Clearly, a home had burned to the ground.

"What do you make of it, Olaf?" Johann inquired.

"I would say we have been on the right path. This has recently burned, and there is a good chance it has to do with Ciarra since we followed her back this way. Who do you think lived here?" Olaf inquired.

"I think William would be a better one to answer that question; he has all the sentries and patrols. I do not know who was out here, but it is clear to me that whoever it was did not want to be discovered. They left no trace."

"How long ago do you think this burned?" Olaf asked.

"Near as I can tell, it is several days old. It may have burned over a week ago. I don't know how much that helps. All I can tell you is that it was a complete burn. There is nothing left to even give us a hint of who was here."

"Well, we won't know until we are able to put all the pieces together."

Johann and Olaf watched as one of the young scouts approached. "I think the goblins have scattered. We chased them this far, but it looks like they have broken up into small groups again."

"Where do you think they went?" Johann asked his scout.

"It looks like most of them are headed in the direction of the volcano."

Olaf thought about what they had found. They had not found any answers this way, just a smoking house that had been demolished up to a week prior. The goblins were disbanding, so clearly they had lost their leadership. The goblins were headed back in the direction of the volcano, so they were no longer needed. Their mission had been accomplished.

"I see no reason to chase down the goblins to the volcano, Johann."

"I agree with you, but what should we do next?"

"I feel as though we are at a dead end. It may serve as valuable information at a later point in time, but I do not believe we will find my daughter if we pursue this route any longer. I am at a loss. We must find Elijah; he is our only hope now. How far is the tower from here, Johann?"

"If we travel swiftly, we should be able to reach the tower by early evening. But is this the right way to go? Wasn't Siobhan sending Elijah back to us?"

"That is true, Johann, but we never encountered Elijah on our way here. I do not know where he is at this moment. If he returned to Nauren, I feel as though he will do everything in his power there to save Ciarra. If we find him at the tower, perhaps he will be able to guide us in the right direction and even come with us to find her!" Olaf held out great hope for Elijah; he trusted and respected the wizard deeply. Elijah had always been there for him, for his family, and for the elven community; he had never wavered, and he had never failed them.

"Elijah, I am sure, assumed we would be able to defend ourselves from the siege that was upon us. Perhaps he felt it unnecessary to come to Nauren to aid us. In fact, he may be working on finding out who was behind the attacks and dealing with them even as we speak. There is no way he could know about the princess because Siobhan left before Ciarra was taken!"

"Well, let us waste no more time!" Johann said. "To the tower we must go—with haste!"

As evening settled in, Siobhan stood by the window in the upper chamber. She had been watching for some time, watching for any indication of the dwarves' movements. She found herself putting her hope in Siv. Clearly, on first meeting Siv, she had underestimated the little dwarf. It was now interesting how all her hopes seemed to rest with the young dwarf. She could not understand how Siv could have seen the boats and the paths below. Siv had said that she received no spell from Elijah, only good wishes. There was something about this little dwarf that captivated her.

Siobhan turned away from the window and began pacing in the upper chamber. She had been doing this on and off again for hours. It was difficult for her to sit by and do nothing. Yet, here she was, relegated to the tower. Her days of wandering were temporarily over. Hopefully, she could get clarification at the next Council meeting. She longed to go with the dwarves, but it was not her place or time. If she had tried, and the prophecy was correct, and they were actually living in the times of the prophecy as Elijah believed, she would not make it to the volcano.

Siobhan wandered to the west-facing window to look out in the direction of Elijah and the home of the dwarves. She wished he would return soon. She should have sent Fallon back after him, but the bird had been worked hard, and it would be impossible for the bird to retrieve Elijah in time anyway.

At first, she couldn't believe what she was seeing. It looked as though fifty or sixty elves were storming the tower. It didn't make any sense. As she watched, Olaf clearly came in to view. Siobhan rushed out of the upper chamber and down to the entrance of the tower to greet him.

When she reached the front entrance, the elves had lined up across the courtyard and only Olaf approached. Upon seeing him, Siobhan ran out and met Olaf on the steps. They embraced each other. "What brings you here, Olaf? I thought you would remain in Nauren."

"Where is Elijah, Siobhan? We all must talk!"

"Elijah is not here. He had a mission. He is one, perhaps two days from here, but he is headed back. What is happening? Is Nauren all right?"

"Can we step inside, Siobhan? We need to talk."

Siobhan escorted Olaf into the sitting area of the antechamber located just outside the great meeting hall. Siobhan brought something for Olaf to drink, and then she waited.

"The goblins, as you know, attacked again from the west when you were leaving. Did you see anything or any other creatures when you flew this way to get Elijah?"

"No, Olaf, there was nothing between Nauren and the tower. We flew up high and very fast, but I did not see anything. What happened that caused you to leave Nauren?"

"Siobhan, I have grave news. Princess Ciarra has been taken from Nauren!"

Siobhan's heart caught in her throat. Elijah had been right! He had acted swiftly. Had he not acted when he did, according to the prophecy, Ciarra would be gone for good this night, and Malkavic would return to oppress all Lavendelle. How could Elijah have known? How could she have had such a hardened heart despite reading the prophecy with her own eyes? How could she have even questioned Elijah, the one wizard she had held in such high esteem her whole life?

The thoughts raced through her mind as Olaf continued speaking, but she was deaf to his words. Her spirit was crushed. How could she even call herself a wizard? Despite all her self-doubt and self-reproach, she just sat there as though she was hearing every word out of his mouth and feeling every emotion he was feeling with him.

"Olaf, explain to me, once again, what happened. This time more slowly."

"Siobhan, it is as I said. The goblins were merely a distraction to draw our defenses away. We countered their attacks from the south and the west, drawing our defenses in these directions. Once we were out of position, they came in and stole Ciarra away from the upper room of my home!"

"Who are they, Olaf?"

"I don't know, Siobhan. The same forces you discovered controlling the eagle a few nights ago apparently used the same eagle to steal away with Ciarra in her bassinet. Although I am not so sure the bird ever had her. We found the bassinet and Ciarra's blanket scattered among the rocks at the southern part of the wastelands, but there was no sign of Ciarra. Then we followed the goblins deep into the forest; however, they reached a freshly burned home and then scattered. We lost the trail and came to find help from you and Elijah."

Olaf hung his head once he had finished speaking. Unlike Siobhan, Olaf's emotions were palpable.

She remained in shock at all she had heard. Elijah was clearly wise beyond her years and her wisdom. Never again would she doubt. Never again would she question. She resolved herself to serve Elijah as Head of the Wizard Council. Thankfully, she had followed Elijah's instructions when she saw the dwarves off.

"Olaf, there is something you need to see. It is something Elijah just discovered when he left Nauren last. He shared it with me just two nights ago before he left for Bradán."

Olaf raised his head and just looked at Siobhan. Why would Elijah go to Bradán with Nauren under siege? Nothing made sense anymore.

Siobhan escorted Olaf into the upper chamber of the tower.

Olaf bounded out of the tower and raced toward Johann.

"What is it, Olaf?" Johann inquired.

"It is the princess; she is being taken to the Chamber of the Gatekeeper in the depths of the volcano tonight! Quick! We must attack the volcano before all is lost. Kill any goblin you see! There will be no stopping us tonight!"

Hearing Olaf's orders, the elves sped off in the direction of the volcano. Siobhan watched from the upper chamber. There was nothing more that she could do. Everything was in motion, and it was just as Solomon had predicted. Siobhan had no idea what lay ahead. They were now at the point in the prophecy where Solomon's words had been destroyed by the fire.

Siobhan sensed that it was too late for Olaf. The evening was upon them, and the moon was just beginning to show above the horizon. The wizards were scattered and out of place. Siobhan now knew it was all up to Siv and her cousins. Everything was coming to pass just as it was written in the prophecy.

CHAPTER LXII
REALIZATION OF
THE PROPHECY

CAEL, Finn, and Drake rested outside the volcano. They were exhausted after a treacherous hike along the northern route to the volcano, but the trek had been worth the effort and time it took to get there.

Drake, though worn out, felt euphoric. He had come to Lavendelle in search of the unknown. He had found the sword and then developed a thirst for more treasure. He thought he had found that treasure when the goblins took him inside the volcano. Instead, he had found even more of a mystery. He was energized!

With careful planning, he had orchestrated a magnificent plan to perfection. He now sat on the precipice of success; he was sure to be rewarded for freeing Malkavic. He would return to Lindisfarne triumphant. He would return with unimaginable wealth. He could not wait to get back and share all his great fortune with Roarke!

There was no stopping him now. No one knew that they were even here. They had remained undetected throughout all they had done. No one had followed them during the night. They would succeed!

Evening was upon them. "How long will it take you to get to the chamber?" Cael asked as he fed Ciarra for perhaps her last feeding ever.

"I must be off as soon as you finish feeding the child," Drake said. "We sure cut it close taking that treacherous route to get here."

"Yes, but it was worth the effort," Finn said. "Not a soul knows that we are here or what we have done. I imagine the elves followed the eagle and the goblins all the way to the forest south of the wastelands. No one could be on to us, and even if they were, they will be too late to act!"

This was just as Drake believed himself.

"Are you two coming with me to the chamber?"

Both Finn and Cael felt a chill rush down their spines. "Master, we could not survive in the heat of that volcano. We would surely perish! We barely survived the last time we were in there with you, and now you are going to someplace even hotter than we were before!" Cael stated emphatically. "Besides, time is of the essence, and you are out of time. We would only hinder you."

"Who will look after the child?" Drake asked incredulously.

"It will have to be you, master. You will have to bundle the child and take her in the sling I gave you. I am feeding her now so that she will be healthy and strong when you offer her in exchange for Malkavic."

Drake drew his sword; he felt a new energy come over him. The ruby on the end of the sword had a faint glow. It was his time. Both Cael and Finn were filled with great anxiety at the appearance of the sword.

"Do you not want to share in the treasure that will surely be ours?" Drake asked.

"Our treasure is different than your treasure, master. Your success will offer us a great reward in and of itself. Why do you think we have been so eager for your journey? How do you think you made it to this point? It is because we have served you in every way possible since we first met. None of us could have pulled this off alone," Finn finished. He felt he needed to offer as compelling a story as he could just to spare his own life. Whenever Drake drew his sword, Finn always felt that Drake had it in for him. He felt no different this time.

"Master, the child has finished and is nodding off to sleep. I think it is time that you take her and be on your way!"

Drake looked at Cael and thought about what he had said. "You are right, Cael; it is now my time." With that, Drake returned the sword to its scabbard and with Cael's help, tucked the child carefully into the sling around his shoulder and neck. The child did not make a sound.

Drake turned and faced Finn and Cael as he said, "Until we meet again. We have made a good team. Perhaps we will again someday!"

Drake turned and walked to the entrance of one of the tunnels into the volcano. Because of his previous trek through the volcano he was fairly certain where he needed to go. Basically, he needed to go to the place all the goblins had avoided the last time he was here.

As he reached the tunnel entrance, he turned and looked down upon the two druids who were quickly fleeing. They were odd creatures indeed, he thought to himself. The night was upon him, and there was little time left for him to get to the chamber.

CHAPTER LXIII
INTO THE FIRE

THE afternoon was passing quickly. The boat had arrived at the shores of the volcano. The three dwarves hurried up the side of the massive mountain.

"Siv, there is no time. We must hurry. Can you keep up?" Ramsey was looking down at Siv as the three scaled the side of the volcano.

"I can keep up. You two are carrying most of the weight. Don't worry about me!"

Teige and Ramsey saw a gritty determination in her eye. There was no turning back. There wasn't even time to think about what they were doing. If there had been time to consider, they probably would all have second thoughts about moving forward.

Siv looked down at her new dagger; the emerald was beginning to glow, just as Elijah said it would. At least now she knew what Elijah meant when he said it was lit from within. Teige and Ramsey noticed it too.

"There is our light for the chamber," Teige pointed out.

"Yes, it is just as Elijah said," Siv added.

Ramsey pointed up to an area that flattened out ahead. "Let us get up to that spot, then we will be able to get our bearings straight and see where we can access the labyrinth of tunnels into the volcano."

Teige was the first to arrive, and he was met by three ghoulish-looking creatures the likes of which he had never seen before. These clearly had to be the goblins that Elijah had warned them about.

The three were on Teige faster than he could react. His axe was still strapped to his back.

Siv had just climbed on to the clearing when she saw the attack on Teige. The three goblins had their backs to her, but Teige had a clear view of her. He was frightened, he was pinned down, and he feared for his life.

Siv pulled out her dagger. The blade glowed and a green light illuminated the area. One of the goblins turned to face Siv, but before the creature could make it all the way around, the dagger slashed its throat and the creature crumpled to the ground, spewing fluid from the wound in its neck.

Ramsey saw Siv in action as he arrived at the clearing. He reached for his axe, but he was much slower than Siv. She quickly moved to the goblin pinning Teige to the ground and buried the dagger to the hilt at the base of its neck. The goblin collapsed on top of Teige.

Siv then pulled out the dagger and rolled her body to the left, positioning herself between Teige and the last living goblin. She buried the dagger in the center of the goblin's chest and then pulled it out. Her arms were now covered with goblin blood. She turned and looked at Teige as she asked, "Are you all right, Teige?"

A weak "I am fine" was all he could muster. In the blink of an eye, he had gone from being pinned down by goblins determined to end his life, to watching his young, delicate cousin snuff out the lives of the three ghouls before either he or Ramsey could act.

Ramsey was equally speechless.

Siv looked at the two. She felt energy flowing from the dagger that she could not explain. She had trusted her feelings and saved Teige. She looked at Teige and then at Ramsey. "This is very real. I suggest you two pull out your weapons and be prepared. It is just as Elijah said: The goblins will kill us if we don't act first."

"It is as you say, Siv," Teige said as he pulled out his throwing axe. "Thank you for your help; I won't be caught unaware again."

They watched the sun dip below the horizon and knew their time was limited. "I believe if we follow this path, it will take us to the entrance to the tunnels," Ramsey stated as he looked up at the volcano. "I think that is why we met these goblins here; they were on their way to or from the volcano!"

"Let's get going!" Siv said. She took off with Teige and Ramsey scurrying behind her.

The path was steep, but the entrance to the tunnels was clearly visible ahead. The sun dipped deeper and deeper and darkness settled across the sky, but the light of the green emerald shone bright. Surprisingly, they did not encounter any further resistance before reaching the entrance to the tunnels.

When they reached the tunnel entrance, they were met with a blast of very hot air. It was going to be a hot, muggy trip to the chamber. The dwarves felt at home when they reached the tunnels. They had spent a good part of their lives mining the mountains back home. They felt like they were on their turf. They progressed forward slowly and found there was no option to go left. The tunnel veered to the right, and to the right they went.

"Thank goodness you have that dagger, Siv. It makes it so much easier to see," Teige whispered. There was a dull light along all the walls that their eyes would have grown accustomed to; however, the bright light from the dagger washed out the other light.

The tunnel widened when the attack came. Seven or eight goblins charged; it all happened so fast, the three couldn't count how many there were.

"Ramsey, look out!" Siv shouted. Just as she did, a goblin swung a heavy club at Ramsey's head. He never saw it coming. He crumpled to the floor and blood flowed from his scalp.

Siv jumped the goblin wielding the club at the same time Teige reacted. Teige nearly cleaved the goblin in half with one swing of his sharpened axe, whereas Siv had jumped on the goblin's shoulders, wrapped her left arm around its head, and twisted it hard to her left. At the same time, she took out the dagger with her right hand and sliced it across the goblin's neck. The goblin sank like a weight to the ground.

Teige turned and caught another goblin and dropped it. Siv cut another goblin down as well.

"Quick, Teige! They have Ramsey!" Siv said excitedly as she saw the four remaining goblins escaping down a tunnel. Siv took out her dagger and flung it at the fleeing goblins. It struck the last in the line in the center of its back. The goblin staggered one step before falling flat on its face and dying.

Siv quickly retrieved her dagger and looked at the area where they had been ambushed. There was a tunnel leading off to the left, and there was another to the right. She had seen them take Ramsey down the tunnel to the right.

Siv looked at Teige. "You must go after Ramsey! There is no time!" She reached down and picked up Ramsey's weapon and handed it to Teige.

"I fear he is dead, Siv, and I cannot lose both of you! I must go with you!"

"Teige, there is no time. Ramsey is alive; I feel it. You must go after him and save him."

Teige hesitated, unsure of what to do. If he went after his brother, it meant that Siv would be left alone. Surely, he thought, she would need his help if she had any hope of success. Siv realized she needed to do more to convince Teige to go.

"If I do not take this tunnel to the left, there will be no time to return and save the princess! I have seen this in my mind for all time, Teige. I cannot explain it to you, but I have known this would be my destiny for my entire life. Only now do I realize where I am and what my visions have been about. I must go after the princess and you must go after Ramsey. You can save him. We will meet back here when this is all over and we will get out of here together. I will need both of you to help me escape with the princess. But in my vision, I take this tunnel alone every time."

"Be careful, Siv, and thank you!" With that, Teige, with rage in his eyes and an axe in each hand, turned and raced down the tunnel after Ramsey.

CHAPTER LXIV
BROTHERS

THE goblins hadn't gotten far with Ramsey and their path was easy to follow thanks to the bleeding from Ramsey's scalp. Teige was enraged; he had been transformed. He thirsted for goblin blood. They had attacked and tried to kill his brother; now they would pay. He lost all objectivity as to the task at hand. He had a new mission: save his brother.

He hadn't given thought to the fact that the resistance they were meeting was relatively light as Elijah had thought. He had nothing to compare this with for he had never been here before. In fact, he had never really encountered goblins before.

He rounded a second bend in the tunnel when he came to a split in the path. His eyes were adjusting to the light in the tunnels, which was significantly less than the light Siv carried with the dagger.

He looked down and saw blood trailing off down the tunnel to the right. He thought he could hear them dragging Ramsey just up ahead and he quickly followed. He slowed his pace as he approached a sharp bend in the tunnel. He peered around the corner and saw more light shining from up ahead. He saw four goblins; one was on top of Ramsey shaking him. It was clear that Ramsey was coming back to consciousness. What Teige couldn't gauge was how many goblins were hidden behind the part of the wall where he could not see.

Thoughts rushed through his mind. What should he do next? It would be infinitely more helpful if Ramsey would wake up, for at the very least, his brother would be able to carry his own weight.

Teige scanned the area and considered his options. There were two tunnels leading out from this chamber. One appeared to head up and to the left, whereas the other seemed to head downward and farther into the volcano. If he could only free Ramsey and they could escape together, it would probably be easier going down until they could regroup and get a strategy to fight their way out.

Ramsey appeared lucid but confused. He was being held down by two goblins who looked unsure as to what to do with him. He continued to bleed from his scalp. Teige knew if he didn't stop the bleeding soon, Ramsey would be too weak to escape.

The time for action had come; Teige could not wait any longer. He could be discovered just sitting there, and then the two of them would have no hope. The thought sent chills down his spine, and he turned to look down the tunnel from which he had come. There was nothing back there.

He turned and focused all his attention on Ramsey. Ramsey looked in his direction, but if he saw Teige, he didn't acknowledge it. Teige took out Ramsey's throwing axe and aimed it at one of the two goblins holding Ramsey down. Teige felt confident that he could take the goblin out, for he was fairly accurate with an axe. He raised the axe, took aim, and flung it through the air. The axe found its home, easily splitting the skull of the goblin in two. The goblin collapsed on top of Ramsey.

There was a moment of confusion among the goblins, and

Teige made the most of it. He dashed across the cavern and swung his axe at the second goblin before it had time to react.

Ramsey saw Teige coming and summoned up surprising strength to twist himself free. He was on his feet as soon as Teige had taken the other goblin out. He pulled his axe from the skull of the slain goblin and turned to face the remaining creatures.

Teige grabbed his arm and quickly pulled Ramsey down the tunnel to the right. They ran like the wind, trying to escape the goblins they had left behind. It was clear they were being pursued.

"Ramsey, you need to go on ahead. I am going to have to drop in behind these creatures and take them out. There is no way we will be able to escape them; they know these tunnels too well. I will stay back as soon as we make that turn up ahead!"

"I got it," Ramsey said. It was hard for him to get his bearings straight as his head pounded and the blood continued to flow.

At the corner, Teige fell back into the recesses of the tunnel while Ramsey moved forward. Teige could hear the pursuers as they raced around the turn and appeared to be making ground on Ramsey. There were three of them and as soon as they made the turn, Teige's axe swung and caught the third goblin square in the forehead. The goblin collapsed to the ground.

The two pursuing goblins turned and faced Teige, their clubs at the ready. Teige pulled his axe from the fallen goblin and took aim at the one closest to him. He unleashed the axe, and it easily penetrated the chest of the approaching goblin.

Teige quickly reached for his dagger. It was not there and he found himself facing one goblin bare-handed. The goblin had a club and was closing fast. Before he could react, the goblin fell at Teige's feet. At first Teige did not understand what had happened, but then he saw the axe buried in the goblin's back and looked up.

He saw Ramsey coming up the tunnel after the last goblin.

"Nice shot, brother," Teige said. Then he ripped a strip of cloth from his sleeve and wrapped it around Ramsey's head to stem the flow of blood. The tourniquet seemed to work, but not without complaints from Ramsey about how tight Teige had tied it.

"Where is Siv?" Ramsey asked, fearing the worst.

"There was no time. You were injured, and I feared you were dead! Siv assured me you were alive and directed me to follow you. It is because of Siv you are alive right now!"

"But what happened to her?"

"She told me that she had to go ahead on her own. She said she had known this moment was coming all her life and that it was her destiny. Then she went to the Chamber of the Gatekeeper all alone."

"Wow," Ramsey said. This made his head spin even more.

"She said she would return and meet us back at the first branch in the tunnels. That is a long way back, and I fear there we will encounter many more goblins on our way back to her!"

"I fear for Siv," Ramsey said as he rubbed his head. "We need to make a plan and battle back. We need to get down to the chamber to help her. How can she do it all by herself? She needs us!"

Teige thought about what Ramsey said before he replied. "I don't know if that is true or not, Ramsey; what I do know is that we have needed her. She saved my life when we first encountered those three goblins. I never knew Siv was so skilled with a dagger! And now, she knew you were alive and sent me after you. I told her that I needed to stay with her, but she sent me after you. She was right, at least right about you. I can only hope she was right about herself and that she stays safe!"

"We need to find her, Teige. We need to get back to her as soon as possible!"

Chapter LXV
Deception

SHE was alone and felt it. She had always known it would come down to this when she heard Elijah speak of the need for a dwarf to save the princess. She was facing her deepest fear—a nightmare that had come to her over and over again as she was growing up. She had seen herself wandering down into the pit, covered in blood, and to the abyss too many times to recall. At least she now understood the source of the blood: goblins. She had always been alone, and that is why she had urged Teige to go after Ramsey. Neither Teige nor Ramsey was to be here with her.

Her nightmare always ended with her wandering down into the darkness below. She never stayed asleep long enough to know how the nightmare ended. She would always find herself waking in a cold sweat, too frightened to stay asleep. Well, today she would find out. She was afraid but displayed no fear. She was resolved to see this through to its conclusion. She would not be running out on the infant princess.

Siv followed the path to the left. She held the dagger out before her in her left hand. The green light was bright and it illuminated the path before her. She felt as though she had dropped down a hundred feet when the path opened up. There was a giant pit that appeared to be bottomless. She stood at the edge, looking down, just as she had in her dreams. There was no bottom in sight.

The walls were thirty feet apart. On the edge of the wall, she could see a stony path wind downward. There were no railings to hold on to. This was not a journey for the faint of heart. In her dreams, Siv did not recall the bright green light being present. She covered the end of the dagger and let her eyes adjust to the darkness. She could make out a faint glow rising from the depths of the pit—a pit that seemed to breathe fire. She really felt as though she were descending into the depths of Hades itself. She wasn't that far off in her thinking.

A small sliver of panic itched at the back of her mind. This was no place for an infant, let alone a princess. Siv placed her hand on her flask. She had plenty of water, and she would make sure that it stayed that way so that she could cool off the baby once she reached her.

She had no idea what lay ahead. A sense of time escaped her and she had no idea how soon the lunar event that would summon the Gatekeeper would take place. All she knew was that time was running out and she needed to be off.

She tested out the path. It seemed secure. She placed the dagger back in the scabbard on her hip and made sure the emerald stone was covered by her cloak. She pulled the hood over her head, covering her long and curly fiery red hair. She was a dwarf and could withstand the burning heat. She clung to the wall on her left as the path led ever downward, spiraling to the right. The steps were quite steep.

Siv moved forward as quickly as she could. The heat became almost overbearing, even for a dwarf. She put these thoughts out of her mind as she continued her descent. Her greatest fear was missing a step and stumbling over the side of the pit into an endless free fall. She was careful with every step, and this took more energy and time as she moved.

Her heart pounded and her breath came quicker as she proceeded. Her senses heightened and her vision sharpened. She took a moment to rest and peer over the edge. When she looked up, she could not see anything but blackness extending out for infinity. Next, she looked below to search for the faint glow that Elijah had said would be present. She sensed, more than saw, a glow in the far, far distance, but she could make out something else as well. A red light that seemed to be quite bright burned far below her. The light seemed to be wandering down the same path she was taking.

Siv's breath slowed and her heart nearly bounded out of her chest. This was new to her; she had never made it this far in her dream. This had to be the evil one who abducted the princess and, in fact, probably had the princess with him at this very moment! Well, she thought to herself, she had a strategic advantage for the moment. How could she use that to her favor? She would have to think about it as she pressed on.

It appeared to Siv that she was right on schedule. The Gatekeeper most likely hadn't appeared yet, and the princess was being carried to the chamber now. Siv reflected back on her decision to keep her dagger covered and realized it had been a good one. Thank goodness she had reflected on the memories of her dreams and realized that she had not seen a green light. She had always listened to her inner voice, and it had always served her well. Her pace quickened as she continued to descend.

Siv had been walking for nearly thirty minutes, and yet the path continued to pull her ever downward. It was going to be a long and grueling walk back to the top, she thought to herself.

She felt certain she would be triumphant, but in reality, she did not know what was about to transpire. She just remained positive, hoping things would work out.

She peered out again over the edge. The red light was no longer visible. The glow from below was stronger. The heat was unbelievable.

Finally, Siv reached the bottom of the pit. She looked around but did not see anyone or anything. She looked up and all she saw was darkness. She took down the hood of her cloak, revealing her long and wild red hair. She imagined she looked as though she belonged in this place with her fiery locks.

There was only one way to go, and it was a narrow path forward that was lined by molten lava on either side. She walked forward as the chamber opened up before her. She shrunk down and made herself as small as she could. She looked around to see where the red light she had followed down would be and who and how many others were down here with her. In the distance, she saw what looked like a man standing with a sword in his hand. The red light emanated from the large stone at the end of his sword, much the same way her dagger emitted light. Her mind instantly flashed back to the time she had been pinned down by the druids. This was the same man! She hoped that the man did not recognize her. Certainly, she now looked far different than when she had been covered from head to toe in paint and animal blood and her hair had been tied back.

She could see fairly well around the room. It was clear that the man had not yet seen her. She was also fairly certain that the Gatekeeper had yet to make an appearance. She didn't know what to expect when the Gatekeeper arrived, nor did she have any idea what the Gatekeeper would look like. For all that it mattered, the man standing before her could be the Gatekeeper himself, but she knew that it was not. The man was clearly waiting for someone. No one was expecting her, including the Gatekeeper!

At first, Siv didn't see her. She had looked, but there was no sign of Ciarra. But she heard the sound an infant would make, and she saw the man look down on his chest. She saw him touch the baby and the baby stopped stirring.

She needed to act fast, before the Gatekeeper arrived. That was her only hope of getting the baby. If the Gatekeeper got the baby first, there was little hope that Siv would ever see the child or be in a position to help her.

Siv looked around the rest of the room. There was a large stone wall at the other end of the chamber. Siv assumed correctly that this was the gate and this was where the Gatekeeper would make his appearance.

Siv considered her situation. She did not know what would happen next. She was fairly certain that the man standing across the chamber didn't know what to expect either.

The man was distracted by the baby, and Siv went with her gut. She stood up and walked toward the man. "I see you have brought the child. It has been a long time indeed."

Siv caught the man off guard. Drake looked at Siv and pointed his sword in her direction, which made her halt nearly fifteen feet from him.

"Who are you?" he asked. There was a familiarity about her, but Drake could not make the connection between the girl he was seeing now and the dwarf he had glimpsed fleeing from the druids.

"You come to my chamber, you bring the child, and now you threaten me with a sword? I can leave, and you will never get Malkavic back!" Siv said this as forcefully as she could. Inside, she was a bundle of nerves, barely able to hold herself together. To Drake, she looked supremely confident.

"You are the Gatekeeper? I find that hard to believe!"

"Whom did you expect to meet down here? I can take any shape or form I desire. The baby needs a comforter and needs to feel secure. I have plans for her. I did not come to frighten her!"

"How did you know I came with a baby? Did you follow me?"

Siv laughed the best she could. She had Drake's attention and he was clearly off balance. She had guessed correctly; he had no idea what to expect.

"Why would I follow you? I don't even know who you are. You are nameless and faceless to me. I haven't given you a thought before this moment, and when I return Malkavic to you, I will not think of you again. I want the child. Is she alive?"

"How do you know I have a child?" he repeated.

"If you don't have the child, then you have wasted my time and your life!" Siv pointed her finger aggressively at Drake. "No one has dared enter my chamber for over seven hundred and fifty years, not since Malkavic was delivered to me by Solomon's agents! I have been waiting patiently for this child, just as I promised I would. Now don't waste any more of my time and let me see this child!" Siv grasped the grip of the dagger in her left hand as she spoke. For whatever reason, she felt energized just by holding it. She could see Drake's eyes take in the emerald's green glow. "I need to see her now and that she is alive, or you will perish! You are out of time!" Siv unsheathed the dagger and its green light matched the intensity of the ruby on Drake's sword.

Something shocked Drake into action. Everything he was hearing was just as the prophecy had said. It was everything he had learned from the druids. This creature seemed knowledgeable and had a confident presence. She did not appear intimidated by him at all. Still, she was so small. He hadn't expected this. But she knew of Malkavic and no one else could have known for the prophecy had been here with the goblins all those years.

The light, the sword, Siv's authoritative command—it was hard to say what drove him—but Drake knelt down and rested his sword on the ground. He took the sling from his neck and presented the elven princess to Siv.

Siv looked down at the child. She was alive but looked limp and weak. She wouldn't last much longer in this heat. Siv reached out for the child but still clutched the dagger in her left hand. Drake was on his knee, holding her out with two hands for Siv. Siv's green eyes bore into Drake's and his stare matched hers in intensity. As she took the child, Drake held on too and said, "Where is Malkavic?"

As the two locked stares, a tremor shook the ground. Siv, never taking her eyes from Drake, took the dagger with her left hand and pointed toward the large stone gate that was beginning to roll aside. "Behold, I give you Malkavic!"

Drake released the infant to Siv's welcoming arms and stood up, facing the chamber door as it opened, fully expecting to see a jubilant Malkavic. He reached down for his sword in preparation to meet him.

Siv acted quickly. She took the child and fled to the back of the chamber. She put as much distance between her and the Gatekeeper as she could. She feared she had been too slow. The Gatekeeper was here, the baby was here, and now she had run out of time and out of places to hide. She had also run out of ideas!

Chapter LXVI
Olaf is Too Late

THE bright moon shone in the night sky, illuminating the way to the volcano. Olaf and his band of elves were at the base of the volcano, but it was bad news on many levels for him. Olaf's heart sank as he watched the moon slowly disappear as the lunar eclipse began. He had not been there for his daughter and he was powerless to save her. This only made his resolve stronger. He had fifty of his strongest elves with him. He had to attack the volcano.

Unfortunately for Olaf, the goblins were ahead of him, and many had reached the volcano first. As soon as the elves began to charge, they met massive resistance by several hundred goblins and were forced to retreat.

"Olaf, we will be unable to withstand them if they attack. There are too many!" Johann shouted in his retreat.

"Johann, look at that ridge up ahead. We need to take defensive positions behind that ridge. If we spread out, we can cut them down with our arrows before they are upon us!"

Johann spread the word, and the elves headed for the ridge. They took their positions and let the arrows fly. They were able to push back the whole-scale attack of the goblins, at least temporarily. The goblins had nowhere to retreat; the volcano was their home.

This time, it looked as though the battle would be to the death.

Olaf crept along the ridge and encouraged his elves to stay strong as he passed each one. His heavy heart ached for his daughter, his wife, and his citizens. He felt as though he had failed Ryanne and his daughter Ciarra. He had to push those thoughts from his mind.

He reached Johann and shouted over the chaos that surrounded them. "Johann, we need to send your quickest man to Nauren. We need reinforcements. If he can run through the night, we could have reinforcements in one to two days. We will have to hold off the goblins or, if we are lucky, cut them down and attack the volcano. Ciarra is in there and I don't plan to leave without her!"

"I will send Merckx; there is none with more stamina and none faster."

"Good! As soon as he is off, we need to attack again! This will give him the best chance at a clean escape. Hopefully, the goblins won't see him go and won't send anyone after him because they will be too caught up defending against our attack!"

"It feels good to give it back to them just as they did to us, Olaf." Johann had blood in his eyes as well.

It looked to be a long battle, and the elves would make sure that if any creatures ever went up against Nauren again, they would pay with their lives.

Chapter LXVII
Fulfillment of
the Prophecy

THE massive stone gate rolled open at the end of the chamber opposite Siv's position. In the blink of an eye, a dark cloud filled the entire expanse.

"Who disturbs my chamber on this night?" a voice bellowed with a depth and fullness that froze both Drake and Siv.

The hair on the back of Drake's neck stood up and a chill ran down his spine. "Malkavic?" he muttered. "Are you Malkavic?"

A laugh bellowed out from the cloud. "Did you call me Malkavic?"

Siv thought about trying to escape, but she realized there was no escape from this beastly vision. She clung to Ciarra as tightly as she dared and remained silent.

"The Gatekeeper," Drake pointed his sword toward Siv. "I gave her the Princess of the Elves in exchange for Malkavic. I read the prophecy of Solomon and I have delivered the child. She promised me Malkavic and you appeared."

The vision of the Gatekeeper slowly turned toward Siv with intense concentration. She turned the baby away from him and returned his gaze with a defiant stare. She would protect this child or die trying. It had all come down to this.

The Gatekeeper let out another loud laugh. "You thought that young waif was the Gatekeeper? What kind of fool are you? I should smote you now! What is your name?"

"I am Drake, I came for Malkavic."

"Well, Drake, you have not delivered the princess to me; you have delivered her to a dwarf! If you want Malkavic, then retrieve her now!"

Drake raged. He had been played as a fool. The dwarf would pay with her life. In an instant, Drake rushed Siv with his sword drawn. The bright ruby was ablaze with fire as he lunged toward Siv.

No one saw it happen, not even the Gatekeeper. Siv had no time to think; she only reacted. She pulled Ciarra tight with her left arm. With her right arm she reached under her cloak and around to the scabbard that sheathed the dagger. With one quick motion she pulled the dagger from its sheath and swiftly backhanded the weapon in the direction of Drake.

The blade blazed with light. The green tail streaked toward Drake. It took purchase high in Drake's left thigh. It drove all the way to the hilt, burying itself in his flesh and coming to rest in the bone of his thigh.

Drake collapsed. This dagger was not an ordinary dagger. It shot fire through his whole body, and he lost all strength in his left leg. He barely remained conscious. Drake shifted his sword to his left hand; he lay prone on the ground, groaning. He took his right hand, reached down, and, using all the strength he had left, pulled out the dagger. He slowly regained his focus. He lifted up the dagger and held it in his right hand. He already had the sword in his left. He sneered at Siv, still bent on destruction as he stared at her between the two blades, but he had no strength left within him.

Drake, as consciousness was slipping away from him, looked from Siv back to the weapons he possessed. He considered the dagger and the sword. Side by side, the hollow portion of the grips aligned the way he was holding them. In fact, they looked as if they fit together. He was compelled to bring them together. He aligned the clefts that formed the hollow of the grips. The emerald pommel slipped into position just under the ruby. The hollow grips came together to form one solid core grip that was no bigger than the individual grips of each weapon. The defects in the quillon aligned and they became one solid piece as well. Slowly, he brought them together and watched in awe as the sword and the dagger became one!

As he brought the two weapons together, Drake passed out from the pain. Blood pooled where he lay. Once the two blades became one, light shot out from the tip of the sword and shot straight into the heart of the gaseous cloud of the Gatekeeper. Light dispersed to all parts of the cloud. The light's intensity was so bright that Siv had to momentarily avert her gaze.

She turned away from the light, shielding the baby. She tied the sling that held Ciarra tightly around her neck so that she could run. She took the extra cloth from the sling and cinched it around her waist, preparing for a quick escape.

The blinding light that had burst from the center of the cloud that was the Gatekeeper finally dissipated, and a being walked toward her out of the bright light. This being had all the appearance of a wizard. Was it Solomon? It did not look like Solomon from the one time she had seen his face. Siv also felt like the danger was not over for her or for Ciarra. Her senses warned her of imminent danger.

This wizard wore a bright red robe with a Kelly green lining, trimmed with silver and gold. Underneath the robes he was dressed in golden clothing. He had a flowing beard and long, thick brown hair that was actually more silver than brown. He emanated strength and power. In his left hand he held a staff that rested on the ground and went up to his shoulder. His cold, piercing grey eyes were distant and difficult to read.

He had Siv's full attention. Her green eyes bore into him. They stood fifteen feet apart. Drake lay prone on the ground between them, showing little sign of life other than an occasional moan.

"What is your name, dwarf?" The wizard lifted his staff and pointed it in her direction.

"I am Siv," she replied with a steady voice.

"Siv, ah yes," said the Gatekeeper. "I have been expecting you for over seven hundred and fifty years!"

Siv considered his reply and said, "And to whom am I speaking? Are you the Gatekeeper?"

"I was trapped under a curse as the Gatekeeper for two millennia! A curse imposed by the Wizard Council of my generation. That spell was broken with the rejoining of the sword and the dagger. My own creations had been used against me!" He paused to let his words rest on Siv.

"I am Aelhaeran, and I have come to reclaim my position in Lavendelle!"

Siv did not know the name Aelhaeran. She showed no fear. Aelhaeran was sure his name would shock her, but he was disappointed.

"You have the elf princess, and it is time for you to give her to me!"

Aelhaeran stared into Siv's green eyes. She returned his stare with her penetrating green eyes, unflinching in her defiance. Aelhaeran was uncertain with whom he was dealing.

"The princess is coming with me and I suggest you do not follow."

Aelhaeran laughed and lifted his staff. "You had your chance." As he pointed his staff at Siv, a bright light illuminated the entire chamber and both Siv and Aelhaeran looked up at its source.

A massive ball of light burst into the room and positioned itself over Drake and between Siv and Aelhaeran. The shape took the form of Solomon and towered over both Siv and Aelhaeran. Solomon stood ten feet tall and focused his attention directly on Aelhaeran.

Solomon's voice bellowed and Aelhaeran took a step back. "You should have never returned Aelhaeran. Siv will take the child and go now. You will not stop her!"

"How do you intend to stop me, Solomon?" Aelhaeran regained his composure and hissed at Solomon.

Solomon lifted his arms and turned his hands in Aelhaeran's direction with his palms open. He did not make physical contact with Aelhaeran, but an unseen energy crashed into the depraved wizard.

Aelhaeran had not been expecting this. He was knocked off his feet and flung back into the chamber beyond the gate. Solomon turned to Siv; his face was alive and intense and his eyes blazed like flames. As he looked at her, he only said one word: "Run!"

Siv glanced at the sword lying on the ground in front of Drake. She thought about taking it but decided not to take chances with the life of the infant cradled next to her body. She ran as fast as she could to the path and ran faster than she ever thought possible, never chancing a look behind her as an uproar crashed through the chasm below and light shot up from the chamber. She knew Solomon was protecting her, and she did her part to escape.

Siv did chance a glance at the infant. The baby still looked weak, but she was alive. Siv did her best to drench Ciarra with the water from her flask to cool off the child. Siv tested the water herself before giving any to the baby. The water was warm and she detected a hint of lemon that left a tart taste in her mouth. She then dripped droplets of water into the baby's mouth, a little at a time. Siv remembered back to all she had learned from Demetrius when he was treating Martha. She applied those same principles as she struggled to resuscitate the princess. She continued her struggle upward, and as she reached the top, she saw Teige and Ramsey running her way!

"We need to get out of here and fast!" Siv shouted to her cousins. They saw Siv holding the baby and running for her life. They all retreated toward the entrance of the tunnels as fast as their legs would carry them.

CHAPTER LXVIII
BLOOD MOON

WHAT they found when they exited the tunnels was that the landscape had changed entirely. The full moon illuminated a battle taking place on the sides of the volcano below, but the moon was unlike anything they had witnessed before: It was a crimson red, like blood, full in the sky, as though it were reflecting the loss of life on the battlefield below. An eerie red light enveloped everything in sight. Dragons swirled overhead, bathed in the light of the blood moon. Lightning bolts randomly electrified the night sky and illuminated the carnage on the ground beneath. Hundreds of goblins were amassed several hundred yards below. Whoever was attacking the volcano that night was not relevant to these three. They realized that the distraction created by the battle had probably saved their lives and the life of Ciarra and offered them the only chance for escape.

There was carnage out on the fields. The dragons were swooping down and devouring the dead goblins spread across the battleground. So far, Olaf and Johann had not sustained any casualties in this conflict. The goblins could not get close to them in their position behind the ridge, and they had no answer for the raining terror of the arrows.

"What do we do now, Siv?" Ramsey asked as they moved to a small collection of rocks that hid them from view below. This place was also out of sight from the tunnel entrance into the volcano.

"There appears to be no way to escape," Teige began. "We may have to ride it out up here."

Siv's attention wandered; she did not seem to be engaged in the conversation. Ramsey and Teige just looked at each other as Siv appeared to be staring out, captivated by the crimson moon, oblivious to their predicament. They did not understand her; they loved her, but at times she was an enigma to them. She certainly followed her own path. She had saved their lives, and she was clearly skilled with a dagger. She never ceased to amaze them.

Ramsey saw it first. He pointed up at the sky as a dragon quickly approached. Siv seemed to be locked on to the dragon as well. Teige finally saw the dragon and his heart skipped a beat. Their deaths were all but certain, they thought to themselves.

The dragon landed on the side of the hill next to them. Before Ramsey could stop her, Siv came out from behind the rocks and walked right in front of the dragon. The dragon lowered its head down to Siv's level. They locked eyes, and Siv reached out and stroked its nose. The very size of the beast overwhelmed her.

As Teige watched, the dragon limped a few steps toward Siv. It was only then that Teige realized it was the same one they had rescued on the side of the mountain. Siv appeared to be able to communicate with the dragon before. How she did this, he would never in his whole life understand. And now she appeared to be doing it again! Teige reached out and placed his hand on Ramsey's shoulder. Ramsey stared in disbelief.

"I think that is the same dragon we rescued from the side of the mountain, Ramsey. Siv can speak to it. Don't ask me how. I think she was calling to that thing to come rescue us when she was staring out into space! How does she do it?" Both brothers stared in disbelief.

"Teige, Ramsey, get out here!" Siv shouted.

Teige peered out over the rock to see Siv holding Ciarra. They were on the back of the dragon! The dragon's head was up and alert.

"This is our only chance. We need to get out of here and quick!"

Teige looked at Ramsey. They couldn't believe what they were about to do. As they saw it, though, there was no other way.

"First a giant bird and now a dragon. No one will ever believe it! I am not sure I even believe it. I have a head injury after all," Ramsey said as he approached the dragon. He rubbed his head as he approached the dragon.

Siv leaned her head against the neck of the beast and the dragon lowered itself down to allow the other two dwarves to get on. Once all were seated, the dragon took off and headed in the direction of Nauren.

Olaf looked up as the dragon flew over. From behind the blood moon lit up the dragon and its passengers. It was very high. He was not sure what drew his attention up, and he quickly looked back to the battlefield. It was going to be a long night.

CHAPTER LXIX
WE WILL MEET AGAIN

Siv, Teige, and Ramsey safely returned Princess Ciarra to Ryanne. Thanks to Siv, the princess continued to show improvement from the time Siv had found her in the chamber. She was grateful for all she had learned from Demetrius.

Olaf and Johann had overseen a massive slaughter of goblins that night. Olaf received word of Princess Ciarra's rescue by the dwarves and her safe return, and he quickly returned home. Nauren would never forget the tragedy. Olaf and the elves took measures to ensure that they would never be caught off guard again.

The dwarves and the elves started on a path to repair relations, thanks to the unimaginable heroism of the three young dwarves who saved the life of their princess. The dwarves, including Elwin, Markus, Teige, and Ramsey, began repairs to the wizards' tower. Siv came along too. Elijah put her in the upper chamber of the tower during her stay.

The wizards met for the first time in their own tower in as many years as any could remember. There were nine seats on the Council. Eight seats were filled. Demetrius was there too, and it was clear that there was much to do to mend relationships. That, however, was not the focus of the discussions this evening. Siv, her heroism, and all that they had witnessed from her dominated the discussion.

"It is not safe for Siv to return to her home unprotected. We still do not know the fate of Aelhaeran, nor that of Solomon!" Elijah said.

The others nodded in agreement. "Siv is not just any dwarf," Demetrius began. "I have spent time with her, and I knew from the very first that she possesses great magic. I believe that she will make a great wizard one day."

Everyone contemplated Demetrius' words. No wizard had ever come from the dwarves. It was something to consider.

"Elijah, you must help her find protection," Demetrius continued. "She could stay here, or she could become a follower to one of us. I know I have much to prove to all of you, but I would welcome Siv to follow me!"

The evening drew slowly into the early morning hours, and Siv tossed and turned in her bed. The fire in the upper chamber burned, but Siv could not get warm. She had goose bumps over her whole body. She was haunted by images of Ryanne. Who was she? She looked so much like Siv! Siv had never come across anyone who resembled her before, and yet when she arrived in Nauren to deliver Ciarra back to her mother, she had met Ryanne. Ryanne, overwhelmed with Ciarra's safe return, did not notice their similarities. But Siv would never forget. Ramsey and Teige noticed the resemblance as well and said as much to her.

She rose from her pallet, pulled a blanket tight around her small body, and walked to the window. Clouds obscured the lake below and reflected the soft white light from the moon. The volcano appeared in shadows.

But as she looked out toward the volcano, in her mind's eye she saw the faint view of a creature limping away from the volcano and heading down toward the lake. Siv moved deliberately forward, squinting her eyes. Her vision took her slowly closer and closer to the creature until there was no mistake about what she was seeing: It was the man from the chamber. Indeed, he was favoring his left leg as he walked. In his hand was the sword she had left behind. A shiver ran up her spine as the man stopped and turned slowly until all of his attention was focused on her. There was no doubt in her mind. It was the same man and yet there was something different about him. Their eyes met and she recognized the cold and piercing stare of Aelhaeran's grey eyes staring right through her! She felt as if his penetrating stare had trapped her in the tower with no way out.

She knew he was looking at her, and then he spoke: "It is not over between us, Siv. We will meet again!"

ABOUT THE AUTHOR

Geoffrey Leigh received his professional education in the United States. He has practiced in the field of medicine and surgery since the mid 1990s. Leigh's passion for writing fiction began under the tutelage of Dr. Carol Ann Moore when he was a teenager. Dr. Moore instilled within him a love for reading and writing which he has carried with him all his adult life. The brilliant scenery of the Rocky Mountains led to many of the descriptions of Lavendelle: the forests, the lakes, the boulder fields, the mountain passes, and the dangerous electrical storms, just to name a few. Growing up, Leigh loved the works of J.R.R. Tolkien, the game Dungeons and Dragons, and all things fantasy. He has returned to the days of his youth to bring us this enchanting and exciting tale.

ACKNOWLEDGEMENTS

First and foremost, I want to reach out to Catherine and thank her for all her support and all that she did to encourage me throughout this process. Without her positive attitude and support, this book would not have made it out of the concept phase.

I wrote a story about a dwarf whose life was predestined long before her birth. Though she had free will, ultimately, her path was known before she was ever born. Despite free will, Siv ended up right where Solomon had seen her seven hundred and thirty-five years before her birth. In much the same way as Siv, despite pursuing a professional career outside of literature, over the course of my life things happened to me that continued to steer me back to my first love: writing. It may be coincidence, it may be serendipity, it may be predestination, but whatever the circumstance, Ronald Chase stumbled into my life at just the right time.

I want to thank Ron for his vision and leadership in getting this project from raw manuscript form to finished project. I want to thank all the professionals whom Ron introduced me to along the way who produced this beautiful book. I especially wish to thank Lisa Workman for giving us the vision of Lavendelle and the face of Siv. I also want to thank Karen Sandoval for her tireless work in seeing this project through.

So many people shaped this project, and I want to reach out to each one and thank you for all that you have done to help Siv come to life. Judy Reveal, thank you so much. I named the Serpent of the Lake "Judy" out of appreciation for all that you have done for me and for Siv!

A special thanks goes out to all who offered input and direction found in the final edition of this book: Dr. Travis Stork, Bob Follett, Dr. Beverly Weiser, Linda Cantrell, Scott Cantrell, Linda Lichtendahl, Wendy Wolfe, Deb Edwards, Dr. Randy Taylor, Gary Lunsky, and Lawrence Herrington! You have all given me great perspective. I wish to thank those in my family who read and critiqued this novel for their input and support as well.

Finally, I would like to end with a special remembrance of one of the most important teachers of my early life: Dr. Carol Ann Moore. Without Dr. Moore, there would be no Siv and no Lavendelle, and my love for reading and writing may never have been realized.